political force, as a huge capitalistic enterprise, and as a fiercely vindictive society that tracks down its enemies wherever they run. His account is a valuable slice of African sociology, an illuminating exposé of the unseen but pervasive grip of African superstition and its very real consequences in the modern world, a thrilling and suspenseful tale of betrayal and revenge, and an inspiring spiritual chronicle that takes the reader out of the dark world of magic and into the light of reason.

Whatever the reader may choose to glean from this absorbing memoir, *Blood Secrets* is a book that can't be put down easily and won't be forgotten soon.

Isaiah Oke lives in West Central Africa. Joe Wright is a freelance writer in Chicago.

BLOOD SECRETS

BLOOD SECRETS

THE TRUE STORY OF DEMON WORSHIP AND CEREMONIAL MURDER

BY FORMER JUJU HIGH PRIEST

ISAIAH OKE

AS TOLD TO JOE WRIGHT

PROMETHEUS BOOKS
Buffalo, New York

BLOOD SECRETS: THE TRUE STORY OF
DEMON WORSHIP AND CEREMONIAL MURDER

Published by
Prometheus Books
700 East Amherst Street, Buffalo, New York 14215,
800-351-0421; in New York State, 716-837-2475.

Library of Congress Catalog Card No. 89-62649
ISBN 0-87975-568-7

Manufactured in the United States of America

Contents

The Initiate

1

At about three o'clock, naked as I came into the world, they stretched me out face-up on the dirt floor of the hut. The *babalorisha* barked, "Don't move, boy," and then, from a soft wicker basket, he dropped a writhing serpent between my legs. The shock of it almost made me jump up in spite of his warning. But I was so tired from the journey that I just froze, gasping for breath, instead of trying an unlikely escape that would only have unmanned me in his eyes.

I was exhausted; we'd been walking since first light. I was required to do all the carrying, which was befitting, of course. Everything had been packed by the junior priests into one enormously heavy bundle. It contained all the ritual objects, the food and water for my guides, and the cages with the smaller sacrificial animals. This I was obliged to carry on my head, after the manner of a woman. The only things they didn't make me carry were the kid and the lamb which my guides condescended to pull along behind them on leashes. We could have completed the long trip before midday, livestock and all, in the old Model-A truck the village owned in common. But that wouldn't have been according to tradition and, of course, tradition was everything.

But whether it was exhaustion that made me freeze up or panic, I felt paralyzed; I couldn't have moved even if I'd wanted to. Not so the frightened snake. As soon as he hit the ground, he slithered up onto my left thigh, seeking the security of warmth. As he did, my guides threw a raggedy net over the pair of us and quickly tapped some small pegs into the ground to hold it.

This made the snake sinuate wildly at first and that frightened me even more. But I kept hearing in my heart all that my grandfather had told me about the ritual: "Nothing your guides do can harm you if you are manly. But the *orishas* will reject you if they sense fear; they will judge you unworthy. So, fear nothing. And above all, remember who you are!"

My eyes were rolling uncontrollably and I was sweating profusely even though—as every Yoruba boy knows—the "poison" snakes in these rituals are always defanged. That's why a python, the true symbol of our religion, is never used; pythons kill by constriction rather than poison and there's no way to fake a python's deadly squeeze.

But the revulsion is the same whether the snake is truly dangerous or not. How would *you* feel if a snake was sliding itself like living sandpaper along your naked body? Even though you knew it couldn't bite?

See what I mean?

I stayed as stiff as one of Grandfather's ceremonial statues, recalling his assurances that nothing in the ritual could really hurt me, and the snake gradually calmed. Eventually it was still, just above my stomach. I think it slept.

I was badly frightened. And the knowledge that other boys of my clan had lived through all this was no comfort. For one thing, no one who completed his ritual had ever broken the taboo by telling any of us younger ones exactly what was in store. Instead, the young men all tried to outdo one another at the evening fire by making up the most frightening yarns, to the horror of us younger boys and the hilarity of our parents.

Furthermore, I knew that *my* initiation would involve far more of an ordeal than most because of my particular heritage, which demanded the most rigorous testing. In fact, both my guides were strangers whom I'd never seen before; it had been bandied about that Grandfather sent all the way to Gabon for them. The man's face supported that rumor. But the woman was so dark that I couldn't read her facial scarring. In any event, they were experts and could be expected to be very good at this.

As the Sun went down, the net and snake were removed and the man took them outside. I breathed freely for the first time since entering the ritual hut. I hadn't moved a muscle in six hours. Humbly, as befits a child in his thirteenth year, I asked for permission to sit up. The woman cuffed me almost absent-mindedly behind the head for my insolence and told me to fetch the two ritual water pots from outside. Normally, of course, carrying water would have been her job, and she seemed to take a special pleasure in making me perform such a degrading act. I scrambled out the doorhole, happy to be free, even if just for a moment.

The pots were gnarly and poorly fired, not even close to the quality of our local workmanship. They looked as if they'd been made by someone who had not the least experience of pottery. But I knew that only a very foolish man would judge juju-water pots by their looks; they were repositories of enormous power, in the hands of a Man of Knowledge.

I wrestled the pots in through the tiny doorhole, then set them down where the woman pointed. As she commanded, I removed the stoppers. The pot with the skulls painted on it contained a foul-smelling brown liquid, viscous and sludgy. The red one with the serpents painted on it contained a clear but equally foul-smelling fluid. Neither liquid seemed to be any of the dozens of kinds of juju-water with which I was familiar.

The woman told me to make a fire in the center of the hut. And again, the corners of her mouth went up a little as I was forced to do women's work. She was much younger than I had thought she'd be, probably even without grandchildren yet. That made my embarrassment twice as deep. I was still burning with shame from the trick they'd played on me with the snake and I almost let my anger show. But the ritual would last for three days altogether and this was only the first night. Who knew what power she could unleash on me in that time? Young or not, insolent or not, she was still an *ayelorisha:* one of the very few women privileged to talk directly to the gods. I made myself hold my tongue.

It was cooling off rapidly. Western people—those from America or Europe—think of West Africa only as a hot, steamy place. But at night it can get bone-chillingly cold. By the time I had the fire going, I was shaking with cold, hunger, and fatigue. I cast a hidden look toward the white robe I'd had to wear for the last three days as a symbol of my approaching initiation. They'd told me to hang it on one of the roof poles as we came into the hut and there it hung still. I wanted to put it back on but I saw the *ayelorisha* follow my glance. She turned back with her small unbearable smile again. "Are you cold, little boy?"

I chose to ignore her, like a man. I raised my chin in defiance and looked away from her. I thought how proud my grandfather would be if he could see me.

She dipped her drinking gourd into the serpent-pot, the one with the clear liquid in it. She stared at the dipper for a moment and chanted under her breath. She looked up at me and laughed, broadly and openly this time. Then she flung the dipper of water all over my shivering body.

I spluttered and coughed, as much at the indignity as at the cool water hitting my chilled skin. No woman, I thought, dares treat a man of the Oke clan in such a way, *ayelorisha* or not.

"But you are not yet 'a man,' " said the *babalorisha.* He was stooped over, squeezing in through the doorway. He was a big man, still strong and fearsome-looking in spite of his years.

"No," he repeated, "you are not yet a man. How is it, then, that it matters how a woman treats you?" It was as if he'd seen into my heart. "*If* you become a man of the Oke clan, then you will be treated accordingly. But only *if* you become a man."

I put my eyes down to the ground. There was silence for a time, broken only by the chattering of my teeth. My two guides went about their business, ignoring me as if I'd not been grievously insulted.

Then they squatted down to enjoy their evening meal of the yams and palm wine they'd made me carry. I'd not eaten all day. And I knew from the other boys that I would get no water nor solid food until my ordeal was over. The smell of the yams, the crunch as they were bit into, made the joints of my jaws ache with desire. I'd never wanted a fresh, delicious yam or a drink of cool water so much in my life. But I took pride in the way I was able to stand by—cold, wet, and silent, enduring all—while my elders ate.

When they finished, the *ayelorisha* removed the remnants and took herself outside. "The woman will sleep now. You will meet the *orisha*," the man said.

As he spoke, he removed his juju from the leather bag around his neck: a carved piece of wood that looked suspiciously like an old table leg; the neck broken off a green bottle; two items as big around as my fist that looked like dried apricots; a rusty knife; and several smaller bags of the type in which one carries ritual herbs.

"First, you will meet *Olu-Orogbo*." He leaned over and pulled one of the little cages toward himself. It was the one with a black rooster, the symbol of *Olu-Orogbo*. He took the bird out of the cage, raised it up, and looked at it face-to-face. Then he began an incantation that I'd heard my grandfather use many times: the one that asks *Olu-Orogbo* to act as special mediator between men and the other gods. Still holding the rooster before his face, he addressed it as "Brother Bird" and asked it to forgive him. Then, with one practiced twist, he wrung its neck.

He called on *Olu-Orogbo* again, this time in a louder voice. I'd never heard an incantation as mournful as this. The song was that of a hyena, morbid and without hope. I began to shiver again, just as I had when the woman splashed water on me.

Suddenly, with a keening cry, the *babalorisha* snapped the bird bloodily in two at the neck. According to custom, he kept the head and offered the carcass to me. We took the hot blood simultaneously from the two parts of the bird.

After I moistened my lips with the rooster's blood and swallowed a bit of it, I went to put the carcass down, since there was no one else for me to share it with ritually. But the *babalorisha* stayed my hand. "Drink deeply," he said.

His words surprised me. Rarely does one take more than a drop or two of sacrificial blood. Blood-drinking is, after all, a *ritual* in Africa; it is not a meal or a way to satisfy one's physical hunger. But I obeyed and put the neck to my mouth once more.

I had never had blood in such a quantity before. The salty, metallic taste of chicken's blood was nothing new to me, of course. But the new sensation of swallowing a whole mouthful of it—a heavy, stringy sensation— almost made me gag. I set the carcass down, the blood dripping off my chin onto my chest.

The *babalorisha* dipped his left hand into the skull pot. He rubbed his head, face, and chest with his wet hand, leaving little stripes of the pasty fluid. Then from the bag at his side, he reverently removed a singlet made of feathers. This he slipped carefully over his shoulders. While he did these things, he began to sing another incantation. This one was more rhythmic, less baleful, than the last. He chanted on and on, lulling us both with the repetitious drone.

Slowly, he began to crouch. His legs seemed to grow shorter and shorter. His arms went akimbo to his waist, palms out behind him. He took a hesitant step and his head bobbed sharply forward and back. He stepped mincingly around the dying fire a few times, letting out soft cackles. At last, having gained confidence in his identity, he stopped and let out a crow of pride in his roosterness. Then he stepped over to me and looked up, his head cocked to one side.

I didn't know at first what was expected of me. He scratched at the ground and crowed again. He was so complete a rooster that I almost saw the comb on his head and the wattles under his chin. After marveling at him for awhile, I asked, "Is it you, *Olu-Orogbo?*"

He toed the ground again and said in a scratchy kind of voice, "I am *Olu-Orogbo.*" He walked around in a tight circle, bobbing his neck which seemed somehow to have grown quite scrawny. He stopped and cocked his head again, looking unblinkingly at me with one beady eye, as if he had just thought of some great truth. "Without the chicken," he said, "the Yoruba could not live."

"That is so, *Olu-Orogbo,*" I said.

He walked around the embers again, scratching the dirt and snapping his beak thoughtfully. "Then," he said, "I shall tell you of our ways so that the Yoruba may live."

He walked around the fire again and again. Every time he completed a circuit, he told me a secret of the chickens. He told me how the egg got its shape and why chickens eat gravel. He told me how to make a baby chick follow around after a frog as if it were its mother. He told me why roosters crow at the dawn and what would happen to the world if they ever stopped.

All through the long night, he told me such secrets—some big and some small. He told me how to read the message of the future in the entrails of a freshly killed chicken. He told me how to make a cure for skin diseases from chicken droppings and how to use polished chicken bones for luck when gambling. He told me why sacrifices of chickens are so especially pleasant to the *orishas*. He even explained how it can be that human beings and chickens are one with all the rest of nature. He told me these and many other mystical wonders. And the more he made me understand, the more I felt at one with the whole world of nature around me.

Finally, as the sky began to lighten in the East, he scratched out through the doorhole, like a rooster leaving the coop. He crowed once, very loudly, and then came back inside.

He dipped his left wing into the other pot—the one with the serpents on it. He rubbed himself with the juju-water and, as he did, he became once again a man.

Without speaking or looking at me, he went out of the ritual hut for the last time. He left me alone with my thoughts, which is the best way to leave someone who has just had a transcendent religious awakening.

I lay there, happy and grateful that the gods were so good and the world so filled with wonder, when the woman came in. I wanted to tell her how childish I felt for having feared the serpent earlier. I wanted to share with her my knowledge that there was no reason to fear the *orisha*. But she was a stranger to me and I couldn't find the words to explain any of these things.

It wasn't until I heard a soft snarl that my attention went to the burlap sack she was carrying. Without taking her eyes off me, she pulled out a baby leopard, surely no more than three days old, its legs bound.

The woman was wearing a spotted collar and her eyes shone like those of a cat in a dark cave. When she smiled her knowing smile at me again, I saw for the first time that her upper teeth had been filed sharp where they poked into her lower lip.

Then she took a gleaming machete out of her bag. She gave me no time to adjust. Still smiling, she drew the machete smoothly across the leopard's throat. She handed the small, still-twitching animal to me and said, "Drink deeply."

All my dread returned at once, washing over me like the flood tide on the Niger. I'd been a fool to feel so secure about my initiation. Now the deepest fear of every African tribal man—the fear of the *orisha*—came into my stomach as strongly as an enemy's blow. It was all the worse for the false sense of security and well-being into which I'd been lulled through the night. It made me want to cry out, to ask for mercy.

But I dared not; the ritual still had two more days to go.

2

I was being initiated into what Westerners know as "Traditional African Religion." Because the real name for our religion sounds humorous to their ears, anthropologists adopted this term so their study of it would be taken more seriously by their academic colleagues. But we Africans still call it what our ancestors did: *juju*. The word is flexible and takes its exact meaning from context. *Juju* can refer to our religion, to the paraphernalia used in its practice, or to the idea of mystical power, as in "so-and-so won the lottery; he has big juju." But however we use the word, it sounds ominous to us rather than humorous.

To us, juju is no laughing matter. We believe it to be a religion of total power and control. It is as formal and as structured as any other religion. And its high priests carry themselves with as much dignity and solemnity, in their own way, as the Archbishop of Canterbury does. Yet the average American or European thinks of juju as childish superstition. He or she calls it "devil worship"—which is not a bad name for it, actually— and thinks it is no longer practiced in the modern world.

On the contrary, juju continues to be practiced in one form or another by most Africans, even many of those who are nominally Christians or Muslims. It is also practiced by those Africans who have been displaced into the New World, whose weak and watery versions of juju are known as *voodoo* or *hoodoo*. So, in terms of the total number of its adherents, juju actually ranks among the world's dominant religions. Yet little about it is known outside Africa.

Juju differs fundamentally from all the other major religions. For instance, whereas Christianity is based on love, juju is based on fear. Where

Christianity seeks salvation, juju seeks only power. So Christians worship a god of love and seek to please him for his own sake. But jujumen seek to appease the gods they fear, the gods of evil.

These gods are many because there are so many things that can hurt us in Africa. Lions and rhinos probably come to your mind. And I suppose they *are* a danger in some places. But many Africans today live in cities that are much like overcrowded cities anywhere: The roars you hear are more likely to be from motorcycles rather than from lions. No, the powers that we Africans fear and need to appease are more subtle than lions. They are all the powers we lack the science and technology to understand or to control. The *tsetse* fly, for instance. And the mosquito. Drought. And famine. Diseases like *kwashiorkor* and others, diseases so horrible that you Westerners found them unimaginable—until that one we call "slim disease" reached you. Western medicine calls it AIDS.

Many of these powers, like the diseases that kill more than half our children before maturity, are invisible. So we find it easy to believe in an Invisible World all around us, trying to do us ill. In fact, we would find it impossible to deny that such an Invisible World really exists; all the spirits who want to hurt us come from this Invisible World. So there are many gods which we need to appease if we're to live in any semblance of safety.

The names of our gods vary from country to country and from tribe to tribe, but their characters remain the same. At the very top of our pantheon is the supreme being. My people, the Yoruba, know him as *Olodumare*. The Dahomeans to the west of Yorubaland call him *Nana Buluku* and the Ibo to the east of us call him *Chineke*. His identity, however, is the same everywhere: He is the one who made the universe and everything in it. We don't worship him, though; he is thought to be so far above us human beings that all we can do is acknowledge his existence.

Olodumare has delegated the daily running of the world to his subsidiary gods. Among these are the principal deities known in Yoruba as the *orishas*. These are very important and powerful spirits. They aren't fond of human beings, either, so we find it necessary to appease them quite often.

Below the *orishas* are many, many minor gods of nature, each with his own department to watch after: the god of this particular river, the god of that particular tree, and so forth. There is no end to these minor gods because we create more of them continuously, as we feel the need to. Suppose, for instance, that a man trips one day over a rock in the path and injures himself. He may give the god of that rock a name and invent a ritual to appease it in order that it might not trip him up again in the future.

Along with all those nature gods are the spirits of our ancestors who, knowing so much about us because they are our forefathers, can be extremely dangerous to us human beings. They need appeasement, too; in a juju household, it is not unusual to set an extra place at table in case any ancestor chooses to drop in for a meal. That place is always set with the choicest food of the household. Our belief is so strong that this practice continues even in times of great famine.

And an ancestor who wants to stay longer than just for dinner can incarnate into the body of a newborn baby. So prudent parents always take a baby to the local juju priest, the *babalawo,* to find out which ancestor lives in their child.

There are two levels of juju: one for all believers, and a special one which is only for those who have had advanced training. One of the characteristics that all the varieties of juju have in common is the secrecy that characterizes juju at that higher level of practice. I was undergoing the initiation to the higher level. Before an initiate undergoes any of the rituals, he is made to understand that death will surely follow if he should ever tell any of the secrets he learns. And, as you'll see, my fellow jujumen would do their best to see to it that the prediction came true in my case.

The secrecy is so complete that one might almost say there is another religion, unknown to the outside world, *inside* the religion of juju. For example, there are two kinds of sacrificial places. The *Temple* is relatively accessible and open. In our cities, there are some big juju temples that resemble Christian churches. Sacrifice is of grain or of paper money or— on some special occasions—of a chicken or a pigeon. Temples are unguarded and unhidden; some even permit tourists to enter—for a price—and observe the juju activities that take place there and which we refer to as *ceremonies.*

But there is another sacrificial place, usually well out in the forest, far from prying eyes and ears, that we call the *Shrine.* It is usually no more than a hut in a hidden clearing in what we call the *igbo-awo* ("the secret forest"). What is performed here is not the innocuous *ceremony,* but rather the gruesome and bloody *ritual.*

Our rituals are designed to appease the most horrid of our gods. And— because those gods are so fearsome—so must be the rituals: We believe that nothing better appeases the fierce spirits of juju than *blood.* We refer to this letting of blood as *ichu-aja,* a word which has been translated as "sacrifice." But, because "sacrifice" has overtones of charity and self-denial to Westerners, you might prefer to think of it as *ritual killing,* which would more accurately describe it.

Blood flows more freely than water in some shrines, but the modern Western world wants to remain oblivious to that fact. It does not want to know that we still appease the spirits of our gods with the blood of animals.

And even less does it want to know that the higher spirits demand the blood of a higher animal: the *human* animal.

Many in the West want to believe that all this—juju, blood sacrifice, ritual killing, human sacrifice—is something from the distant past, a relic of darkest Africa from the days before it was "civilized" by the white man. That belief is far more comforting than the truth.

But juju in its bloodiest forms is still alive and well today. Not only in Africa, but among Africa's transplanted children in the New World, where it has now spread to whites as well. Hardly a week goes by that news of juju rituals is not reported somewhere in America by the press. But it's such a big country that the incidents seem isolated, the work of individual psychotics. Only when one becomes aware of how many such incidents there are altogether can one begin to see them as parts of a pattern. For example, the Cable News Network reported on September 1, 1988, that the remains of sixteen animals had been found in a public park in Newark, New Jersey. The remains were in plastic bags and included chickens, dogs, and a goat, the head of which was never found. But only a few days earlier, the Chicago television station WGN carried a film report about an apartment on the west side of the city which was used as a "holding pen" for sacrificial animals. Dozens of animals including chickens, pigs, goats, and dogs were kept in their own filth until sold to jujumen for sacrifice. Amazingly, the neighbors in this densely populated area claimed that they saw, heard, and smelled nothing.

Juju is in the midst of America now. It may be known by other names and some of its rituals may have been updated. But, basically, it remains the same as we in Africa have always known it to be: the religion that is believed to give power through blood. And that thirst for bloody sacrifice will explain much that has been happening in the West lately. As we will see, it may have an impact on even that most overwhelming social problem, AIDS.

Before I would come to recognize any of that, though, I would go through a mystical odyssey. My initiation was only the first step in that odyssey, but it was one that had been ordained for me from the day I was born.

3

The position of juju high priest—*babalorisha*—is not, strictly speaking, a hereditary one. In my case, there was no reason to believe that the honor would ever fall to me. Especially since my family had moved from Nigeria to another country altogether.

Our migration was a result of the Gold Rush that took place in West Africa in the 1930s. It was in the area called the Gold Coast which we know today as the country of Ghana. Visiting Americans often remark that it reminds them of Florida. On a map, it's a little closer to the West than my ancestral homeland of Nigeria.

In many ways, our Gold Rush must have been like the one that occurred in the American Wild West. Almost overnight, people from all over the world converged on one small spot on the West African coast. Few could understand the language of those working next to them. Fewer still could understand the other's culture or religion. Drunkenness and violence were common; it was not a good place to raise a family.

I was born in a mining camp there. Today the area is much more built up and modernized with a big port where the new cities of Sekondi and Takoradi squeeze the river. The people of Ghana call them the "Twin Cities," just like Americans refer to Minneapolis/St. Paul. Sekondi/Takoradi is somewhat warmer, of course, especially in January.

My father brought my mother there from Nigeria some months before I was born. He supported my brothers, my mother, and me by laboring in the state mines. Whenever he felt he could spare the time and money, he would go off and search for a strike of his own.

The harsh, vagabond life we led surprises some of my American and

European friends. After all, my grandfather was a *babalorisha* back in Nigeria—one of only a very few. That's an exalted position, roughly equal to a Bishop in the Anglican Church. My friends wonder why Grandfather didn't take my father into the "family business," so to speak, rather than let him scratch out a meager living in the mines of Ghana. But inheritance in Africa usually goes to the first-born son and that was not my father.

Sadly, Grandfather's first two sons both died in infancy. And in both cases, they died shortly after he officially named them as his successors. This seemed to discourage him from designating any other heir. He even ignored some of those who had strong cases to succeed him: Joshua, for instance, the seventh son of Grandfather's seventh son, should have been a strong candidate, But *nobody* was training to be the next *babalorisha,* so all the sons of my grandfather were required to earn a living any way they could, including my father.

To be designated as our next *babalorisha,* a man had to be chosen by the gods themselves. And that's why some sign was needed from Grandfather as to who the residents of the Invisible World had identified. But apparently, neither the gods nor the ancestors ever spoke to Grandfather on behalf of any of his sons, grandsons, or great-grandsons, even though he faithfully presented each of us to the *orishas* in elaborate juju rituals.

These rituals begin with circumcision—the boy's first experience with blood ritual. Also, facial cuts are often made which will heal into distinctive scars later. To accentuate the scarring, certain herbs are rubbed into our wounds. These inflame them so that a good, deep scar will eventually result. These scars can be used to identify a man's tribe, his clan, even his family. This practice has declined in favor of chalked facial markings; juju is, more than ever, a secret religion, so it's unwise for modern jujumen to wear permanent signals on their faces.

It is that willingness to adapt to changing circumstances that protects juju. A European friend recently asked me what my name was before I changed it. "What do you mean?" I asked him.

"How could your name have been given to you in a juju home? 'Isaiah' is a Christian name," he said.

"Ah, yes. But many Africans have Christian first names, even though they're jujumen."

I explained that Africans are resilient people. When any new concept comes to us, including a new religion, we take from it what we like and add it to what we've already got. The rest we throw away. The new idea doesn't replace the old one, but gets mixed into it like an ingredient in batter. It happens so consistently among us that the anthropologists have even invented a pretty name for it: *syncretism.*

So, many Africans who are nominally Christians or Moslems continue to practice juju in private. On the surface, they are all piety, and the minister or the mullah may count such people as members in good standing of his local congregation. But in reality, they are "closet jujumen."

Like most Central Africans at that time, my people were still thoroughly juju. But they were smart enough to prevent the outside world from knowing that. So when I was born, my parents took me to the local missionary and asked him to select a fitting Bible name. He chose Isaiah, a major Old Testament prophet.

Then my father turned right around and took me, Christian name and all, to the local *babalawo* for juju ritual.

A *babalawo* is a juju priest of the junior level who can lay curses, cast spells, and participate in public ceremonies. He cannot, however, officiate at secret rituals, not can he speak directly to the gods as a *babalorisha* can. *Babalawos* network among themselves just as members of every other profession do. They pass along information and establish each other's reputations for power: one might be very good at helping you curse an enemy, for example, while another might be renowned for lifting the curse that made your wife or your cow barren. Periodically, they even have international conferences and get-togethers, just as if they were hardware manufacturers or insurance salesmen.

The local man to whom my father took me turned out to be an old friend of my grandfather. He accepted the baby goat that would be sacrificed, but he firmly declined the few coins that would be his official fee; it was sort of a "professional courtesy," I suppose, toward my grandfather.

After what my father said was a very lengthy interview, during which he asked all about our family, the *babalawo* told my father to go away and to return two days later. In the meantime, he said, he had to consult with some of the local "specialists": the necromancer, the astrologer, and so forth. It was clear, he said, that a very important ancestor had become incarnate inside me and he needed to do some research and some tests and to consult with his colleagues in order to know who that ancestor was. In the meantime, he told my father, be very careful: You don't know who might be inside this child. This was all big news to my parents; they hadn't counted on anything except just another human baby.

The next couple of days must have been very difficult for them. Who was in me? A favorable, helpful spirit who would bring them good luck? Or . . .

Two days later, the *babalawo* dropped a bombshell. "In this child,"

he said, "is incarnated *Orisha-Oko.*"

So! I wasn't just a spirit—I was a *god!*

Well, a godling, anyway. *Orisha-Oko* was the name of one we call a "household god." This was a special private god for the clan Oke only. Actually he was a demigod: half-god and half-ancestor. Legend has it that he was born with part of the amnion covering his head; the Europeans would say he was "born under a caul." This, of course, was very big juju, an omen of greatness. So he adopted the name *Oke,* which means "membrane," and became the founder of the clan Oke. The rough equivalent in the United States would be to say that the spirit of George Washington had been reborn in me.

My father was both proud and stunned. He was proud because a god had come into his child. Certainly the baby would grow to be very important and influential—perhaps a *babalorisha* or even an *oba* (king). Who wouldn't be proud?

But at the same time, he was scared and confused. How do you treat a baby who is the miraculous incarnation of somebody special? How was he to discipline me? How could my mother bear to feed me? Or change my diaper? None of this was the *babalawo's* concern, of course. Juju priests, as a rule, feel themselves to be above the daily concerns of ordinary people; they do not show the care for their congregations that a Christian would call "pastoral."

So, without giving my father any counsel or advice about handling a child with a god inside him, the *babalawo* finished the ritual. With appropriate incantations, he killed the kid my father had brought two days earlier. It had to be a baby goat, rather than a calf or any other kind of young animal; in the secret symbolic language of juju, jujumen refer to themselves as "goats" and everyone else as "sheep." He smeared some of the animal's blood on all of us. Then, with the same knife, he circumcised me, thus making me a "brother in blood" of the goat.

Finally, he gave me my Name. The juju belief is that one's Name is heavy with juju, that it summarizes and symbolizes one's entire person, that it is the essence of one's soul. No one else—except my closest family members and my first son—was to know it. No woman—including my mother and my future wife—was *ever* to know it. Should it happen that my Name was ever learned by a tabooed person, the belief is that they would then have enormous power over me. I like to think of myself these days as educated—a traveled man, perhaps even a bit worldly. I no longer subscribe to juju beliefs or engage in juju practices. Nevertheless, even today, I would need a very good reason to reveal my Name.

This business of giving a baby a special Name, spiritual and hidden, seems at first harmless, trivial, even a bit silly. But it exemplifies the way juju thrives on secrecy. It shows how juju maintains its hold long after it has been consciously renounced. It demonstrates the *true* power of juju, the way juju can—and does—flourish unrecognized in the midst of any group of people. Even Western people—educated, sophisticated, rational people like your neighbors there in America.

But there was no reason to keep *Orisha-Oko's* incarnation in me a secret. The only "secret" was how my grandfather would react.

4

They tell me that Grandfather killed a valuable ox when the good news reached back home about *Orisha-Oko* being inside me. He also sent a gift of two cows and a wife to his colleague in Ghana who had divined my true identity.

He immediately went into consultation with other important *babalawo* in the district. Many chickens and lizards were killed and their entrails studied. Every rain cloud was carefully examined by those who practiced that form of divination. And the graveyard was crowded with all the necromancers, seeking omens from the dead. In the end, these sorceries confirmed the news for Grandfather: His grandchild had been chosen as the earthly vessel for the great spirit *Orisha-Oko*.

It was inevitable, he declared, that I should succeed him as the next *babalorisha;* who was more worthy?

He sent detailed instructions to my parents about my care. Everything possible was done to assure my well-being. In effect, my parents and my brothers became my slaves. I always got the best and biggest portions of any food. And if I wanted some trifling trinket, I always got it. Even if that trinket already belonged to somebody else. It must have been easy for me to learn to walk because I don't think there was ever a time when anybody got in my way. Even out in the streets of our village, people stepped aside for me. And anybody who had a sweet or a piece of fruit shoved it in my mouth, hoping for the smile that might indicate a blessing. So I quickly became very fat and very spoiled.

In my fifth year, my mother took me back home to Nigeria, to be with Grandfather and to learn the ways of juju. I never again saw my father after that. He hadn't ever been comfortable around me, always peeking at me out of the corner of his eye, afraid to raise his voice lest I curse him. It must be frightening to have a little god for a son. I understand he took another wife. He died some years ago.

As to my brothers, all of them still live in Ghana. We had no chance to be close, the way African brothers are supposed to be. Fortunately, there was a new family waiting for me at Grandfather's compound.

The name of our village in Nigeria was Inesi-Ile. It was a rural place in those days. It took a walk of about an hour through the savanna grass to get to the bus stop on the closest of our very few roads. And the district capital of Ilesha was more than two hours' additional journey away by bus. So those who had business in the city faced a lengthy commute.

There were a hundred or more homes in our village. They covered a very large area because a Yoruba home is more of a compound than a structure. It's a group of small buildings, sometimes only single-roomed, rather than one large building with many rooms, like in the West. The compound of my grandfather befitted his station as one of the principal *babalorishas* of Nigeria. It consisted of several buildings around a small yard and a little garden plot; the town's main square was just outside, in accordance with Grandfather's position as the principal man of the place. Juju ceremonies were conducted there as well as in our market.

Four of the buildings were quarters for Grandfather's wives. Each wife had her own room in one of the women's buildings and he took his dinner at each woman's place in strict rotation. There was also a granary, two livestock barns, and several outbuildings of the type one finds on farms anywhere.

In the garden we raised vegetables like cabbage and carrots, and also some annual plants. The larger plants, like bananas, and the produce that required several years to yield, like our local apple, were grown on a somewhat more spacious field that was a mile or so from the compound. In that cleared area, which we called "the farm," we also grew rice, beans, and several varieties of yam.

Toward the rear of the compound was the building that housed Grandfather's private quarters. When the women snickered among themselves, they referred to it as "The Palace." In actuality, it looked no different from any of the other residential buildings; it had but two rooms and an enormous porch.

Just in front of the Palace was Grandfather's Temple: a building which was used for consulting with other *babalawo,* which Grandfather did frequently, and for certain ceremonies. It was also the place where I was to receive much of my juju training over the next several years.

The whole of the compound was surrounded by a kind of stockade fence with a single gate giving off onto the village proper. These fences (or *odi*) are characteristic of Yoruba architecture and have religious, rather than military, significance. They are designed to keep out not people, but *evil*. To do this they naturally rely on juju.

The fence around a Yoruba city has seven gates, seven being a sacred number. The *orisha* in charge of gates is *Legba*. *Legba* is not a friend of man; no *orisha* ever is. But he is the enemy of Fate. And it is Fate that sends bad fortune to men. So we propitiate *Legba* in order that he will trick his enemy Fate into leaving us alone.

Whenever an *odi* is built, therefore, *Legba* must be appeased. This requires that three persons captured at random be buried alive, still kicking and screaming, under each of the seven gates.

One of our legends about the power and the impartiality of juju involves just such a sacrifice. It seems that the firstborn son of a certain *oba* was weak, greedy, and despised by the people of the city. Yet it was he, the firstborn, who was designated to take over when it would be time for the old man to die.

The people of the city were at a loss at what to do. There was no democracy, of course, so the son couldn't be voted out. And a violent *coup* was out of the question because of the family's powerful juju; it would avenge anyone who lifted a hand against the son.

But it happened that the fence was being replaced at that time and the *oba* had ordered victims to be captured so the appropriate sacrifices could be made.

One morning very early, the firstborn son stepped out of his house to respond to a call of nature. He was set upon by a group of the junior priests. They bound and gagged him and hid him in the forest. Then they went to the *oba*.

"Great *Oba*," the priests said, "we have secured victims for the sacrifice to *Legba*, just as you commanded."

"Well done," said the *oba*. "We will make ritual tomorrow morning. See to it."

But the men just stood there, looking from one to the other with worried looks on their faces.

"What's wrong?" said the *oba*.

"Great *Oba*, we captured the last man only this morning. It was still dark and we could not see him. He turns out to be an important man with great and powerful friends."

"Hmmmm." The *oba* thought for a moment. "But all men are the same to the *orisha*. If any man wanders into your grasp, surely it must mean that the *orisha* intended for him to be caught. It is his destiny. Do not think about it further."

But the men continued to look frightened. "Great *Oba,* he is a jujuman, a Man of Power, a *babalawo.* His juju is great and powerful."

The *oba* half-rose out of his throne. "Wha-a-a-t? Do you think that *his* juju is more powerful than *my* juju?" He relaxed when the men quaked satisfactorily. "I order you to prepare for sacrifice tomorrow morning—"

"But the man we caught this morning—"

"Enough!" The *oba* boomed. "No man is greater than the rituals! Were it my very own son, I would carry out the ritual exactly as given to us by our ancestors."

Having said this, there was no turning back. His honor required him to bury his own firstborn son alive the next morning, which he did. History does not record what happened to the plotters.

During my years at Grandfather's compound, the fence never had to be replaced. A good thing for me. I had an enemy there who felt about me the way the plotters felt about the *oba's* son: he was Joshua, the son of my father's brother. That may seem a roundabout way of saying he was my cousin, but I have no other way to express the relationship: We have no word such as "cousin"; all are brothers.

My brother Joshua was twice my age when I came to Inesi-Ile and was already looking forward to his own initiation. His father was the seventh son of our grandfather and Joshua was the seventh son of his father. To be the seventh son of a seventh son is very big juju. I understand the same is true in Europe, where supernatural powers are often ascribed to the seventh son of a seventh son. No one in our village—especially Joshua— could understand why Joshua had not been made Grandfather's heir.

Of course, the day the news came that *Orisha-Oko* was inside me, Grandfather's peculiar behavior suddenly made sense to everybody; he'd obviously waited so that he could name me to succeed him. If anything, his reputation for wisdom was enhanced. So when my mother and I arrived in Inesi-Ile, everyone chanted and bowed down to me. Except Grandfather, of course. And Joshua.

Even as a child, Joshua's hatred of me was profound. I remember how he used to try juju on me, to make me sick. At first, everybody thought he was cute, making his little hex signs at me and cooking up his little charms.

But in fact, shortly after my arrival, I did take quite ill. I developed a mysterious fever and nearly died. It was the end of the dry season before I recovered. People said it was young Joshua, strong with juju even at such a tender age.

For years, he was my constant torment. He would pinch me when we attended the adults so that I would cry out. Then, of course, I'd get cuffed on the head for disturbing my elders: God or no god, there were standards of behavior in the compound.

Even as we grew, so did our enmity for each other. It was a relief when his heart was finally captured several years later. Her name was Rebecca Abanogu. I remember once when I was about ten years old, he tried to trouble me in her presence and she rebuked him for it. She hugged me close and called me "little brother." It was the first time I'd ever been near the breast of a woman who was not my mother. Her breast was warm and firm and smooth. It yielded like a bag filled with duck feathers when she held my cheek to it and rubbed it comfortingly across my face. I became confused about my feelings toward her at that moment and finally decided that what I was feeling must have been gratitude for her kindness.

It infuriated Joshua, of course. But he never again taunted me when she could hear. And since he followed her around constantly, it neutralized him as a threat to me.

In any event, there was less time for me to come in contact with Joshua than there might have been. Most of my time when I was growing up was spent at Grandfather's side, watching him officiate at juju ceremonies. Because I had not yet been initiated, I was not allowed at this time to see or participate in any of the secret rituals out in the forest. That was good because it gave me time for school.

School was Grandfather's idea. Usually, our people didn't hold much with school, believing it to be "white man's magic." But Grandfather made an exception in my case. It was his long-range plan that I should record on paper the whole of juju knowledge. This had never been done before and he felt that it would make me the most powerful jujuman not only of Nigeria, but of all Africa.

Of course, that meant I had to learn to read and write. Rather than let me go to school to be "polluted" by outsiders, he found a tutor willing to stay on in the village: Mr. Olungwe.

Mr. Olungwe was a sad man, impoverished and wifeless. All his study had not helped him to get a job in the Civil Service, which is where most educated Africans wound up in those days. Nor was it his fault. During his last year in school, a kinsman of Mr. Olungwe's had led an abortive and well-publicized uprising in neighboring Cameroon in which hundreds were killed. The name "Olungwe" became a kind of curse and seeking work became futile for anyone of that name. His family's property had been seized, including the little money he'd sent them to save for him. Lacking a "bride price," his options were limited. But even families that had women who were difficult to marry off wouldn't allow them to go to an Olungwe.

So he taught me in return for his keep. I learned reading, writing, and arithmetic. He taught me in Hausa, English, and French. But the textbooks were left over from British colonial days, so I thought history consisted only of the Battle of Hastings, the Magna Carta, and Lord Nelson. Of African history, I was totally unaware.

Mr. Olungwe's difficult job of teaching me was made harder still by Grandfather's insistence that no "missionary juju" or "white man's juju" find its way into my young head. In other words, he was to teach me the mechanics of the "three Rs" and nothing else. As a graduate of the mission school and a European university, and as a consumer of Western books, he must have found it difficult to always avoid sensitive issues.

Whenever there was public juju ceremony (which seemed to be most of the time), school was out for me. For days at a time, my classroom would become my grandfather's side. The result of all these interruptions in my formal education was that it took me a long time to learn a little.

But gradually, the primer on juju that Grandfather wanted grew fat. In fact, I became somewhat of a fanatic about the white man's magic known as writing. The way the little black marks could make the paper talk seemed to me very big juju. Among our people, the mysterious sheets of marked-up paper were known as the "talking leaves." Through them, a man could speak to other men even after his death without a necromancer as a go-between, as our verbal system required.

I began to write down everything: the ceremonies that Grandfather told me to record, of course. But also chants. Curses. Charms. And, most of all, herbal recipes. Recipes for curing every kind of illness, for bringing luck, for male potency. I wrote with yellow #2 pencils sharpened with the edge of a machete. I wrote on big yellow tablets with green lines; those tablets had a wonderful pulpy smell about them that I remember to this day. I stored the pages in a big metal box which Grandfather hid for me at his Shrine way out in the forest. He carried the box back and forth himself, but he let me keep the key to it, which was a great honor and trust. I wore it around my neck, clanking against my cowries and all my other juju.

There seemed no end of information: Every jujuman adds something of his own to the standard procedures and recipes, and I tried to record it all. But, big as my manuscript was becoming, it still contained no information at all on the secret rituals that were for the initiates alone. I'd only witnessed the harmless public ceremonies—the ones with which we amused ourselves by charging tourists and anthropologists to watch. In spite of my exalted position as the heir apparent to my grandfather, in spite of all I'd seen at his side, in spite of all I'd written during six years, I'd not even gotten close to *real* juju.

But that would be rectified as soon as I completed my initiation.

5

During all the rest of my initiation ritual, my guides spent time with me by turns so that I was never permitted to sleep. Nor was I allowed solid food or water in all that time. Instead, I was supposed to be sustained by the mystical wonders they served up for me. They took turns introducing me to the spirits that were important to my people.

The way of it was always the same. If the woman was finished with me, she would leave the ritual hut. Sometimes the sound of drums would then begin to come from outside but at other times, all remained silent; so, unlike me, my guides may have had opportunities to sleep. If the woman left, the man would come in. He would first conjure with various juju before sacrificing an animal of the type that was pleasing to the specific *orisha* he wanted me to meet. Then we would share the blood of the sacrifice.

After that, he would wash himself with the juju-water from the skull pot. Immediately, the animal whose blood we had just consumed would possess him. The animal would then proceed to tell me all that is good for a man to know about the secrets of its kind.

When it was finished, the animal would dip its paw or wing into the juju-water. Only this time, it would use the serpent pot. As the animal washed with the juju-water, the man would repossess his own flesh. He would leave the hut, drained and weakened. But the woman would shortly take his place and the cycle would begin again.

In this way, I met many benign spirits: the wise tortoise, the loyal and brave dog, and the fun-loving monkey. We laughed together and they became like my brothers.

But I also met darker spirits: the slinking hyena, the traitorous jackal, and the brooding vulture. Those spirits called forth the horrifying *orisha* whom they represented. *Isa,* the god of evil and illness, threatened me with every kind of sickness. *Ifa,* the god of understanding, cursed me and threatened to make me go mad. And *Ogun,* the god of metals, threatened to cook me—"slowly and forever," he said—in his forge.

I lost track of time and place. As I did, the world of the ritual hut became more and more terrifying to me. At one point, I felt my body was covered by masses of our huge African termites. Later, I recognized snow falling from the roof of the hut, even though I'd never seen snow except in pictures. It buried me alive; I was colder than I imagined anyone could ever be.

Toward the end, the woman appeared. She was wearing a wrapper around her body—yellow with large black spots surrounded with green rings. It was a very beautiful pattern—familiar, though my mind seemed unable to make sense of it. From her bag she brought forth a snake with spots similar to her wrapper, but of different colors. I wondered if it might be the same snake that had slept on my stomach back when the initiation started.

She knelt by my side. "Now," she said, baring her pointed teeth in a grin, "you prepare to meet *Orunmila.*" She was panting slightly, as if she was short of breath, and her skin glowed with perspiration, even though she'd not yet started. It was as if she was excited, the way I'd heard a woman was when she was with a man.

"*Orunmila?*" I repeated weakly. My mind seemed as if it was full of smoke. I felt a perfect fool, aware that the name was that of one of our most important and powerful *orishas,* but still unable to place it.

"The god of all secrets," she breathed, stroking the snake. "Only he can tell you the ways of the most dangerous animals of all—other men." She rose gracefully, like an Ibo queen, still stroking the snake. In a few moments, it became limp. The woman slid her hand down to its tail and let the rest of its body dangle toward the dirt floor.

Suddenly, she snapped it—BANG!—over her head like a whip. Every bone in its body must have broken at once.

With a mighty jerk, she pulled the head off and dropped the rest on my chest, with the usual reminder to drink deeply of it. As I did, I saw her tilt the skull pot up on its side to scoop out the last of the juju-water. I remember how seeing her do this brought me joy; it meant the end was near. All I had to do was tough out this final exercise and manhood would be mine.

Drums started outside the hut. The woman began to writhe in time to them. As if by magic, the patterned wrapper she wore around her body seemed to stretch as I watched. It began to get longer, until it covered her feet. And it began to get higher, until it covered first her neck and finally her face. At the same time, it began to get tighter and tighter, stretching until it fit her as tightly as the skin of a . . .

Python!

It opened its glassy eyes and wiggled its forked tongue in my direction, tasting the air to see if I would be as juicy as I looked. It was a very long snake—every bit as long as the woman had been tall. And it seemed very, very strong, heavy with juju.

There was nothing of the intangible about this giant snake, nothing that could have come from lack of sleep or food, nothing that could have resulted from the power of suggestion or from all the blood I'd ingested. The snake was even more real than the other visions I'd had. It was as real as I was, as real as my grandfather, as real as Africa itself. In fact, I heard it tell me somewhere deep inside myself that it was the very *soul* of Africa.

I had to face the most powerful symbol of a society rooted in symbols and I couldn't do it. I screamed and ran in a panic to the doorhole of the hut, willing even to give up my manhood to escape. But the tiny hole undid me; before I could wiggle out, the snake was on me.

I had already screamed all my air out. I could take no more in because the python's coils bound me from knees to neck and they were tightening. I cried out—but only in my heart—to my ancestors, that they might receive me well in the other world.

But suddenly, the pain of the python's coils was gone. I took in air . . . no, I was as *light* as air! I opened my eyes and saw the roof of the hut almost touching my face; it was so close, I even blew away a fire ant from a piece of thatching an inch in front of my nose.

I rolled over in space and saw my body below me, wrapped in the coils of a huge yellow and green python. A hot feeling came up to me from the great serpent, as if it hated me. Even as I watched, the coils tightened until I heard popping noises come from my body. But, somehow, I was not afraid. Could this be the secret of Initiation? Did it explain the warning my grandfather had always given me that, "Nothing can ever *really* hurt you"?

I heard a rushing sound, like the wind from the tropical cyclone. I looked down again and saw the *babalorisha* leaning over my body with a drinking gourd in his hand. He was calling my name loudly enough for me to hear him over the sound of the wind.

Suddenly, without having made any effort to get back to my body, I was down on the floor again, looking up at him. Next to him was the woman, the *ayelorisha*. She was wearing a spotted wrapper, no different from the kind any other Yoruba woman might wear.

I drank from the gourd. It was blood again. Not chicken blood, which we tasted almost daily in my village. Not snake, which I'd had earlier, either. Something I'd never tasted before. A little like pig blood. But rather different, actually. I looked around, but could not see what animal they had killed to get the blood.

"Are you well?" the woman asked.

"Y-yes," I said. "But the serpent . . ."

"Serpent?" the man asked. "Look around you. Do you see any 'serpent' here?"

"No, but . . ."

"Take this," he said. He ripped a long narrow strip from the white robe I'd worn on my pilgrimage to the ritual hut. The robe had been hanging from the roof pole ever since we'd arrived, a silent witness to all that had happened here. While I held one end of the long strip, he twisted it into a tight, rope-like braid. "This," he said, "will become your *ibante.*"

I closed my eyes and nearly wept with relief: The *ibante* is a jujuman's source of power. What he was telling me was that I'd made it, that I was "in." From now on, I was going to be a *babalawo,* a Man of Power, among my people. Even more, I would become their *babalorisha* when my grandfather died. I would be privileged to talk to the gods and to all of our ancestors directly. It meant that the way was now cleared for me to become eventually the supreme juju leader of all West Africa.

The *babalorisha* produced a needle from his bag. It was threaded with some very strong, clear material. Then he and the woman both emptied on the ground the last of their bags, out of which fell many pieces of juju. He handed me the needle and thread.

At his direction, I picked the juju from the dirt one after the other and sewed them to the long skinny braid of white cloth. Most of the juju were either cowries or small, polished bones, although there were also a few metal and wooden objects: buttons, they looked like. Sewing was another of those tasks which were not appropriate for men in my clan to perform, so I made slow and sloppy work of it. But at last I was finished.

Then they helped me to drench the *ibante* in the last of the unfamiliar blood that the *babalorisha* had given me from his drinking gourd. I held one end of the braid just below my navel while the two of them crawled around, winding it between my legs, around, and back again. When they were finished, it looked as if I were wearing crotchless, bloody briefs, my manhood protruding from the stringy triangle so formed.

It was intended that I should wear this power garment under my outer clothes for the rest of my life. But the taboo required that it be worn in the utmost secrecy. I could never undress in front of anyone and, even when alone, I could never undress in the light. I could never submit to an examination by a medical doctor. And, when I married, I would oblige my wife to wear a hood whenever we coupled, lest she accidentally glimpse the source of my power.

The *babalorisha* threw me a pair of old khaki shorts and told me to cover myself. Then the *ayelorisha* carried the last of the drinking water to me, which was as things were meant to be. She also brought me some fresh-dug yams, the best I'd ever tasted. There were no congratulations to accompany the meal, though—those would come later at my celebration ceremony. Instead, I just fell asleep, half a yam still in my mouth.

When I awoke, my two guides were gone. I have never seen either of them again. Nor would I care to look for them.

As custom demanded, I knocked down the ritual hut and scattered the pieces. To the eye of any anthropologist or tourist who ever stumbled on the spot, it would be as if nothing had happened in this place since the dawn of time.

When the Sun was barely above the horizon, I set off toward home. The three days of private ritual were finally over; the seven days of public ceremony were about to begin.

The Juju Scholar

6

I made my way back to Inesi-Ile through a forest that had become different
to me in the past three days. It was warmer, lighter, and less threatening
than the ominous place it had always been before.

Still, I knew it was me who had changed not the forest. The spirits
that lurked behind every rock and inside every tree were still there. And
they were as vicious as ever; I still wouldn't want to be caught out in
the forest after dark or on a day that had bad omens.

But I felt more secure because for the first time I had a *defense* against
the random evils that befall men. I now knew that the ancestors and the
nature spirits and even the *orisha* could be appeased and thus (to some
extent anyway) they could be controlled. I was sure I would learn countless
ways to deal with them during my development as *babalorisha:* charms,
hexes, and chants. But already I understood the most potent appeaser of
all: blood.

Nor was I unaware of the power my new knowledge would give me
over others—over many of the men and all of the women. They would
know I was different, reputed to be a new and mighty man of knowledge.
I was only just beginning to flatter myself with the fantasies of all that
such a reputation could mean.

Because I no longer felt the need to move especially silently, a raggedy
band of children heard me when I was yet some distance from the village.
I barely saw them before they ran away from me in mock terror, a tangle
of little brown arms and legs. In an instant, they were out of sight, racing
toward Inesi-Ile. Every one of them wanted to be the first to have the
honor to shout, breathless and wide-eyed, "A strange man approaches!

A strange man approaches!"

The drums started almost immediately. So by the time I made my way to the ceremonial clearing by Grandfather's Temple, a large group of men had gathered. They closed in a big circle around me as I went to the center of the clearing. Spears in hand, they danced flat-footed and fierce-looking to the beat of the drums. They took turns stepping forward, shaking their spears menacingly in my direction and yelling dire threats. When the turn came round to him, Joshua glared at me as if he really did want to kill me.

For my part, of course, I simply stared indifferently off into space, as befits a Man of Knowledge. Out of the corner of my eye, though, I looked to see if Rebecca Abanogu was near Joshua. But, of course, it would have been taboo for a woman to be present in the warriors' circle.

Finally, after the last man had his chance to show his determination to defend our village against all comers, it was time for someone to step forward and "recognize" me. Custom dictated that it be my father. But in his absence, my grandfather himself honored me by stepping put of the circle of townsmen. He performed his part well, approaching me haltingly with much hesitation. When he was close enough to touch me, he stopped and squinted up into my face. He blinked a few times, as if trying to place me. Then, he let a big, toothless smile split his face. "People of Inesi-Ile," he shouted, "fear not! For this is my son, Isaiah—now a man!"

It was the signal. The men all threw down their spears and came forward, laughing, to embrace me. The women, who had all been inside, presumably quaking in terror, now came out singing and dancing in time to the music. Even the children dropped their act and joined in. All except for one little fellow who obviously hadn't been briefed; he picked up a dropped spear, charged me, and jabbed me painfully in the calf. I scooped him up and held him over my head. "This one is as brave as a man already," I shouted, and everyone laughed some more.

Everything from that point on is in progressively hazier detail because someone shoved a shell of palm wine into my hand and I downed it in salute. It was not the milky, mildly alcoholic drink that accompanies our food, but the strong stuff—"man's wine," we call it.

The first group of sacrificial animals were brought out immediately: the seven calves. There would also be seven he-goats, seven she-goats, seven cocks, seven hens, seven lambs and seven antelopes, all of which would be consumed with much palm wine in a seven-day feast of gigantic proportions.

One of the great things about a "new man" festival is that it's one of the few times we can celebrate in a purely "secular" manner. That is, the drumming, the fiddling, the dancing, and the drinking that accompany the ceremonies lack the religious overtones that color most of our activities. This festival is just for fun, an outcome of our exuberance for life.

And we certainly took advantage of the opportunity. The dancing and the music were as spirited as I've ever seen. Few of the celebrants even stopped their merrymaking to observe Grandfather's first ceremonial cut.

The calf was first anointed with the appropriate herbs by a group of women, one of whom was Rebecca Abanogu. Then they dragged it out and tethered it to a pole in the square. Two of the men, already giddy with palm wine, grabbed the calf's hindquarters and pulled backwards to make the animal stretch its neck.

Grandfather inspected his sacrificial knife with a practiced eye and bobbed his head in satisfaction. He pulled the calf's head back and swiftly drew the knife across its throat in the prescribed manner, from the left ear to the right. The left side being unlucky, this was a prayer that bad luck should turn to good.

But his knife missed the jugulars and he had to make another pass at the bleating creature. This was a major embarrassment for him because he was usually far more precise in his work. When he sprinkled the customary handful of blood on the crowd, his mouth was tight with shame. I noticed that, after that, he declined any more palm wine.

The women set on the carcass at once. Within minutes, it was skinned, gutted, split in two, and spitted over the fire. It smelled wonderful.

The men continued toasting me and each other; the palm wine flowed like water. There were strong, homemade cigars for all of us to share while we sang all the old songs to the accompaniment of the musicians.

People soon began to behave peculiarly. Men I knew to be quiet and serious became boisterous. Others who were always industrious and hard-working now lay around the fire, barely half-conscious. Well-behaved daughters and sisters were telling secret jokes to one another and laughing out loud quite unbecomingly. Of course, that was the whole idea of all the drinking and the other activities.

By the time the Sun was down and we were into the fifth calf, I noticed something that I'd never noticed before. Some of the women would roll their eyes, sort of, in the direction of the men. The men would grin and knock each other in the ribs until, after a while, one of them would get up from the circle and go speak to a woman. Then, full of palm wine and laughing, they would go into the bush together.

I had no doubt that this sort of thing went on at every big celebration, but I'd never noticed it before. Of course, this was the first time I'd ever had any cause to pay attention to it; initiation in our culture is chosen to coincide with sexual maturity. So, for the first time, I was a man in more ways than one and that meant I found the women interesting, especially Rebecca Abanogu.

She was one of the women standing around behind the squatted circle of singing men, so naturally I just couldn't help but notice her. Joshua had chosen his spot in the circle to be directly in front of her, as always, and if I craned my neck to see over him, I could just make out Rebecca's breasts bouncing over his head. They were shiny with sweat from the exertion of dancing and, as I watched them, I felt myself becoming aroused.

As I explained, this was a new sensation for me and I was embarrassed lest anyone should see my shame. For I was wearing only a loose loin cloth over my *ibante* and it did nothing to either hide or suppress my erection. So I sort of hunched over uncomfortably and leaned in toward the fire, trying to act casual and natural. I don't think I fooled anyone because more of the rib-knocking immediately started up and I could hear some of the women giggling even above the sound of song. I was mortified, certain with the self-consciousness of the newly pubescent that they were laughing at my lack of self-control. But I still found it impossible not to stare at Rebecca Abanogu.

Then I looked up to her face and saw that *she* was looking at *me*. To be specific, she was staring at my lap, in which I'd placed my folded hands as a desperate attempt at camouflage. Her wide-set dark eyes were big and she appeared to be breathing through her moist mouth. Her sweat was coming harder now, and the area around her full lips was glistening with it. I was both panic-stricken and aroused almost to the point of release but she didn't seem to notice my discomfort.

When she finally raised her eyes to my face, she stunned me by smiling pleasantly, as if she wasn't shocked by me in the least. In fact, she started rolling her eyes at me the way the other women had been doing to the men of their choice. I heard the newness of my loin cloth rustle in time to my throbbing. The thought that she was inviting me to go into the bush with her was almost more than I could bear.

I tore my eyes away from Rebecca and down to Joshua. He was rocking back and forth to the drums, his eyes glazed like those of a man with yellow fever. He held his wine gourd at an angle and the milky fluid was dripping onto the ground. Rebecca started dancing a private dance of her own behind Joshua. It was not a formal ceremonial dance, just the slow swaying of her hips from side to side, and then forward and back. Yet

I knew instinctively that it was perhaps the oldest dance of all.

Grandfather leaned over to me, winking and laughing in rare good humor. "Joshua sleeps," he laughed, pointing, "even in the midst of much song. Clearly, he prefers wine to a woman tonight, eh?"

I could not speak.

He leaned even closer in the kind of conspiracy older men feel with the younger in such matters. His voice fell almost to a whisper. "You are a man now," he said quietly. "You may do as a man does."

I continued to be too embarrassed to answer; I just hung my head. When I didn't respond, his lecherous grin faded. "Unless you prefer otherwise, my son. We know, of course, that some men prefer for themselves the way of a woman, although I thought you . . ."

"No, Pa," I said. "It's not that. It's just that, well, how does one do it? I mean . . ."

He laughed again, his gummy mouth wide in mirth. "Is it for nothing that you have watched over our livestock all your life? That you were initiated as a Man of Knowledge? That the cock and the he-goat told you their secrets and gave to you of their blood?"

He was right, of course; it wasn't ignorance that was holding me back. The real explanation for my hesitancy was the same as it was for every other young man: fear of falling short of expectations. Fear of failure. Especially with this much older woman, the woman of my brother, Joshua.

But in the end, desire won out over prudence. Which, I understand, is the way it works in every culture. I rolled outwards from the circle, saving myself the embarrassment of standing up before the light of the fire. I walked uncertainly around the outside of the clearing until I was behind Rebecca. She turned to look at me, still swaying. I knew I was supposed to "talk her up" as the other men had done.

"Uh," I said, "uh."

Joshua was slumped forward now, but I didn't want to be too loud anyway. Rebecca didn't seem concerned about him at all, though. She laughed and said in a loud, mocking voice, "Is this some magical chant from the new Man of Knowledge? Some powerful new juju? Will it charm the birds from the trees, perhaps?"

I cleared my throat and started over again. "Uh," I said. "Uh."

Rebecca threw back her head and laughed heartily. "How can I resist the eloquence of this 'new man'?" She laughed again. "Very well, Spirit-Man," she said, "I am bewitched by your chant. Come." And with her leading me by the hand, we went off together into the bush so that I could learn the last secret of manhood, the one only a woman could teach.

7

The question of sex always comes up when I discuss juju rituals with my American friends. They expect to hear that not only is *sex* central to our rituals, but that *perverted* sex is. They seem to want me to tell them how juju high priests perform unspeakable sexual perversions in their dark and hidden shrines in the forest. And when I tell them that sexual perversion is not a primary factor in juju rituals, they seem disappointed.

However, it's true that for certain cults (mostly those dedicated to the *orisha* we know as *Esu*), violent and perverted forms of sex have an almost sacramental status. One such cult in Uganda, for example, practices *bestiality* (sex between humans and animals) as an essential ingredient of its rituals. After the private ritual, there is a public ceremony in which the animals so used are slaughtered and consumed raw by the population.

But such behavior is the exception rather than the rule in juju. The reason is that we Africans make less of a fuss about sex than do Americans. That may be because we live closer to nature than do many other peoples and our children are in a position to observe and understand sex from an early age. What juju perverts are those things that it regards as *secret*. And, among us, sex is no secret. So it follows that our rituals emphasize aspects of life other than sex.

But our juju ceremonies are something else again. Our ceremonies are less "religious," more "secular," than our rituals. And they are very sexy. But rather than being an *ingredient* of these ceremonies, as most Westerners expect, sex is a *consequence* of them.

Consider how some of the characteristics of our juju ceremonies make sex among the celebrants almost inevitable. For one thing, our juju ceremonies often go on for days, during which we continuously consume enormous quantities of palm wine. While it's true that our wine is weak compared to Western whiskey, it is quite intoxicating when consumed in sufficient quantity. Even when consumed moderately, it weakens inhibitions (or so claims any man caught in the bush with his neighbor's wife during a ceremony).

Drums are another feature of ceremonies that contribute to free availability of sex. They are played literally without stop for days during a long ceremony, and their effect is indeed hypnotic.

Then there's our local tobacco: very, very strong, and rolled by the women into enormous cigars. And sometimes, there's more than tobacco in them: Every village herbalist knows more than a few recipes for hallucinogenic brews. We use these concoctions to spike the palm wine and to "sweeten," as we say, the cigar smoke.

Of course, the jujuman will never admit that his potions are being used "recreationally," for the purpose of inebriation; that would be too frivolous an application of juju powers. Rather, he says that he is "awakening" the people, "enlivening" them, so that they can participate more fully in the ceremony. The ultimate goal is for the celebrants to achieve an intoxicated and uninhibited state in which they can do the things that our closely-regulated tribal way of life ordinarily forbids.

All these activities—plus the general mood of fun and merrymaking—tend to stimulate sexual desire. Adding to that desire are our marriage customs. Marriage among us tends to occur quite late: when the woman is in her mid-twenties or so, and usually, the man is even older. So there is a long time, often ten years or more, between the onset of puberty and marriage—just when sexual curiosity and desire are at their peaks, in other words. During that time, we nonetheless expect both men and women to remain officially celibate. But note the word "officially." The reality is that sex is quite common.

Then, there's the issue of polygamy, though it's frowned on now in most modern African nations. But Islam tolerates it and juju positively encourages it—for the higher-ranking men in the society, anyway. You can imagine how the ordinary "man in the street" feels about it, how it adds to the tension in the community.

So juju people release their sexual tensions at festivals like our harvest ceremony, which occurs only after all our millet and maize have been safely stored. It's a four-day ceremony that falls on a different date every year. One of the high priest's jobs is keeping the calendar and telling the people when it's time to perform such activities. The method by which the date for the harvest ceremony is determined gives insight into the surprising depth to which juju belief penetrates African life.

First, the high priest with his lesser priests in attendance tours the whole town and all the surrounding countryside to make sure all work is done. Then he calls for various predictions from all the area's diviners. He will consult with every prognosticator and fortuneteller from the *ifa* man (who employs a wooden instrument something like a *ouija* board) to the astrologer (astrology being a very important art in juju). Finally, he'll secrete himself in his Shrine in the forest for a few days where he'll make sacrifice, drink blood, and talk directly to the *orisha*. Only then will he be able to direct the people to prepare for a feast. Several days will be required for the community to get ready.

Part of getting ready involves the unmarried young women. Through what is supposed to be an naive dance of thanksgiving, each girl can show the community how devout and innocent she is. But she really has a strong sexual interest that our social rules do not let her satisfy. The juju dance gives her a way to behave erotically while outwardly appearing to be chaste.

The dance goes on all through the ceremony and is for unmarried young women only; their ages are from about thirteen or so, on up to the late twenties. Each girl has to balance a grain pot on her head, so the dance is actually more of a *walk*. Anyone watching her will understand that to keep the pot balanced, the walk has to be slow, and very rhythmic. Apparently, walking with the hips thrust sharply forward while swinging the buttocks works well for most of the girls. Of course, a young woman out in the Sun so.much during festival time ought to oil her body frequently with her best scented ointments. And it would be wasteful to rub off all that luxurious, fragrant oil, so she parades through the town naked. Well, not completely naked: All the girls in the long, writhing-snake line wear jewelry made of gold, cowries, and beads, and they also wear rouge on their faces and their nipples.

The effect on our young men (and our old ones, too, for that matter) is about what you'd expect it to be—the same as it would be anywhere.

Of course, any man who desires to take one of these young women into the bush has to do his part to foster the deception, too. So he may paint his face or wear a cloth mask. Then both the man and the woman can claim that her seduction was by an unknown spirit who temporarily possessed the man.

In this way, behavior that might have been condemned is transformed into something that is socially acceptable. What we actually wind up with is our young girls being ravaged repeatedly by men wearing grotesque masks, which you could probably sell tickets for in Times Square. But we soothe ourselves with the notion that it is an innocent ceremony of thanksgiving and no one is to blame if it gets out of hand. And, because this ordinarily contemptible behavior goes unpunished, it is repeated at every juju ceremony.

An obvious result of all this freely available sex is our unacceptably high rate of venereal disease in Africa. People intoxicated by the many raptures of a juju ceremony do not trouble themselves to practice safe sex. Nor is it likely we can ever convince them to do so; they are simply too carried away to think of such precautions. The ready availability of sex under juju may also explain some of the high rates of our other communicable diseases, although the link with diseases that are not sexually transmitted is less obvious.

But there is one tragedy that we may be *certain* results from juju sex practice: the distinctly African phenomenon of "throwaway babies." It is one of the saddest chapters of our history and a growing shame. What to do with all the unwanted children that result from our wild juju ceremonies? Abortions are almost unknown among us: They are too expensive and they seem contrary to our philosophy of life. So a woman who conceives during a juju festival will likely carry the baby to term.

But she can't keep it. A suitor might overlook her lack of virginity, especially if he can be persuaded that it resulted from a spiritual encounter. But what are the chances of convincing him that *he* has to raise the child? A child makes a young woman nearly worthless in terms of bride price. So she needs to get rid of her unwanted child *after* its birth rather than *before,* as is done in the West. Her parents may even have made it a condition of allowing her to stay in the family home during her pregnancy.

Juju has ritual uses for babies. And, given that the problem is especially prevalent among jujuwomen, the answer would seem obvious: Present the child to the head priest. But *unwanted* babies are taboo to juju ritual; anything *unwanted,* anything *valueless,* doesn't comprise much of a sacrifice, does it? Juju can use only things of value for its blood rituals. So a *babalawo* must obtain a newborn baby before its mother has the chance to throw it away, which act would obviously alert the *orisha* that it's unwanted. If no cooperative mother can be found, jujumen will steal a baby for rituals that require one.

But the typical juju ritual does not require human sacrifice. So a woman who has an unwanted infant generally adopts the simple expedient of abandoning it, usually in the dead of night. For the woman who lives in the country, the nearby forest makes a convenient dumping ground. Clearly, a newborn infant can't be expected to last long there and the hyena and jackals ensure that there will be no carcass. City women have brought this abandonment practice with them, leaving their babies in the town garbage dump, where rats fill in for the hyenas.

Guilt is seldom a problem after these abandonments. Remember that a jujuwoman is quite accustomed to blood and violent death. Remember, also, that she considers the baby to be the spawn of an evil spirit who seduced her in the guise of a man. Her parents accept this too. And the real father may not realize the baby is his. Or he may even be unknown. So it's really not a matter of conscience for anybody involved.

The number of newborn infants abandoned in this fashion is incalculable. The dumping procedures automatically eliminate the evidence so people can plausibly deny that it happens. It makes it possible for tenderhearted Americans to doubt the truth of the whole ugly story. But there's an objective, scientifically verifiable fact that helps to convince them: If one calculates the ratio of pregnant women to live births, it is clear that there are far more pregnancies in Central Africa than there are infants.

So what happened to the "missing babies"?

The answer we often hear shows how the West misleads itself about Africa. Officials from such groups as the World Health Organization are certainly aware that there are fewer infants in Africa than the incidence of pregnancy would indicate. But these officials have been trained in Western modes of thinking; they can't imagine the world as it is under juju. The educated officials have to find some rational, acceptable explanation. So they assume that the missing babies were stillborn or that they died of natural causes shortly after birth. They ascribe the causes of these deaths to unspecified "poor health practices." Then they put out a report citing the poor health practices they just invented as the reason for Africa's "high infant mortality rate."

Happily, some people who have taken the trouble to understand Africa have now begun to address the problem. Pastor Danny Curle is one who comes to mind. With the support of sponsors like Diane Lewis in the United States, he cares for hundreds of these "throwaways" at "feeding stations" throughout Zimbabwe. And, in my own modest way, I am trying to follow his example in southern Nigeria. But we know we're just lighting one candle against the darkness of juju culture in Africa.

Sex and its aftermath represent one example of the way juju perverts normal human tendencies. Of course, I acknowledge that we Africans would still have our fair share of unwanted pregnancies and venereal disease even without juju. But the important words are "our fair share"; our problem would be more or less like anybody else's, rather than the crushing burden we now bear.

Juju lets people escape the social blame for the counterproductive behavior that would otherwise remain suppressed. And as long as it does, we Africans will be held back. This makes juju more than a religion—it makes juju the enemy of a modern Africa. It makes our people free to blame any ills not on themselves, but on a distinctively African phenomenon—spirit possession—which was the next thing I learned about.

8

The day after the ceremony began, I felt like a lion. I strutted about the town like one of the roosters that Grandfather was to sacrifice that day.

That afternoon when I saw Rebecca Abanogu at the feast, I almost committed the unpardonable blunder of acknowledging her. Fortunately, she was more experienced in these matters than I was and had better sense. When she saw me coming toward her, bright-eyed and eager, she turned and walked casually toward her girlfriends as if she didn't know me at all. Which, in a sense, was the case; from her standpoint, her lover had been a "Spirit-Man," not me.

I didn't see her for the next couple of days. She kept herself to her gaggle of girlfriends and ignored all the men of the village, Joshua and me included.

I mooned around a bit at first, barely aware of the celebration going on in my honor all around me. I cheered up only gradually as all the women of the town fed me morsels of the food their daughters had been preparing ever since they heard a festival was scheduled. I don't want to appear shallow about my feelings for Rebecca, but even the pain of unrequited love must give way when a teenage boy savors the delights of smoked goat, marinated cowrie meat, and fermented cabbage.

Besides, Grandfather took me to one side when he saw me so miserable. He explained how any woman of the village would find it a great honor to give herself to *Orisha-Oko,* the spirit that possessed me. I quickly tested his theory and found he was right. After that, I felt just fine.

By the time of the song circle on the third evening, I had recovered myself considerably. I sat in front of the fire, just listening rather than joining in, thinking about how we juju people really live two lives. One is our everyday life of work and family, and living by the rules of our society. The other is a life of wild and reckless abandon, quickly lived and easily forgotten—the life of the spirit-possessed.

Rebecca Abanogu had returned to the circle and I had half an eye on her when I saw Joshua rouse himself from his customary position near her. He was glassy-eyed, as though he'd had too much palm wine again. Without speaking, he left the circle on unsteady feet.

I leaned back and watched him leave us. I had good reason to watch him: Every time he'd looked at me the last few days, spears had come out of his eyes. I think he suspected what had happened between Rebecca and me. That would have been enough to get him angry at any man, let alone me whom he'd hated since I came to Nigeria.

He walked like a man in a dream to the garden area off to the side of the ceremonial clearing. He reached up to Grandfather's pecan tree and pulled on its lowest branch. He bounced it up and down several times and it finally broke with a loud snap. Sitting on the ground he quickly forged from it two long, skinny sticks, each with a V-shape on one end like a crutch. He stood, propped the crutches under his arms, and began to walk back toward the song circle.

And then a remarkable thing happened. With each step he took back toward us, he seemed to grow older. He began to bend over in the pain of advancing years. His back became hunched and he hobbled noticeably. Even his clothes seemed to go limp and hang from him like rags. A mangy old dog came out from somewhere and started hopping in excited circles, eyeing the sticks as if he expected a game of "fetch."

When Joshua got back to the group, he swung one of his crutches feebly and grunted, as old people do. The woman he struck turned to give him a piece of her mind, then stopped and gasped in amazement.

I saw her lips say, "Babalu-Aye," but I couldn't hear her. Then she said it again, louder this time so we all heard. She kept repeating the name over and over, rising in hysteria: "Babalu-Aye! *Babalu-Aye!*" As they figured out who was amongst them, the whole group in the clearing took up the chant: "*Babalu-Aye!* BABALU-AYE!"

For it was no longer Joshua among us; it was Babalu-Aye, the father of all *orisha.* He looked exactly as he did whenever we dared to depict him: a ragged old man supported on walking sticks and accompanied by a dog. In the flickering of the bonfire, even his skin looked old and lined, nothing like the young face of Joshua. It was the first public possession of the festival and the greatest.

Grandfather stumbled forward and greeted the *orisha*. "Great Babalu-Aye, how can we appease you? Is our ceremony not pleasant to you? Are the animals we sacrificed not. . . ."

Babalu-Aye waved his crutch and waited until there was complete silence. The dog seemed to lose interest as Babalu-Aye came to a standstill in the center of the circle. He scratched behind his ear a couple of times and then loped off into the darkness. When all was quiet and respectful, Babalu-Aye spoke softly in a hoarse voice, heavy with its coating of age. We all strained to hear.

". . . ceremony is acceptable," we heard him say. We all breathed a sigh of relief. "But I have a few things against some of these here," and we all held our breath again.

He started to turn slowly, sweeping his crutch slowly past the people like a cameraman panning a camera. Every time the crutch lingered over someone, that person shrieked in fear and cringed. Finally, the crutch came to rest pointing at a man who lived over on the other side of town. I knew him slightly as one of our local blacksmiths but not a good one, apparently: Joshua had bought some *nganga* pots from him and complained about the poor workmanship.

"That one," said Babalu-Aye. The blacksmith's eyes got wide and he quivered with fear. "That one is a cheat."

The cowering man shrieked, "No, Babalu-Aye! Please! I—"

"Silence!" boomed Grandfather in his best ceremonial voice. The blacksmith fell to his knees.

"That one," Babalu-Aye repeated, "is a cheat. Now, a cheat is the same as a thief. So he will suffer the justice of the thief: His right arm will wither up and will no longer know its former cunning with metals."

It was a sentence worse than death for a blacksmith. The man groaned once and fell face forward in a dead faint. No one went to his aid.

The crutch moved on.

"That one," said Babalu-Aye, pointing at a woman, a cranky old crone who sat on her porch all day and yelled insults at anyone who passed her yard. "That one's tongue has condemned her. She will die. Tonight. Even before the Moon rises!" The old lady's lips flapped up and down a few times, but for once, she could find no words.

The crutch moved again. It stopped at Rebecca Abanogu.

"That one. That one is a harlot. She dishonors the people of Inesi-Ile." Everyone gasped and moved away from the hapless Rebecca. "She, too, will die. For her harlotry." Rebecca started to cry.

"But first, her beauty will decay. She will become a hive of open sores, so that no man can look upon her and hold his eyes open. Flies will breed in her body and fly out into the world through her sores."

People were staring at Babalu-Aye in amazement. Truly, this was big, big juju! Surely the father of all *orisha* would not have chosen just anybody for the delivery of such a powerful curse. Perhaps a mistake had been made in not choosing this Joshua to be the next *babalorisha* after all.

"And when the flies have consumed all of her that they wish," Babalu-Aye concluded, "then she will die." He cackled with laughter and started his crutch slowly moving again. In my direction.

When he got to me, he stopped. Then he lifted his other stick from the ground; he pointed *both* his crutches at me and my heart turned to wood within my thirteen-year old chest.

"And *that* one," he shrieked in his creaky old voice. "*That* one . . ."

The mangy dog picked an ideal time to return. Running at full tilt, he playfully grabbed one of the sticks, spun the old *orisha* around, and sat him down irreverently in the fire.

I was the first one to run forward and help the leaping, hooting Joshua to put out the fire on his shirt. I knew the *orisha* had left him; it's common knowledge that spirits don't like fire.

We never heard what the *orisha* was about to say. But Grandfather fulfilled his duty as our *babalorisha* to interpret what Babalu-Aye *would* have said, had he been permitted to finish: That the *orisha* were most pleased with the progress Orisha-Oko was making in his spiritual development inside the body of Isaiah Oke and that he would become one day the greatest *babalorisha* in all Africa! Joshua made a face as if he wanted to challenge the authenticity of this interpretation. But nobody paid any attention to him; he was only Joshua again.

Rebecca Abanogu was helped off to her home by her friends, as was the devastated blacksmith. The gossipy old woman shook off all attempts to help her back to her home. She stomped her feet and feistily demanded to stay for the rest of the evening's sing-sing.

The drums started up again but the heart seemed to have gone out of the festival after the apparition. Still we tried. And eventually, with more palm wine, we were able to resurrect at least a semblance of our former good humor. Until the old sharptongue suddenly let out a loud, shivering wail and fell over, stone dead.

Grandfather hurriedly conferred with his lesser priests. The remainder of the festival was canceled by unanimous agreement.

In silence, we all watched the Moon finish rising.

9

A few days later, Grandfather dealt with the curse on the blacksmith and healed him completely. The news spread rapidly around town that *babalorisha* Aworo Oke's power was equal even to a curse laid by the *orisha* themselves.

Grandfather later confided to me that the cure had actually been an easy one. He was able to completely skip the first step in the typical juju healing: finding out who bewitched the victim in the first place. This can often take a good deal of research—consulting with the various diviners, and so forth. But in this case, we had all seen the curse laid by Babalu-Aye himself.

The next job in a healing is to find a counter for the curse. Suppose, for example, that someone lays a curse of diarrhea on his victim. This is a very common scourge in Africa, especially in those areas where there are no rivers to flush away wastes. Americans sometimes make a joke of diarrhea, considering it to be, at worst, an embarrassing inconvenience that ends in a few days. But we lack the medicine and the technology to deal with it and, with us, it is serious indeed. In fact, it has been estimated that between two and three million children under the age of five in Africa die each year of the dehydration that results from diarrhea. The World Health Organization even lists "emergency rehydration therapy" as one of its top priorities for Africa in the 1990s. The West, of course, blames our high incidence of diarrhea on dysentery from stagnant water. But we Africans know that it comes from a curse laid by some enemy.

There are many counters for diarrhea cases; each herbalist has his own. Grandfather preferred this one (being unaware, as far as I know, that diarrhea which persists for more than about seven days will kill its victim):

> Put a piece of raw pig tongue in a *nganga* pot. Add *kudu* urine to cover. Add several water hyacinth leaves. Boil until urine is gone. Remove tongue and discard. Add juju-water and honey to remaining leaves. Bring to boil again. (Make this up every month or so because it has a short shelf life.) Administer seven drops to victim for seven days and diarrhea will go away.

Grandfather's cure of the blacksmith was somewhat less unpleasant. According to my notes made over the years, I subsequently used the cure for other paralyzed limbs—legs as well as arms. I always found it at least as effective as the more elaborate cures of other *babalawos:*

> Call on *Ogun* to observe the cure. Lay three copper coins on the affected arm. Light a white candle and wave it over the arm. Walk around victim nine times while shaking *ase* (a ceremonial gourd) and burning tobacco in a dish. Have the victim extinguish the candle flame by spitting on it. Then tell him, "As you have extinguished this flame, so I extinguish your pain." Then spit on his arm and pronounce him cured.

Having discovered the source of a curse and countered it, one task remains for the *babalawo*: turning the curse back on the originator. Obviously, this revenge can only be used when the originator is someone the victim dares to hit back at; turning a curse back on an *orisha* is not a good idea.

This "turning back" is responsible for the "juju wars" which break out between rival *babalawos* and which can continue for years. What happens is that the original curse-worker's reputation is damaged when his curse is turned back on his client. So he counters the counter with another curse, even stronger than the first. This needs a stronger counter measure which, if successful, becomes a further challenge, and so on. There are juju wars that have gone on for generations. The sad families of the victims troop back and forth from one *babalawo* to another for their entire lives. Whole villages can go to waste in the meantime (though whether from the "war" or from neglect is debatable).

So with relatively little effort, Grandfather further enhanced his already considerable reputation by curing the blacksmith. This brought many requests for his help. People whose families have fought a curse for generations will search all over Africa for help; they believe that the side which finds the most powerful *babalawo* or *babalorisha* of all will eventually win the feud. Grandfather had to begin turning away business from as far away as Togo; he had enough juju wars of his own right in Nigeria to worry about, and he didn't care to go looking for more.

His crowded schedule had an unplanned effect: He'd sent all his lesser priests out to other regions on his behalf, so he had to call on me to assist when Rebecca Abanogu's mother brought her for a cure.

Even though only a few weeks had passed, Babalu-Aye's curse of Rebecca was already being fulfilled in every particular. I cannot admit to any tender feelings for her; her condition was so gruesome that one noticed only the condition itself, not the person. She had lost a great deal of weight. She was dazed and listless and had to be carried into the compound on a litter by two of her kinsmen. There were two enormous, festering sores on her face: one on her right cheek and the other on her forehead. They did not give the appearance of being on the skin, like ordinary sores. Rather, they seemed to be deep, almost cup-shaped, as if the skin were being eaten away by acid, down to the bone and beyond.

Apparently, no one had had the courage to approach the sores and Rebecca seemed unable to care for herself. So the wounds had been allowed to become filthy, surrounded with a ridged corona of dirt and pus. They gave off the smell of rotting meat. Grandfather leaned over and studied them closely, his professional curiosity overcoming the revulsion that the rest of us in the Temple felt. "Hmmmm. This is not an ordinary sore. Isaiah, see this!"

I swallowed hard and bent lower.

"This is the work of an exceptional spirit," he said, poking his bony index finger into a prominent bulge in the pus pile. The bulge seemed to slide easily around under the mucus that covered it. He centered it between the thumb and index finger of each hand. But it still slipped and slithered under his pressure like a balloon filled with oil.

"Push here," he said to me, gesturing with his chin toward the center of the lump.

I looked around in the vain hope that he meant someone else. "Me, Pa?" I squeaked.

He sighed. "Are you not a *babalawo*? Are you not he who will follow me? Do as you are told!"

I swallowed some more. The fish I'd eaten last night felt as if it had come back to life and was swimming about in my stomach. I bent over and stuck my trembling finger into the mess.

With my first touch, the bulge split open with a pop and a little splattering of pus and mucus. The smell that came forth was sudden and overwhelming. I jumped back but Grandfather continued to lean over Rebecca, studying her with intense professional interest.

After a few moments, he said again, "Isaiah, see this!"

"Aw, Pa!" I said.

"*Isaiah!*"

I bent immediately and at first wondered whether the old man just wanted to torment me, to "toughen me up," as he always liked to say. There was nothing about the vile sores that I hadn't already seen.

No, wait. . . . The bulge that I broke had released some grainy material from inside it. With their covering of pus, the grains looked like rice under a saffron sauce.

Then, as I watched, some of the grains moved.

I was too shocked even to faint, I think. I just continued to watch the wiggling grains, fascinated by the sight.

One of the grains separated itself from the mass of decay and shook itself, like a tiny wet dog. It was alive and, even as I watched, it flew unsteadily away. Others immediately did the same and in seconds, a swarm of flies flew in a black line out of Rebecca's cheek.

To my relief, I never did actually faint. Just almost. I remember the sight to this day: the flies zipping out of Rebecca's face in tight formation like a line of tiny, buzzing fighter planes. My Western friends always try to reassure me that a fly simply laid her eggs in the sore and, the sore never being cleaned, the eggs just happened to hatch as we poked at the egg case.

But being there was different from talking about it. What I saw was "flies coming forth into the world out of Rebecca's body," just as Babalu-Aye's curse had said.

"This is serious," Grandfather said in a masterpiece of understatement. "I suspect an evil spirit of extraordinary power and malignancy is inside her; she has been possessed." The assembled kinsmen gasped as one.

"Bring the truck," he told one of the men. "We must take her to the Shrine. We must make sacrifice."

10

We had seriously overloaded our old Model-A pickup truck, so I made sure to sprinkle a little "luck powder" over it before we set out. Rebecca Abanogu was stretched out on a makeshift cot in the back. Her mother and her two kinsmen rode back there with her. Also in the back were two big sacks, loaded with all the juju that Grandfather thought he might conceivably need. Grandfather himself rode up front with our usual driver, David, and David's brother, who came along to help us carry. The brother sat in the middle and held the goat between his legs. There was no room left for me except on the running board, where I held on for dear life.

Grandfather muttered juju chants under his breath the whole way; he never trusted anything with a motor. "White man's stink juju," he used to call engines. But we made much better time bumping along the forest path than we would have if we'd tried to walk. We reached the site of the shrine in about an hour, despite the fact that the last half-mile was almost virgin bush.

The Shrine was in a well-hidden clearing; one who did not know where it was would have to search for it very diligently. The site would have been disappointing to an outsider who expected it to be something grand. It was only large enough to hold maybe a dozen or so people standing close together. But there was no need for it to be large. What went on there was always secret; there would never be more people there at one time than had to be. There were only two small buildings: the Shrine itself and a shed used for storage. Attached to the shed was a small corral for penning the sacrificial animals.

Even someone visiting it for the first time would conclude that the site had been used a great deal. There were well-worn depressions in the ground at intervals around the clearing. These were the places where rituals required that fires be lit or that libations of water, oil, or blood be poured. Over the years, these spots had grown into little pits so that one had to be careful where one walked. And in the center of the clearing, there was a low flat stone where sacrifice was made. Where the original surface still showed through (in a few spots on its sides), it looked as if it had once been almost white. But now it was a streaky rust-brown from all the blood that had been shed on it.

Before starting his ritual, Grandfather needed to make sacrifice. He told Rebecca's kinsmen to set her cot down out of the way. He told me to get the he-goat from the truck and tether it to the sacrifice stone.

Meanwhile, he searched around in his big sacks, removing juju items that he then lined up neatly next to Rebecca; it was as if they would give her strength just by being close to her. Among the items were an old broken sword, a large round stone with symbols painted on it, several bottles with liquids of different colors, a little metal box that rattled when he handled it, and a human shin bone.

He also removed from one of the sacks several little pouches. He peeked furtively into each until he found one that contained a purplish powder. He poured some of this material onto a banana leaf and burned it. It produced the same kind of incense smell that sometimes used to come out of the Catholic church back in Sekondi/Takoradi. I wondered if it was some powerful juju that Grandfather had stolen from the Catholics. I became convinced of it when he dipped a stick in some juju-water and sprinkled it on everything and everybody in the clearing, just the way I'd seen their priests do.

He directed me to hold the goat for him while he killed it. He was in such a hurry he used his everyday pocket knife, not even bothering to find his sacrificial blade. He scooped up some of the goat's blood in a gourd and mixed it with a little green juju-water from one of the bottles, He poured some of this mixture directly on Rebecca's sores. Then he directed her mother to remove Rebecca's clothes and rub the rest of the blood mixture over her body.

He rummaged in his sack again and discarded several of the homemade cigars that he had in there until he found the one he wanted. It must have been special in some way but to me it looked exactly like the ones he had discarded. He lit it and passed it around after taking a few puffs.

He dug in the sack some more and produced a box containing a handful of little brown knots, like dried cat turds. He handed three to me and told me to suck on them until they were gone. I stared at them in my hand until he took three for himself and, sighing at my lack of trust, popped them in his mouth. Then I followed his example; they were porous and had a vaguely peppery taste. Finally, he opened Rebecca's mouth and dropped three of the pellets under her tongue.

He slit open the goat he'd sacrificed and told me to remove the entrails and place them in one of the depressions in the floor of the clearing, all except the liver. This he sliced up himself, putting one slice of it over each of Rebecca's wounds and eyes.

He took his own clothes off and put on a considerable amount of juju jewelry that he took from one of the sacks: necklaces, arm bands, even a gaudy headdress of feathers and cowries. As a humble assistant, I did not rate any special costuming.

Having suitably prepared both his patient and himself, he directed her kinsmen to move Rebecca into the Shrine. He followed and called me in with him, but told everyone else to wait outside. With Rebecca laid out flat on the floor, there really wasn't room for anybody else in there anyway, especially with the way Rebecca was thrashing around.

At first, I thought it was just her fever. But no. She was moaning and writhing—not with pain, it seemed, but with pleasure. Her legs were apart and as I watched, she slid her hands slowly and voluptuously up to her waist, brazenly spreading and displaying herself to us. What shocked me even more than her wantonness was the sight of another of the huge, weeping sores in her private region, its discharge mingling with her own juices.

She was panting and her lips were drawn back to show her white teeth clenched as if in ecstasy. Her hips, which had been rolling in a slow, even circle now began to thrust forward, harder and faster.

"Pa!" I said. "She looks like . . . uh, she looks like she's, uh, ..."

He interrupted his private prayer and looked down at her. "Yes," he said calmly. "This is not uncommon. She is with her 'heaven husband' now."

" 'Heaven husband?' "

"Yes. What you see now is 'spirit rape'—what we call '*oko-orun*.' "

I tried to look away, but I couldn't. She was twisting her body as if in a fury, screaming and cursing—not at all as she had done with me a few weeks earlier.

Suddenly, with a great cry, she was done. She was covered with sweat by that time and the smell of her sex mixed with the blood of the he-goat was overpowering. I was embarrassed but Grandfather kept on with his work as if nothing had happened. He squatted next to Rebecca, shaking his *ase* gourd while he called softly, "Esu (*rattle*): We seek you. Esu (*rattle*): We call you. Esu (*rattle*): . . . ." And so on.

The use of Esu's name so surprised and frightened me that I almost forgot about Rebecca altogether. I had not seen Grandfather perform any acts of divination, yet somehow he seemed to have learned that the spirit possessing Rebecca was none other than Esu himself. Esu is the *orisha* that most closely resembles Satan; all of our Christian churches in Africa equate the two. Esu is called upon for help in all evil purposes, such as laying down an *epe* (a curse) on one's neighbor. He is the cause of all misfortune as well as of death. He is vicious and ranks near the very top of our pantheon. In fact, he is the most powerful—and so the most feared—of all the *orisha*.

I may have been a *babalawo* but I knew I wasn't ready to deal with the likes of Esu. I had to keep reminding myself of what my initiation had been about: Nothing in the spirit world can *really* hurt a Man of Knowledge. But it wasn't easy to control my fear. The cases of possession by Esu are among the worst on record. The behavior of the Esu-possessed is always evil, even to the point of abomination. A person possessed by Esu may go wild, hacking away on a crowded bus with a machete. Or, as one possessed woman recently did in Angola, kidnapping randomly-chosen school children and gouging out their eyes, only to set them free to a life of total blindness.

Grandfather droned on, calling on Esu for what seemed to me a very long time, during which I could only sit by. It was a perfect chance for me to study every step of Grandfather's procedure, trying to learn my future craft, and I wanted to. But incredibly—despite everything that had happened, even despite the fear that was creeping up on me—I found myself passing into sleep as I listened to the dreary, droning litany. "Esu (*rattle*). Esu (*rattle*)."

Then I heard a third voice in the shrine—a man's voice, deep but nasal: "Leave us be, old man, me and my horse." I started out of my doze and looked around. Grandfather seemed to be in a trance state. The voice hadn't sounded like his anyway. But there was no other man with us.

Grandfather continued his chanting in that steady, rhythmic way of his, never missing a beat. "Esu (*rattle*): Come to us. Esu (*rattle*): We rule you."

About then I noticed a peculiar thing: Even though it was still day outside, the shrine seemed cold—almost as cold as night in the dry season. I looked down at Rebecca. The liver slices were no longer covering her eyes, which were open and shining as if with a light of their own. "Who dares speak so to such a one as me?" she demanded in the deep masculine voice.

Grandfather's eyes were still closed. He seemed to be ignoring the spirit completely.

"You, old man," the voice boomed. "Why do you molest me?" The voice suddenly took on a wheedling tone. "I am merely a meek old ancestor, come for a nice visit. Can I not ride this mare in peace?"

Grandfather continued to ignore the voice, shaking his rattle and calling on Esu to come out and show himself.

The whine disappeared from the voice. "What do you want of me?" it roared.

Grandfather finally roused himself. "Are you Esu?" he said calmly.

"Yes, damn you. Yes, I am Esu!" As the voice said this, a vapor came forth from Rebecca Abanogu's mouth, like from a tea kettle. Only it was cold.

Then something like recognition passed over Rebecca's face. "So you still live, old man?" the male voice said with Rebecca's mouth. "You surprise me; I would have expected you to be worm food long since. Ah, well—it will happen soon enough, an old bag of bones like you."

Grandfather sat back on his skinny haunches, ignoring the taunts. Except for a certain tightness around the mouth, there was nothing to indicate he'd even heard. His eyes were still closed and his voice remained calm. "We command you to leave this person."

"*You* command? *You* command?" The voice roared with laughter. "How can *you* command? You are only a little old naked black man in a dirty, miserable hut in the middle of nowhere."

I felt compelled to take a slow look around. Then I blinked with shock: It was true—our Shrine really was just a wretched hut. Then I looked over at Grandfather's bony frame. For the first time, I saw what a frail and puny specimen of manhood he was; before, I'd always seen him as ten feet tall.

"You are good for nothing," the voice went on more quietly, "nothing but to grow old and die and molder in the ground. This is your only value, for you are just a foolish old man."

My heart was breaking for Pa. Surely his weary and worn old body could be no match for an evil spirit of this calibre. "Oh, Pa," I said, "let's stop this. You can't possibly—"

"Hush!" he hissed at me. "Never listen to Esu. I know this one from long ago; he is a deceiver and a liar. He will tell you any lies that suit his purpose. And he can make you believe them." Then, for the first time since he started the ritual, he opened his eyes. They looked sadly into mine. "Even worse, he may tell you the truth about yourself."

"Do you fear the truth, then, old man? Is it truth that makes you tremble so before me? Will I see you wet yourself before we are done?" asked the voice with a laugh.

It hurt me to hear Grandfather insulted so. Anger replaced my fear, giving me a false courage. "My Grandfather fears nothing! He is a great man, a Man of Knowledge; he is a *babalorisha!*" I said, addressing the spirit.

Grandfather reached out and slapped my face, hard. "No! Never talk with the spirit. If you do, you are undone!"

But it was too late. Rebecca turned toward me, her eyes as shiny as obsidian. "What have we here?" The voice took on a taunting tone. "Oh, I see who it is. He who can read! And write! Now I am truly frightened. Indeed, the whole Invisible World trembles at the name of Isaiah Oke." He laughed heartily. " 'Isaiah Oke, Boy *Babalawo,*' we call you."

"Remember," Grandfather said to me, "he cannot harm you if you don't acknowledge him. Pride cannot tolerate being ignored and Esu is the King of Pride. Ignoring him is the only way to hurt him."

The voice laughed even harder. "I know you, boy! You're the one who took my horsey here out for a ride at his initiation ceremony. Do you want to know what she said about you, little boy? Do you want to know how she laughed at you? Eh, *little* boy?"

I felt rage rising, taking the place of my judgment. Grandfather's hand was resting on my arm, as if to show he was with me. But I shook him off violently.

The voice just kept laughing. "This is not much of a grandson you have here, old man. He will never learn to please a woman; he will be a *little* boy always." It was as if the voice was physically *rubbing* its obscene, oily laughter all over me. "No, he is not much of a grandson for you. A bookworm. Or maybe just a *worm,* eh? He is very fast for a worm, though. Do you want to know, Grandpa? Do you want to know how *fast* your little bookworm is with a woman?"

"Stop it!" I was losing control. "Stop it!"

Grandfather grabbed my arm with a grip stronger than I would have believed and dragged me outside the Shrine. Then he slapped me again and threw me to the ground. "Learn from this!" he shouted.

I was weeping with rage and shame and barely heard him. "You have let the Invisible World see your emotions," he said, "and you are vulnerable now forever." He shook his head at me and then turned to look back toward the hut.

"I will have to finish with him by myself," he said, quietly. "It is now for you to wait and watch. Do not fail me further." He turned his back and straightened his scrawny shoulders. Resolutely he walked back into the hut to face the Devil alone.

Maybe he *was* ten feet tall, after all.

*   *   *

It took four days.

At times, the hut was silent for hours on end. At other times, we heard voices shouting and screaming; they were voices both of men and of animals. Once, there was a rumbling noise something like distant thunder on the northern mountains. It shook the ground on which we stood.

During the second day, I tiptoed to the hut and called out timidly, "Pa? Would you like something to eat?" But the only answer was a roar of such ferocity that it sent me scurrying backwards to the edge of the clearing. After that, I gave up any thoughts of trying to show courage and just huddled at the fringe of the forest with the others.

It was mid-morning when it finally ended. There had been no indication that the battle was over; all had been quiet for hours. I was dozing in the truck when I heard Rebecca Abanogu's kinsmen cry out at the sight of her. She looked as if she were three times her twenty years; most of her shiny black hair had fallen out and her formerly firm and voluptuous breasts sagged halfway to her waist.

But of the sores with the flies issuing forth, there was no sign.

Grandfather was the most tired man I'd ever seen. He and Rebecca had to hold each other up, literally. Everybody in the clearing ran at the same time to help them but they both waved off questions. We headed immediately for the truck where Grandfather was unable even to boost himself up into the passenger's seat. I finally had to lift him; his body felt like an old sack of bones and weighed only as much.

He never talked about the incident later so I don't now what happened. As for Rebecca, she *couldn't* talk; she had been struck dumb at some point during the ritual and she never spoke again. She lived for about another ten years but seldom left the porch of her house.

Whenever anyone asked her, she indicated by gestures that it had been worth the price she paid—and that she would have been willing to pay even more—to be free of possession by Esu.

11

After that, changes came very quickly.

Grandfather changed. He started to age. He'd always been lean, but vigorously so. Now some of that vitality deserted him. He ate less and kept to himself more. He gave one the impression that he'd become somewhat frail. It was almost as if he was trying to make Esu's slanders about him come true.

My relationship with him also changed. Previously, I'd been at his side almost constantly, learning from him and recording his teachings. We had been almost like brothers, despite the enormous difference in our ages. But now we were both too aware of how badly I had let him down during the confrontation with Esu.

And I changed, too. I redoubled my efforts to absorb my formal education: Perhaps that was one way in which I could fulfill Grandfather's expectations for me. Certainly, it was a change for the better from the standpoint of my tutor, Mr. Olungwe. I suddenly became a very earnest pupil. Before, I'd always hurried through my lessons so I could go work juju at my grandfather's side. But now that he called for me less often, I retreated to the few books that Mr. Olungwe felt were "safe"—that is, devoid of any real ideas that might pollute my mind. Remember, it was Mr. Olungwe's job only to teach me reading, writing, and arithmetic, not thinking.

One day, Mr. Olungwe decided to change his job description and defy Grandfather by actually *teaching* me something. He had been making me read aloud from *The Theory and Practice of Colonial Administration in Africa* by Lord Emsworth. It was the wet season and, between my droning and the steady rain outside, I'm pretty sure I was close to putting us both to sleep.

"Stop," said Mr. Olungwe. "That would bore even an Englishman."

When I obediently closed the book, he stepped onto the porch and looked out into the heavy rain. He looked first one way, then the other, like a thief about to make off with someone's goods in the market. It wasn't really necessary to act so guilty; people stay indoors a great deal during the rainy season, so no one was about.

He came back in and carefully closed the door, despite the humidity. Then he pulled the shutters on the windows closed, as if we were going to start a secret juju ritual. He took something out of his rucksack and hesitated before finally handing it to me.

I studied it for a moment. "Honorable Olungwe, this item is like a book."

"It is a book," he said.

"But it is small. And it has no cover."

"It's what the Americans call a 'paperback.' It's about this man."

He pointed to the picture on the cover. The man had the familiar facial structure of the Ashanti but his name was quite foreign and unpleasant to my ear: George Washington Carver. "I do not recognize the name, Honorable Olungwe. What clan is he?"

He shook his head. "He is an American person. They do not have clans."

"No clans?" I was shocked; the clan is central to life in Nigeria. I had never conceived of such a strange thing. "How can they survive, Honorable Olungwe?"

"That is why I want you to start reading some other books, my son— to find out that there are other ways to live than our way: other societies, other economies, other philosophies."

I guess I looked pretty dubious because he said, "Have you never wondered how other people live? What other places are like?"

I shrugged and munched a *kola* nut from the bowl between us. His question was meaningless: Why should I care about some other place when the only place I am is here?

I wistfully eyed the *ugbo-azigo* board over against the wall; Mr. Olungwe and I always had a rousing match at our national board game after one of our tedious reading sessions. He saw my attention wandering and cuffed me smartly on the side of the head. They have their own form of juju, these scholars, and can get away with treatment that would earn anybody else a good, solid curse from a *babalawo*. "Read," he said, pointing to the little book.

I made the bow of apology and started to read out loud. But it was even more boring than the book about colonial administration. And besides, the closed-up room was becoming stiflingly hot. All in all, I was very unhappy, but I kept reading. I was turning over in my mind whether to take the unprecedented step of rebelling against Mr. Olungwe when I got to the part about the peanuts.

Peanuts are a staple of life in West Africa. They are an ingredient in many of our foods and supply much of our protein. We also press them for the oil that we use for cooking. The husks that are left we grind into a kind of flour. The peanut is second only to the yam in importance in our food supply here. And not only for food. We make a die for cloth from the shells and certain medicines can be made from the little stem portions, if one knows how.

This Ashanti man with the funny American name knew all our secrets for living off the peanut. He told them to his American kinsmen, it seemed, and became renowned—very clever of him, I thought. The book related many of the secrets he had learned, some of which I hadn't heard before. It was a great deal like learning some new juju. Besides which, I enjoyed the story of the man's trials and tribulations for itself; we Africans love a good story.

So when Mr. Olungwe reached out and closed the book on me, I was startled to see that it was almost dark outside. "That's enough for today; more tomorrow," he said. "Perhaps."

"Oh, yes, Honorable Olungwe. Please," I added.

He returned the book to his rucksack. While he was looking in there, something else seemed to take his interest. He looked around the room, both ways again, as if someone might have snuck in while I was reading the forbidden book. Then he pulled out two more books.

One was thin with beautifully decorated pages. It was titled Koran and seemed to be associated with a man named Mohammed. He must have been from a very numerous clan because I'd met many men of that name on one of my trips up north with Grandfather. But I didn't think any of those fellows were capable of producing such a fine-looking book.

The other book was bigger with very small print. It was beautifully bound and was obviously of some great importance because the edges of its pages seemed to be covered in real gold, if one could believe such a thing.

The title was printed in gold on the cover: Holy Bible. I looked inside and saw what I assumed was the author's name. " 'Gideon,' " I said thoughtfully. "Sounds like he might be an Ibo."

Mr. Olungwe took the contraband books back from me and hid them back in his rucksack. "Perhaps when you are ready," he said. "Now, you won't tell anybody what you've been reading, will you? Especially the Honorable Aworo Oke?"

"Of course, Honorable Olungwe. If you wish it so. Although I don't see why—"

I got another smart rap on the head and wisely shut up.

Two happy years passed in that way. Mr. Olungwe frequently smuggled in books which turned me into an avid, though not very selective, reader. They seemed to have some magical power to shrink things, because my village sometimes seemed a smaller place after I read one.

The books came from Ilesha where there was supposed to be a thing called a "library," according to Mr. Olungwe. He told me this was a building bigger than Grandfather's complex and that it held nothing but books. I didn't believe him, of course. I figured there was a point or a moral to his story, just as there is to all the fables we tell in Africa, but I confess that it eluded me. I had plenty of time to read all the material he brought me, though, especially during the rainy seasons. I never spent much time on my juju training at that time of the year, anyway, because Grandfather made few trips out to the Shrine. But ominously, on the few trips he did make, he took Joshua as his helper.

It was all the more surprising, then, when Grandfather called me to his meeting room late one night in my fifteenth year to discuss my training. "Until now," he said, "you are only *babalawo*. If you ever hope to become *babalorisha,* you must progress further along the path of understanding and knowledge."

"Yes, Pa," I said meekly, assuming that he was going to correct me for spending too much time on my reading and writing. But the written collection he commissioned me to make of juju recipes, charms, and practices was becoming truly enormous; I wondered if I could get away with using that as a defense.

"So, I have arranged for you to go south," he said, "to study in Lagos."

I was struck speechless. Lagos! To a village boy, it was more than a legendary place—it was almost mythical! The biggest, most dynamic city in Nigeria: crowded as Hong Kong, dirty as Calcutta, busy as New York. A crossroads for international business, bursting at the seams with millionaires and with poverty. An exciting but wicked place.

Inesi-Ile had begun to seem to me pretty isolated, so part of me was happy at the prospect of going to the Big City. An equally large part of me was frightened, of course.

Grandfather stared hard at me for a moment. I thought I saw a glimpse of something like pity in his expression. "You will be given the special opportunity," he told me, "to learn from Doctor Drago."

The frightened part of me suddenly flowed over the happy part and smothered it. Drago was a name pronounced throughout the whole of Africa.

But only in whispers.

They called him the "devil doctor of Lagos." He was said to be a *babalawo* of truly exceptional power. There were rumors to the effect that he refused to speak to the spirits, as the *babalorisha* do. Instead, he *commanded* them to do his bidding. He was supposed to be a deeply menacing figure. Some reports even said that he was the incarnation of Esu. I didn't want to believe those reports any more than I did Mr. Olungwe's wild tales about a whole building filled with nothing but books. But still . . . .

I tried to swallow whatever it was that had suddenly made my throat so dry. "Pa," I croaked, "this Drago—"

"*Doctor* Drago," he corrected.

"*Doctor* Drago . . . they say his power is unusual. They say he works evil. They say . . . ."

" 'They say,' 'they say.' Do you listen now to the women while they wash clothes?"

"No, Pa. But if you could just tell me why. . . ."

"Why? To give you a second chance, that's why. To give you the chance to redeem yourself, to show that you have what it takes to be *babalorisha* after me."

I looked down humbly. "Yes, Pa."

He nodded. "That's better. And you can thank your brother Joshua; it was his idea to arrange this chance for you to prove yourself. Now, make yourself ready; you leave for Lagos tomorrow morning."

"Tomorrow morning? But that's so soon. I've got some more pages for my juju record. I ought to go out to the Shrine to put them in the strongbox."

"You may leave them with me. I'll take care of them for you."

"But it needs a key. . . ."

"You may leave that with me as well." He held out his hand.

I trembled as I removed the key from around my neck. It had been there so long, clinking among all my other juju, that it seemed a part of me, like the *ibante* cord crossed between my legs. But I handed the key over humbly and obediently.

"Can I at least say farewell to my friends, to Mr. Olungwe and to. . . ."

"I will give your regards to everyone in Inesi-Ile."

There seemed nothing more to say. "As you will, Grandfather." I turned to go.

"Wait." He came forward and gripped my shoulders. He looked into my eyes and said, "I want you to succeed, son. I want to be proud of you. You know that, don't you?" I nodded.

Then he shocked me by falling forward and embracing me tightly. He held me that way for a long, long time, as if he didn't want me to go. He'd never done a thing like that in my memory.

At last, he stepped back. He instantly became his usual dignified self again—the *babalorisha* of Ile state. "You leave for Lagos at first light," he said briskly.

It was a dismissal.

12

In those days there was no direct route to Lagos from our part of the country, which is between the banks of the Shasha and Oni rivers. So I walked the hour's walk to the bus stop, getting there just after full light. Our buses out in the country operate on a timetable that answers only nominally to the movements of the Sun. So I had to sit by the side of the road for another hour or so, until the bus came along. It was a lovely morning, though, and I had a breakfast of some of the *fufu* that my mother had packed for me. She made the world's best *ofe,* too, which went so beautifully with the doughy *fufu* cakes. At home, we always refer to *ofe* as "palaver sauce" because every good homemaker always keeps some heated and ready to entertain any guest who wants to come over and "palaver" a while. But there was no convenient way to carry any with me, so I ate my *fufu* dry.

The "bus" I refer to was actually an old flatbed truck, which was far better suited to our modest dirt roads in the bush than a more comfortable vehicle would have been. It ran only between the various rural villages and the district capital of Ilesha. Its paint job was unique, exhibiting every color in the world, like an explosion in a paint factory. A big hand-lettered sign on the front shouted its name to waiting passengers: GLORY.

In Ilesha, I switched to a slightly more modern bus, bright yellow and fully enclosed. But the road to the south was still dirt in those days, and the machine broke down frequently with one malady or another. In the end, the complete trip of about two hundred kilometers took three days. Today, of course, there's a paved road between Ilesha and Lagos city. But it's always so choked with traffic that it can *still* take three days to drive. Or so it sometimes seems anyway.

The city of Lagos is on an island. But it has hills all around it that are crammed with the little homemade shanties of all the poor who leave the countryside to seek their fortunes in town. So we say that Lagos is the only island surrounded by people as well as by water.

My first sight of the city marked me as a country boy, I am afraid. But I couldn't help it; I'd never made such a journey all by myself before and I was excited. I leaned out so far to get a good look as we approached that I almost fell out my bus window. The driver stopped his machine in the middle of the road to pull me back in. He scolded me more than I thought appropriate. It reminded me of the way Grandfather always carried on and I found myself homesick even before we screeched to our final stop in Lagos Central Bus Terminal.

Lagos has between two and three million inhabitants, making it comparable to cities like Boston, Berlin, or Sydney, though, in reality, we fear that it may well be larger than any of those. There has never been an accurate census. One barrier to accuracy is the truly astounding number of squatters who have always lived on the hillsides around town. Another is our general reluctance to reveal too much about ourselves. Part of this reticence results from simple practicality: If the government doesn't know how many you are in your family, it's harder to tax you.

But there's another explanation, equally valid: We have carried our juju beliefs with us into the cities. Juju teaches that the more that's known about you and your family, the easier it will be for someone to lay on *epe* on you. That's why we always try to hold something back—from our neighbors, from the government, from everybody. So, no matter how bustling and modern the city of Lagos seems, no matter how much a Westerner is tempted to say, "Why, it looks just like Pittsburgh!" it's good to remember that appearances are surface only. Underneath, the old ways still rule us. In fact, we have a saying: "When a man moves to the city on his feet, juju moves in his heart."

So it really wasn't surprising that a renowned jujuman like Drago had chosen to hang out his shingle in this modern metropolis. What was surprising is how extremely *well* he did. I began to understand just how well when I stumbled out out of the terminal, blinking in the light and heat and stench of Lagos city.

A very short man in purple livery waved and ran toward me, laughing out loud as if he were happy to see me. His uniform couldn't have fit any tighter if it had been painted on. His cap had a shiny black visor and a high peak with a bright gold medallion on it. His knee-high boots looked like they were made of flexible black mirrors. He had two gold teeth gleaming in front and I thought I had never before seen a man who looked so important.

I assumed he must be a general in the Nigerian Army, maybe even a field marshal. He started speaking to me very loudly and very rapidly in a language I didn't know. Why he would want to talk to me was a mystery, but I recognized my name in the flood of unknown words.

"Yes," I answered in Hausa, "I am called Isaiah Oke. Do you speak Hausa, please, sir?"

"Hausa, yes!" he yelled with a laugh. "Also Arabic, Swahili, Fula, French, English . . . what you wish, Boss?"

"Hausa, if you please, sir."

"Hokay, we speak Hausa! Very good, Boss! Welcome to Lagos!" He stepped back, clapped his boot heels together with a bang, and saluted me. I gave him back an embarrassed little gesture, a kind of weak and fluttery imitation of his salute. But it seemed to satisfy him and he laughed uproariously again.

Next, he leaped forward, grabbed my hand, and pumped it up and down vigorously in the manner of Americans. "Ojike, Boss—Nnaia Ojike, that's me!" He spoke loudly, and so rapidly that I could barely understand him. "But call me 'Speedy,' Boss. Everybody calls me 'Speedy'! That's right, Boss. Good old 'Speedy,' that's me!"

Before I had a chance to respond, he reached out and grabbed my arm tightly. He started to run across the street with me in tow. It occurred to me was that maybe I was being arrested, though what crime I'd committed or why the officer kept calling me "Boss" was more than I could make out.

We ran over to an automobile that was the same shade of purple as Speedy's livery and as shiny as his boots. With a big grin, he ripped off his cap. Then he opened the car door with a flourish, and bowed low, his arm across his chest. It seemed that he wanted me to do something, but I didn't know what. So I just waited as respectfully as I could. We stood there in the hot afternoon Sun—him bent over and waiting, me confused and frightened—until he muttered a cue under his breath: "Get in, Boss! Get in!"

"Me? In there?"

"Yes, Boss! Of course!"

I still hesitated. The car was shiny-clean and enormously long, nothing like our village's truck at home or the buses that had brought me here. The rear was a comfortable, glassed-in compartment of purple leather and polished wood. Farther forward, there was an open area for someone to sit while operating the machine. And all the way up in the very front, in a place of great honor on top of the radiator, was this beautiful silver goddess with wings—*Shamanga,* I thought; or possibly even *Oya* herself. Obviously, she was there to watch the road and to protect one from the *epe* of flat tires, breakdowns, and accidents. It was like a shrine on wheels.

I paused in the doorway to wipe my feet off on the hem of the caftan that I was wearing for travel. I stepped into the car gingerly and instantly jumped out again, shocked.

"What's wrong, Boss?"

I backed away. "What juju is this? It's cold in there, cold like the rainy season. Has my family given you some offense, sir, that you should place such an *epe* of chills on me?"

Speedy laughed until he had to hold his sides; I'd never before seen a man of such easy and constant cheer. "That's just what we call 'air conditioning,' Boss. It's something new; a good thing—not juju." He took my arm and guided me gently back into the car. "Don't worry, Boss, you'll get used to it."

I sat down carefully, even though there was room enough for me to stand up back there. Speedy shut the door with a heavy thunk, instantly cutting off the sound of his laughter and all the other sounds of the busy city. I hadn't realized until that moment how noisy a place Lagos is.

Up front, Speedy leaped over the side of the car, landing in the operator's seat. He must have started the engine, though I couldn't hear it, because it began to get even colder in the back as we pulled out effortlessly into the jammed street. We were sharing the pavement with all sorts of lorries, carts, and bicycles. It was remarkable how they would all move out of our way after just one brief glimpse of the big purple car, though other cars on the street seemed not to intimidate them at all.

We rounded a corner onto a road that ran along the waterfront. For a few blocks, the traffic remained dense. Laughing all the way, Speedy worked the car through spots tighter than I would have believed, people miraculously making way for us. Then, traffic suddenly thinned out as we passed a line of warehouses marking the edge of the central city. In minutes, we were cruising easily along a blacktop road at about sixty kilometers per hour. Speedy pushed a button in front and the glass window between us went down into the back of his seat.

"So, Boss," he said over his shoulder, "What you think of Lagos? Crowded, huh? Noisy, huh?" I opened my mouth to answer him.

"Yeah, Boss," he said around another of his big laughs, "you're right about that. I know what you mean. Yes, indeed. Say, Boss, how you like this car?"

I cleared my throat and leaned forward, determined to try harder to catch his attention.

"Yeah, it's great, huh, Boss? A Rolls-Royce, the only one like it in Lagos: all custom. All of Doctor Drago's stuff is the very best. He insists on it; but you probably know that."

He paused and, for once, he didn't laugh. "How well you know Doctor Drago, Boss? You know him well?" I just shrugged, having concluded that conversation with Speedy was a road on which traffic could go only one way. But as I sat back to take in the sights for the rest of the ride, I saw his face in the rearview mirror: His whole attitude changed when he mentioned Drago. For the first time since we'd met, his face was drawn and tense.

"Yeah, Boss. I know what you mean; I sure do. But just do like he says, Boss. Yeah, do like he says and you'll be okay." He blew the horn at a farmer passing along in an ox cart. "Don't ever cross him, Boss. 'Cause he's a big man, the Doctor. That's right, Boss. A *big* man. *Big* juju. But you know that, right, Boss?" The farmer almost upset his cart, hurrying to get all the way off the road for the purple car.

"Don't ever cross him, Boss," he repeated. "You know what happened to the last man crossed Doctor Drago? That's right, Boss, that's right."

He went on cautioning me like that for the remainder of our trip. On the whole, I liked the overly cheerful Speedy better than the morose Speedy. But neither gave me a chance to say a word on the whole trip. That was how I learned the value of talking loud and fast in Lagos.

He was right about Drago's air conditioning, though; I got used to it real fast. Being the "devil doctor of Lagos" might cause people like Speedy to fear you. But it appeared to have its compensations. I thought that the Doctor must surely be an exceptional man. I couldn't wait to meet him.

13

Nothing had prepared me for the actual sight of Drago's compound—not the limousine, not the liveried chauffeur, nothing. Actually, we'd been on the grounds of the estate for ten minutes, Speedy told me, before we even came to the sprawling collection of buildings that made up the compound proper.

We pulled into a circular drive and stopped before what Speedy called the "Big House." It was the biggest building I'd ever seen up this close, bigger even than the Lagos Central Bus Terminal. It was as white as a chicken's egg and all of its many windows had glass in them. The roof of the front porch was balanced on four tall white pillars that looked like smooth tree trunks. The sprawl and height of the place made me think of our hills at home. But this was a hill squared off, hollowed out, and made into a dwelling for a race of giants. I suppose a European would have called it a palace but I'd never seen one and didn't know the word.

It seemed that Speedy didn't like to spend any more time than necessary around the "Big House"; I was barely out of the car before he roared off. I went up the stairs and stood before the two huge doors, carved wood and solid, not at all like the simple hides we hang across our doorways at home to keep out the drafts. I called out for permission to enter, as is our custom, and wondered how anyone inside the huge place could possibly hear me. But they did. Either that or else I was expected, because a tall, dark man opened one of the doors.

I stepped back a step, startled. His eyes were as black and shiny as Rebecca's had been when Esu was riding her. They seemed fixed toward the front, as if he'd have to move his whole body if he wanted to look at something that was not directly in front of him. He wore a black tunic and pants, filigreed with silver piping. My first thought was that he might be the master of the house, considering the cut of his clothes and the stiffness of his bearing. But my meeting with Speedy had showed me that all was not always as it appeared at first glance in Lagos. So I decided to wait before jumping to conclusions.

The man stepped to one side, still staring straight ahead and never blinking. "Come," was all he said. I stepped past him and found myself in a hall so vast that I had trouble thinking of it as a room. A room is just someplace to keep one warm and dry, so it's made in sizes that are right for a man. But this hall was more like a forest clearing than a room. It was as long as the main street in my village and the ceiling seemed as far away as the sky.

The tall, dark man closed the door, turned, and walked past me as if I weren't there. "Come," he said again as he passed me. There was a stairway off to one side which he began to ascend, slowly and methodically. He never looked back to see if I was following.

At the top of the stairs we turned down a much shorter hallway. He stopped before another of the solid wooden doors which seemed to be everywhere in the house. This one was carved with many juju symbols, only a few of which I could place. He opened it for me, stepped silently to one side and said, "Enter."

The room was as big as Grandfather's whole house back home. Yet it was clearly intended for a very small family. Or maybe even for just one person, because there was only one of everything. There was only one bed, for example, rather than a mat. But it was big enough that four people could sleep in it comfortably. It was raised up off the floor in the European style and had its own little cloth roof overhead on four long poles.

There were other doors set into the walls of the room. The tall, dark man went to one of them and removed a suit of the type favored by Nigerians who live in the city: a long tunic, loose pants, and a visorless cap. He glanced at my feet, then produced a brand new pair of sandals from the same place. He laid all this out on the bed in absolute silence.

He turned in my direction, still staring unblinkingly over my head. "Wash," he said. He made gestures, rubbing his face and body, as if to make sure I understood him. He pointed to the new clothing. "Wear," he said, pantomiming a man shrugging into a shirt. Then he turned without another word and headed toward the door to the hall.

"Please, sir," I said, "where is the stream?"

He stopped dead in his tracks. "Stream?" he asked in a hollow voice, still facing the door; it seemed he could only look straight ahead.

"How else am I to wash myself, sir, as you have directed me to do? Such a fine house as this must surely have a good stream nearby."

He turned around and bent slightly, as if to better bring his eyes to bear on me. For just an instant, I thought a look of amusement moved across his impassive face. Then he straightened and walked in his stiff way to another of the doors set in the wall. Behind this one was another room, much more the size a room should be. It was a lavatory, like the ones I'd used in cities and on trains. Only it was very clean. There was no one else in it and, like everything else he'd showed me, it seemed to be for use by me alone. He stoppered a big white tub and ran water into it for a few minutes from a metal pipe coming out of the wall. At last, he left without saying anything further.

I was afraid to dawdle in the tub. But I did, anyway: It was hot and clean—luxury like I'd never known before. Even my *ibante* came fairly clean and the rash that all jujumen get from it subsided a bit.

The sandals were slightly snug. But the rest of the fine embroidered outfit that had been laid out fit me perfectly. I dressed and then sat quietly in my room's one chair until the tall, dark man came for me. He knocked instead of calling out as we would have back home. I opened the door and he stood there, staring over my head at a spot on the wall behind me. "Come."

I followed him downstairs to another huge room. It faced out onto a sort of courtyard. The principle piece of furniture was a long table of dark wood, like the one Grandfather used for conferences, but even bigger and much better made. Two chandeliers sparkling with electric candles hung from the beamed ceiling above the table.

There were twelve high-backed chairs upholstered with red brocade around the table but only two of them were occupied. Seated on the long side was a man around my age, maybe eighteen or so. But there were tight little lines around his eyes that made him look somewhat older. He was lightly bearded and wore a *djellabah,* loose-fitting and hooded, after the style of the Moslems who live to the north. He rose and looked at me as the hawk looks at the pigeon.

Then I turned to the head of the table: There was a man there. A man with something not right about him. He didn't rise; he sat perfectly still, smiling like a statue. But his hands kept crawling slowly around the table in front of him as if they had minds of their own.

My eyes went to those hands and watched them, like a man helplessly watching a python. On each of his fingers, including his thumbs, he wore gold rings with massive colored stones. And the fingers themselves kept moving always, slowly and aimlessly, like the legs of a spider. Sometimes, the hands would stop and one or another of his fingers would raise up and rotate a little, like the tongue of a serpent tasting the air. I knew I was being rude, standing there dumbstruck, watching his hands. But I couldn't help myself.

He broke the spell when he spoke. His voice had the kind of rasp one hears when a carpenter saws wood: not exactly unpleasant, but high-pitched and impossible to ignore. "Ah, my new pupil," he said.

I started, then bowed deeply with greatest respect. For, surely, this was Doctor Drago. When I straightened, I was able to see the rest of him for the first time. His face looked as if it had been chiseled out of mahogany, the bones standing out in sharp relief against his shiny, stretched skin. His spectacles caught the light from the chandelier and made his eyes look like two solid white discs. He wore Western-style clothing: a three-piece suit with a white shirt and necktie. Across his stomach were several heavy gold chains, each of which ended in a pocket of his vest. Certainly, no one needed so many watches, so there must have been something else attached to them.

The tall, dark servant pulled out a chair opposite the younger man and I sat. Two more servants immediately came into the room, a man and a woman. They were dressed less well, but had the same look as the tall, dark man: stiff bodies with eyes made of glass. They held silver utensils for us while we served ourselves. The woman offered two kinds of cooked vegetables—fried cassava stuffed with *yabas* (our strong local onion) and a stew of mixed greens in chicken stock. The man brought around a tureen with a steaming *ragout* of well-spiced meat. It made me realize how hungry I'd become since eating the last of my mother's *fufu* for breakfast. My mouth started watering and I'm afraid I took rather too much on my plate. I tried to eat with the fork that was laid out by the plate but I'd never used one before and made a sloppy job of it.

Doctor Drago laughed with a sound like the cicada makes in the forest. "It is good to see a boy with a healthy appetite. I must always have some young man around to remind me of how precious is youth." He nodded toward the young man opposite me. "Mustafa here is leaving me today to go back to his people. And today you come to take his place. One goes, one comes; tell me, is it not wonderful how the *orisha* provide?"

I nodded, my mouth too full to speak. The food was the best I'd ever tasted. The vegetables were crisp and snappy; we do not like our food cooked until it's gummy. As for the meat stew, it was superb. Some of the spices were familiar to me and the whole had a rather minty flavor. So I decided it must be pork because we often prepare pork in a mint base.

Then I noticed that Mustafa was eating it, too, with almost as much relish as I was. This was strange because even a Moslem who is a secret jujuman will not break his cultural taboo against eating pig. I shrugged and helped myself to another big helping. It was the best meat I'd ever eaten.

"You will see much during your time here, Isaiah. Here you will see juju that is a little . . . different from what is practiced out in the country. Is that not so, Mustafa?"

Mustafa peeked furtively out of the corner of his eye toward Doctor Drago. He'd done the same thing earlier, before sitting down when I came in. And he'd done it also before helping himself to any food. He acted as if he would dare nothing without first trying to gauge Drago's reaction. "Yes, Doctor, that is so," he finally murmured.

Drago ate far more fastidiously than either of us boys. His elegant hands seemed to enjoy the fork more than the food, stroking it and twirling it so it reflected the light. He barely touched his food, preferring to talk and to watch us while his hands amused themselves. I suppose it explained his cadaverous look.

"But for some days, Isaiah, I want you to simply get comfortable here. Later, perhaps, you can assist me in some small ways. I am very low on 'Gambling Soap,' for instance, and must make up a new batch soon; it is much in demand in Lagos. Perhaps you can help me with that."

Mustafa dropped his fork with a clatter onto his plate, splattering *ragout* everywhere. The two stiff-limbed servants stepped forward to wipe his *djellabah* clean.

"Hmmmm. Well, we shall see," said Drago, "we shall see. No real hurry, eh? Plenty of time. Meanwhile, if you should need to go into town, Speedy is at your disposal with the Rolls. Lucien, my *major domo,* will see to any of your other needs; you have but to ask."

Lucien moved stiffly into the room at that moment and said, "Speedy." Then he backed out with no more grace than he'd shown coming in.

"Ah, Mustafa. It is time to go for your train. I will miss you, my boy."

Mustafa rose from the table. "Thank you, Doctor. I . . . I will think of you often."

The Doctor came over to his side and embraced him briefly. It lacked the feeling that Grandfather had shown when I left the village. The Doctor's fingers twitched idly and impatiently on Mustafa's arms. "I know you will, my boy. I know you will. Now, go. And, until I see you again, take care of your soul for me." Which struck me as an odd way of saying farewell.

Mustafa turned. He hesitated a moment, as if he wanted to say something to me, then thought better of it. Without another word, he left us. We heard the front door close and the car drive away.

The Doctor took his seat again. "A strange boy. Juju on top of Islam. It's one of those combinations that never works out as well as one hopes: Something always gets held back." He turned his fixed smile toward me. "That's a problem your grandfather promises me I won't have with you. No confusion lurking in the back of your mind, is there, Isaiah?" I couldn't see his eyes through the milky reflections in his spectacles. "No Islam? Or worse—no Christianity? No 'higher education'? Nothing that might make a boy independent, might give him doubts?"

"Oh, no, sir," I was able to tell him honestly. Apparently, Mr. Olungwe had never decided I was "ready" and so had never allowed me to read his contraband religious books. Now I could be grateful for that omission in my education.

"Ah, good." He sat unmoving, his eyeglasses aimed at me and his fingers restless as seaweed in the current. He stared at me until I got nervous, feeling that there was someone *inside* me, turning me over and studying me as a boy might study a beetle.

Finally, he roused himself and said, "You must be tired after your long trip. Go to bed now. We'll talk more in a few days, after you've settled in."

I belched loudly to show my appreciation of the excellent meal and went up to the wonderful chamber that I had already begun to think of as "my room." I undressed and got into the four-poster, luxuriating in the comfort of a soft mattress and smooth, clean sheets. I fell asleep thinking how lucky I was and blessing good old Joshua for the great idea of sending me here to prove myself.

14

There came a day when a motorcade pulled up in front of the Big House. I'd been with Drago for about two months. Two very pleasant months, I should add, marked by frequent dinners of the delicious *ragout* that we'd had the first night. I ate so much of it that, for the first time in my life, I was beginning to put on weight.

My duties were rigorous and time-consuming, but on my infrequent free days, Speedy drove me into town where I enjoyed the wonders of the Lagos Central Library; there really was such a place! He would roar away in the car after dropping me off but he always rejoined me for lunch. I enjoyed his manic conversation and we were becoming friends. I still didn't understand why he looked as if someone had damaged his car every time I mentioned Drago.

On the day of the motorcade, I was in my room, making a few notes on a juju recipe the Doctor had taught me for arthritis. Because my room looked right down onto the driveway, I'd learned over the past couple of months not to be surprised by fancy cars coming to Drago's compound. Men would step out of the cars cautiously, glancing around as if they were afraid to be seen. Sometimes Drago would get in the car with his customer and they would go off somewhere, occasionally for days at a time. But more frequently, the caller would leave after a few minutes, his hand buried deep in his tunic pocket. Most looked relieved when they left. But they all looked around just as furtively as they did when they'd arrived.

But this was different. There was a big, big limousine preceded by a jeep full of soldiers and followed by another. The soldiers were very tough looking. They wore helmets and balanced carbines on their knees. Bringing up the rear was a white ambulance with red crosses on its sides and roof. Nor was the sedan itself the usual Mercedes, Peugeot, or Rolls that always brought the most important men to the Doctor. This was an American car, like nothing I'd ever seen before. It was huge, with big fins sticking up in back like the sharks that sometimes appear off Lagos Island. The windows were greenish and seemed very thick, much thicker than ordinary automobile glass. The rear windows were fitted with gray drapes that had been pulled closed from the inside. The shiny, black car was longer than some of our public buses; there must have been room inside for a dozen passengers.

But only one figure stepped out when the car stopped. He was a mountain of a man, as big around as he was tall. His uniform was that of a senior military officer, although not of the Nigerian army. He wore his chest full of medals like they were juju. He didn't look embarrassed or afraid, as did most of Doctor Drago's customers. Instead, he laughed loudly when Drago himself came down the front stairs to meet him. His face was round and shiny, like a dark Moon.

For the first time during my stay, I saw Drago humbled. He bowed and scraped before the big man. "Colonel, I was not expecting you until sometime next week," he said in English.

"In my business, my frien', one get away when he can do," Colonel Moon-face answered in a deep, loud voice. Then he laughed again, heartily, and embraced Doctor Drago, much to the Doctor's distress. Even from my second floor window, I could see that the big man's features were not those of the Yoruba nor the Ibo, the Hausa, the Fulani, nor any of the other nearby peoples. Nor did he know any of the languages in common use around Nigeria. Otherwise, the Doctor wouldn't have chosen English, a language in which the Colonel was obviously not very skilled.

The Colonel released Drago, turned, and snapped his fingers. The soldiers immediately jumped down and removed small wooden boxes from their jeeps. Small or not, it took two men to carry each inside while a third man stood guard.

The Colonel stopped the men before they entered the Big House. He slammed the palm of his hand against one of the boxes with a slap hard enough to make the bearers groan. "Here," he said to Drago. "Here you fee, Doctor. Gold, jus' like we agree on. You like inspec' it?"

The Doctor's fingers fluttered greedily for a moment over the boxes, as if they wanted to fondle what was inside. But instead of telling the soldiers to open them, he said, "No need, Colonel. You are an honorable man."

The Colonel threw back his big head and laughed with a sound that shook the windows in their frames. "Ah, yes! 'Honorable man.' Ver' good, Doctor. I like you. You my frien'." He flung his right arm around Drago again and shook him. Even behind the white discs of his glasses, I could see the Doctor's distaste for this big, loud, uncouth man.

While this was going on, two men in white suits removed a litter from the ambulance. The body on it was strapped down and covered completely with a sheet, as if it were a corpse. But I could hear some muffled noises and could see movement under the sheet, as if the person was trying to get up from the litter. I concluded that it was a case of possession and that we were about to see a healing of a very important person.

The entourage went inside then, the Colonel and Drago bringing up the rear. The Colonel kept laughing and babbling all the while in his broken English, as if he and Drago were old friends.

I suppose the men had some private business because it was more than two hours before Lucien came to get me. I had grown accustomed by this time to the lethargy characteristic of all of Drago's servants, with the exception of our driver, Speedy. I'd even gotten bold enough to amuse myself at their expense sometimes. For example, I used to see how long I could keep Lucien in the doorway, saying, "Come," over and over again at one minute intervals. In the end, I became bored with the game before he did; otherwise, I think he might have been standing there passively to this day.

But obviously, I wasn't about to try any childish mischief when it was Drago who had sent Lucien for me. Especially when someone as imposing as the Colonel was with him. So this time, I obediently lined up behind Lucien who, much to my surprise, did not turn toward the Doctor's study. Instead, he led me out the back door and across the lawn to Drago's *ile-agbara*—literally, his "Power House."

The Power House is a mystical place. It is sort of a private Shrine, and each jujuman provides one for himself according to his means. A poor man might have only a corner of his home with a curtain that can be drawn across it for privacy. Those of greater affluence try to set aside a room where no one but the *babalawo* will ever enter; it may only be the size of a closet, but it is still a special place to the jujuman.

In Drago's case, his wealth was such that he had a separate small building behind the Big House to serve as his *ile-agbara*. It is only by comparison with the Big House that I can call it "small"; a few months previously I would have been awed by its size, thinking it fit to be the home of the *oba* of some entire nation of people.

Drago's Power House was several times the size of Grandfather's Shrine. It was built of beautiful, cold, white limestone blocks and was surrounded by its own well-tended grounds. I'd been inside it many times, but only in the central room, the one set aside for sacrifice. Drago required me to do all the sacrificing while he and his lesser priests negotiated prices with the customers in the smaller rooms around the outside.

And it was long and hard work, I can tell you. I've lost track of how many hours I had to labor over the killing table. We used a special one made of stainless steel that the Doctor imported from a place called Sheffield in England. It had been designed for use in the embalming trade and had little gutters cut into it so the blood and other bodily fluids could drain away into an *abattoir* down at the foot of the table. Sometimes the blood was saved in buckets for use in further ritual. But often, I was liberating so much of it during my day's work that Drago told me to just let it go down the drain. There were times when I went to bed with a sore arm from all the ritual killing work I was obliged to do to earn my keep. I may not have been learning as much new juju from the Doctor as I'd hoped, but there was probably no equal in all of Africa for my skill with the blade.

And it was to the large sacrifice room that Lucien brought me once again. Only this time, I had company. The staff had been pressed into service as musicians and were all sitting glassy-eyed on the floor just inside, softly playing ritual drums. Doctor Drago was standing at the head of the table, his eyeglasses like silver coins under the fluorescent lights. The Colonel was there, too, next to Drago; every few seconds his big belly shook as if with silent mirth at a joke no one else could hear. They were both dressed completely in white, the juju ritual killing color. Two of the soldiers, apparently picked at random to represent all six, had been given white tunics to wear over their fatigues. They stood along the wall, huddling into themselves as if badly frightened. I was a little amused by their nervousness; they probably weren't jujumen at all, just common soldiers. They probably had never even seen a blood ritual, let alone participated in one.

Well, boys, I thought, *there's a first time for everything.*

"Colonel," said Drago, "this is my new assistant, Isaiah."

"He look like good boy. You good boy, Isaiah? Is good to be good boy."

"The Colonel," Drago said, "has asked that you be present. The soldiers are here at his request, too."

The Colonel beamed. "I like many witness. Juju too secret, too quiet.

But I like many people to know how I do things—to know how I get power, how I use power. So you be witness—tell other jujumen. These men be witness—tell other soldiers."

I bowed politely. "Yes sir, as you wish." I turned to Doctor Drago. "Do you wish me merely to observe, sir? Or would you like me to execute the sacrifice?"

"You will do the killing, Isaiah. But this is the first time you will be performing this particular ritual. I want you also to observe closely, to learn all you can. It is not often we are find ourselves commissioned by some great patron"—here he bowed in the direction of the grinning Colonel—"to perform a ritual as powerful and important as this."

"Really, sir?"

"Yes. Even I myself have had the opportunity to perform it no more than two or three times each year during my career."

I found myself becoming excited. This was the kind of training Grandfather had sent me here for! The only thing spoiling it for me was the two soldiers who looked so out of place. In fact, one fellow looked as if he might faint at any moment. I suppose just the thought of seeing a goat or a ram sacrificed was curdling his stomach because he kept staring at the table behind the Doctor, swallowing and swaying. I found it distracting; I would have asked him to leave, if the matter had been up to me.

"This ritual is called 'iko-awo,' " the Doctor said. "Do you know it?"

I shook my head thoughtfully. It translated roughly as as "spirit slave." Not only did I not know it; I'd never even *heard* of it. It was that way with much of this big-city juju, though. The Doctor sold juju remedies through distributors all over Africa. Trucks were always pulling up to be filled with items we'd never heard of in the countryside: *Gambling Soap. Better Luck Candles. Lover's Oil. Lord Mnube's Health Elixir.* I assumed they were the same kind of remedy our herbalists back home made up out of local ingredients. But Doctor Drago had a large wholesale volume, so I figured he just made them up in bulk and packaged them under his trademarks.

There was only one sure thing: Doctor Drago had made his reputation by guaranteeing that every remedy was *absolutely authentic.* It was a good answer to those who said that the Doctor didn't even really believe in juju, that he was just in it for the money. But his insistence that every remedy, every curse, every ritual be 100 percent authentic showed his true juju nature. And if Drago said a ritual was important, it was *important.* And if he said it was authentic, it was *authentic.*

"So this ritual is new to you?" he asked.

I nodded.

"Well," he said lightly, "there's a first time for everything, isn't there?" He stepped to the side, his active hands fluttering about as if they were congratulating each other.

And there, bound with leather straps to the table behind him, was this skinny white man.

15

The ritual we were about to perform was an example of a new style of juju—what we sometimes call "money juju." That's actually a slang term for the brand of juju in which making money seems to be the *babalawo's* only motivation.

That is, juju's traditional objectives—curing or preventing misfortune by appeasing the *orisha* and one's ancestors—seem to be not at all important in "money juju." The only goal seems to be the acquisition of obscene power for oneself (or for one's client) in the Invisible World. So the rituals of "money juju" are deliberately cruel and vicious because the customer is supposed to receive enormous power from the diabolic behavior.

"Money juju" is a product of city life; it could never exist in the country, at least not on any large scale. It depends on the anonymity and fragmented society found in big city life. In our cities, people of many tribes and cultures are thrown together into an amorphous heap, so that there are no community standards. In the countryside, everyone knows everyone else and we all have the same rules by which we have to live. In such stable communities, word spreads quickly about any jujuman who is insincere, because taking juju lightly might bring the fury of the *orisha* down on his whole village.

So, if a man is thought to be guilty of perverting juju, he will receive the tribal man's ultimate punishment: He will be shunned—ostracized, ignored, psychologically exiled. He will be cut off from all those with whom he has a common culture. No one will speak to him, his wives will ignore his needs, his children will withdraw their respect, and his neighbors will pass him by, paying him no more notice than they would a goat turd drawing flies in the road. He will be completely alone in the midst of many others.

Life without community is not worth living for one who has grown up in a tribal culture. Being shunned is even worse than being rejected by one's own family. In fact, for the tribal member, being shunned by one's fellows is the worst punishment possible, short of death.

But the city dwellers are already cut off almost completely from their traditional culture. They no longer have a community to ostracize them. So they no longer fear the shame of standing guilty before their peers. In the city, they can be punished only by the impersonal written law of the courts. And the law's only eyes are those of the policeman, while the village has eyes everywhere.

So there are few controls on the city dwellers, and they feel they can get away with anything. In the first place, there are not the thousand prying eyes of the village to find them out. And in the second, what can city people do to them even if they catch them? Put in them jail? The threat is hollow: For tribal members, being in the city and away from their people is *already* something like being in jail. Where village members are held back by their fear of what the community will think, city dwellers *have* no community to fear. They simply don't care what you or I think and are quite candid about letting us know that.

This indifference to the good opinion of one's fellows has let *cruelty* become the primary characteristic of the modern phenomenon of money juju. In fact, the crueler the ritual is in money juju the more power it is believed to have. The idea probably stems from one of the most ancient of our ceremonies: the annual ritual killing of the scapegoat.

Each spring, the *babalawo* sacrifices a goat in the town square. The ceremony is a solemn one. It is three days long and starts with a period of quiet, during which no citizen may work. Rather, each member of the community is expected to examine his or her conscience during this time. Each tries to remember anything done during the last year that might cause those who populate the Spirit World to be angry with the people. On the third day of the ceremony, the people assemble and symbolically pile all their moral transgressions on the goat. The belief is that, with the animal's death, all these sins will die as well, and the citizens of the Spirit World will have no cause to harm the community.

This custom is not unknown in other parts of the world. But whereas the ancient Israelites, for instance, used to send their goat out to wander to its death quietly and alone in the desert, we take a more direct approach. At sun-up, the *babalawo* begins to make slow, shallow cuts all along the flanks of the sacrifice. Then he pulls off the long, thin strips of skin between the cuts and throws them to the watching crowd, who eat the flesh raw.

Our traditions say that an animal will survive two hundred such cuts, if they are made with an extremely sharp knife, which is why we call the ritual "The Two Hundred Cuts." But just because the ritual is thought to be survivable does not mean it is painless. In fact, it's intentionally hard on the poor animal, deliberately brutal and inhumane. The belief is that the "soul" of the goat must be "charged up" by pain and agony, and that makes the animal's suffering an integral part of the ritual. Indeed, the more the beast suffers, the better, from the standpoint of the believer who wants forgiveness of his or her sins.

To make it all as gruesome (and, therefore, as "powerful") as possible, the poor animal is never gagged; the more noise it makes during its ordeal, the more the *orisha* will come to see what all the fuss is. In between cuts there's a good deal of celebration, so the whole procedure takes about twelve hours, running from sunup until sundown.

Finally, the 201st cut is administered. It's the only one that's supposed to cause death, so it's always across the throat. It's the only one that's deep. Not until that 201st cut is the poor animal finally put out of its misery and sent to the Invisible World to intercede on behalf of its tormenters. Just to make sure it does so, its head is removed and placed in a specially prepared *nganga* jar. The head is held as ransom until the next year, when a new victim is chosen.

This ritual is unusual for its cruelty. For the most part, it is blood that plays the sacramental role in juju, not pain or suffering. Admittedly, we adorn our bodies with blood, we sprinkle it over each other—even *drink* it. But the animal from which we take that blood is almost always killed *fast*. To deliberately torture a sacrificial animal is not our way.

The difference was defined by a man with whom I appeared on an American television talk-show recently. He was a professor from the American city of New Orleans and billed himself as an expert on *voodoo,* the watered-down imitation of juju that slave owners grudgingly permitted their slaves to practice in the American south and in the West Indies. The talk-show host is widely known for his liberal views and had been assailing me for cruelty to animals. I was getting the worst of it, I'm afraid; my English was not adequate to debate someone so glib.

"The thing you fail to understand about voodoo ritual practice," the professor told him, "is that it's basically humane."

"*Humane?*" the liberal host yelled. "*Humane?* How can you say it's humane when they kill helpless animals?"

"And where do you think meat comes from for your table? 'Helpless animals' are killed to feed you and your family, aren't they?"

"That's not the same thing at all," the host said.

"You're right," the professor admitted. "The African jujuman kills his sacrifice with a single stroke. Death would appear to be almost instantaneous. As far as we know, the sacrifice is painless—"

"Aha! 'As far as you know'!"

"That's right. Did you know that the jujuman uses the same technique required by *Leviticus* for *kosher* slaughter? It's supposed to be the least unkind method. That's not how our American packing houses do it, though."

"What do *you* know about packing houses? You never worked in one. You're a *professor*." The host said the word as if it were a curse.

"No," the professor admitted, "but I read Upton Sinclair's novel, *The Jungle*. That's where I learned about how cows and pigs are really killed in our packing houses. Do you know how a cow is killed? They chase her into a chute that runs down to the slaughtering floor. The chute is so steep that she can't stop herself from falling and bouncing all the way to the bottom once she sets foot on it. When she finally hits the bottom, her legs may be broken and her skin is all ripped. The man at the bottom of the chute is supposed to put her out of her misery by slugging her between the eyes with a sledgehammer."

The audience started acting restless and the host said, "That's not what we're here to talk about."

But the professor continued. "This usually doesn't kill her right away, though. So the workers jam a metal hook with a chain on it through her neck. Then they drag her off with a tractor to this huge pile of other slowly dying cows. They all lay in their own blood and filth for hours, blind and bawling in terrible pain, until they they die.

The host broke for a commercial at that point and some of the audience left. I think it was a less-than-successful show for the host. The professor had been right, though: Compared to other methods of slaughter, juju does tend to treat its sacrifices humanely—except in those special instances where we want the animal to carry messages for us into the Invisible World of the spirits. Then we use rituals like "The Two Hundred Cuts" that are so deliberately abusive, painful, inhumane, and cruel that they make Mr. Sinclair's slaughterhouses look like amusement park rides.

Now here's a pretty obvious idea: If juju like "The Two Hundred Cuts" works with a goat, it should work even better with a man, right? The *babalawos* are not fools; they figured that one out ages ago. So they have long believed that the ritual torture and killing of a human being should gain enormous power in the Invisible World. But because of the social scrutiny that's a part of tribal life, that kind of murder was really only an isolated problem with us.

Until, that is, we Africans found freedom from social judgment in the anonymity of the big cities like Lagos, where I was living. And also— as you'll see later—New York and London and Los Angeles, where *you* might be living.

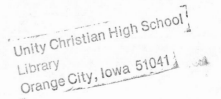

16

There was a tennis ball stuffed in the skinny white man's mouth. A leather thong had been passed through two holes poked in its sides and tied behind his head. It made a very effective gag. His eyes were bulging, but that seemed to have been due to fear, because he didn't appear to have been injured in any way. Rather, he seemed quite fit. He was lean and wiry, like a runner, and there were no cuts or scratches or bruises on him anywhere.

In fact, he appeared to unblemished.

The situation couldn't be what I was afraid it was. It just couldn't be. "Do you know the 'Two Hundred Cuts'?" Doctor Drago's voice asked. I don't think I was aware at first that it was me he was talking to. My complete attention was given over to the man on the table.

My surprise at finding a stranger restrained against his will was understandable, I think. But there was also the fact that I'd never before seen a white man this close up with no clothes on. It was fascinating, of course, to see a body so *pale*—almost the bleached color of a leper's scars. But what really drew my attention was that the fellow had a thin coating of *hair* all over his body, stiff and straight, just like a goat. I couldn't stop staring at him.

Doctor Drago whacked me over the head with his *ofo,* the staff of office that many *babalawos* carry whenever they are at ritual. An *ofo* is usually only a couple of feet long and maybe an inch or so in diameter— more a switch than a staff, in fact. So it just sort of naturally lends itself to helping a student focus his attention. But Drago's *ofo* was made of almost indestructible *ahayan* wood and was as thick as a man's wrist. It was about seven feet long and shaped like a big, dark question mark.

A leather sack of sacred alligator pepper was bound to the foot of the staff and rattled whenever he shook it. When Drago hit you with his *ofo,* it did more than get your attention; it hurt like the devil.

And it also made the Colonel laugh hysterically. He seemed to enjoy watching someone inflict pain.

"Isaiah!" the Doctor said. "I asked you a question, boy! Do you know the 'Two Hundred Cuts'?"

"Oh, yes, Doctor," I said fearfully, rubbing my head. "Sort of, that is; I've seen my uncle do it."

Drago was wearing a starched, white tunic buttoned up high around his neck, and white trousers over white shoes. He looked like a medical doctor from an American movie. "Hmmmm," he said, "but you've never performed the rite yourself, is that correct?"

I became aware that I was trembling. I desperately wanted to believe that I misunderstood what he had in mind. I reminded myself of the strange tourists that would offer Grandfather exorbitant sums to watch one of our sacrifice rituals. One of them—an Englishman, I recalled—had himself tied up by a companion while he watched us sacrifice a ram. His behavior made no sense to any of us, but surely something like that had to be the explanation for the skinny white man.

"The 'Two Hundred Cuts'?" Oh, no, sir," I said. "I never did. Not me. You see, we only did, the 'Two Hundred Cuts' once a year back home— just before spring planting." I was babbling, hoping to get myself off the hook. "I suppose Grandfather always meant to have me start doing it, but he never actually—"

"*Atoto!*" Drago said. "Enough! I see that I shall have to perform the ritual on this sacrifice myself. You have evaded this task successfully, Isaiah." He turned away from me shaking his head in apparent disappointment. I took a deep breath of relief.

Then, just as I felt I'd been spared, he spun and faced me again with a knowing leer, as if he had timed my reaction. "Very well. I will perform the ritual myself. But you—and all the others here—will watch." As always, the discs of his eyeglasses reflected light so that they looked like two bright headlamps coming at me fast down a dark highway. But I was learning to tell when he was pleased with himself by watching his hands. Such as now, when his fingers fluttered their soft dance up and down the *ofo,* like spirits of the forest swaying to a melody that no human could hear.

"And at the end," he said quietly from behind his glasses, "you will administer the Final Cut for me."

My heart ran back up into my throat again. For a moment, the only sound in the sacrifice room was the Colonel's greasy chuckling. It was the same laugh men use when talking about their first time with a woman.

"I trust you can handle that?" Doctor Drago asked.

"Oh, yes, sir. That is, I . . . I guess I can. But. . . ."

His *ofo* rattled softly, like an annoyed snake. "Why do you hesitate, boy? Is there some reason why you don't want to give the Final Cut to our sacrifice?"

I shook my head mutely. I could hear the Colonel in the background, giggling like a girl with an inexplicably deep voice. It was becoming impossible to believe that this was going to be an ordinary, everyday ritual. But I kept trying to fool myself nevertheless, denying the evidence, as one will when reality begins to look unacceptable. I told myself that we would soon go outside into the grounds where a lamb or a calf would be tethered. That's how it would have to be, I thought, because there was certainly no sacrifice in sight in the Power House.

At last, I cleared my throat. "Doctor, I . . . I see no sacrifice here; what animal will we use?"

"Ah." He beamed the lights of his glasses on me again. "Well, as to that, we shall sacrifice the animal that eats salt."

I put my head down so no one would see my face. His use of the phrase "the animal that eats salt" had confirmed my fears: He had spoken in "the hidden language." Although the practice of juju is protected as a civil right in most African nations, some individual juju acts remain against the law, which makes it prudent for jujumen to adopt the habit of being indirect when speaking about rituals. And the Doctor had used one of our most well-defined code words: The animal that puts salt on its food is *man*.

The Colonel stepped forward. He seemed impatient, his big, round face cleared for once of its customary smile. "We start now, yes?"

"As you wish, Colonel." The Doctor turned to a surgical tray next to the stainless steel table. In the short time I'd been with him, I'd become accustomed to his somewhat westernized ways. So I was not surprised to see the tray laden with surgical implements rather than the homemade knives more traditional *babalawos* would use. He laid his *ofo* aside, took one of the scalpels and turned back to the man on the table. He peered down the edge of the blade with a squint, as if judging the instrument's sharpness. The white man became even whiter as he watched, utterly helpless.

The Doctor leaned toward the table, his eyes unreadable as always. Slowly, he brought the knife down toward the white man's throat. The white man's eyes followed the blade until it seemed they would go down into his cheeks. The tennis ball was heaving in and out of his mouth with the exertions of his breathing. And the air was filled with that peculiar sharp scent that a man's body gives off under extreme fear.

At the first touch of the scalpel, the white man urinated on himself. Drago slid the flat of the scalpel along the white man's neck, as if he were shaving him. My testicles tightened as I watched, as if they were trying to pull themselves back up inside me. The blade slid under the leather thong just below the white man's left ear. And Drago slowly, lingeringly rotated the scalpel, bringing its razor-sharp edge to bear.

Then, with one quick motion, he slashed the thong holding the tennis ball and the white man spat it out.

"Oh, thank God," the white man said breathlessly. "Thank God."

Drago returned the scalpel to the tray. He looked at the white man solicitously. "Do you understand what is happening here?"

"Yes! I mean, no. I mean. . . ." He had a British accent and must have been one of those holdovers from colonial days because he recovered himself in a matter of mere seconds. In fact, although he lay there tied up, naked, and wet, he spoke to Drago as he might have spoken to a house boy. "I was simply standing about outside the Club, waiting for my transport, when a local military vehicle pulled up. Well, I naturally assumed the Embassy had asked them to come collect me."

The Doctor's fingers swayed like reeds in the wind. "But not so, eh?"

"Certainly not!" said the white man. "Rather than taking the road toward the Lake, which they should have done so I could rejoin my unit, the buggers headed for the airport!"

"The airport? My, my. Then your trip must have been a long one."

"Yes. Six hours on the metal floor of an old Dakota, me trussed up like a Christmas goose! When we finally arrived here—wherever 'here' is— they threw me in some sort of old ambulance and . . . well, here I am!"

"Tsk-tsk. Your story is most sad."

"Yes, well. Now, you appear to be an educated man, not like the rabble that kidnapped me; I should be grateful if you release me at once. There's no point to holding me because I'm really not worth much in the way of ransom."

Drago made a surprised look. "No? Hmmmm. Then it appears we shall have to find some other use for you." His fingers caressed each other like lovers.

The white man's face began to lose its confidence again. "Now, see here. This is most irregular; I shall be missed, you know. Now unless I am released immediately, I refuse to answer for the consequences."

"You do, eh? Well, sir, Africa is a dangerous place. Disappearing here is not the same as vanishing from your Trafalgar Square at high noon, is it? Is it not likely that your countrymen will feel you've met with some unfortunate mishap?"

"Nonsense! I am an 'old hand' in Africa. *I* know my way around; *I* know how to take care of myself here."

"Indeed? You'll forgive me if I point out that you've not done well recently."

"None of your cheek, now, Boy-o!" the skinny white man said. "When word of this outrage gets back to my unit—"

Drago held up one of his elegantly swaying hands. "I regret that your unit will never hear of any of this. I think they are very far away."

The white man considered. "Nonetheless, I feel it safe to say that my Embassy—"

"I think, sir, that you should try to understand that you are quite alone here. 'Here,' by the way, is Lagos. We *do* have a British embassy, of course. Rather close by, in fact. But since they have no reason to believe you are anywhere within two thousand kilometers of Nigeria. . . ." He shrugged.

The Colonel's voice boomed out. "Doctor, please: Is time to begin, no?" For the first time, he stepped into the white man's field of view.

"*You!*" the white man shrieked.

The Colonel grinned down at the white man. "Is good of you to reco'nize you ol' frien'."

" 'Old friend,' indeed! What is your part in all of this?" the white man demanded.

"My part? I am the man you will serve."

"Not bloody likely!"

The Colonel roared with laughter. "Oh, but yes. *Very* bloody likely. Is not so?" he said to Drago.

"Yes, indeed," the Doctor answered. "You see, sir, you will truly become the Colonel's servant, his representative. Not here, but in the Invisible World. You will become his messenger, his Spirit Slave—what we call *iko-awo.*"

The white man's eyes showed that this was not the first time he'd heard the word.

"Ah," said the Doctor with pleasure. "I see you know *iko-awo.* That is good. The more you know about this ritual, the better. Because then, the more you will go to the *orisha* in a 'charged-up' condition. Yes, I think you will make a very strong messenger for the Colonel."

"Please," the white man said with an unexpected whine in his voice.

"Please, let me go. I won't tell anyone, I swear I won't! Do all the juju you want, just let me go. I'll make it worth your while, both of you."

Drago looked as if he wanted to taunt the white man some more. But the Colonel seemed bored by the change in his attitude. "Begin," he ordered.

"No, look, I've got some money saved up. English money, sterling! It's yours, all of it. Only you can't do this thing. Especially you, Colonel. Why, you and your troops are the reason I am in Africa, don't you remember? I came here to help you!"

"Good," said the Colonel. "Now I give you the chance to help me ver', ver' much." He suddenly grabbed up a scalpel and thrust it into the white man's side to a depth of several inches.

The white man screamed and flecks of blood flew from his mouth all the way to the ceiling.

The Doctor grabbed the scalpel out of the Colonel's hand and threw it to the tile floor with a clang. "Do you wish this man to go to the *orisha* having died an ordinary death? Can you afford to indulge your anger if it creates such *waste?*" he shouted. The Colonel instantly looked regretful and almost abashed.

Drago bent to study the wound. He examined it critically and made the kind of quick, competent judgment that only a man who has inflicted thousands of such wounds can do. He sighed. "Four hours. No more. We shall have to work faster than I'd planned."

He went to a cabinet against the wall and brought back several packets with red crosses on them. Within minutes, he'd expertly cleaned and dressed the white man's wound. Then he pulled a chair alongside the table and leaned to the white man's ear.

"Listen to me. You will go to the spirits in pain. They will hear you above all others because your pain will be so great. You will plead for good fortune for the Colonel. If you fail him, he will burn your body and scatter your ashes to the winds. Is that clear?"

He snapped his fingers at the Colonel. The Colonel looked insulted, though I didn't know whether it was because of the Doctor's attitude or because he was being obliged to do something for himself. But in any event, the ritual required the Master of the Spirit Slave to bring forth by himself the vessel in which the remains of the sacrifice would be imprisoned. So the Colonel bit off his anger and went through the doorway into a small room in back that was always kept dark.

He returned puffing under the load of a portable clothing wardrobe. He set it down just beyond the foot of the sacrifice table, where the white man could see it. It stood almost as high as the ceiling, and was made of pressboard. It was the same color blue as a cloudless sky and it had a label on it: Sears, Roebuck & Company. Such cabinets were a common sight in Drago's *ile-agbara*. There were probably a dozen or more just barely visible through the doorway to the darkened room. I'd always before assumed they were just shipping cases for juju, because sometimes one of the men with the fancy cars would take one of them away with him. I'd never looked in any of them because Drago had never told me to; it wasn't any of my business. Besides, it always *smelled* so bad back there.

Drago pointed to the cabinet. "This is your 'hostage home,' " he said to the white man. "Look upon it and know fear."

But the white man was moaning and tossing his head from side to side, though whether from the pain of his wound or from the terror of what was to come, I did not know. Drago chose not to repeat himself to the white man. Instead, he reached into one of the packets he'd brought from the cabinet and produced a little white cylinder wrapped in gauze, about the size of a peanut. He twisted it in his elegant fingers and the astringent smell of ammonia spread instantly through the sacrifice room.

But rather than simply waving the smelling salts some distance under the white man's nose, as would have been normal, he jammed the capsule up one nostril.

The white man's head thrashed wildly in an involuntary attempt to escape the noxious fumes. His screams nearly drowned out the popping noises that came from his overtaxed neck muscles. If the stainless steel table had not been bolted down, I'm sure it would have been dancing in place from the white man's exertions.

It wasn't until the smell began to dissipate that the Doctor removed the capsule. "Now," he said calmly, "you have had a lesson: You must understand all that will happen. You must pay attention to me and you must answer when spoken to. Do you understand?"

The white man glared at Drago in defiant silence. The Doctor was still holding the broken ammonia capsule, massaging it sensually between his fingers. When the white man failed to answer, he dropped it to the floor. With a sigh, he took a fresh capsule out of the packet.

"Yes!" the white man shouted, his eyes large. "Yes, I understand!"

Drago smiled and patted the white man on the head. "That's good. Thank you for responding to me."

Then he broke the capsule anyway and shoved it up the white man's other nostril.

I looked around the room. The two soldiers seemed to be as shocked and unsettled as I was. But the Colonel was vastly amused by the incident. He was holding himself with laughter, leaning backwards with his face toward the ceiling. I was surprised to see an erection bulging under the sharply creased pants of his uniform.

When the Doctor finally removed the capsule, he said to the white man, "Now you have had another lesson: Pain will be your constant companion for the remainder of your life. There is no way you can change this fact. Think on this and know fear."

He dropped the capsule on the floor and turned to look at his collection of scalpels on the tray. "It is right that you should be afraid," he said over his shoulder. "That is the purpose of this ritual, to send you to the spirits in a state such that they cannot help but notice you. Only then can you be effective in pleading the Colonel's case. I will put you into such a state by using pain. Think on this and know fear." He turned back to the table, his fingers stroking the handle of a gleaming scalpel. "You are alone," he said to the white man. "You are lost. There is nothing you can do. Think on this and know fear."

The white man was gasping for air. He still had a defiant look on his face, but much milder than before. Perhaps the Doctor's urging for him to "think on this and know fear" was working.

The first cut made by the Doctor was much more disciplined than the Colonel's wild stabbing. He set the blade just above the sternum and a bit to the left. He let it sink into the white man's flesh to a distance of perhaps a centimeter or so, just enough to separate the top layer of skin from the underlying tissue. He drew it downward evenly in a perfectly straight line until he got to the pubic hair. I could see the skin spread back behind his knife; it reminded me of plowing a furrow. But it would have had to be a furrow in a place like Georgia, where the soil is red, because a thin trickle of blood oozed up behind the blade as it passed. Without pausing, Drago went back up to the starting point. He moved his blade a little farther to the left and proceeded to cut another track, as straight as the first.

Then he made a short cut up at the top of the man's chest, connecting the two long parallel cuts. He turned the blade toward the foot of the table and undercut the meat to an extent of maybe ten centimeters, just enough to provide a flap of skin which could be grasped by a man's hand. This was all done so skillfully that the skinny white man never even cried out.

Cutting the tracks and creating the flap had taken only seconds, during which there had been silence in the room, except for the sound of heavy breathing from both the white man and the Colonel. Drago set the scalpel down gently and took up his *ofo*. Then he turned to me.

"Isaiah," he said, "please remove the first strip from the sacrifice."

I'd been so fascinated by his work that my horror had subsided momentarily and I nearly forgot what would come next. This isn't as crazy as it sounds; remember that I'd been studying juju for years and this torture was actually a demonstration of my craft by a master. But now, it suddenly hit me: This was no innocent ritual, culturally enriching us through "traditional" religious observances. The white man, for all the pale and sickly ugliness of his skin, was a human being.

"Doctor, I . . . I . . ."

Drago said nothing to me, but the glare from the flat plates of his glasses were burning a hole into my very being. I knew I was disgracing myself, my grandfather, and all my ancestors. Not to mention my village and my whole tribe. But even knowing all this, all I could do was stand there, stammering like a frightened child.

The Colonel stepped forward. "I see this before. When we hunt zebra, back home. Often, young man afraid to kill first time. We call 'buck fever.' Is easy to fix." He grabbed my skinny arm in his hammy hand and pulled me to the table. With great precision, he pushed my hand forward toward the flap of skin hanging from the skinny white man's chest.

I tried to resist, but it was useless; the Colonel was twice my weight, maybe more. In spite of how badly I was shaking, he guided my hand unerringly to the bloody flap of skin hanging off the white man's chest. "Oh, God," the white man was muttering. "Oh, God, please don't!"

I tried to clench my fist, but the Colonel easily pried it open. He positioned the palm of my hand directly under the dripping flap. And then he squeezed it closed.

The flap was just the right size for my grip. As the Colonel painfully compressed my hand around it, the skin exuded blood and bits of marbly fat, which oozed out from between my clenched fingers. I felt my stomach revolve and then I vomited.

The Colonel didn't even seem to notice. He just leaned back, pulling my hand along with him. Slowly. The soft, squishing sound as the flap of skin unzipped itself from the white man's body was nearly drowned out by his pitiful screaming. I was transfixed by the sight of the flap, becoming longer and longer at the end of my arm, until it was a bloody, rubbery-looking strip. We pulled at the lengthening piece of bloody skin—the Colonel laughing and me weeping with horror—until the resistance of the attached flesh finally ceased just above the white man's penis. I would have fallen over backwards if the Colonel had not been there to hold me up.

The white man stopped screaming then and fainted from his agony. The Doctor revived him with more smelling salts while the Colonel laughed in that hearty, yet threatening, way of his. When no one joined in, he turned to scowl at his men. Even though he looked somewhat younger than they were, the soldiers clearly feared him. One of them was so unnerved by the possibility of the Colonel's displeasure that he even tried to force out a weak laugh of his own. But he only succeeded in producing a kind of breathless sound. The other soldier couldn't even try; he just rolled his eyes back into his head, slumped against his fellow, and slid quietly to the ground.

This seemed to amuse the Colonel anew and he roared again, holding his shaking stomach. His face was as round as one of our local pumpkins and he was missing two teeth in front. When he laughed like this, it made him look like a leering, jack-o-lantern of the sort that American children carve. The same look of plump, obscene menace was there.

I kept staring at my hand—the one that had pulled the strip of flesh from the man's body. Drago looked down at me with what was almost a look of kindness. "Did it feel any different than any other skinning you've ever done?"

I couldn't speak, but I shook my head. The fact is, it had felt just like all the countless times I'd pulled strips of skin from calves and from lambs to make the leather thongs with which we attach spear points to their shafts. The only differences were that this time the animal was alive. And, of course, this time it was "the animal that eats salt."

"If it is the same," said the Doctor, "there is no reason you should not continue to remove the strips while I make the cuts." There were tears in my eyes, but he was as cool as ever. His fingers twined sinuously through my hair as he tried to comfort me, just as though he were my grandfather.

"I *do* need your help, you know, Isaiah. There is much to be done and little time to do it. I know this ritual can be difficult the first time. But remember your Grandfather; do it for his honor if for no other. . . ."

"Grandfather?" I said. "Surely my grandfather could never have carried out this kind of ritual!"

A slight smile cracked the Doctor's face. "No? Who do you think taught it to *me?* Of course, the old man only did it for your village, because he thought it would bring your people power and good fortune. I don't think he ever did it for a client, in fact, I doubt if he ever made ten *naira* in his whole life from his juju."

The vague air of sympathy disappeared and he became all business again. "Now," he said, "let's finish the job. And remember, Isaiah: You can no more change what will be happening here today than that poor white man can." He made a motion to the Colonel, who slid into the chair up alongside the white man's head.

For the next three hours, the Doctor cut and I pulled. As we did, the Colonel talked to the white man, which was difficult at first. But it soon became easier: The white man screamed his voice hoarse and made very little noise after the first few minutes.

I don't remember much of what the Colonel said to the white man; I felt like I was in one of those dreams in which you work all night and wake up tired in the morning. But I remember the Colonel's main objective because he repeated it to the white man over and over again: to eventually take over his country. He said he knew it could take ten more years, but that he was prepared to wait. Esu himself had appeared to him in the form of a monkey, he said, and had told him that it was his destiny to become the supreme ruler of his country. This the Colonel said again and again until at last, inevitably, the white man became the Colonel's *iko-awo*.

It took a little less than the four hours the Doctor had anticipated. By the end, the floor was almost carpeted with the little capsules of ammonia, as well as with empty syringes. These had contained the drugs that the Doctor injected into the white man as the ritual entered its later stages, when it became harder and harder to bring him back each time he passed out from the agony of his ordeal.

I have always told myself that the unknown white man was probably dead anyway by the time I administered the *coup-de-grace*. Or that he wouldn't have wanted to live in the kind of shape he was in and that I actually did him a kindness. Those are the things I've always told myself about that 201st cut, which I had to administer.

*   *   *

After a break during which the Doctor had coffee and the Colonel drank some French wine from a squat bottle one of his men carried, we removed the white man's entrails. That was a trivial procedure compared to everything else: a couple of quick cuts and done. The Colonel saved the liver in a plastic box that had a blue flower on its side and had a matching top which snapped in place; it looked very festive. Everything else was discarded. The hollow, skinned corpse was much lighter than it had been in life. We washed it and shoved a big iron hook through its back. Then we hung it up in the sky-blue wardrobe, like a butcher might hang a chicken in the window.

The white man had been tall and his toes nearly dragged on the floor of the cabinet. The Doctor told the Colonel they'd need to be "trimmed back" as the now-empty body stretched out over time. I have since heard florists advise people on the care of houseplants in much the same tone of voice.

The Colonel had his men carry the wardrobe out to the ambulance. I was detailed to carry the big carton of spices and herbs that he would have to apply to the body weekly, to keep the insects and smell under control, until it was fully "ripe," which would take about a year or so.

Then the motorcade set off for the airport and the long trip back east, leaving me a day older.

17

After that, I was ill for some time. I'd apparently caught some sort of fever, because I was unable to keep my food down.

It very much disturbed the Doctor for me to be sick. For one thing, he now seemed enthusiastic about my prospects to become a *babalorisha,* as my grandfather wanted. I think this was because, in spite of obvious misgivings, I'd still been able to carry out the Final Cut on the white man in the *iko-awo* ritual. I got some hints that my predecessor, Mustafa, had failed to perform when he was called upon in a similar situation. Drago told me he was going to send a glowing report about me back to Grandfather.

But at the same time, he was annoyed that my illness made me unable to "go and fetch." This was one of the duties he always demanded of the boys who studied under him. There was a rigid schedule of visits through the surrounding countryside which had to be made on time or else the Doctor's operation suffered. They involved his money juju—picking up fresh ingredients or delivering prepared products.

Some of the tasks were boring: About five days of each month were spent just delivering the Doctor's various aphrodisiacs, always to the same fancy addresses. And of course, while I was running around doing the deliveries, my duties in the sacrifice room of the Power House piled up on me. So I seldom looked forward to "go and fetch" days.

But on occasion the errands were fascinating. For example, one rainy day toward the end of my first month in residence, an unusually quiet and grim Speedy drove me out to a distant swamp in the forest. The way was marked by big, leathery-looking trees with trunks as gray as the day was. When we came to a marshy clearing surrounded by yellowish reeds, he turned off the engine.

For a long time, nothing happened; we just sat there. I asked him several times to tell me what we were waiting for, but he acted as if he hadn't heard me. Finally, he just rolled up the window between the sedan and his open compartment. We waited for the better part of an hour like that, not speaking, staring insensibly straight ahead out the windshield.

Finally, some of the bushes around the car stood up. They were men covered from head to foot with garments made of reeds. They also wore masks made of reeds that had only slits to see out of. They walked slowly toward the car and stared in through the windows at us for a few minutes with what I took to be a mixture of curiosity and hostility.

"Don't look at them, Boss!" said Speedy's voice over the speaking tube from the front compartment. "Just ignore them. Pretend you don't see nothin', Boss!"

Following his lead, I continued to look ahead fixedly, as if the frighteningly silent men weren't there. They didn't exhibit much in the way of interesting behavior anyway; they just stared and stared, cocking their heads at times as if to get a better look. Finally, one of them rapped with a spear in the hood of the car, at which signal Speedy pushed a button on the dash, popping open the big trunk of the Rolls. The silent men stepped to the rear of the car and filled the trunk with a number of sacks, so many that I felt the car lower toward the rear. Then I heard the trunk slam behind us and, by reflex, I looked back in Speedy's mirror to try to see what they would do next.

But they were all gone. They had just evaporated into the forest like morning mist. Only a few birds broke the damp silence of the marsh.

Speedy started the engine and we drove slowly out of the clearing. I had no idea what it had all been about until I heard some hoarse croaking sounds from the back as we pulled away.

"Frogs, Boss. Stinkin' frogs. Once every couple months, we gotta go see those creepy guys and get their stinkin' frogs. You know what my trunk smells like after I carry frogs in it? Huh, Boss?" He shook his head, but then he laughed loudly, his gold teeth glinting in the rear-view mirror. "That's right, Boss—it stinks! It smells like being right down inside a great big ol' stinky frog, is what it smells like."

And on he went, griping and laughing at himself at the same time. It was a relief to hear Speedy's rapid-fire monologue of complaint after the silence in which we'd passed the previous hour. But the croaking from the trunk kept getting louder and louder during the trip back, eventually drowning him out altogether. It had almost driven me to distraction by the time we finally reached the Doctor's palace.

The Doctor made me decapitate the toads while Speedy cleaned out the trunk. There were thousands of them and it took me several hours. Only the heads had value, the Doctor told me, so I enlisted Lucien and several of the other servants to carry away the bodies, except for a few dozen of the biggest ones, which I held out for that night's dinner. We took all the bodies to a spot in the western section of the grounds, toward where the Sun goes down, which is where the Doctor had instructed me to bury them.

The Doctor killed a piglet and sprinkled its blood over the pile of toad heads. Then he had me shovel them all into a big vat of salt water along with leaves from the *peregun* evergreen tree and several handfuls of white beans. He added eleven pieces of iron and boiled the mixture for three hours. He decanted the liquid that came off into a big flat pan and dehydrated it over a fire. It produced a dark slag which he covered with a paste made of mashed fresh fish and bananas. This he let "breathe" overnight—out in the yard, much to my relief.

The next morning he directed me to scrape off the paste, rinse the slag well with red palm oil, and then grind it up in a mortar. After a morning's hard work, the slag yielded about a kilogram of a dark reddish powder which the Doctor called *eru oku* ("spice of the dead"). This he caused Lucien to put in large salt shakers. I understand the spice was always taken at meals by every one of the principal members of his staff, except for me and Speedy.

But during my illness, I was too sick to "go and fetch" the toads on the appointed day. The Doctor was cranky about it, but all he could do was wait until I recovered enough to go, which wasn't until four days later. We found the toad men were still hiding in the clearing, just as they had been the last time, apparently having waited there unmoving for the four days.

By the time we made up a new batch of *eru oku,* the Doctor's whole staff was getting restless. Work around the palace was being done sloppily. And noisily: Lucien had begun to speak without provocation. And in words of more than one syllable. One of the housemen had even dared to question an order he was given. Things were getting out of hand. But the usual quiet routine of the household was restored as soon as the spice was put on the table for that night's dinner. From the mesmerized and lackadaisical way servants at the compound always acted, I always figured that the Doctor had some secret way of making them cooperative and docile. But this was the first time I realized how dependent Doctor Drago was on his own money juju to maintain control.

Of course, during the time I was so sick, I made the same assumption that jujumen always make: That I was suffering from "juju sickness." So I asked the Doctor to work a charm on me and to turn the curse back on whoever had placed it on me. But he declined; like most of our root doctors and herbalists, he was able to distinguish quite reliably between disorders caused by juju and those brought on by other causes. For example, a compound fracture of the arm sustained in a road accident clearly requires the techniques of Western medicine. So even the most devout jujuman today will demand modern treatment for such a condition, although he will probably require that it be *in addition to* traditional (*i.e.,* juju) treatment. In many localities, the local root doctor has had at least a minimum of Western first aid training and may be competent to stop the bleeding, clean and suture the wound, set the bone, and immobilize the arm in a cast. But he will also charm the evil spell that caused his customer to break his arm in the first place. So instead of working a juju cure on me, Drago sent to town for Doctor Sese, one of the medical doctors who practiced in Lagos.

Dr. Sese gave me some medicine that tasted worse than any juju medicine I'd ever had. He told me to stay in bed for at least two weeks. His instructions depressed me, since I had no desire to be alone, with nothing to think about but the Colonel and the recent *iko-awo* ritual.

But Dr. Sese also told Drago that it was a good idea to let me read the books that Speedy offered to bring from the library. And for this I was indebted to him, because Drago looked on Western books with almost as much suspicion as my grandfather did.

Drago assigned his most junior wife to tend to me during this period. She was about fourteen years old, a girl from one of the more isolated regions that belong to the *Egba* people. People from that region tend to be stumpy and muscular, with a corresponding lack of alertness and a perpetually sleepy look. They are referred to among townsmen as *omo igi*—the sons of sticks. They are considered by most of us to be old-fashioned; they are considered by some of us to be good-for-nothing. And, no matter how harshly they are characterized by the rest of us, they never seem to object.

The girl was representative of her people. As far as I could tell, she was totally uncontaminated by modern ways. She wore the traditional garb of the juju wife and was so festooned with cowries and beads and charms that she literally clanked when she walked. She was a strong girl, big-boned, and I estimated that she was wearing about three heads of cowries (six thousand cowry shells). In the old days, when cowries were used as money, it would have been a fortune, exchangeable for the heads of three enemies. But in modern times, when cowries have lost all but their decorative or symbolic value, it was only thirty pounds of junk. She also kept her face fully chalked at all times, after the old custom. This was a good idea in her case, because she was the most homely young woman I'd ever seen. Her looks and temperament notwithstanding, she was several months pregnant.

For the first several days of my illness, she refused to speak to me. She would bring me my broth and my medicine, and would fetch my books and so forth, as she was supposed to. But when she had no specific assignment from me, she would simply sit scowling on the floor in the farthest corner of my room. Occasionally she would flash one of the various juju hand signs that ward off danger. It wasn't until the Doctor struck her with his *ofo* and ordered her to speak that she finally did so.

Even then, her story came out only in short and grudging portions. But I eventually understood that she'd had a very hard life. Her mother had been a minor noblewoman among her clan while her father had been only a casual worker on the Lagos docks. He had been thought socially beneath the family and, as if in fulfillment of those opinions, he ran off before his child's birth.

The mother returned to her family, humbly asking them to take her back in. But they refused, saying that they'd never approved of her choice of man in the first place. Had she not gotten pregnant, they said, it might have been a different story. Their attitude could have been summed up by the popular American expression, "You made your bed; now lie in it."

The child was born friendless and into abject poverty. Her embittered mother named her Oba-bunmi, which means "the god of smallpox gave me this." Rather than simply abandon her, though, her mother was clever enough to sell her for a few coppers to a childless woman.

But, almost immediately, the woman died of unknown causes and everyone said that little Oba-bunmi was cursed and would bring bad luck to anyone foolish enough to buy her. After that, of course, selling the child was out of the question. But so was abandonment; the townspeople forced her mother to take her back, lest evil befall the village.

But that didn't mean her mother had to treat her well. Oba-bunmi was beaten regularly, for little or no reason. As she grew older, her mother repeatedly tried to sell her to people passing through town who didn't know her history. But the child had been so disfigured by abuse that there were no takers, even for free.

Oba-bunmi ran off as soon as she was able. For a while, she lived in the bush. As soon as she began to menstruate, she offered herself as junior wife to an extremely old man and woman. She made it sound unlikely that it was he who put her with child. But in any event, he died soon after taking her in. She must have thought she stood to inherit his land, which amounted to several hectares, because she began to lord it over the other women of the town. But instead of inheriting, she found herself willed to Doctor Drago, much to her surprise, as payment of some long-standing debt. The Doctor would rather have had the cash, it's safe to say.

That was the way the Doctor got most of his fifty or so wives—through inheritance. Which points up one of the commonly misunderstood aspects of African polygamy: Not every juju wife need be a sexual partner to the *babalawo* who owns her. Actually, it's only commonsense: Most men can deal successfully with (at most) three or four "mat wives." This innate physical limitation is recognized even by Islam, which limits the number of a man's wives to four (although modern Moslems frown on any polygamous practice at all).

But an important man in the tribal society—an *oba*, an *olowu*, or a *babalorisha*—might have dozens or even hundreds of wives. It is even said that the semi-legendary founder of the Yoruba people, Oduduwa, had over a thousand wives. The obvious question is, how could he possibly have dealt with them all? And the obvious answer is that he *couldn't.*

That gives rise to the distinction of a "jujuwife": a woman owned by a man with whom she does not necessarily have a long-term sexual relationship. In actual practice a man will probably take a jujuwife once or twice before going back to his regular mat wife. Although the new jujuwife becomes an official part of her husband's harem after that, any infidelity is conveniently unnoticed, unless she is betrayed by pregnancy. And of course, the inheritor of a wife may choose to have no relationship with her at all, as was almost surely the case with Drago and Oba-bunmi.

Oba-bunmi was not exactly pleasant to have around; her hard life had taken its toll on her personality. She was morose in her behavior and morbid in her outlook. She even told me that she thought the child in her womb was an *abiku*, a child born only to die. We believe that the *abiku* children are possessed by members of an evil fraternity of demons who live out in the forest, in the largest of the *iroko* trees. Each *abiku* who comes into the world arranges beforehand the time he or she will die, thereby breaking the poor mother's heart and amusing all the other evil demons.

The object of an *abiku's* mother must be to persuade the spirit in her child to stay beyond the time he or she has agreed to return to the forest. Only if the spirit is convinced to stay away from the forest too long will the demon forget the company of his or her fellows. He or she is then free to become a normal, loving child.

Needless to say, this puts an incredible burden on the mother of an *abiku*. She has to devote her full energies to spoiling the baby, living only for him or her, so that the spirit will be enticed to stay on. And, since humans cannot know the time the spirit planned to depart the child's body, the spoiling must go on for the rest of the mother's life.

Oba-bunmi did not seem to be the type of woman who was up to the formidable task of raising an *abiku*. She understood this, I think, and was resigned to whatever fate might bring; she even told me she intended to name the baby Akuji, which means "awake, and then dead."

By the time I recovered, with only modest help from Oba-bunmi, it was already June and time for the *egungun* festival in town. My people were never strong followers of the *egungun* cult and neither was the Doctor. However, a good friend of his was the *alagba* (master-of-ceremonies) for the big *egungun* festival in Lagos, so the Doctor and his staff of lesser priests were expected to participate. Actually, *egungun* is another of those demonstrations of how easily the West fools itself about Africa.

The *egungun* cult believes that spirits of ancestors can come back and inhabit our bodies. Just like all other forms of juju, *egungun* celebrates with festivals. Because they are so colorful, these festivals have been the subject of numerous books and travelogues in the West. You've probably seen the pictures: The celebrants wear masks and dance through the streets of the town to the accompaniment of drums and whistles. Western anthropologists comfort themselves that *egungun* is nothing more than a public party; a carnival; a fun-loving *mardi gras* staged by innocent primitives.

But *egungun* is a full-fledged African religious festival. And it has this in common with the other religious aspects of Africa: There's only so much we're willing to tell white people.

Which is reasonable because there's only so much they're willing to believe. The reality is that all of our "masked festivals" share the well-documented juju penchant for blood and lust.

Egungun begins with a night of prayer and fasting during which there is much sacrifice and blood is poured over the graves of our ancestors. This is so that they can participate in blood ritual in death, just as they did in life. This night of prayer and sacrifice which we call *ikunle,* meaning "the night of kneeling," is the *real* justification for *egungun*. Yet, I doubt if any Western visitors have ever paid attention to it.

What they notice are the next seven days, which are filled with visits from departed ancestors, those we call the *egungun*. They take over the bodies that are closest in physique to those they had when they were alive. They also cause the host to cover his head with a mask, so that no one will make the mistake of thinking that a mere mortal is in the body.

It is thought to be obvious that no man is responsible for what he does when the spirit of an ancestor is in him: His will is no longer his own, after all. So rape, looting, and murder are common occurrences, and no man possessed by an *egungun* may be punished for these crimes. Only the *spirit* that inhabits the man deserves the punishment; catch him if you can.

Like most aspects of juju, *egungun* has become more serious and widespread in recent times. One reason is that our people—just like people everywhere—have discovered chemicals. It used to be that our people could only become drunk on palm wine or on *ogogoro,* the local whiskey. Both liquors are weak, compared to Western standards, and you have to consume them in large quantities to get inebriated; relatively few people go to all the trouble to get really drunk. Most Nigerians, of course, were unable to afford Western whiskey or cocaine, so a relative sobriety tended to be the rule among us.

But oil money has changed all that, as it has changed so much in the coastal part of our nation. Now the *egungun* weave wildly through the streets day and night, often waving a whiskey bottle in one hand and a machete in the other. Both cocaine and marijuana are considered "sacraments" and are taken in large quantity, as are others of our indigenous hallucinogens, all of which become more powerful when mixed with alcohol. These days, the number of deaths in large cities after every *egungun* festival is in the hundreds.

The civil authorities have found it impossible to stop *egungun*. The best they can do is arrange a sort of "safe conduct" for innocent citizens: For one hour during each of the first six days of the festival, women and children are allowed on the streets to tend to normal business and police do their best to protect them. During the rest of the time, curfew is imposed. Then the streets belong totally to the *egungun*—the same ones Westerners laugh at in the travelogues—and even the police have learned to stay out of their way. By the seventh day of an *egungun* festival, even this modest effort at civil control is abandoned and curfew lasts all day and all night.

And the situation as described by the *Lagos Times* has deteriorated recently. The *Lagos Times* is our national newspaper of record, equal in the eyes of Nigerians to *The Times* of London or the *New York Times.* Among the many stories about the excesses of the *egungun* cult is one that appeared on February 19, 1988. It said that the governor of the state of Kwara felt he could be forced to impose an indefinite curfew *throughout the entire state* because of the number of *egungun* killings there.

Of course, at the time I accompanied Drago to the Lagos festival, *egungun* had not reached the level of fever pitch toward which it is tending today. Besides, we spent most of our time at the various state and social functions that are given because many educated Africans pretend that *egungun* is a purely cultural activity. Even so, it was pretty rough and the Doctor recommended that whenever we had nothing scheduled we should all stay indoors just like the women and children.

I felt uncomfortable all the time we were in town and was glad to get back to the compound. For a couple of days, anyway. Then Oba-bunmi's water broke and the Doctor told me to bring her to the sacrifice room because she was "ripe." I suddenly understood that her dread about her future and that of her child had not been misplaced after all, but only premature.

18

Westerners find it difficult to believe just how important the products of money juju are to the daily activities of the tribal peoples of Africa. The notion that substances so common and trivial as water or oil can be empowered with potent spirit magic is almost laughable to the Western mind. Yet, consider the jujuman's view of life. He believes that *Olodumare* intended for his favorite creation—us human beings—to be happy. Nonetheless, our world is full of danger that subjects us to great pain and misfortune. How can these two ideas be reconciled?

It's obvious to the jujuman that evil can exist only because forces from the Invisible World are interfering with the happy fate that has been intended for us. So he seeks power to control all those evil forces. Pacifying them in order to restore his natural, happy condition is what the religion of juju is all about.

But if an evil influence comes into our lives anyway, we're taught that it can be cleaned out with the products made available by the practitioners of money juju. So all sorts of everyday items can assume enormous superstitious importance to us. This is particularly true of items that suggest power, like anything with a sharp edge. But it's also true of household items like brooms and even soap that suggest the idea of sweeping or cleaning away the evil that the spirits have dumped on us.

Because juju artifacts are often so common and homely, the West finds it easy to ridicule them. And so money juju thrives, even when scholars insist that the old traditional religion is dying out. It permits juju to be treated far too lightly, especially by Americans.

For example, it is not uncommon for an American who has been in New Orleans or in Haiti (where the variant of juju known as *voodoo* is practiced) to bring back voodoo artifacts. Other travelers to such popular vacation spots as Southern California and South Florida (where there are large Hispanic populations practicing another variant of juju known as *santeria*) invariably bring back some of the items they found in the "funny" little local store called the *botanica*. You've seen the kind of stuff: maybe a "saint" candle, a can of "Queen Oya's Good Luck Spray," a bar of "Gambler's Soap," a bottle of "voodoo water" or a vial of "Love Oil of High John the Conqueror." They pass this material around as a joke, sniffing it or spraying it or otherwise scattering it all over the office without a thought about what might be in it.

But consider *Doctor Drago's Gambling Soap,* which is sold in many cities in Africa. And elsewhere, for all I know. It's billed as "the soap that washes away bad luck." It starts out like the soap African householders have made for thousands of years. All you need is some fat which you boil along with an alkali. Our most common source of alkali is the ash from something that we've burned. Although ash from an ordinary woodfire is fine from the chemical standpoint, juju always burns the body of some newborn sacrifice, such as a chick, to produce "pure" ash.

Money juju always goes farther. It always corrupts traditional juju practice by emphasizing juju's most brutal aspects. And, in the case of soap-making, the form of corruption is obvious: If a newborn chick will make "cleaner" ash, how much more so will a newborn human infant make it?

On the day that Oba-bunmi gave her child over to the cause of Drago's profits, she could hardly have failed to know the purpose to which her baby would be put. After all, Drago made no secret of the viciousness of his rituals. To do so would have hurt his business; money juju entrepeneurs like Drago need a certain amount of publicity to prosper. Believers in juju generally accept that the more gruesome a ritual is, the more powerful it must be. So a man like Drago can use his reputation for brutality to convince his customers of the power embodied in his charms, potions, and other artifacts. And everybody knows that Drago's juju products are 100 percent authentic; if the recipe calls for a human baby, then a human baby is what's used.

As soon as we arrived at the compound from Lagos, Drago directed me to go and fetch Oba-bunmi. I ran to the Big House to get her, enlisting helpers from among the men who were always lounging around in the Doctor's yard, waiting to be assigned odd jobs. We carried Oba-bunmi, cot and all, out to the Power House. Her eyes were empty and glassy, though whether from the rigors of her labor or whether from *eru oku,*

I couldn't say.

When we brought her into the sacrifice room, Drago was just finishing up his preparations. Two high stirrups had already been bolted to the foot of the stainless steel table and he was directing one of his junior priests in the drawing of juju symbols in bright lipstick on the white tile floor.

I don't know what got into me. But when the men and I had placed Oba-bunmi on the table and positioned her legs in the stirrups, I became dizzy. My mind filled with uninvited thoughts, most of which seemed to be shouting inside me, "I don't want this to happen!" Yet there was really no reason for me to feel that way. Nobody wanted Oba-bunmi's child, including the girl herself. It would wind up in the dump outside town anyway if Drago didn't get to it first. So why should I care?

But my thinking, for a jujuman, seemed to be going out of whack. I kept remembering all those books Mr. Olungwe had given me that talked about the dignity of human life. I kept remembering the skinny white man whose name I had never even learned but who I'd been required to kill. I kept wondering if Oba-bunmi's baby would ever get to open its eyes or if it would be murdered in darkness. And for the first time in my career, I began to feel guilty. It flashed through my mind for just a moment that maybe juju was *dirty* and *cruel,* the way Western people always said it was. That—at its best—juju was only a simple-minded and misguided attempt to control nature. And that—at its worst—it was a barely opaque cover for greed and for blood lust. After countless sacrifices, I was losing my stomach for killing.

I asked Drago if I could leave. To my surprise, he agreed. Moreover, he appeared unbothered by my reluctance to stay for Oba-bunmi's delivery or for the subsequent immolation of her sacrifice. Maybe he felt that, with the death of the white man, I'd already passed the test that had been set up for me. Or maybe he saw me swaying a bit and thought I was suffering a relapse of my earlier fever.

But I don't think so. Though I could not justify it, I got the unmistakable feeling that the death and burning of Oba-bunmi's child was simply no big deal to him. He'd apparently performed the ritual so many times with other unfortunate infants that he saw it more as a chore than as an atrocity. He seemed almost bored. In fact, when I asked him if I could be dismissed so that I could work on my notes, he said, "Yes, Isaiah. There's not much for you to learn from soap ritual. I'm sure you'll develop your own as you go along; there's not much to it. Besides, have I told you that it pleases me for you to write down so much of our lore?"

"It does, Honorable Drago?" He'd *never* said anything like that to me before.

"Yes, the Western people think they know such a great deal. But they do not even know which plants an old man can use to make his penis hard or which a woman can use to keep a wandering man at home. Someday, your writings will show them who knows what!"

I thanked him and started to back out of his presence, bowing as he always liked for me to do. "Wait," he said. He gestured at Oba-bunmi with his *ofo,* then set it aside. "Help me prepare this one before you go. She will be of no further use to me when we finish. Would you like her for yourself as a gift?"

"Me, Honorable Drago? Oh, no, thank you, sir." I automatically started to flatter him a bit, by commenting on his dedication. "Like you yourself, sir, I am much too busy for a woman."

He had been taking instruments out of the sterilizer that was against one of the white tiled walls; it seemed bizarre to go to such trouble for an infant who would be sacrificed before he or she could draw a second breath. But that was how the Doctor did things: to perfection.

"Indeed?" he said. He stopped removing the instruments and turned to beam the light of his glasses at me. "How strange. This is not at all the same story I hear from my eunuch."

I found myself too embarrassed to speak. The fact is, I'd been amusing myself with the daughter of one of his wives almost since the day I'd arrived. We used to meet out behind the compound's corn storage house, in a glade of fragrant lime trees. But I never thought the Doctor knew about it.

I stammered for a few seconds and then the Doctor laughed. "Calm down, my boy." He handed me some leaves from the "sandpaper tree" which we call *epin.* "You have done nothing to injure her bride price, have you?"

I started rubbing poor Oba-bunmi's stomach with the leaves, as called for when delivery is expected to be difficult. She still made no sound, even when the leaves began to rasp her skin slightly. "No, sir. I always give her a potion of *akara-aje* after."

He nodded, rolling his instruments to the sacrifice table. The root which we call *akara-aje* or "witch's bread" makes an effective, if unpleasant tasting, birth control potion. I always prescribed it because women could take it after sex, rather than before. The drawback to it, of course, is that it tastes so absolutely awful that many women only pretend to drink it. They toss it in the bushes when they get home, preferring to trust the whim of the *orisha,* rather than science, to prevent pregnancy.

"Good, Isaiah. You have behaved responsibly. But next time, use *imiesu*. Do you know it?"

" 'Devil's dung'? Yes sir, of course I know it. But I thought it was only for cancer."

"When chewed, yes." He kept working while he talked, laying out the same obstetrical tools a Western doctor would use to assist delivery. "But if you crush the nuts along with a few red tree ants and mix it up with a little sweetened *orombo* [lime juice] it prevents pregnancy. Furthermore, it tastes good, so you're sure your woman will take it. And there's something in it that makes the woman want to come back to you again."

He was full of tidbits like that. After my first week or two at Drago's compound, I wrote up several sheets daily about the remedies, rituals, and curses I'd learned that day, most of which proved remarkably effective over the years. He typified juju's hold on its believers: Just when you think nobody in his right mind could accept any more of its cruelty or silliness, juju shows you still another thing that *actually works*.

I stood there for a moment, marveling at Drago's practical knowledge of the natural world, until he asked, "Have you changed your mind? Do you wish to stay for the ritual after all?"

"Oh, uh, no, sir. Thank you. My writings, you know. I have to, uh. . . ."

He tested the big forceps a time or two. "Well, then be off with you, before I find some work for your idle hands." He was actually whistling as I left.

*   *   *

I never again saw Oba-bunmi nor, of course, her child. In fact, I almost never saw Drago again; a message was received early the following morning from my grandfather. He required me to return home.

I must confess to a certain relief. My confusion about myself and my place in the world had become even greater, I think, than that of most other adolescents. It made the warm familiarity of home sound especially good to me. I packed my few belongings immediately. These amounted mostly to piles of notes on Drago's rituals. I actually ran down the steps like a child when it was time for my last breakfast in the formal dining room.

The Doctor was wearing one of his three-piece suits from London. He looked up as I came in. "Ah," he said, "I see you received your grandfather's message."

"Yes, Doctor," I said. I bowed. "Please let me tell you how much I—"

"No time," he said briskly. "You must leave right now or you will have to wait another whole day." He got up from his breakfast and started pushing me out the door. When we got to the big front porch, he said, "My regards to your honorable grandfather, my boy." He shook my hand, as an American might do. His whole body was expressionless, except for his fingers which danced in my palm. Then, without any further ceremony, he closed the door on me.

The purple Rolls was waiting in the driveway at the foot of the stairs. The engine was running and Speedy revved it a couple of times to get my attention. I hurried down the steps and jumped into the rear compartment of the big car. Speedy was careful to pull away in the stately fashion he always adopted around Drago.

"Well, Boss, you goin' home, huh? How long you been here anyway? Oh, yeah, around four months. Well, that's not very long, is it, Boss?" He looked somber, as if he would miss me. "But I bet you're glad to be goin' back, huh?"

He caused the wheels to squeal as we made the turn out of sight of the Big House and I bounced back into the leather upholstery. He immediately relaxed and laughed loudly. "Yeah, Boss, I know what you mean. Always good to be goin' home." His eyes looked at me in the mirror. "You know, Boss, you look pretty good for a guy who just been trained by the Doctor. Some guys come away from there, they look like they been goosed by *Shango* himself." He laughed again. "But, like you say, Boss—you weren't there very long. I bet you still saw some stuff, though. Huh, Boss? Sure you did. You really saw some stuff."

He paused. Then, without his laugh, he surprised me by saying sadly, "I'm sorry you had to, Boss."

Suddenly, we were on the crowded main road again and Speedy directed his attention to driving and horn-blowing. His silence gave me time to reflect on the thoughts he'd shared with me during our trips back and forth to Lagos. I suddenly realized that he was the only one I would miss from among the two hundred or so people who populated Drago's compound. Perhaps it is a measure of the loneliness of Drago's brand of juju that the only friend I'd made while staying with him was this man whose face I saw mostly in a mirror.

Nobody else could have gotten me to the bus terminal on time; there were a few times when I thought even the sight of Drago's purple car would be unable to clear a path fast enough. But we roared up in front of the terminal, horn blasting and lights flashing, with only seconds to spare.

There was no time for goodbyes, no time for me to remind Speedy to return my library books or to thank him for having been my friend. The only bus north to Ilesha that day had its engine running already, so I jumped on board. I pressed my face against the window, watching the dirt of Lagos go past. It was going to be very good to get back to the warm love of my village.

The White Man's Juju

19

Some of the men from the village met me at the bus stop in our truck. They bowed and addressed me as "Honorable," which hadn't happened to me since I left. I admit that I enjoyed the attention. I had been kept so busy at Doctor Drago's compound that I almost forgot that I was a god of sorts.

I was concerned at the impatience this implied, though. A sense of urgency is not part of our lifestyle in West Africa and I worried that it might mean Grandfather was sick. But the men assured me that that was not the case, even though it was Grandfather himself who told them to come and get me in the truck, in order that no time should be wasted.

My first sight of Grandfather did little to reassure me. His descent into old age and decay probably went unnoticed by the village people who saw him every day. But to my eyes, four months made a noticeable difference in his appearance. He stooped a little now when he walked and the bones of his face were more prominent. He was not yet what I would have termed "an old man," but his feet were on the path to that sad, ultimate destination.

The Council of elders and lesser priests surrounded him like a protective shell. I saw that Joshua now stood scowling among them. He had taken the place of Moses Obuko, son of my father's brother's son and father of many, who had been killed by a fall while hunting in the forest. There were those who whispered that it was a juju killing: Moses had been a hunter of renown and they found it unthinkable that he would stumble while running after a wild pig and fall fatally onto his own spear.

Juju killing or not, the Honorable Obuko had to be replaced and a general meeting of all the men of the town was called. Joshua astounded everyone by rising and putting forward his own name. He said that he should be chosen because he was a "Man of Action." That seemed to be his entire platform. It also conveniently explained why he was bold enough to nominate himself. But it was unlikely he could have found an elder to do it for him anyway because, while it was not exactly taboo for a young man's name to be placed ahead of the hundreds who were older, it was a distinct violation of our social customs.

No sooner did Joshua, the Man of Action, propose his own name as Council member than his friends, Yesufu Owure and David Akuko, leapt to their feet. They showed plenty of action on his behalf, yelling and jumping about, exhorting the assembly to approve Joshua. So great was their energy in support of him that some townsmen became convinced that the two were possessed. A rumble began to go through the crowd to that effect. If true, it would be a momentous sign that Joshua's election was favored by the *orisha* themselves.

And so, as his two friends shouted and leapt ever more furiously, the conviction grew that Joshua should be the chosen one. Yesufu sensed it and acted to push the decision over the brink. At almost six feet, he was well-known as the tallest man in the village and was highly visible. He drew his machete and took a large slice out of his own left arm to prove his frenzy for Joshua. He waved the meat aloft as a token of his earnestness, which the crowd could not deny, the way his blood was spattering down on them. First by one voice, and then by dozens, the cry went up of *Mopade okorin na!* Translated, this means "I have met the right man!" Among us, it signals an affirmative vote. Within only minutes of convening, the meeting was adjourned, Joshua having been elected by acclamation. It had been the shortest open meeting in the memories of even our oldest chroniclers.

A few of the more querulous old men let it be known that they felt cheated: Meetings to decide something as trivial as the ownership of an axe had been known to go on for days. Joshua and the younger men he represented, on the other hand, seemed pleased at the efficiency his rapid election had brought to an old process. Social implications aside, though, Joshua had carried the day and was now the youngest member of the Council by a good twenty years. It was rumored that he was also the most vocal.

But what surprised me most about the assembly that greeted my return was that *so many* people had turned out to welcome me home. Not only the entire Council, but hundreds and hundreds of our local citizens—maybe even the whole town—had gathered in the big square by Grandfather's compound. Grandfather came forward and saluted me with his *ofo*. It was not so big nor so grand as Drago's, but the crowd ceased its murmuring the instant he raised it. I bowed toward him. To my utter astonishment, he bowed back, just as if we were peers!

"We welcome home our brother, Isaiah Oke, and he has our blessing," he shouted. And the crowd repeated the phrase. I was moved and deeply honored.

After repeating his blessing loudly six more times, he stepped forward from the supporting circle of elders. I noticed for the first time that he was dressed in what could be called finery. His *girike* appeared to be of the silk we call *samayan* and it looked brand new. It was bright blue and much embroidered, extending down to his ankles and beyond his arms into ample, sweeping cuffs. Down below the hem of the garment, he wore brand new sandals. And he'd even been shaved. Grandfather was never a man to pay much attention to appearances and I wondered what could be so important that he would trouble himself in this way.

He held his *ofo* aloft again and the crowd quieted. "People of Inesi-Ile," he shouted. "Today you will hear important news. I have had a report about our brother Isaiah. This report comes to us from Doctor Drago of Lagos." The crowd had been hanging on his every word. But at the mention of Drago's name, they became even more still, if such a thing were possible. They ceased to move, even to breathe.

"Doctor Drago," Grandfather went on, "reports that our brother Isaiah has distinguished himself. He reports that our brother Isaiah has faithfully recorded much wisdom through the juju of *reading* and *writing*. He reports that our brother Isaiah has brought honor to us, the people of Inesi-Ile."

The crowd went wild—cheering, stomping, whistling, and generally making as much noise as possible. After an appropriate interval of celebrating, Grandfather again signaled for quiet.

"Doctor Drago," he said, "has recommended that our brother Isaiah should continue to learn of Western ways. And so, we announce today an action never before taken by this village." Everyone remained quiet, even though Grandfather had made no further call for it. "Our brother Isaiah shall soon leave our village once again. Only this time, he will not go to Lagos, to study *our* juju, as he has for the last season. No, this time, he will go away to Oyo.

I couldn't believe my ears! Oyo had been the capital in the legendary "old days" before the British came, back when we were the proud nation of Yorubaland. Much smaller than Lagos, but far nobler in its traditions, Oyo transacted little in the way of international business, so Westerners seldom went there anymore. Yet it had a fine university and was thought by many to be the cultural center, the honorary heart, of all Nigeria.

Grandfather kept right on. "And in Oyo, our brother Isaiah will study at the Normal College where he will master . . . *the white man's juju!*"

The crowd "ohhh'd" and "ahhh'd" because this statement was beyond its understanding. Most of them knew that my tutor, Mr. Olungwe, had already taught me reading and writing; what more could there possibly be?

"Not only will our brother Isaiah learn more reading and writing, but also . . ." Here Grandfather paused and peered dramatically around the circle of anxious faces. "But also . . . *accounting*—the secret of the white man's increase!"

The crowd went mad with pride and delight. They had no more idea than had my grandfather what "accounting" was all about. But if it was, as he had said, "the secret of the white man's increase," it must be powerful stuff indeed. Besides, it had a grand sound about it and they began chanting it: "Ah-kown-TING! Ah-kown-TING! Ah-kown-TING!"

Only when some of the men began to throw their spears in the air in glee did Grandfather once again signal for quiet. He waited until the last echo of the last yell had died away before continuing. Finally, he looked around and said calmly, "And there is yet more to be told."

More! Was there ever such a day in Inesi-Ile? Several of the women were suddenly possessed by ancestors who wanted to be present on this most auspicious of all occasions.

"My youth," Grandfather said, "is spent. Soon, age will be heavy upon me. I must begin readying myself to become an ancestor." There was a sudden, shocked roar of disbelief and disapproval at this announcement. Some of the men rent their garments as they cried, "No, *Babalorisha,* no!"

He let it wash over him briefly; there is probably no greater pleasure than hearing the grief of one's people over one's death while one is yet alive to enjoy it. After a bit, he held his *ofo* aloft again and the crowd quieted, although there was still some weeping to be heard. "But the *orisha* have told me that my death will not come for some years yet."

The people erupted into spontaneous cheers. Some of the men ran forward and began turning somersaults, demonstrating their joy at this happy news. The women wept and raised their eyes and their palms to heaven in thanks.

Again, Grandfather calmed the crowd. "But a prudent man lays plans for his death, just as the tree ant lays up food for the rainy season." Many of the elders of the Council nodded their gray heads at this saying. "It would not be good for you to be without an intercessor between you and the gods. And so, I will name to you today the one who will succeed me as *babalorisha*."

The crowd caught its breath and held it. Even though I had been fated since birth to the position, it could never be official without Grandfather's blessing. But he had become disappointed in me when we faced Esu together. And I was always writing up notes on juju cures when there was ritual to be performed, so that Joshua or some other junior priest seemed always to be filling in for me. The truth is, I had long since despaired of ever having Grandfather's mantle transferred to my shoulders.

And, to be candid, I wasn't sure that would be so bad.

So, even though it would shame me, I expected (and hoped, to be honest) that Joshua would be named. And I think much of the crowd did, too. Joshua even moved forward a bit from the ranks of the elders. His chest was big and his mouth was hard in a sneer, as befitted his reputation as a Man of Action. He knew there were grounds to justify his appointment. After all, he was a Council member now as well as being the seventh son of Grandfather's seventh son, whereas I had never been more than a disappointment—a coward and a bookworm.

The only thing in my favor, besides my skill at reading and writing, was Drago's praise. And that was only because I'd found it in myself to put an unknown, skinny white man out of his misery.

"You must be protected," Grandfather told the villagers, solemnly. "For terrible times are coming; the *orisha* have told me so. And you must have a protector who is fit to lead in terrible times. Therefore, when I rejoin my ancestors, you will be protected by . . ."

Joshua's friends, Yesufa and David, started shouting and congratulating themselves.

". . . our brother Isaiah, a Man of Learning."

20

The Normal College at Oyo could not be confused with Oxford or Harvard. It is, in fact, what Americans would call a "junior college." There are many such institutions in West Africa because, even though we modern Nigerians are a very literate people, our educational system is somewhat spotty. That is, our city children receive their primary education in schools that are no different from ones in Pittsburgh or Pasadena. And today, our oil wealth has made our secondary schools more or less the equal of modern schools everywhere. They have well-trained teachers, up-to-date textbooks, and computers. But many of our rural children are still taught in the old "one-room schoolhouse," where books are outmoded and methods slow to change. So, for us, reading and writing are not in themselves enough to justify moving our children on to the next level of education. We need a common educational experience if all our young people of widely differing ages, cultures, and levels of preparation are to attend the same university. And that's where our junior colleges come in; they are "the equalizer" for our students.

Normal College is built on a site that is especially rich in history; it is said to be the location of the original military college for the warriors of the semi-legendary Oranyan. Oranyan was an important character in Yoruba history. He was the first *Alafin,* or "supreme king," of the Yoruba people. He was our version of George Washington and is said to have unified 1,060 separate kingdoms into the one vast empire known as Yoruba-land. Some estimates put the territory under Yorubaland's control as an area larger than the United States, although this has never been proved. It is generally accepted, though, that eight of the independent nations of contemporary West Africa were eventually carved from the Old Empire.

Even though we now live in modern republics, many Yorubas remain loyal to today's *Alafin*. But he is less a political authority these days than a cultural figure. He is also a religious symbol, because the *Alafins* have always been hereditary priests as well as kings. In fact, if juju could be said to have the equivalent of a pope, it would be the *Alafin* at Oyo. To this day, the dynasty that Oranyan founded holds court in and around Oyo, where the modern *Alafin* lives in regal splendor.

The same, however, could not be said about students at Normal College in the early sixties. Conditions for us were just short of wretched. Normal College was started just after World War II and several of its buildings when I went there dated from that time. Most of them were prefabricated, so the campus did not make a favorable aesthetic impression. Nonetheless, it was a chance for genuine formal education and most of the students took it as seriously as they would have taken Cambridge, me included.

My room was in a dormitory (actually a mobile home) that we called "The Palace of the *Ejo*." *Ejo* is our word for the number "eight" and eight of us shared the place. As for the word "palace," that was an example of youthful sarcasm. Actually, it wasn't as bad as I make it sound; West African homes tend to have very small rooms anyway, so I was used to cramped quarters.

Besides, when they heard who my grandfather was, the others all voluntarily turned over to me the lion's share of the space. This worked out well for me because, like all *babalawos,* I took my juju with me wherever I went. So I hung a cloth between the plywood partitions that defined our individual rooms and the space behind it became my own *ile-agbara*.

I immediately began to use what I'd learned from Doctor Drago— not his strong and brutal rituals, but his marketing know-how. From the moment of my arrival at Normal College, I let it be known that I was a *babalawo* of great power. I could manufacture charms that would assure good grades. I could prepare potions guaranteed to arouse the interest of the girls of Oyo. I could recite chants that would bring money from home by the very next post. In short, through the power of my juju, I was prepared to supply all the necessities of college life.

There were already two senior students vying to be known as the head *babalawo* when I arrived. But neither of them was the grandson of the great Aworo Oke. Neither of them had studied under the dreaded Doctor Drago. Neither of them was fated by birth to become *bablorisha* of all Yorubaland as soon as he graduated from college. And, of course, neither of them was the incarnation of the god *Orisha-Oko*. When I let all these distinctions be known, both men dropped prostrate before me and offered to be junior to me.

Except for two Europeans and one Asian, our teachers at Normal were all West or Central Africans. And, regardless of their educational attainments, they carried juju in their hearts. So they treated me with almost as much deference as did my roommates and my fellow *babalawos*. One of my professors, the Honorable Omo, even became one of my best customers.

The Honorable Omo was a man of extreme years, having received his education in England back in Colonial days just after the turn of the twentieth century. He came to me the second week I was in residence. With much embarrassment, he told me that he had not experienced an erection in over twenty years. (What he intended to do with one at his age he did not make clear.) But he had long sought both Western medical treatment and traditional juju treatment for his condition. The doctors he consulted simply shrugged and told him it was a part of growing old, that it happened to all men, and that he must learn to accept it.

The answer to his problem was simple, of course. At first, he was frightened when I showed him the *ishin* nuts I'd collected for him. Westerners know the *ishin* as the "king tree" and call its fruit "Bligh's cashew," because it is said to have been first described scientifically by Captain Bligh of the HMS *Bounty*. The Honorable Omo did well to be afraid of it; the unripe nut is one of the deadliest poisons known. Fishermen on the Osse River extract its oil, a few drops of which in the water returns a plentiful harvest of dead fish within minutes. It is a curious detail to the study of juju medicine that the plants we use to help men increase their sexual powers all seem to have use as poisons as well. Consider *akato*, which means "the executioner." It is said to be even stronger than *ishin*, whether used as a poison or as an aphrodisiac. But when used as an aphrodisiac, it must be administered as an enema, which cuts down on its popularity.

I had no wish to be the death of my professor, so for the Honorable Omo I made certain to collect only *ishin* nuts that were fully ripe. One handful of them—marinated, dried, ground into paste, and mixed with vinegar and the pulp from an *ejirin* (an African cucumber) would make even a piece of cooked macaroni hard. The Honorable Omo looked doubtful as I explained how it was to be rubbed on, left for half an hour or so, and then thoroughly washed off with juju-water containing peppercorns. After all that, I promised him, he would be his old young self again for the following two days.

Of course, I also warned him about how the mixture would burn. I told him to apply it to himself out in the forest because people might hear him yelling and, for just a moment, I thought I saw his resolve weaken.

But then he said it would be worth it if the potion worked as promised. I again assured him that he would find the results satisfactory but, because of the undesirable side effects I'd just explained, I gave him the first treatment free.

When he came rushing back to me three days later, I informed him that I would not accept payment in the traditional (but now valueless) form of cowry shells. Rather, I required compensation in good, hard *naira*. He pointed out that my two predecessors had agreed to accept cowries. But I pointed out that I had made him as hard as *iki* wood and they had not. He stopped grumbling and handed the money over. He quickly became one of my best customers, calling on me twice weekly from that time on.

I made sure that everyone I helped told his friends about me. Just like Drago, I profited from word-of-mouth notoriety and business boomed. By the end of my second month at Normal College, I was able to hire a manservant from the town to see to my needs. He was reputed to be a worthless fellow. He had no land and no trade and lived on handouts. He kept moving around the town continuously, never standing in one spot long enough for anyone to get really angry at him and chase him away. So he was called *Akunyun;* that is, "one who wanders to and fro."

I changed his name to Speedy. He lived under the Palace of the Ejo and turned out to be a decent servant; all he'd ever needed was somebody to tell him what to do. He was a slow and clumsy fellow, it was true. But he was cooperative. He turned out to be a good helper at the many blood rituals for whjch fellow students paid me handsomely every time exams drew near.

Naturally, I was enjoying my advantages. Money came in freely. Teachers and students alike feared me. People who met me in the road on my way to classes bowed respectfully. Now, this kind of treatment may be common for college basketball players in the American midwest, but it is extremely rare for a student in Africa. The result was that I very quickly became what Americans refer to as a "big man on campus" and my head grew large with pride.

Best of all, classes at Normal turned out to be almost easy, compared to Mr. Olungwe's intense tutelage. I breezed through my first term effortlessly and with quite creditable marks. I went home during the midterm break, astounding everyone in my village with my erudition. Some of my townsmen kept pestering me to "say something in accounting," while others asked me to "work some accounting" on behalf of their ancestors or for a sick baby.

It was on that first trip home that I rejoiced to see the dour Mr. Olungwe happy at last. Grandfather had gifted him with two hectares of land, an ox, and a wife as a reward for having helped make a man of me. The Honorable Olungwe was now a gentleman farmer as well as a scholar, and he took to strutting around the town with a self-satisfied grin all the time, as if he were the father of many.

And so my life went for nearly three more years: Pleasant schooling was punctuated by rewarding trips home. It was almost perfect. The only sadness was Grandfather's increasingly great burden of age. The advancing years had a peculiar effect on him: Every time I returned home, he seemed to be lighter and smaller than he had been the previous time, although his health otherwise remained good, except for a persistent cough. I began to think that he would not die, after all; he would simply shrivel up to nothing and disappear one day. I'd never before seen anyone become quite that skinny and sick just from age and I couldn't shake the feeling that he had some terrible, unknown disease.

A couple of days after I returned to Normal College for my last term there, I was eating with some of my friends in the building where we all took our meals. I suppose I could call it the "cafeteria" but that might be stretching the truth. At Normal, every student prepared his own meals; we simply consumed them in that common place.

But I was always popular in the cafeteria because the new Speedy prepared my meals for me. I'd even taught him to make a pretty fair replica of my mother's "palaver" sauce. No one else at school had a personal servant and I always made sure Speedy prepared enough that I could invite friends to dine with me.

This particular evening, I was sitting with my friend, Simon Meji, when a new group of freshmen was ushered through on their orientation tour of the campus. They were every bit as scared-looking as Simon and I had been three years earlier. So naturally we hazed them by throwing bits of *fufu* at them and yelling, "Better save this; the only food for you in this place will be *ayan* and *ekun* (cockroaches and tears)." Of course, this frightened the poor nervous newcomers even more, which Simon and I enjoyed immensely. Some of the young women among the group even sniffled a little.

The temptation to give them a really bad time was too much for Simon. "Look at the women in that mob, will you?" he asked loudly. "Have you ever seen such an ugly bunch of worthless women in your life? I'm glad we're going on to university before we get desparate enough to think they look good." He flipped three or four quick juju signs at them. Then he cursed them with a phrase that means, roughly, "May you be rejected, even by the bush"—"*Igbekoyi!*"

Some of the youngsters literally shook. I didn't know whether they shook with fear of juju or with the simple tension that is part of being a freshman. But their reaction amused Simon, who nudged me in the ribs and laughed.

I shook my head and tried a gentle expression. "Aw, leave them alone, Simon. They're just scared kids. Give them a break." I smiled benignly up at the group. As soon as some of them looked a little relieved, I yelled, "Even though they really are ugly!" Simon howled with laughter and slapped my hand in congratulations.

None of the boys in the tour group had the nerve to tell us off. As for their guide, he was one of our teachers; he certainly wasn't about to mess with *me*. As I said, I was a "big man on campus," *plus* I was a powerful *babalawo*. And besides all that, I was a senior, too.

But one of the girls looked more scornful than scared. She was young, no more than sixteen or so, and dressed after the fashion of the West: blue jeans, sneakers, and tee-shirt. Her hair was very full, not plaited into the small strips that unmarried women displayed. She stepped out from the group and approached Simon and me, just as bold as anything.

She put her hands on her hips and glared at us as a man, even a warrior, might do. Then, in a most unseemly fashion, without being first addressed by one of us men, she spoke to us. "You know, you're not very funny, either of you. That's not nice—throwing food at people. And I think you've been calling us names; that's not nice, either." She spoke in English with the most peculiar accent I'd ever heard. Her speech was full of growls, like the language of the wild dog.

Simon was shocked at her behavior and again levelled his curse at her: "*Igbekoyi!* Be gone, Woman."

"Be gone yourself," she said to him. She seemed not in the least frightened, as she should have been. Or at least, as she should have given the *appearance* of being; that's what would have been appropriate for a woman, especially one of her tender years.

The freshman group was staring at us with big, round eyes, eager to see what was going to happen next. This was doing no good for my image as the strongest *babalawo* on campus.

"Woman," I said gently, but firmly. "You forget yourself."

She turned from Simon to me. "Stop calling me 'Woman.' " She showed no more fear of me than she had of him; she probably hadn't been on campus long enough to know who I was.

I smiled at her, although Simon looked as if he thought I should lay an *epe* on her for her insubordination. But one thing I've learned: Some people respond better to friendliness than they do to threats. So I always try friendliness first. It's like that old saying in my village: "You can catch more termites with honey than with you can with vinegar."

"We address you as 'Woman,' " I said, "only because we do not know your name. What is it that you are called?"

She relaxed a little. "My name is Janet."

It was a strange name. I rolled it over in my mind. *DJA-net.* It sounded vaguely Arabic, but she didn't look like an Arab. "Are you Fulani?"

"Am I what?"

"Fulani. Are you Fulani, *DJA-net?*"

She wrinkled her brow. "I don't think so. What is it?"

I saw Simon roll his eyes back in his head. He was probably thinking that such ignorance could only come from an Ijesa. "He means, Woman, what tribe are you?"

" 'Tribe?' " she said. "Oh, you mean what African tribe. Well, I'm just over here for a year while my father gets your new power plant built. But I'm not African; I'm an American."

"*Hepa!*" I said happily. "I have always wanted to meet one of your tribe. I know of all your great men."

She looked startled. "You do?"

"Oh, yes." I puffed up a little, pleased at being able to show off such esoteric knowledge. "I admire greatly your President of the clan of Kennedy." I signed on the table top the sign for good fortune and then raised my face toward the *orisha* and added the exclamation "*Kabiyesi!*" This is really a juju prayer we offer on behalf of royalty and it means, "May long life be given to him." Several people in the room who had been listening in (there being no such concept as "privacy" in tribal life) picked up my prayer and repeated it so that it became a chant: *"Kabiyesi! Kabiyesi! Kabiyesi!"*

She was a strange girl: Here I was praising her *oba* and yet she looked uncomfortable about the signs and juju prayers I offered.

"Ah," I said. "Perhaps you wish to rejoin your group and finish your tour? Very well, we will talk later. For now, you are dismissed."

She looked as if she were about to say something again, but thought better of it. Instead, she smiled wryly and shook her head. Then she turned to rejoin her group. I nodded my permission to the group's teacher/guide, who looked relieved and immediately ushered the group out.

"What is your interest in this woman?" Simon asked as they filed out. "She is too young for you. Besides, she is very plain and she behaves badly.

Why, she is even more arrogant than a *babala* . . . I mean, her behavior is a disgrace."

"Yes, but she knows things you and I do not."

He put on a pious and conservative look. "If we do not know a thing, Isaiah, then our ancestors did not mean for us to know that thing. We know only what is good for us to know."

"Tell me, Simon, do you never wish to discover new things, to consider new ways? Do you never wish to look beyond our rigid social customs, to look beyond juju?"

"Never!" he shouted. He immediately began to ward off the evil my words might bring.

"Well, I do" I said. "I am interested in hearing the words of this foreign girl."

He gripped my arm, tightly. "Isaiah, my brother: No good can come of it. Foreign ideas are not for us. They lead only to trouble."

I laughed and pushed him away. "I will hear her words, Simon, but I will not fear them. After all, what could a foreign child like her possibly do to hurt a powerful *babalawo* like me?"

21

A day or two later, I planned a feast in honor of the new student from whom I would learn so much about America. First I went into town and bought a choice pig and a large jug of the local maize beer. While I was at the market, I also spent much of my previous month's juju fees on the ingredients for a side dish of *Jollof* rice, which many people consider to be our most aristocratic dish.

At the little Shrine I'd built in the nearby forest years earlier, I sacrificed the pig and ordered Speedy to butcher it into small cubes. I discarded all the entrails, sparing only the kidneys; these I planned to present to my guest as a special treat to take home with her. As long as I was in the forest anyway, I took time to gather some mint and other herbs for the sauce. I was never able to get my *ragout* to turn out quite as good as that we used to have at Doctor Drago's; I couldn't get that musky taste in my meat that his had. But my guests always complimented me on the quality of the mint sauce I served with it.

That day, we took over the cafeteria just after midday for our principal meal (which, among us, is lunch). Also present, in addition to Janet and a freshman girlfriend of hers (an Egba girl whose name I didn't catch), were my friend Simon Meji, three of our teachers, and the headmaster of Normal College, the Honorable Doctor Abraham Olubiwi.

Speedy, of course, served the meal, though not without considerable grumbling. It is customary among us for servants to take their meals with their masters. The number of people present was such, however, that Speedy knew he probably wouldn't be sitting down to eat until everything was cold.

In spite of all my planning, we got off to a rather rocky start. After introductions, everyone sat and I blessed the assemblage and our food with a juju chant. Such a thing is not really customary, but this was a special occassion and I wanted my ancestors to observe how actively I was seeking enlightenment. Janet had only the slightest familiarity with our language; she couldn't possibly have understood more than a few words of what I was saying. But she appeared uncomfortable nonetheless.

She only picked at her food, trying to be polite, I think. But it was clear that she liked it not at all. As for the maize beer, she never even tasted it. The only aspect of the feast that really interested her was the fact that I'd worn my *ejigba,* the knee-length necklace that I brought out only on special occassions. Mostly, *ejigbas* are worn by kings or high public officials as a badge of rank. They are usually made of very costly beads, including even precious stones and the rarest of pearls in the case of the *Alafin.* Of course, the *ejigba* of even the most important jujuman is far less grand than those worn by our secular leaders. But it is more powerful.

Janet stared and stared at my *ejigba.* Finally, as I ran low on small talk while Speedy was clearing away after the main course, I asked her whether there was a problem. "Those bones you're wearing," she said, pointing to them. "What are they?"

"This one," I said, proudly showing her the biggest, "I inherited from my grandfather's father. Where he got it, I don't know. This next one is the sternum of a hyena which I killed myself; he was possessed by an evil spirit at the time. Then there's this whole row: the backbones of a serpent, which is our most sacred animal. Here, of course, is the finger which I use for divining purposes. This next one—"

She stopped me. "Did you say 'finger'?"

I looked up. "Yes. It is the forefinger of a man who was a famous soothsayer; I am extremely fortunate to have it. See, the joints are glued together, so the whole thing makes a kind of pointer. Now, when I want to divine something—say, if I want to find water, or if I want to know whether today will be a good day to hunt—all I have to do—"

She offended me by interrupting yet again. Headmaster Olubiwi had enough presence of mind to turn toward Simon and comment on the quality of the meal, as if her behavior posed no problem. But I could see the three teachers peeking out from their lowered gazes, watching. "You mean to say it's the finger of a human being? A regular *person?*" Janet asked.

I paused for a second to collect myself. Her voice had an accusing tone about it that I didn't like. "Of course. What else would a soothsayer be? A horse?"

Everyone laughed and I saw her make an effort to pull her attention away from the bones.

"But you must tell me more about America," I said, seizing the opportunity to change the subject. "I understand that many children of Africa live there. Tell me, is it true that they all live side-by-side? Yorubas and Ibos and Hausas, all together?" *That* got Headmaster Olubiwi's attention. He looked shocked by the idea that such different peoples could possibly live together.

"Well, I don't know about that," Janet said. "I don't think there are many of us black Americans who can trace our histories all the way back to Africa. The fact is, most of us don't have any idea where our ancestors came from. Or even who they were."

It was my turn to be shocked. *Not know who one's ancestors were?* I could not conceive of the possibility. Knowing and honoring one's ancestors was only the most important duty of one's life, that's all. How could her people go on living under such conditions of depravity?

"Ah, yes," I said nervously, trying again to change the disgusting topic. "Because of the disruption brought about by slavery, is it not so? A very bad thing, slavery. Especially the way the whites practiced it, which was much different from the way we did. But I have heard it said that the adversity of slavery gave you black Americans some of your great leaders."

"Like who?"

"Well, like . . ." I remembered the only black American I'd ever heard about—probably the only black that white Americans at that time had ever heard about, too—and I thought to dazzle my guests with my extensive understanding of faraway America. ". . . like George Washington Carver!" I finished triumphantly.

She rolled her eyes in what was almost a juju gesture. "Oh, puh-leese! Don't drag up those old names from a hundred years ago. Get with it, Isaiah! What about all our modern leaders? What about Ralph Bunche? What about Martin Luther King? What about . . ."

I could take no more of it. She'd spurned my food. She'd gawked rudely at my juju. She'd interrupted me repeatedly. Now she even ridiculed my knowledge. I rose to my feet and slammed my hand hard against the table. "*Atoto!*" I shouted. "Enough of your noise! Will you continue to shame me before my guests? Do you not know meekness?"

She jumped up and slammed her own hand against the table, just as loudly as I had. My other guests jumped at the boldness of the child. " 'Meekness?' " she repeated. "How can you—a Nigerian—say that women have to be meek? Nigerian women have more power than any other women in Africa—maybe even in the world!"

It was true. The economic power of Nigerian women was only just beginning to be felt in those days. But already the message was clear to anyone with the wit to read it and it was becoming a sore point among our men. In southern Nigeria, buying and selling has always been thought of as "woman's work"; men here have always believed that commerce is unmanly. So women have always been the ones to take any extra produce of the family farm to market. Women have always transacted the sales and women have always handled the cash. The inevitable result, especially when petrodollars began to flood the country, was that the economic power of the nation would tend to flow toward women.

And so it happened. Many of the major international companies of Nigeria are owned, or at least controlled, by women, including some of the big oil interests. Even the office towers of Lagos and Ibadan are often owned by women's "clubs."

But Nigerian women still knew how to behave meekly, keeping up appearances in accordance with our customs. And that's what this little slip of a girl from America was *not* doing.

I controlled my rage. I tried to make my voice icy as I told her, "I bear you no ill will. Simply admit that you have behaved shamelessly and apologize to me and we will say no more about it."

I really felt I was being more than fair.

Janet did not seem to share my feeling. "Apologize to *you?* Well, I like that!" She picked up her purse and grabbed the arm of her Egba girlfriend, who looked as if she was about to faint. "Go try to make conversation with some guy who's wearing soup bones around his neck!" she said to the girl.

So now, she was belittling the sacred juju of a *babalawo*! Really, it was too much. It had gone beyond even insolence; this was sacrilege!

I fully expected that *Shango* would unleash one of his thunderbolts on her and split her in two. But for some reason known only to himself, the god refrained from taking this perfectly justifiable action; strange are the ways of the *orisha*.

"Stop!" I commanded. "You cannot leave. You must apologize; I am a *babalawo!* You must apologize!"

She stopped in the doorway and turned back toward me for a moment. She said, "Oh, drop dead, creep." She spun on her heel and left, dragging her hapless friend behind her.

Simon grabbed my arm and squeezed it in fear. "You heard her, Isaiah? You heard her? 'Drop dead,' she said. It is an *epe,* a curse on you!"

I reached under my tunic and clutched my *ibante* reassuringly. "We shall see about it," I said grimly. "Who this 'creep' is, though, I don't know—maybe one of her gods."

Then I understood why *Shango* had not struck her dead; he had left that task for me. "Soon, Simon," I said, "we shall see if her 'creep' is a match for my *Shango*. We shall show all the world who has the stronger gods!"

Headmaster Olubiwi knew when things were too close for comfort. He rose, bowed, thanked me, and took his leave immediately. We did not even go through the usual charade in which I would beg him to stay and he would decline and we would do this again and again until finally we would agree on just one more mug of wine for each of us.

The three teachers did not even think to add their thanks to the headmaster's; they just took to their heels, leaving the cafeteria free for me and Simon to plot our juju revenge on the American girl.

The only one who seemed happy about the way things turned out was Speedy. He sat himself down at the end of the table and took a big swig of Janet's untouched maize beer. He followed it up with a huge chunk of *ragout* dipped in mint sauce.

"Good sauce, Boss," he said cheerily.

22

Simon urged me to turn Janet's curse back on her, to cause her to "drop dead." And I suppose I should have; turning a curse back on its originator is, of course, the jujuman's version of justice.

But I wanted to teach her a lesson more than to destroy her. After all, she was only a child. And an American, at that, totally ignorant of our ways. So the first curse I put on her was a mild one. It's a popular one, though, among the *babalawos* where I come from:

> Call upon *Olofin-Aye* (the *orisha* who controls famine and food) to witness. Sacrifice a pigeon. Then insert two pins or needles into its stomach. Tell *Olofin-Aye* to "sour all fruit and meat in the stomach of" your victim. Then transfer one of the pins to a piece of any fruit or vegetable, leaving the other pin in the belly of the bird. Bury the carcass of the bird. Place the piece of fruit on top of the burial spot and let it rot there.

This is a well-known curse, for which success is often claimed. It produces symptoms indistinguishable from those of common food poisoning. Its power to induce real sickness is taken for granted by most *babalawos*. This is despite all the unbelievers who argue that, in a land where refrigeration is uncommon and where Western standards of hygiene are not always observed when food is prepared, frequent bouts of mild stomach problems are to be expected anyway.

I laid the "belly curse" that very night. I did not go out of my way to look for Janet or to get news of her for some time after that. There was no trick to avoiding her because she didn't live at Normal with the rest of us. She lived in town with her father who dropped her off every morning on his way to work on the power plant. But even if she'd lived in the next dorm, I would still have avoided her. It's always best to give one's *epes* time to work. In fact, sometimes months elapse before one gets to take credit for the belly ache every victim experiences sooner or later.

When I finally did see her, it was purely by chance. Simon and I were walking to a class and spotted her across the central square.

"Huh! She looks okay!" Simon said, shocked.

"Give it time to work," I reminded him.

"Yeah? Well, it's been weeks now. Maybe something went wrong. Why don't you go talk to her, see how she's been feeling?"

"Me? Not a chance. I don't ever want to talk to that girl again after the way she behaved."

He stopped walking and stared at me, hard. "Is Isaiah, of the Oke clan, afraid of a girl's juju?"

I laughed. "Don't say ridiculous things, Simon. I just don't see any reason to start up with her again, that's all."

He thought about it a second before he said, "Okay, then. I'll see to it myself." He trotted across the open square to challenge her.

From where I stood, I couldn't hear what they said. But it clearly wasn't friendly because, after a few words had been exchanged, he raised his hand as if to strike her. She put her hands on her skinny little hips and said something that made him freeze like a statue. Then she shook her finger at him and he backed up, as if she were cursing him as well. He turned and ran, a man being chased by an invisible lion. He slid to a stop and tried to hide himself behind me, just like a child hiding behind its mother.

"Now she has cursed me, also! She told me to 'drop dead,' just like she told you. Only she shook her finger before my face as she said it. Right in my face! This is some powerful American juju, I know it! Oh, Isaiah, will I die?"

He was panicking while Janet walked away toward her class as if the incident was trivial. Others around the square stood looking at us with open curiosity. It was mortifying.

"Stop that!" I hissed at Simon, pulling the hem of my garment out of his hands. "You will not die. Have I died because the witch cursed me? No! Therefore, you will not die, either."

He came out from behind me and faced the spot where Janet had stood. "Forgive me, Isaiah. But I am not a *babalawo* like you; I cannot face up to juju by myself. Protect me!"

"Come," I told him. "We need not attend our class. Instead, let us prepare to destroy her."

As we went back toward the Palace, I thought I saw where I had gone wrong: I had neglected to let her *see* what I was doing to curse her. With another Yoruba, it would not have been necessary to go to such trouble. Often, the very knowledge that one has angered a *babalawo* is enough to cause intense physical pain, even before a curse is laid. But this young witch apparently had a background so different from ours that she failed to appreciate power unless she saw it for herself.

So this time, we laid our plans more carefully. I sent Simon to the market square with some money and instructions to buy a young monkey and some other items. Meanwhile, I went into the forest to begin gathering the other necessary materials. It took several trips over the course of two or three days until I was able to gather together everything that would be needed. Then I invited Simon and two other men, whom I did not know well but who came well recommended, to accompany me out to my shrine in the forest. They would act as my seconds during the ritual.

It took place at night, naturally. While Simon and I got the monkey ready for sacrifice, the other men started a rhythm on the *sekere* drums I'd brought. Both of them had the reputation of being good musicians and they justified it. In perfect unison, they snapped the sleeves of cowries that surrounded the calabash bodies of the drums. I could have enjoyed it purely as music; the fact that every beat was putting power into the ritual I was about to perform was an added bonus.

I passed around several of the hollowed-out fruits of the *osuigwe* plant which I'd filled with palm wine. The British used to claim that *osuigwe* and alcohol was a remedy against malaria. But we West Africans know it as the kind of mild hallucinogenic that plays a role in both our public ceremonies and, to a somewhat greater extent, in our secret rituals. Today, of course, some jujumen use street drugs for their rituals. Such traffic is usually ignored by our law enforcement authorities, because the drugs are said to be for devotional rather than recreational use. But in fact, the drugs they buy are often resold.

For our ritual, I needed to heighten the effect that *osuigwe* would produce. I considered having everyone chew raw seeds of the candlewood plant. But I've always regarded it as dangerous; I've known people to become so enamored of the seeds we call *ata* that they become addicted to the stuff.

So instead, I brought some thin latex which I'd bled from an *ayan* tree. I dipped a parrot feather into the powerful stuff. Then, very carefully and gently, I drew the feather across the eyeballs of each of us, starting with myself so the others could see there was nothing to fear. Between the two hallucinogenics—the *osuigwe* and the *ayan*—it required only the least suggestion from me that something was about to happen to the monkey. They stared toward where the little animal was tied up with a mixture of dread and excitement on their faces.

Simon was the first to see it. He'd never been to any but the simplest rituals before so it was no surprise that he was almost overcome by what he saw.

"Look!" he cried out in a shaky voice. "The monkey . . . it grows!"

The rest of us then saw that it was true; before our eyes, the monkey became taller. First to the level of a man's waist. Then to his chin. Then it was as tall as a man. "Keep playing," I said to the men, as I walked toward the monkey.

"Who is in you?" I asked it.

But the monkey just stared at me.

Again, I asked, louder this time, "Who is in you?"

It still refused to answer. I turned back and scooped up the pack of "bribes" I'd told Simon to buy in town: a string of brightly colored beads, a baby's rattle, and a can of snuff, which I opened before setting it down. To these items, I also added some bananas. I laid the whole before the monkey.

"Please accept these gifts," I told it, bowing. "Now, tell me: Who is inside you?" The monkey reached down (it was now taller than any of us men) and took up the can of snuff.

Aha, snuff! Snuff is a thing for men, not for animals or spirits. So it made sense, I thought, that he who was residing in the monkey must have been a man at one time.

The monkey looked at the snuff for a moment as if he was wondering what it was. Then he raised it to his nose and took a big sniff. He dropped the can abruptly, as if startled, and for the first time, I heard him: "Baba-Tunde!" he barked through his nose. And again, "*Baba-Tunde!*" rubbing furiously at his nose. "BABA-TUNDE!"

Tranlated, this means, "an old man."

So. The next question to be settled was, *which* old man? Not my father, certainly. Nor my grandfather; he was living in *this* world still, as far as I knew. Could it be the father of my grandfather? Yes, perhaps that's who it was.

"O, great Baba-Tunde: A witch has cursed your servant. Will you not help the son of your grandson?"

Baba-Tunde took up the rattle, looked it over still rubbing at his nose, and then shook it.

"He shakes his *ase!*" Simon cried. "Hear it? What can this mean?"

"It means he will help, you fool! Now keep silence while I speak with this, my great ancestor! I spat on the ground to show my displeasure. Simon put his head down, properly chastened at interfering with the work of a *babalawo.*

When I turned back to Baba-Tunde, he had grown to where his head touched the lowest branches of the trees. "O, great Baba-Tunde: What punishment will suffice for this witch? Please choose a scourge and visit it upon her. For by insulting me, she has insulted all our generations of the clan Oke."

Baba-Tunde threw the rattle aside. He shook his head, which was now up in the tree branches, and he rubbed his nose again. He barked out his name some more—*"Baba-Tunde!* BABA-TUNDE!"—and his eyes started watering heavily, the huge drops crashing to the ground around me like buckets of water dropped from a tree. For a moment I was reminded of the sneezing and weeping reaction of one unaccustomed to snuff. But I knew that couldn't be: My great-grandfather used it all the time and, having decided it was he in the monkey, it made no sense that the monkey would be sneezing from snuff.

Then Baba-Tunde reached up and rubbed his eyes, hard, shaking the tears off his paws when he was done. And at once, I understood.

"O, great Baba-Tunde, I understand: She has seen our shame. Therefore, she should see no more, ever again; you will strike her blind!"

I bowed respectfully in recognition of the favor he was granting me. At that moment, one of the men playing the drums screamed. I looked at him in time to see his head go back, as if he was watching a bird fly high in the sky. A look of maximum horror crossed his upturned face. Then he passed out, his mouth open and dripping spittle. I reflected that I should have warned him not to be afraid of learning the secrets of the monkey. Or of *anything* that might go on during the ritual, for that matter. But it all happened too fast for me to prepare him.

Fear is contagious. The first man's fear spread to the man next to him, and then to Simon. They both looked upwards, screamed, and fainted, just as the first man had done. I offered a prayer of thanks that, as a *babalawo,* I was immune to such fear.

Then I turned back to find that Baba-Tunde had grown again. Now he had grown even taller than the trees. His feet filled all the clearing. His body was bigger than any mountain. He let out a roar so loud that it seemed to come from right inside my head. But I knew it was real because

I could feel it shaking the earth I was trying to stand on. Then, even as I leaned back as far as I could to watch, his head went higher and then higher yet, until it became the Moon overhead, grinning down at me.

*   *   *

By the time we all came to, Baba-Tunde apparently had gone back to the Spirit World because the monkey was back to normal size again, tethered right where we'd put it earlier. I felt foolish momentarily because I'd forgotten to get Baba-Tunde's permission to sacrifice it. That would have been seemly in as much as it had been his host, however briefly.

But Baba-Tunde knew the rituals as well as I did; he would expect me to complete this one. So I drew my blade across the monkey's throat and caught some of the blood in one of the *osuigwe* cups. We all took a taste, even Simon, who took just enough to wet his lips. Then I removed the left paw and wrapped it in a banana leaf to preserve it.

Monkey is a delicacy among us, so I skinned it and butchered it quickly. I discarded the entrails and the head, which we buried in one of the pits in the little clearing. The meat I split with the two musicians because Simon didn't want any. He took the skin, though. Then we hiked all the way back to Normal College.

The others must have been as exhausted as I was. When we finally got to the campus, they all split up as fast as thieves and, without even a whispered word, they all ran to their rooms. I yawned, envying them.

But it wasn't until I completed my last remaining task that I finally tumbled onto my mat for a righteous, well-deserved sleep. After all, the whole idea was for the witch-girl to *know* she'd been cursed. Anonymously . . . mysteriously . . . mystically.

When I fell asleep at last, it was with a smile, wondering what the witch-girl's reaction would be when she opened her door the next morning.

23

But she didn't go blind. Nor did she ever get that belly ache. In fact, it was difficult to tell exactly *what* effect my juju was having on her.

Other than to make her quite angry, of course. She awakened me the next morning with such a pounding at the aluminum door of the Palace that it shook in its frame. I answered it myself; my juju fees had been dropping steadily while she remained so healthy, so when they finally fell off to nothing, I'd had to let Speedy go.

Janet stood defiantly in front of the trailer. She was accompanied by Mr. Agura, one of our younger teachers. It was a condition of his employment at Normal College .that he act as "resident student advisor" in addition to his other duties. The title meant that, until a newer and more desperate teacher was hired, he had to live on campus, available at a moment's notice to any student who might claim his help. Times were hard just then and positions for educated Africans were few. But at that moment, with a *babalawo* looking down at him, Mr. Agura appeared unhappy that he'd ever accepted the job.

Janet held up a hunk of newspaper. She peeled back a corner and exposed the monkey's paw. The blood was dry and the paw had begun to look rather dessicated. "Is this your idea of a joke, you creep?" she demanded.

I blinked. Perhaps "creep" was not so good a word as to describe one of her gods after all. Then I smiled blandly in an attempt to recover. "I have no idea what you mean."

"No? Well, somebody tied *this* to the doorknob of my house last night." She shoved the paw toward me and shook it in my face. "I've asked around and they tell me it's more of your stupid juju." She flung it at me, newspaper and all. I ducked and it splatted up against the wall inside the Palace.

"Now you listen to me, Mr. Jujuman Oke: I don't want any more of your juju junk around me. I'm a good Christian girl, so save it for somebody who believes in it, okay? And Mr. Agura is going to see that you do. Isn't that right, Mr. Agura?"

Mr. Agura seemed unable to speak. He was so unnerved that I wondered whether he might be a jujuman himself. I rolled my eyes in the pattern that makes up one of our many juju recognition signals—the left, back, up, back, repeated very rapidly three times. It was the kind of thing that a non-jujuman would not be likely to notice. Or, if he did, to discount it as just a facial tic. But a jujuman, of course, would give another secret signal in reply. Among us, whole conversations take place in this way without a word ever being exchanged. But the only response in Mr. Agura's case was a rapid oscillation of that lump in his throat that Westerners call "Adam's apple." It wasn't any juju signal that I knew of so I concluded the poor fellow was not one of us; he was merely scared out of his wits.

His reaction was typical, though, of even educated Africans: We still find it difficult to confront juju. In fact, it's much easier to simply pretend it no longer exists. Admitting that juju continues to be such a potent influence on our people is an embarrassment to our determination to be modern. So the most sophisticated among us simply deny it. And, when forced to face it, we're as ill-prepared and uncomfortable as Mr. Agura was in the presence of a real, live jujuman.

Janet continued to accuse me. "If you didn't hang that disgusting object on my door, who did?"

I smiled at her condescendingly. There was no need for me to intimidate the child further; it was enough that she knew she was under a terrible curse. "Now, young lady, you accuse me falsely. I tell you I have no idea what you're talking about."

She shook her head in disgust. "You aren't even man enough to own up to it. Doesn't it bother you to lie like that?"

Actually, it didn't; there is no moral standard in juju against lying. What *did* bother me, though, was that a small crowd had begun to watch the exchange. They were waiting not to hear the truth, but to see my power. The problem was, I'd already used some pretty heavy-duty curses on Janet to no visible effect. She remained unharmed even though others had confirmed for her that she was the object of a juju attack mounted by one who was reputed to have access to overwhelming power in the Invisible World. Yet, here she stood: not only unafraid, but defying me—

challenging me—in front of everyone.

And for the first time in my life, I saw the courage that comes from an independent will. This little girl didn't fear me because she didn't fear my gods. On the contrary, the fear had become all mine; I was afraid to try any more of my huge store of traditional curses on her. It wasn't that I was afraid she would turn them back on me, as I would if I were cursing another *babalawo*. It was even worse than that; I was afraid that nothing—absolutely *nothing*—would happen.

I continued to proclaim my innocence. But I knew that I no longer held any conviction of power or of faith in myself. I could feel it: I was becoming afraid of *her,* rather than the other way around.

She scolded me a while longer. I tried to bluster my way through, but I didn't fool anybody; even Mr. Agura dared to snicker toward the end. I glared at him and he choked off his laughter, so at least I still retained that much influence. But it was small consolation.

When she'd said her piece, Janet turned and left with Mr. Agura in tow. I tried to save face by saying loudly, "Yes, you may go; you are dismissed now." But there were some titters from the crowd and, embarassed, I retreated into the Palace of the Ejo.

There was no denying it: It was time to get tough. I would have to use the Power that frightened even me.

24

I got ready to meet the Power. It was something I'd dared to do only three times previously in my life: Once when Grandfather told me to go into the forest and fast and seek out my own special spirit helper; again shortly after my initiation; and finally, after my encounter with Esu. It was not an experience I looked forward to; the Power helped me but that didn't mean it was my friend,

I journeyed in secret back to the forest around Inesi-Ile to make my preparation. Without letting anyone know of my presence, I hid myself near Grandfather's Shrine. For three days, I took no water when I thirsted, but drank only a mixture of palm wine, vinegar, and a little blood from a chicken I'd killed. I took no solid food either, but chewed only the yellowish root of the plant we call *iboga*. *Iboga* is a deceptively innocent looking shrub of the family scientists know as *Tabernanthe*. The name by which we call it is designed to deflect suspicion that the plant might be important; it means only, "This belongs to the Ibo people." *Iboga* grows wild in the Ibo territory down in Gabon and probably originated there. But jujumen all through West and Central Africa have cultivated it since time immemorial for its narcotic effects,

I prayed continuously during the three days, demanding help from every god I could think of, while I accompanied myself on a drum to get their attention. I slept almost not at all. Whenever I did drop off, my sleep was of poor quality, troubled by vicious, colorful gods who leapt from branch to branch in the surrounding trees, screaming and jeering at me.

The third night, a great serpent came to me in my sleep. It tried to crush me in its coils, just as it had at my initiation. Only it succeeded this time. After forcing all the air out of me, it opened its jaws wide and swallowed me whole.

There was a terrible pressure all around me, as if the hand of God was squeezing me like a rubber ball. I remember thinking as I was forced down the serpent's gullet, *Being born must be something like this.*

There came a moment of relief when I popped out into the comparative roominess of the serpent's stomach. But it was short-lived as I saw all the others the great serpent had eaten: a hyena, a parrot, a horse, a leopard, a giant spider, and many others.

They knew everything; they took turns reciting the secret doubts and fears that I had tried to keep inside me. They all kept telling me that they hated me because I'd shamed my people, whereas they never had: The spider claimed to have been a good spider, the leopard a good leopard, and so forth. But I had not been a good man, they said. Certainly not a good *juju*man, because I'd let myself be influenced by foreign ideas until I'd begun to doubt the ways of my own people. They were offended, the animals told me, at being compelled to share the serpent's stomach with such a traitor to his ancestors. They kept saying that they would like to kill me and eat me. But they couldn't since the serpent had already done that and now we would all have to be together in its stomach forever.

That dream was the worst of them. But all the others I'd had over the three days were of a similar quality. Yet, unpleasant though the period of preparation was, I dreaded its end. Because that meant going to face the Power. As the Sun's descent marked the beginning of my fourth day in the forest, I could put it off no longer. With dread pulling me back at every step, I walked the short distance to the mahogany grove,

Mahogany is the most noble of the woods produced by our forest. It is durable, yet not so hard that it cannot be worked. It is abundant and it is beautiful when finished. We have long used it as a primary building material. In addition, it provides a wealth of medical products to whomever is knowledgable.

And in our forest, there is what we call a "grove" of mahogany trees, although it is really an entire section of forest—more mahogany than my people can use in one hundred lifetimes. And in that grove, there is one special tree, one sacred tree—a living giant, hollowed out untold years ago by one of *Shango's* lightning bolts.

I first found the sacred tree when I was but a boy. I had been training under Grandfather for just a few years then, so I was only about ten years old. He sent my into the forest to seek out my "special spirit," the private one that is unique for each *babalawo*. He promised it would become the ultimate Power in my life. But he warned me that this Power could only be experienced as the product of a long, hard, and lonely quest.

I'd been wandering alone in the woods, hungry, cold, and frightened, for perhaps ten days before I saw the hollow tree. *Struck by lightning,* I thought when I first saw it, *and yet it lives!* I was small for my age and the hollow was ample for my frame back then. I climbed inside, oblivious of the weevils and the other vermin, and called out to the Great Spirit who must surely rule such a magical tree.

A deep voice spoke authoritatively inside my head, demanding to know who dared disturb his repose. I said my name, but there was no further response. I brushed some of the bugs away from my face and said my name again, out loud this time. There was still no answer,

Then, trembling inside the tree, I whispered my Name, that secret word given to me the seventh day after my birth that identified me uniquely and forever to the residents of the Invisible World.

Immediately, the Power of the mahogany tree began to say *his* Name in my mind. It was more than just a label; it was a Name that embodied the Power's whole history and identity. His Name was so long that it took hours for the Power to tell. It boasted of the forces he could control and the demons he could command. It remembered what men he had possessed and it predicted who he would possess in time yet to come, even out to ten generations from now. It conveyed his hatred of mankind in general and of *me* in particular. It made me tremble and weep at the malevalence, the hatred, the sheer evil that were the sources of this Power.

And yet, when the recitation was over, the Power was under my control, because I had heard his Name. But the Power was so wicked, so vile, that I should never dare to call upon it, except in times of extremity. Now, as I squeezed myself into the hollow space which I'd long since outgrown, I cringed with the thought of what the Power would say when I confessed that a mere *girl* had caused me to come running for his help.

But, unlike the previous times I'd sought the Power, there was no answer in my mind. For hours I called, weevils nestling in my ears and nostrils, my skin rubbed raw from the tight, woody little womb, my bones sore from the cramped confinement. During all that time I praised the Power; I begged him; I pleaded with him; I condemned and cursed him. But all to no avail. My mind remained empty of an answer.

I called all night, while the *iboga* wore off and I started to become aware of how much physical harm I was doing to myself. With the coming of the dawn, the bugs became less vigorous in their attacks on my squashed, naked body. But that was the only difference. There was still no answer from the Power.

It wasn't until the Sun started heating the hollow tree like an oven that I finally tumbled out, sore everywhere and sick from the smell of my own sweat. I lay on the ground for a while, looking at the home of the great Power that had lived in a dark part of my mind since childhood. I was tired, hungry, and lonely. I was bruised and bloodied, achey and sore.

But I was also sober for a change, free from the narcotic effects of both *iboga* and religious ecstasy. For the first time, I was able to see that the mystical home of the dreaded Power was nothing more than an old hollow tree.

I picked myself up and washed in a nearby stream. I ate a breakfast of wild plantains and water from the stream. But it couldn't fill up the hollow feeling I had inside; my own private god had turned out to be a shadow of a starved, drug-numbed brain. For me, juju had turned out to be such a powerless joke that it could be jeered at safely, even by a child like Janet.

And, if all that was true of the supposedly omnipotent juju, what of *me*—the *babalawo* Isaiah Oke, a god and the son of gods? Did I have no special power over nature after all? Was I to be just another struggling human being, like everybody else?

*   *   *

I eventually made my way back to Normal and let myself into the trailer, ignoring all the notices taped to my door that, in the opinion of the headmaster, I was seriously truant and faced possible expulsion. But my need to act out my new resentment of juju was stronger than any concerns over school. The first thing I did was to dismantle my *ile-agbara,* my private "power house." Until I started to remove it all, I hadn't realized how much my juju collection had grown over the years: an old perfume bottle with a squirt bulb at the end of a long rubber hose, a piece of somebody's grave marker, the rusty breech of a World War I rifle, a colorful umbrella that I'd found on the grounds of the Lagos Colony Golf and Country Club, the mummified head of a lizard, a glass doorknob, a dried beef heart, and on and on and on. I'm sure it would have filled several boxes, had I troubled to pack it. But I just scooped it up, armful after armful, and flung it out the front door of the trailer. There was no reason for me to be ceremonious; I'd begun to think of it as "junk" rather than "juju."

My last act of sacrilege was to cut off my *ibante*. I slipped a knife under it, but then found myself unable to make the cut. I had worn it for so long that removing it would be like amputation. It had become the same color as my skin. It looked like it was part of my body, like a small roll of fat around my middle; I hadn't thought of it as anything other than a part of me for years. In spite of everything, it still took an effort for me to see my *ibante* for what it really was: a source of rashes, a home for fleas and ticks, and a generator of strange smells.

Pulling together my courage, I slashed through the *ibante* violently, first at my waist and then on each thigh. It crackled like dry dead reeds when the knife blade bit through. I went to the door and threw the filthy, petrified rag as far away as I could. Then I fell onto my sleeping mat and, for the first time I could remember, I felt naked.

I wept and then I slept. At one point, one of my roommates—Lazarus, a premed student—rapped on my door and asked whether I was all right, but I ignored him and he went away, I guess he told the others that I didn't want to be bothered because nobody came by after that, though I kept waking up at the sound of people coming and going,

I must have gone off my head for a bit because they eventually had to break my door down. I hadn't eaten anything substantial in over a week by that time and I'd also suffered a series of very painful emotional shocks. I remember being tended by the school physician and by my friend Simon, who knelt at the side of my sleeping mat and fed me because I was too weak to do it for myself.

When I finally came out, I learned that I'd been expelled for unexcused absence. There was a time when nobody would have dared take such an action. But now, after witnessing the impotence of juju before the defiance of a little American Christian girl, everybody around me seemed to have found his or her courage. Nobody feared the future *babalorisha* of Yorubaland anymore.

It was at that point that I understood my loss was total, a loss of public status as well as of private faith.

And I went looking for Janet.

Freedom

25

I caught up with Janet in the school's cafeteria. She was chatting amiably with her fellow freshmen, just as if she'd not destroyed every belief that gave my life meaning. The group scattered when I sat down across from her, all except for Janet. She stood her ground, even though she looked frightened.

"Hey," she said, "I don't want any trouble."

"I do not intend any trouble for you," I told her. "I merely want to talk with you."

She looked suspicious. "About what?"

"About why you did not fear my juju."

She looked as if she really preferred not to discuss the subject. But, with an air of exasperation, she said, "I already told you, Isaiah: I'm an American. We don't believe in stuff like juju. We don't believe that it can hurt anybody. We think it's just silly superstition."

Then, as an afterthought, she added, "No offense."

I waved her apology off. "Whatever its source, I must possess this power of yours," I said. "I can give you some things of value. I own a nice piece of land, for example, near my village—it could be sold for hard currency. Also I have some jewelry, items I used to wear sometimes on special occasions for juju ceremonies. I no longer have any need of it." I coughed to cover up my horror at what I was saying. "All of it is yours, if you will just sell me your gods."

At first, she looked confused. Then, after a moment, she shook her head and smiled. She said slowly, as if I were a baby, "There's nothing for me to sell. I mean, we Americans are the way we are because we're free. And nobody has to sell you freedom. It's what we call a 'right'; it belongs to everybody already."

"It does?"

"Sure. And if you don't have any, it's just because somebody took it away from you. So what you have to do is take it back." She nodded her head sharply, as if to say that everything was settled.

I stared as her in total confusion. What was the child on about? Nigeria had been free from Great Britain for almost three years. It hadn't made any great difference that I could see. Not in the lives of ordinary people, anyway, except maybe to make things worse. In fact, there was constant strife between our dozens of political parties. There were even those who said that a bloody civil war between us and the Ibos was inevitable. If that's what she meant by "freedom," she could have it.

"But what about your gods?" I said. "I have seen you Christians before and I have not understood you." I remembered the strange people in Ghana, who sang and performed their rituals in broad daylight, in white buildings with open windows, where anybody going by could see in. "But I did not know you Christians possessed a power greater than juju. Please," I said, "sell me your gods. I will worship them vigorously; I will feed them all their favorite foods. They will be happy if you sell them to me, you'll see."

She was beginning to relax a little in my presence, I thought. She even rolled her eyes up in her head the way I'd seen her do before when she wanted to express impatience. "There are no gods to 'buy,' " she said. "Christians pray to *Christ*. And Christ is free."

" 'Free?' " I repeated. "Ah! Then he, too, must be an American, this Christ fellow. Is it not so?"

This time she even managed a little laugh. "Well, lots of us would like to think so. But no, we can't get away with saying that." She idly traced patterns on the table with her finger. *Juju!* I thought instantly and automatically. Then I mentally slapped myself for thinking it. I had lived so long under the spell of juju that it was going to take a while for me to learn not to be what this American child called a "creep."

Janet glanced at me from a lowered head, as if she were embarrassed. "Look, Isaiah, if you're so interested in Christianity, I can fix it for you to talk to somebody who can explain it better than me."

I was surprised. "Better than you? You mean, you do not know all? You are not one of the high priestesses of this Christianity?"

She showed impatience again. "Not hardly. I'm just an ordinary school kid. I mean, I go to church on Sunday and I read the Bible and all, but

I'm hardly the one to preach to heathens. No offense. I mean, I'm nobody special."

"And yet, you speak of your religion openly," I said with wonder, "as if you did not even fear your god. You discuss him with strangers. You hide nothing."

"Yeah, well. It's that same freedom thing again, that I told you about before. If you become a Christian, you'll understand."

"*Me?*" I said, shocked. "Me, a Christian? Is it so easy to become one, then?"

"It's a lot easier than becoming an American, that's for sure. Look, why not have a talk with Dr. Osborn? You'll like him—he's a wonderful man, very understanding and warm. He's our local pastor here."

" 'Pastor?' "

"Kind of like a, what do you call it, a '*babalulu*'?"

"*Babalawo,*" I corrected. "He speaks to your god for you, this Osborn?"

"We *all* speak to God for ourselves. But a pastor is . . . well, he's kind of our teacher. Our spiritual leader, you might say."

So! A *babalorisha*. Just what I'd spent my own life preparing to be. Surely he and I would have so much in common that he might condescend to share some of his great secrets with me.

I felt myself perspiring with anticipation. "Do you think he might be persuaded to regard me as a colleague, this Osborn?" It was difficult to keep the excitement out of my voice. "Do you think maybe, if I worked hard, I also could be a *pastor?* This is the kind of work for which my grandfather trained me, you see, and—"

"Whoa, Isaiah! One step at a time. First, let me set up an appointment for you to meet Doctor Osborn. Then see what you think, okay?"

*   *   *

I liked Doctor Osborn very much and I have always flattered myself that the feeling was mutual. He was small and slight, but very strong-minded. He reminded me of Grandfather.

He must have had vast experience in relating to those who were troubled, He visited the headmaster on my behalf and asked him to check with the school physician to see how ill I'd been. It was only through Doctor Osborn's efforts that the decision to expel me was modified. True, I had to spend the rest of the year on probation, but that was quite mild compared to expulsion.

Doctor Osborn made a place for me in his beginning Bible class at the mission church. His classes gave him a chance to display one of the reasons for his great success as a missionary: his skill as a storyteller. That's an essential quality for anyone who wants to communicate effectively with African tribal people, given our oral traditions. He kept us all so spellbound with Bible stories interspersed with tales of life in America that some of us failed to notice he was also converting us to the Christian faith.

But Christianity did indeed answer a need in my life that juju had left vacant. The innocent spontaneity of Doctor Osborn's little church refreshed me after all the blood and the exacting ritual of juju. And Christianity's emphasis on love through faith cleansed me after juju's lust for power through fear and violence.

That's not to say that my decision to become a Christian was immediate; my renunciation of juju had made me understandably suspicious of all religions. So I spent as much of my final year at Normal as possible examining this strange, nonviolent, monotheistic faith. I took every break I could from my academic studies to pester Doctor Osborn to teach me the Bible. In fact, I spent so much time reading the Bible and then trying to explain it to my classmates that I nearly flunked out. You know how new converts to *anything* are, right?

But Doctor Osborn went to bat for me again and convinced the administration to give me one last chance. Thanks to his many reminders about "Rendering unto Caesar what is Caesar's," I forced my concentration back to academic work. In the end, I achieved such a healthy balance between religious and secular concerns that my final grades turned out to be quite commendable after all.

As I began making ready to accept my diploma from Normal, I also accepted baptism from Doctor Osborn. For me, it was the culmination of a process that had begun long before; maybe in the old hollow tree, when I first admitted the bankruptcy of juju. Or maybe when I came away to college and was exposed to ways of seeing the world other than through juju eyes. Or maybe even back when Mr. Olungwe first taught me to read and opened my mind to the existence of philosophies other than juju. But no matter when my process of rebirth began, it was fulfilled when I heard the words of the baptism ceremony about "renouncing Satan and all his works." I took to them be a formal renunciation of juju and I felt clean afterward.

I sent word home—not about my conversion (I was not yet independent enough for *that*) but about my graduation. I had been allocated four tickets for people to come and witness the ceremony. I knew Grandfather himself could not come, of course. Nor would he be likely to send any of our young people who might be contaminated by this strange Western idea, this nonjuju "ceremony of the graduation." In the end, he made the decision to send four of our bravest and handsomest warriors, all staunch jujumen.

They attended the graduation ceremony in full battle regalia—spears, shields, parrot feathers, and all. The problem was, several other tribes were represented as well, and they all displayed their chalked facial markings with as much pride as my own kinsmen did. I thought that a war would break out right on the spot, the way they started glaring at each other. But the administration of Normal College had grown accustomed to such problems in our culturally diverse society and were prepared. They had volunteers on hand to go through the crowd welcoming each delegation in its own language and thanking it for letting all the others live.

I received my diploma amid wild shouts of pride from my contingent. They kept carrying on the same way all during the headmaster's "farewell tea" out on the parade ground. Since they'd been convinced not to fight with anybody, they apparently decided they would out-shout another band of warriors over on the opposite side of the field. The other warriors thought this a good idea so the two groups hurled verbal threats and imprecations over the heads of the tea drinkers for a full hour. They were so disorderly and loud that I wanted to dismiss them. But they had been ordered by my grandfather to give me an escort home, so the decision was not mine.

At first, Doctor Osborn chuckled at the thought of how embarrassing it would be for me, now an educated man and a good Christian, to ride the train with these fierce warriors and their weapons. Then he grew more sober and said he hoped they weren't dangerous. I told him they weren't, and that the really dangerous part wouldn't come until I got home.

When I faced Grandfather to tell him that I was no longer a jujuman.

26

But Grandfather knew. I don't know how he knew, but he knew. This time, he had prepared no feast, no celebration, no homecoming welcome for me.

As soon as we entered the village, I figured out that the men who'd been sent to my graduation were not really my honor guard after all; they were my jailers. They took up positions all around me, boxing me in. I tried to turn off into the lane toward my mother's house, but they pushed me back into their midst with the hafts of their spears. They refused to explain themselves and continued trying to walk me in the direction of Grandfather's compound. When I became insistent, one of them turned his spear's point toward my ribs, which convinced me to go with them meekly.

The old man was hoeing his garden. I wasn't sure at first that it was him. He'd lost still more weight but he moved as if he were carrying heavy weights inside of him. Performing such an everyday task as gardening was a tribute to him. Not just because he was no longer the man he once was, though that would have been reason enough. But there was also the confrontation with me that he clearly knew to be imminent. He had planned for me to be his legacy to his people, to be his claim to immortality. But no one can live another's life for him, and he somehow knew that I had chosen otherwise. His disappointment must have been deep to the point of despair. And still, he hoed his garden.

My guards came to a stop, boxing me in. I bowed and greeted Grandfather respectfully. He looked up from his work, leaned on his hoe and just stared at me. At first, I thought it was the same dispassionate look with which one might study a bug before stepping on it. But after standing under his gaze for a long time, I saw a tear come down his wrinkled cheek.

He shook himself and gestured toward his private quarters. Two of the men took my arms, resolving any doubts I might have had that I was being welcomed home. A jug of palm wine and two mugs had been set out on a little low table. Grandfather and I squatted on opposite sides of it like enemies across a contested field. I hoped it wouldn't turn into a yelling match, the way the parade ground had for the warriors back at Normal College. We both held our tongues until the men left.

When Grandfather finally spoke, his voice was very soft. "Our ancestors have been crying out to me. They say they are displeased with you; can you say why?"

"Honorable sir," I said with lowered head, "I know you will be hurt by what I have to tell you and for that I am sorry. I hope you will understand. But please do not talk to me about 'communicating' with our ancestors; I no longer believe in such things."

"Indeed?" He poured some palm wine for each of us, a good host in spite of the pain on his face. Behind his naturally dark complexion, there were large spots of a still darker hue on his hands. Age, I thought, was overtaking him faster than it had ever overtaken any other man. Either that or. . . .

But I could not think it. I told myself that he was no thinner, that his movements were no less smooth, that his cheeks were no hollower than they had always been. That I was looking at the early stages of "slim" disease in my beloved grandfather was something I could not face. Nor could he, apparently; he waved aside all my polite, but sincere, questions about his health and returned instead to the topic of religion.

"What do you believe in now," he asked, "since you no longer believe in communication with our ancestors?"

"I believe in Jesus, Honorable sir."

He sipped at his refreshment. "This is an *orisha* with whom I am not familiar. What is his power? What forces does he rule?"

Responding was pointless and I should have known it; there was too big a gulf between us now for me to make him understand. But I was filled with the kind of consuming zeal that religious converts so often show at first. It made me feel that I had to seize every opportunity to display how determined my new faith was. So, I answered him humorlessly, as if he were asking me sincere questions instead of baiting me. "He has all power," I said. "He rules all forces."

"So this going away to school has taught you much—you have discovered a new, very powerful *orisha* for us. This is good." He offered me a kola nut from a bowl beside him. As I reached out, he seized my arm and peered suspiciously at my new wrist watch. "Is this part of the juju of your Jesus?"

"It's not juju; it's a gift," I answered stiffly. "From a dear friend, Doctor Osborn. He presented it to me to honor my graduation."

"Hmmmm." He cocked his head to one side and listened. He nodded in time to the ticking. His hearing must have been exceptionally acute for one of his years and poor health. Either that or Doctor Osborn had given me less of a watch than I thought. But after a few seconds, Grandfather seemed to lose interest and dropped my arm back into my lap.

"And what of that?" He pointed to my Bible, which I now carried at my side always.

I lifted it and shook it above my head, as I had seen Doctor Osborn do so often when he preached. "This is the word of God!" I said in my best pulpit voice.

He leaned forward and cocked his head over again toward my Bible. Then he leaned back and shrugged. "I hear nothing."

"It is a *written* word, a word which *I* am able to read. If you like, I can read it to you, Honorable sir. It will help you see how Jesus can save you."

"Thank you. Perhaps another day." He was being painfully polite but clearly wanted to.get down to the *important* matter. "Now, tell me—how shall we appease this new *orisha* of yours? What is his food? How shall we sacrifice to him? What blood does he prefer?"

I shook my head. "It is very difficult to explain. Jesus demands no sacrifice. He wants no blood other than his own, which he has shed for all of us."

"Really?" Grandfather sat back and thought about that a bit. "He sounds like a most generous fellow, your Jesus."

"Oh, yes, Honorable sir: He is!"

"He sounds much more pleasant than our other *orisha;* I certainly hope he will get along with them."

I wouldn't let myself consider that Grandfather might be taunting me. But even if I had, I probably would have welcomed it at that stage of my life: It would have made me a martyr, in a way. And that would have made me feel good. "There are no *orisha* for him to get along with," I said, a little stiffly. "Jesus is the *only* God."

Grandfather raised his eyebrows. He calmly took another kola nut and munched on it. "No *orisha?* This will be a surprise to all the spirits who serve them—the spirits of the forest, the spirits of the air and the water, the spirits of the rocks and the trees and the grain and the animals."

I took a deep breath. "There are no such spirits, either, any more than there are *orisha.* There is only Jesus."

He sat back on his haunches again and appeared to think about this for a while. "So. No *orisha.* No spirits of nature." He shook his head as if confused. "Next, you will inform me that you have discovered some new facts about our esteemed ancestors: Perhaps that they are *not* all around us, after all, watching all our doings as we have always believed."

"Yes," I said gravely. "That is so. Our ancestors are in heaven, with Jesus." I stumbled a little over this last statement. My grounding in Christian theology wasn't very firm yet. I didn't know at that time how to respond to the charge that our ancestors didn't know Christ and, therefore, hadn't been saved. But there was no way I would dare tell Grandfather a thing like *that.*

The appearance of an open-minded seeker of knowledge began to fade from his face. "No ancestors? Then, who is it that I talk to when I seek help? Who is it that I see when I make ritual at my Shrine? Who is it that shows me hidden truths when I divine the future?"

I took a deep breath before answering. "All these things," I said with a sadness that masked my insensitivity, "are imagination and superstition. They are what Western people call hysteria."

"I see. You no longer believe, then? You no longer have any faith at all in our traditions?"

"No. Not in juju, anyway." I was burning with the desire to Witness, even to this poor, sick old man who had not the slightest chance of profiting from my testimony. I raised my face heavenward. "The only true religion is Christianity; all else is idolatry and nonsense."

The look of shock on his face was painful to me. "I'm sorry to have to tell you that," I added with a slightly smug air.

But the funny thing was, I really *was* sorry. Saying it in that superior way reminded me of Janet saying, "No offense," every time she insulted me. I suddenly realized that I was being pointlessly cruel to a dreadfully ill old man whose beliefs were as genuine as my own. And, even if his *ideas* were crazy, I had every reason to love *him.*

Instantly, I was ashamed of myself. Why is charity always the last of the virtues to be learned by Christians? And by everybody else, for that matter? All of a sudden, I wanted desperately to find some way to make things right with the old man; I didn't want him to go to his grave hating me. But my remarks about our ancestors had taken things too far. He was actually shaking with rage, no longer bothering to hide the anger that I had so carelessly kindled. "Very well," he said. "Bring on this Jesus of yours. I would meet him. We will match him against *my* gods; then we will see who is who! Show him to me!"

"I cannot. He is not like *your* gods—pieces of old junk that you pretend are sacred. He is different. If I could only make you understand . . ."

"You will not permit me to see him?"

"I *cannot,* I tell you. He is only in my heart."

"Then, that's where we shall have to see him, isn't it?" He got to his feet and kicked the bowl of kola nuts across the floor. He drew himself up to all the height he could muster. "Take yourself out of my home. I place on you this Obligation: Go right now through all the streets of Inesi-Ile. Go far and wide. Tell all the people to make ready for a sacrifice tomorrow at dawn. No one is to stay in bed. No one is to go to the fields at that time or tend his flocks or start the firing of a pot. All must come to my square outside and witness the sacrifice."

A sacrifice? I didn't want to believe what he had in mind. But I could think of no other interpretation.

"Pa," I said, "look. Let's start again. I really didn't mean to offend you—"

"Me? Worry not about how you have offended me; worry about how you have offended your ancestors! Only this Jesus who you keep in your heart will appease them!"

"Aw, Pa. Can't we just—"

"Enough! You have been placed under Obligation. Must I remind you what that means?"

It was more than a request, more than a suggestion. More than an order, even. Being placed under an Obligation by an elder meant performing the assigned task no matter the cost. Even if one's life was endangered, an Obligation had to be met. It had always been so in our clan. Especially after the confrontation we'd just had, I couldn't bring myself to let Grandfather down any further.

"Yes, Pa," I said, and ran from the house to do as the old man wished.

I'd gone through only two or three streets, stopping before each house to call out Grandfather's demands, when I heard a heavy tread behind me. I turned and saw Joshua's cruel face grinning down at me. We are not a tall people, and Joshua would have been judged big even by the standards of Americans. Towering over me, face heavily chalked, he was a sobering sight. Especially as he was carrying his machete casually at his side.

"So," he said, "the great Isaiah Oke has returned from his *school.*" He said the word "school" as if it were as bitter in his mouth as the *oruwo* fruit from the brimstone tree. "You have learned the ways of the *white* man well, have you not, son-of-my-father's-brother?"

I tried to overlook his obnoxious tone as I ran on toward the next house to fulfill my duty. "Why do you molest me, Joshua?"

"I do not molest you," he said. "I escort you. On the wishes of our grandfather."

So, Grandfather no longer trusted me enough even to believe that I would carry out his Obligation voluntarily. It was a bitter realization, made no sweeter by the face that he'd chosen Joshua to be my shadow. I stopped before the next house and yelled out Grandfather's invitation to anyone who might be inside. It struck me as incongruous that I should be clutching my Bible for comfort while I invited people to my own juju execution. Logically speaking, it made no sense.

But I had to fulfill the filial duty imposed on me by Grandfather. It was something my whole tribal experience had conditioned me to do. To ignore an elder's direct orders would have been unthinkable. "It is not necessary for you to watch me, Joshua." I told him as I set off again. "I will do as I have been Obligated to do; I am not without honor."

He merely laughed and threw me the juju hand sign which means, "May your lie choke you."

It took about three hours to go all through the town. I was hoarse and my feet were sore by the time we finished. Joshua had stood loftily behind me at every house, idly slapping his machete against his leg. The impression he gave was that he was my keeper. It augmented my shame, and he enjoyed it.

As I started back, I again tried to turn off down the path toward my mother's house. She had not come out when I stood before her door, shouting out the shame of my coming sacrifice. But it was almost dark now, and maybe she would let me in if I snuck around the back. Or maybe not. But I thought I would try.

Joshua stepped in front of me, making the hand sign that means, "May you lose your way." He blocked the lane like a big, grinning wall.

"Please, Joshua, I want to go see my mother. I've been through the whole town, as Grandfather ordered. So you can go back now."

"Yes," he said with the kind of leer one sees on old men who covet young girls at a festival. "I will go back. But you will come with me."

"Joshua, I told you: I want to try to see my mother now."

The look on his face became still more obscene, it seemed to me.

He was getting real pleasure from being Grandfather's watchdog. "It is forbidden," he said. "You may never see her again. You are to come directly to our grandfather's compound where you will be held in the storeroom. Until it's time for sacrifice." His chest puffed out. He was enjoying his assignment. "And Grandfather has chosen me to ensure all this, Little Man."

"But I don't understand, Joshua. Have I not done all that Grandfather asked?"

"So far, yes. But he wants to be sure you're present for tomorrow's sacrifice. He'd be very hurt if you happened to miss it." He laughed down at me. His breath had the smell of one who is too lazy to clean his teeth well.

It was true that I hadn't yet made up my mind as to what I would do. Part of me was afraid that reconciliation with Grandfather was no longer possible, that his decision to sacrifice me was unchangeable. That part of me kept telling me to behave intelligently—to run for my life.

But another part of me wanted to believe that I could still reason with him—that if we could just talk to each other calmly, I could make it all well.

Joshua laughed loudly again, as if he already knew what the outcome would be. And that helped me decide. "Now, Joshua," I said in a hollow voice, "prepare for your end. Today may be your last day."

He gave me a haughty look. "Oh? What will you do, Little Man? Can you overcome the best warrior in Inesi-Ile? Can you outrun the fleetest legs? Can you prevail against the strongest arms?" He laughed at me again.

"No, Joshua," I looked up at him and very deliberately closed one eye while keeping the rest of my face as immobile as possible. "But can you stand against the power of . . . MY EYE?"

The derisive laughter cut off with a sharp intake of breath. His mouth fell open and he let out a kind of frightened squeak. It was an incongruous reaction from such a big, strong, well-armed man. But that's what juju does.

He dropped his machete and threw his forearm across his eyes. He aimed his other hand in my general direction in the universal hand sign for protection against "the evil eye." I saw his index finger and pinkie quiver like the horns of a nervous bull in the brief instant before I hit him in the stomach with everything I had. His breath exploded out of him, but he didn't go down. He just dropped both hands to his midsection and looked surpised.

So I hit him in his slack jaw, which did the trick. His head snapped back and he went over backward; it was like felling a giant mahogany tree.

As he hit the ground, I turned and started running in a near panic. But I remembered that I had almost no money at all on me. What good would it do me to run?

I didn't dare go to my mother's house now. And I had nowhere else to go. So I went back to Joshua. He was out cold and there was a bloody space where one of his front teeth used to be, but otherwise he looked okay, for which I offered up thanks. I reached under his tunic and untied the money purse we wear around our middles. Then I grabbed up his machete and took to my heels again.

I ran without thinking for a few minutes before I calmed down enough to make myself stop and think of a plan. I was well into the forest that surrounded the town and headed south. Of course, that's exactly where they would expect me to go; back toward Normal College, territory that I knew well.

So I turned east, toward Grandfather's juju Shrine, the direction he'd least expect me to take. Somewhere well beyond it, I recalled, there was a road. I had to outwit the posse that would be out after me as soon as Joshua came to and reported. There was a time when I wouldn't have had that worry; I would have killed Joshua so there would be more time before the alarm spread. But I couldn't do that anymore. I had truly become, in the words of the scriptures, "a new man."

But I found myself praying fervently that the new, Christian Isaiah could still run as fast and as far as the old, juju one.

I made good time and, after an hour or so, recognized the area: I was close to Grandfather's Shrine. I ran into the clearing I knew so well and collapsed exhausted in front of the little corral where we penned the sacrifices. I promised myself to rest only long enough to catch my breath and then to go on again toward the distant East Road.

I set down the machete and opened Joshua's money purse. It offered no help: only some worthless cowries (and a few nearly worthless one-*kobo* pieces) fell into my hand. I tossed the cowries away and dropped the *kobo* into my own money pouch. I went to toss the purse away, but there was still something inside it. I shook it again and a key fell out.

Keys were uncommon at that time in rural West Africa and I'd only seen a few in my life. My experience with them was so slight that they all tended to look alike to me. And yet, there was something familiar about this particular key.

Suddenly, I recognized it: It was the key to the box that held all my juju notes of the past fifteen years, ever since I'd first learned to read and write.

Grandfather had given it to Joshua.

It hurt me more than anything else that had happened to me. I could deal with the loss of my faith in juju; I had something better to replace it. I could deal with disgrace in the eyes of my people; I had gone a different way by choice. I could even deal with the forfeiture of my grandfather's love; people will love whom they will and no one can force the love of another. But to give my writings to Joshua—*especially* to Joshua—was a pain that could hardly be borne.

My pain didn't last long; it transmuted itself into rage, the way a truly serious hurt always does. I ran across the clearing to the Shrine and kicked in the door. I dug up the big tin box from its burial place under one of the altar stones and used Joshua's key to open it. The papers were so tightly packed inside that the top of the box popped open as if it had been on a spring. I grabbed the pages, filling both arms, and ran outside. I left behind me a trail of yellow paper with green lines.

I sat, dropped the stack down on the ground, and, in the moonlight, squinted at what I'd written. Some of the pages surprised me with their childish scrawl; I would not have thought there was ever a time when I'd printed so poorly. Others surprised me for their length and for their precision of detail. Many of the pages were insightful, recording the reasons *why* jujumen believed certain things. Others had a certain semi-scientific logic about them, as if there might be something to them other than simple superstition. Taken altogether, the record was more than juju recipes; it was, in its way, a window into the minds of my people. I sat there until the sky began to pink in the East, rereading it all and letting the pride of the accomplishment wash over me.

I heard a sound. It startled me out of my fixation; otherwise I might have remained there until I was caught. What should I do? There were too many pages, far too many, to take with me. But one thing I'd become sure of during the night's reading: Joshua was not to have them. In his hands, there was no telling the evil which could be worked.

Besides, they were mine. And they were too good for him.

I grabbed up as many of the pages as I could carry. It made a pile well over my head and individual pieces kept blowing off as I made my way toward the stream from which Grandfather always got his "juju-water."

I have no idea where the stream eventually emptied. Not that it was important; where it flowed behind the Shrine, it was straight and fast, though shallow, which was all that I needed to know. I flung the papers over the water with all my might, as if I were throwing them with the strength of my resentment toward Joshua. They separated and fell like dead dreams.

For a moment, they floated randomly, bumping into each other in the swift current as if they couldn't make up their minds where to go, same as me. Some of the pieces tumbled and sank, but some of them clumped together to form big mats, reminding me of the way tribal people cling to one another to survive. The mats became so big I was able to see them all the way down to where the stream turned and got drunk up by the dense forest.

I sat there for a bit, watching the empty stream. Then I went back to the Shrine and made trash of it. I kicked over the two little buildings and the sacrifice corral. Using one of the corral rails as a lever, I pried up the main altar stone, with its generations of caked blood, and rolled it toward the stream. I blessed the slight downhill stretch that made the job easier. It rolled like a wheel clear to the middle of the stream where it tipped and disappeared under the swift water.

Lastly, I broke and scattered all the juju: the strings of beads, the bones, the shells, the broken bottles, the old pieces of iron, the scraps of cloth, the jugs for juju-water and all the rest. I did a very thorough job and by the time I finished, it was full light.

I looked around at the mess and understood that it was not only the wreckage of juju, but of my tribal life as well. There was no way I could ever go back now, not even if, through some miracle, Grandfather were to have a change of heart some day. I was cut off forever from my people.

And yet, I was still a tribal man inside and that part of me wept. I stood in the midst of all the wreckage I'd made and asked myself the question that always comes at the turning point of one's life: "What now?"

Flight

27

There was nowhere for me to go but onward, toward the faraway East Road which more or less marked the boundary of our territory. I ran quickly, not knowing whether my fleetness was due to the rest I'd had at the Shrine or to the guilt that was pursuing me through the dark forest. If I reached safety and started a new life, that life would have to include some way to live with the memory of how much harm I'd done to my people. As I ran, I prayed through my tears that they would find something to replace their juju. In time, of course, they would. My people have resilient spirits, as do all people.

But for Grandfather there would not be enough time. He could not live long enough for the wounds I'd inflicted on him to heal. He would never find another form of security to replace his lost juju, nor would he live long enough even to forgive me. His death was certain; no one with "slim disease" ever survived.

The people of the West have not yet lived with AIDS long enough to know its true face. Movies are made about it and books written, and they think they know it. But, for most, the movie is about someone else's life and touches them only when the victim happens to be somebody famous, or if the story is especially poignant.

But we Africans have had to live with AIDS for longer than they. We were living with it in our very midst a whole generation ago. We watched our village people die without even the meager comfort provided by Western medicines. And they died just as inexorably, just as inevitably, just as painfully as people anywhere.

At first, the affliction was doubly mysterious and fearful because it was so unusual: Few villages of any size failed to see at least one brother or sister wasted by it, but those cases were still isolated and rare. To us, AIDS was indeed more like a curse than a disease, inexplicably singling out one person from a large village. But that aspect of AIDS, of course, was soon to change.

My personal experience makes the spread of AIDS more than just numbers to me. Some years ago, I attended in evangelical conference in the interior of Africa, well east of my native Nigeria. I decided to make a holiday of the long trip, so I stayed on an extra week to trek around in the bush country. One of the villages where I stopped was a particularly progressive little place, neat and tidy. It was located on the bank of a picturesque river and the people were extraordinarily pleasant. I stayed there only two days but I never forgot the beauty of the place nor the kindness of its people. They had no problems that I could see, except one: There were four cases of "slim" disease that nobody knew what to do about. This was a very large incidence for a village of that size. The people wondered who it was that had cursed them so. For only a juju curse, it was thought, could have brought on such a concentrated misfortune.

Last year, I found myself within fifty kilometers of the place and decided to look in on the friends I'd made there years earlier. The driver I hired to take me there refused to get out of the car when we arrived, but told me he'd wait, even though I hadn't asked him to, as if he expected that I would not be staying long.

I couldn't believe it was the same town that I had so admired. Grass was growing in the street. Starving cattle, their ribs showing, tried to make a meager meal of it. Not one of the roofs in sight seemed to have been thatched any time in recent memory and several of the homes had crumbling walls as well. Flies were everywhere, crawling about in congealed masses like living carpets.

The few people who moved about did so listlessly and seemingly without hope. They looked weak, hungry, and . . . slim. The town square was nearly empty, except for several sacks of rags propped up in the shade of a wall. One of the sacks moved or I wouldn't have known that it was a man.

That made me look closer. I saw that all the rag sacks were *people*— people so bedeviled by the swarms of black flies that I wondered how they could even breathe. I tried at first to chase some of the flies away from them, but it was hopeless. I tried to ask them what had happened to them, but they obviously didn't want to talk and just turned away from me. And who could blame them, in the shape they were in?

I wandered around for a few minutes, but saw not one person who was healthy. Nor did I see anyone I recognized, although "slim" changes one's appearance so much that I could have walked right by an old friend without knowing him or her. The town, which I thought to have a population of about a thousand on my first visit, was now a ghost town with maybe fifty or so citizens.

And, so far as I could tell, every one of them was sick unto death with AIDS.

The mystery of AIDS in Africa versus AIDS in the West is that women and men in Africa get it in more or less equal numbers, while in the West, it's more common among men. Scientists have concocted many elaborate theories to explain this discrepancy, many of which depend on bizarre sexual habits on the part of the entire African population, children included. But one of the things I've wondered about is whether there couldn't be a simpler solution: AIDS is a blood disease, spread by contact with infected blood.

And who has more exposure to raw blood than a jujuman?

We cut ourselves and we cut others. We splash blood about. We even drink it. It's part of our ceremonies, part of our rituals, part of our everyday lives. Men, women, and even children drink blood—human as well as animal—as casually as Americans drink cola.

Could this be how AIDS was spread among us? How it was able to spread so fast and so far? And how it affected our men, women, and children so universally?

I haven't heard of any Western doctors or scientists who have seriously considered the possibility that our juju blood rituals are responsible for the unique pattern AIDS has made in Africa. In fact, those scientists to whom I've mentioned the idea dismiss it because they refuse to accept that human sacrifice is as common in Africa as I say it is. I can't blame them; scientists no more want the gruesome facts of juju to be true than laymen do.

And, unless you've been born and raised in Central Africa, it's easy to argue that I'm lying. That happened to me on an American radio show recently. The other guest was a very young anthropologist. The topic was "Traditional African Religions." She became so heated when I told the truth about juju that the host cut to a commercial earlier than planned so he could calm her down.

When we came back on the air, she had regained her control and said she could prove that jujumen no longer offered human sacrifice. Juju sacrifice these days, she insisted, was only *symbolic:* just a little corn or a handful of rice thrown on the fire. A chicken, maybe, a couple times a year; on rare occassions, maybe even a goat.

But humans? Never!

How did she know? Simple: She asked a jujuman, she said, and he told her so.

Besides, she reminded me, human sacrifice is against the law, had been ever since 1886, when Her Majesty The Queen of England directed us to "abolish the said abominable practice."

"Now, if that doesn't convince you," she said, "I don't know what does."

Okay. Try some of my evidence, from the January 19, 1988 edition of Nigeria's *Daily Sketch*. A thirty-year-old news vendor was found in Onitsha with his throat slashed and his ears and his genitals removed. The report said that his room had been "sprayed with blood" and that the murder weapon was found hidden under a cushion: a decorated machete.

Or how about this from the *Nigerian Tribune* of July 29, 1987: A man wanted a spirit slave and hired a "native doctor" to create one for him. The victim was the client's thirteen-year-old nephew. In this particular ritual, the boy's head was severed from his body, which was then thrown into a canal. There was no testimony as to what rituals transpired prior to the decapitation. The head was preserved in a small box in the client's room. It was subsequently admitted as particularly gruesome evidence in his murder trial. Two other participants who helped out with the killing were tried separately: the client's mother and father—the victim's grandparents.

It may be true that juju practice, including blood sacrifice, almost died out at one time in the more sophisticated parts of Africa, just as "experts" would have us believe. But lately, circumstances have conspired to renew its appeal for the masses. Beginning in the 1950s a series of laws was passed protecting and guaranteeing "the practice of traditional religion."

That seems to be the same principle one finds in the First Amendment to the United States Constitution, guaranteeing freedom of religion. But our governments in Central Africa do more than take a "hands off" attitude toward juju. They actively endorse and sponsor something called the "Festival of Arts and Culture," known locally by the acronym "FESTAC." This is supposed to be a periodic celebration of our folk dances and, as a "cultural activity," it is paid for out of government funds. But, its grandiose name aside, it is really a thinly disguised promotion of juju, attended by herbalists and *babalawos* from all over Africa.

Juju, in the guise of culturally primitive innocence, is taking over all our institutions. We built a fine, new school—the Benue Polytechnic— which we hoped would help us move into the modern world. But in the Nigeria *Daily Times* of August 1, 1987, a front-page report describes the court-ordered closing of the new school. The judge who chaired the commission of inquiry on the matter, Mr. Justice Eri, said that the staff practiced "juju and witchcraft" on the premises to the point that the school became unworkable. He did not identify the specific rituals that were going on, but he referred to them collectively as "nightmare sorcery." They must have been even more grotesque than the rituals I used to practice because Mr. Eri said they made the school "administratively bankrupt, financially archaic, and intellectually emaciated and redundant."

So there's really no question that juju, including human sacrifice, is being actively practiced once again in Africa, as shown by these current newspaper reports. The Nigerian writer, Wilson Asekomhe, however, may have gone too far; he states in his essay, "The Menace of Ritual Killing," that "human sacrifice will soon become *the number two cause* of accidental death in West Africa, second only to automobile accidents" (emphasis added).

But just suppose that the ritual letting and consumption of blood—including human blood—is a reality in today's Central Africa, just as I have said. Could it explain not only why AIDS befalls women as easily as men there, but also why AIDS spread so quickly? And, if so, what are the implications for America?

Robert C. Gallo, of the National Cancer Institute (U.S.), and Luc Montagnier, of the Pasteur Institute (France), are the scientific investigators who discovered human immunodeficiency virus. More easily referred to as HIV, this is the virus that causes AIDS. Gallo and Montagnier wrote an article entitled "AIDS in 1988" that appeared in the October, 1988 edition of *Scientific American*. They ask why the virus appeared so suddenly and spread so fast:

Where was HIV hiding all those years, and why are we only now experiencing an epidemic? Both of us think that the answer is that the virus has been present in small, isolated groups in central Africa or elsewhere for many years. In such groups, the spread of HIV might have been quite limited and the groups themselves may have had little contact with the outside world. As a result, the virus could have been contained for decades.

That pattern may have been altered when the way of life in central Africa began to change. People migrating from remote areas to urban centers no doubt brought HIV with them. Sexual mores in the city were different from what they had been in the village, and blood transfusions were commoner. Consequently, HIV may have spread freely. Once a pool of infected people had been established, transport networks and the generalized exchange of blood products would have carried it to every part of the world. What would have been remote and rare became global and common.

I call your attention to the statement that "blood transfusions were commoner" in our cities. Perfectly true, no doubt. But common enough to account for AIDS? From my experience, exposure to ritual blood is far more common among my people than is medical transfusion. But that's my only quarrel with the statement. Perhaps adding a line to the effect that "Central and West Africans frequently and willingly expose themselves ritually to raw blood" would complete the picture. Recognizing ritual blood-letting as an additional source of exposure to contaminated blood makes the rapid and widespread distribution of HIV throughout Central and West Africa not only understandable, but inevitable.

At first, the rest of the world experienced AIDS only in certain well-defined segments of their populations. These were groups which science could have predicted were vulnerable to a blood disease: homosexual men, people who'd received transfusions, and users of shared intravenous needles. But there was one other group that seemed especially susceptible to AIDS, too.

Haitians.

Science never did come up with a convincing reason why Haitians should be singled out above all other peoples in the Western Hemisphere for the tragedy of AIDS. But, just as was the case with us Africans, nobody wanted to seriously consider the idea that Haitians practice ritual letting of human blood through the religion called voodoo, the New World offshoot of juju. Instead, theories were advanced based on tortured logic to suggest that the entire Haitian population—including octagenarians and infants, heterosexuals and celibates—made a habit of bizarre sexual practices.

Suppose it is more than coincidence that AIDS has hit hardest in Africa and on Africa's children in the Caribbean, both of whom are exposed to human blood during religious ritual. Are there implications for America's population, *as a whole?*

I believe there are. Satanism (a form of juju) is not unknown in America. On a recent "Geraldo" television show about Satanic cults (aired October 6, 1988), the guests were all former devil worshippers. They appeared—to my eye, at least—to be educated, articulate, middle-class American youngsters.

All of them were white, incidentally—another sign that juju practices are spreading. Every one of them confessed to having participated in human sacrifice, to having consumed human flesh and having drunk human blood.

And these nice, white, American teenagers knew of the "spirit slave" ritual—the *iko-awo:* One of them explained how he obtained power from the creatures he was killing. He confessed that the power was his motive for ritually sacrificing to Satan, whom we Africans know as Esu.

Another young man, identified only as "Kurt," admitted to ritually cutting and scarring his body, to drinking his own blood mixed with the blood of others during ritual, and to sacrificing goats and dogs.

Sound familiar?

Now, if Americans are beginning to practice blood ritual, we may see an increase in the kinds of diseases that follow from exposure to blood—including, most prominently, AIDS. And the disease would not be confined to the "risk groups" already identified. Rather, the disease would spread more evenly than in the past.

In other words, if I'm right, AIDS will break out into the general population. It will begin to look more like our African disease: It will infect women as well as men, heterosexuals as well as homosexuals.

Notice that this is a prediction for the future; we know that AIDS has not broken out into the general population in America *yet.* There is evidence to that effect from the state of Illinois, which conducts a mandatory HIV test for any person applying for a marriage license. According to the *Chicago Tribune* of October 11, 1988, 125,000 people were tested. Out of that large number, who are more or less representative of the general population of the United States, only fifteen were found to contain the virus in their blood.

So here's an easy way to know whether I'm telling the truth about human sacrifice in Africa and about how the practice is spreading to where you live: Look for an increase in the incidence of AIDS in the general population. It will begin to show up in women, in heterosexual men, in children, in older people. It will become an epidemic among you as it has among us.

That's the only way I was ever able to understand my grandfather's AIDS: I think he got it from exposure to blood during juju ritual. The certainty of his death was just one more burden for me as I ran away from Inesi-Ile that day. How long he would last, I didn't know; the disease seemed to work differently from person to person. But I was sure death would overtake him before he had a chance to forgive me.

Even so, I didn't dare turn back to apologize; running on toward the East had taken on the same inevitability in my mind as had Grandfather's death from AIDS.

28

I made it all the way to the East Road without running afoul of the search party that I was certain had to be breathing down my neck by now. They would be going slower than me, of course, because they were tracking while I was just running. But they would be pretty mad, too, and wouldn't be taking any rests. Fearing a spear through my back at any moment, I hid in the bush until I heard the cross-country bus come bumping along.

I stepped out into the middle of the road to flag it down because I could imagine the reluctance with which the driver would stop to pick up this dirty, sweaty vagabond. He apparently decided that stopping would be better for his rickety bus than running me down, because he squealed to a dusty stop just inches from my knees. He studied me with obvious distaste for a moment after I got aboard. He couldn't have listed himself as a bus driver anywhere else in the world: He had only one eye and the fingers of his left hand were missing. "Where do you want to go?" he asked gruffly.

I had run off with only a few *kobo* in the money pouch around my waist and had been able to add only a few more from Joshua's purse. I opened the pouch now and dumped the pitifully small collection of bronze coins into my hand. "How far will these take me?"

He sniffed disdainfully, "Just out of sight, maybe. But that's all."

"Look," I said, "I really need to get as far as I can. How about letting me ride for free? Please."

He shook his head and pointed to the door. "No money, no ride."

"I'm desperate, sir. If you take me with you, I promise to pay you back. Double."

"The company can't put your promises in the gas tank." He glanced at my watch. "Now, if you had something of value, something that I could give to the company that they could turn into money . . . ." The watch was worth many times the price of a fare even to Port Harcourt, the easternmost city in Nigeria. But I pulled it off anyway and handed it over. He studied it critically. "Okay," he said, "this will take you as far as Benin City."

"But that's not far enough. That's one of the first places they'll . . . I mean, couldn't you take me farther than that?"

He held my watch as if it were a dead fish. "Farther?" he repeated. "For this?" Nevertheless, he slipped it over his wrist and held it up before his good eye. It looked incongruous next to the stump of his hand.

After a moment of study he shook his head again. "I only drive to Benin; I can't divide this watch up to share with the fellow who takes over from me," he said. "No, Benin City is as far as you can go for this watch, boy." He dropped his hand to the gearshift and depressed the clutch as if about to get under way again. But he was looking at the machete I'd taken from Joshua rather than at the road. "Unless, of course, there's something for the other driver, too."

So I handed over the machete. I hated to part with it; it was a good one, English-made. He appraised it as he had the watch. It met with his approval and he shoved it down between his seat and the wall of the bus. "Okay," he said with a grin that showed he knew I was in his power, "what else you got?" I noticed that he had dropped all pretense of "compensating the company"; I felt like I was simply being robbed. I again offered him the few *kobo* I had in my money purse, but he acted as if these were beneath his dignity. "What's that?" he asked, pointing at my Bible.

I held it closer to me. "It is only a book."

The eyelid of his one good eye narrowed. "The way you hold it so close, it must be worth something. Maybe I can find somebody who will give me money for it, eh? Give it here."

I stepped back. "No, Honorable sir, this is of no use to you. I've already given you everything I had that you might value."

"I said, 'Give it here,' boy!"

"Please, Honorable sir. It is only my Bible; I am a Christian."

"A Christian?" He spat on the floor near my feet. "Okay, boy, keep your book; who wants a thing like that, anyway? You can ride until somebody tosses you off, for all I care, but you don't ride in here with decent people who fear their ancestors." He jerked his thumb toward the roof. "Up top with you." He laughed raucously.

It wasn't fair, of course. The watch and machete I'd been forced to surrender were worth far more than the price of an inside ticket; they may have been worth as much as the frail old bus, for that matter, but I grabbed the edge of the roof and swung myself up without complaint, anyway; what other option did I have? The driver grated the gears when I was still only halfway up and tore off down the road in a cloud of dust.

The roof top was like a griddle. I spread my garments out as well as I could to keep my skin from blistering on the hot metal, but that let the Sun beat onto my exposed skin. Between the Sun and the dust from the road, it was torment; I didn't know if I could take it for more than a couple of hours.

But I did. I hid up there hungry, thirsty, dirty, and tired through two dust storms and eight drivers until we eventually reached Port Harcourt. Altogether, it had taken four days hard journey from Ilesha. Following me would have been an enormous undertaking for my kinsmen. So at least I felt physically safe when we finally arrived at the absolute end of the line. What I could *not* feel, of course, was financially secure. So my first priority was to find a way to get some money in this strange and very unpleasant town.

I decided to get a job as an accountant. After all, I'd had good training at Normal College and the main business of Port Harcourt is shipping, an industry which requires lots of accountants, auditors, and so forth. So a job in accounting seemed a logical and potentially rewarding choice. But there were a couple of impediments.

First, although I really was quite skilled, I had no way to prove it: My diploma from Normal College was still back in Inesi-Ile. It wouldn't have been very smart to write and ask them to send it on to me. Besides, I told myself petulantly, Grandfather had probably found it and given it to Joshua by this time anyway.

Then there was the problem of my appearance: I didn't exactly look the part of a successful accountant. I'd slept outdoors for want of enough money to rent a room and my clothes looked about the way one would expect. And somebody had stolen my shoes while I slept.

I tried to wash in the public fountain but a policeman chased me away. If he hadn't been so muscle-bound, he might have caught me. But I gave him the slip and then went back and got the newspaper I'd used for a blanket the previous night. I figured out where all the offices were that had advertised for an accountant and then confidently set out.

The first place had a buzzer on their door; they looked me over through the window and refused to open up for me.

The second place was run by a huge Ibo man who chased me down the stairs when I admitted I was Yoruba.

The third place wouldn't let me in, either. In fact, when I kept insisting through the closed door that they give me a fair chance to interview for their job, they called the police on me. Then I wasted time trying to apologize until the policeman showed up—the same Hercules who'd chased me away from the fountain that morning. I had the pleasure of my second race of the day, barefoot and on an empty stomach. All in all, my first morning in Port Harcourt had not been a good one.

After a couple days of the same treatment, I was reduced to begging. But even that didn't work—there was too much competition. Some professional beggars beat me up and warned me to stay out of their territory. I had nothing left by then but my Bible and I was beginning to get too weak from hunger to read it. I could have asked help from the nearby Christian church, of course, but that was something I avoided as long as possible; the church in Africa has burdens enough without adding my hunger to the list. But in the end, hunger overcame my scruples and I went around there, begging a handout.

The pastor, Reverend Mervyn, was a gaunt and distracted young man, laboring under the guilt of not having saved all of Africa single-handedly. He had given away everything he had until his own appearance was not much better than mine. He invited me in.

He turned out not to be a real missionary, after all; he was only serving two years in Africa before going back home to a place with the beautiful name of "Forest Hills." Just hearing it spoken made me homesick. There was little he could do for me because he'd stretched the meager funds of his little church past the breaking point already. And he'd tried to stretch his personal energy the same way. The more I studied him, the more it seemed good to me that Pastor Mervyn's "hitch" was almost up: He was tormented by our endemic poverty. He'd come to us, as so many young missionaries do, full of plans to feed every hungry belly in Africa. Some Westerners learn to live with the realization that it can't be done; some, like the Reverend Mr. Mervyn, never do, and if that kind stays too long, Africa consumes them.

He scrounged us some stale bread and a few *kobo* for me, anyway. I had the feeling that they were to have been for his own supper that night and I felt very guilty about taking them.

But I took them anyway.

He listened to my story while I chewed the hard bread; to this day, I think the listening may have been more important than the bread. He suggested that I go to the hiring halls down at the docks because many members of his congregation had found work there.

I hadn't considered that before because of a problem that I share with other contemporary Nigerians: Since oil has brought so much easy wealth and corruption, no one wants to labor anymore. Everybody wants to be an entrepreneur, an agent, a middleman, or a go-between. Anything but a *laborer*. Many of us would rather stand in the hot Sun all day to sell one *kobo's* worth of matches than swing a pick or lift a shovel, because that would be "dirty" work. The work at the hiring halls was for porters, cleaners, stevedores, and so forth. Not accountants.

But the luxury of looking for a professional job was one I could no longer afford. So I joined the flood of men who converged on the waterfront sheds each morning, just before dawn. Each shed contracted a certain type of work and men who wanted that type would go there to apply. We had to show up in person every morning because the jobs were awarded only for one day at a time. "The hiring master" sat up in the front of the room on a high stool behind a big desk and called out numbers apparently chosen at random from a jug by his side. If the number he called matched the number a man received as he entered the shed, that man got a day's work.

I went to the shed for common laborers, declaring myself to be available for any type of work. But my number didn't get called the first day, nor the second, nor the third. By the end of the week, the few bronzes Mr. Mervyn had given me were gone, spent on food of the very meanest sort just to keep myself alive, and I was on the edge of despair again.

I went back to the church but found that Mr. Mervyn had been recalled in disgrace to his beautiful Forest Hills. He had bankrupted the little mission church through his excesses of charity. His fate back home was uncertain because his failure had done little to endear him to his American parishioners. They had agreed to foot the bill for his mission and had expected a going concern for their money rather than a soup kitchen. As for the church building itself, some men were boarding it up when I went by to beg another handout. They said there were no plans to reopen it.

It was then that I hit bottom. I just sat down in the street outside the little church and wept. I was unmindful of my safety, and oblivious to the calls of "Get out of the road, fool!" I was broke and alone, a stranger in a strange land. I had no one to lay claim to the title of "friend," no one to acknowledge me as family, no people to accept me as one of their own. I had nowhere to stay, nothing to eat, and no hope for the future. Even the comfort of the little mission church had been denied me. It was the low point of my life. I just rocked back and forth on my heels, hugging my Bible close to my chest and asked quietly, "My God, my God, why hast thou forsaken me?"

The next morning, I walked down to the hiring halls, more out of habit than for any other reason. They gave me my number when I went in, like always. I dragged myself up to the hiring master to plead, like always. He called out the first batch of numbers and mine was not among them, like always.

I almost didn't even care. I turned back to sit down and spend the day staring passively into space along with the other hopeless men. I bumped into someone and dropped my Bible to the floor. When I picked it up and brushed it off, the thin coat of reddish dust it picked up from the floor went all over my hand, so I rubbed the back of my left hand with the palm of my right, making a clockwise circle as I did.

I looked up and saw the hiring master watching me intently. He stared at me for a second, as if making a silent judgment of some sort. Then he popped his eyes to the left, then back, then up, then back. He did it three times, rapidly. It could have been a facial tic.

But I knew it wasn't.

The hiring master looked around the shed quickly, as if to see if anyone was watching us. Then he yelled at me, "Hey, you. Country boy. Come here!" I approached his desk warily. "Give me your ticket!" he barked and I handed it over.

"So! Here's my 'missing man,' " he said, loud enough for everyone to hear. "Why didn't you come up when I called your number, fool? You tryin' to throw my reports out of balance?"

"N-no, sir," I said.

"Well, be sure it doesn't happen again. Now go out back and report to Mr. Luganna; he'll give you your day's assignment." He turned back to the papers on his desk, apparently having lost all interest in me.

"Oh, and one more thing," he said as an afterthought. He took another quick glance around the room. When he spoke again, his voice was as soft as the forest nights around home. "Don't line up with those sheep anymore. Come up with the other goats no matter *what* number I call. Got it, Country boy?" He winked and went back to his paperwork.

I stood in shock for a moment. This was my first insight that juju is more than just the old-fashioned, out-of-date, rural superstition that good people like Pastor Osborn think it is, but is alive and thriving in our modern cities. In fact, it exists even among literate people in positions of power and influence.

I wasn't sure what to do. On the one hand, a day's work meant food, shelter, money. All I had to do was pretend to be a jujuman. In fact, I didn't even have to pretend; all I had to do was keep my big mouth shut.

On the other hand, that was the same as denying my Christianity. Wasn't it?

Maybe I had become even more deeply religious than I'd realized. Or maybe I was delirious from hunger. In any event, I walked up to the hiring master's desk and cleared my throat. He looked down at me.

"Honorable sir," I said courteously, "I am grateful to be chosen for work. But I have no wish to deceive you."

"Deceive me? How do you mean?"

I thought about the food. About the chance for a warm room and some clean clothes. I thought about all these, and then I blurted out, "I am a Christian."

He just looked at me for a while, unmoving, as if he expected me to say something else. "Yes, and . . . ?" he prompted.

"That's all, Honorable sir. I cannot accept work under false pretenses. I am a Christian."

He blinked a few times, then started to shake as if he were trying to hold in a laugh. After half a minute or so, he wiped his eyes with a rag. "So am I, boy," he said in a shaking voice. "So am I. And so are most of us. Except for those who are Moslems, of course. We have to be *something,* don't we? Why, I'm in church every Sunday without fail. Right down front, too!"

"But, sir, you called me a 'goat,' a jujuman, and I am now a . . ."

He dropped his amused look. "Shhhh!" he hissed. "Listen, Country boy, if you don't want to work, that's fine with me, but don't waste my time with nonsense about religion. Anybody who's ever been a jujuman is one of us, no matter what he pretends for the bosses and the whites. Now, if you're too lazy to work, I can always give the number to somebody else."

"Oh, no, Honorable sir! I'm happy for the chance to work."

"Then get out back like I told you and stop wasting my time." He shook his head and muttered to himself, " 'You can take the boy out of the country, but you can't take the country out of the boy,' " and sort of chuckled quietly once more. Then he started moving his papers around again as if I no longer existed.

So I walked out back in a kind of stunned condition and reported for my first day's work. The job I got may not have been much by some people's standards (scrubbing out the hold of a big cattle barge), but I thanked God for it. I worked so hard that some of the other fellows took me aside at the midday break and told me to take it easy so I wouldn't make them all look bad.

I ate like an *oba* that night: *three* bowls of rice cooked in coconut milk and laced with juicy hunks of antelope meat. I was too worn out to go all the way into the "native quarter" of town so I took a room in what passed for a hotel just off the business district. Being in the "international" part of town, it was segregated, and the room that I got was only marginally better than sleeping in the bush. But at least it was dry, and with the rainy season just around the corner, that was a blessing indeed.

The hiring master, who I found out was Mr. Mamuyo, seemed to remember me with fondness after that first exchange, though whether for my honesty or for my naivete, I never learned. When he found one day that I could read, write, do sums, and balance books, he took me off the boats and gave me a try as his clerk. After a few days, he made the position permanent, and at a handsome salary, too.

A few months later, I rented a small two-room house for myself on the outskirts of the town. It was one of a series of little houses all owned by the same landlord, a short Moslem man. He acted as if he were renting me a Fifth Avenue penthouse, the way he questioned me. But that was good; I wanted peace and quiet from my neighbors and this landlord seemed the kind of fellow who could provide it.

The long walk from the house plus the long hours spent clerking for Mr. Mamuyo kept my days very full. What time I had left I spent at the mission church in the neighborhood where I was living. I began to teach Sunday school and enjoyed it very much. I organized a social group, set up the men's club, and started a youth choir. It was the kind of socially conscious leadership I'd been trained for by Grandfather and I turned out to be pretty good at it. So much so that the pastor recommended me to his bishop. A new "daughter" church was being planned for the future and the bishop was kind enough to consider me to be its lay-pastor. My life was beginning to fill up.

Mr. Mamuyo was so pleased with my progress after a year that he introduced me to his daughter, an attractive and pleasant girl of marriageable age. I did not have time to court her but my pastor agreed to act *in loco parentis* on my behalf in arranging a marriage with Mr. Mamuyo. The pastor and the jujuman began to meet on a regular basis to hammer out the details of bride price and so forth. They seemed to like and respect each other and would linger over their palm wine and kola nuts far longer than was necessary. The two men were the closest I had to family now, so the fact that they enjoyed each other was a source of delight for me.

I'd been in Port Harcourt for nearly two years and everything was going beautifully. I don't remember ever being happier. Best of all, my conscience was clear: Mr. Mamuyo never raised the issue of juju again. As time went on, I all but forgot that such a grotesque thing as juju even existed.

Until the morning that I found a monkey's left paw tied to the doorknob of my little house.

29

The Honorable Mamuyo was visibly shaken at my news that someone was trying to curse me. We sat and reviewed my life since coming to Port Harcourt, but we could think of no enemy I'd made who would want to take such an action against me. Finally, he leaned back and shook his head. "I do not understand," he said. "You say juju has been worked against you. And yet, it is no juju that I know."

I sipped the palm wine of his hospitality. "We call it 'monkey hand.' It has long been used by my clan; how popular it is with others, I don't know. It's an *epe* that is supposed to produce death gradually and after much suffering."

"How do you mean?"

"Well, the victim's brain is supposed to deteriorate. His hands start to shake and his memory fades. His understanding fails and he may even begin to act like a child. All this goes on for a long time, getting worse and worse, until the victim finally dies."

"Hmmmm. It is powerful, this *epe*."

"So it is said. But it has always claimed its greatest success against older people. That's the way juju works—it takes credit for something that would have happened anyway." I remembered how angry I was at Janet's immunity to this same *epe* when I used it on her. Looking back, I realized that no really clever jujuman would have tried that particular curse in her case. It would have produced a result only if she was a true believer: Then she would have started to hobble around, shaking like an octagenarian. Or, if she had been an elderly person, those same symptoms might have eventually manifested whether she believed in juju or not. But in either of those cases where the outcome was what he'd wanted, the astute jujuman would claim credit loudly. His credibility would be enhanced in the eyes of all potential victims. And that would put more people into the "true believer" category, improving the probability of his success with future curses.

But the Honorable Mamuyo was having none of my explanation. He made a hex sign that showed he disclaimed my words. "You say that this *epe* is a powerful one, Isaiah, and popular with your clan. But around here. . . ." he shrugged. "So it must be that your enemy is someone from your past rather than your present."

I nodded. His words made sense: My enemies had found me at last. And a lump of dread began to grow in my stomach from that moment. It wasn't the juju that threatened me. Rather, it was the thought of a hatred so implacable that it could drive my kinsmen for years across half of Nigeria just to seek me out for vengeance.

But the Honorable Mamuyo, a typical jujuman, was more concerned with the *epe* itself than with its implications. "How is it that I, who have travelled much in my life, have never heard of such a ritual?" he asked.

"Have you been west?"

"Yes, of course." The Honorable Mamuyo took great pride in the exploits he had performed when he was younger, including serving in World War II. He puffed up a bit now. "I have been to Lagos itself, and even beyond."

"Well, I've studied in Lagos and my people are from near there, though a bit farther north. A little place, just the estate of my grandfather, really. Inesi-Ile: You probably never heard of it. . . ."

He froze, a nut halfway to his mouth. "Are you . . . are you part of *that* clan Oke?"

"Why, yes," I told him. "My grandfather is Aworo Oke."

He dropped the nut from fingers that suddenly began to shake like river reeds when the winds of the rainy season blow. His mouth fell slackly open. He thrust his hands toward me and began to sign for the various *orisha* to protect him: "*Shango*, protect me. *Oduduwa*, protect me. *Osanin*, protect . . ." I reached out and took his hands to stop him.

"Honorable sir, please do not fear me. I would never harm you. You know I am a Christian; I no longer work juju. Besides, you are my benefactor and I have come to look on you as my father. Why would I harm you?"

"*You?*" he shouted. "Who fears *you?* It is your clan I fear! Your grandfather is," he gulped audibly, "a *babalorisha!* Think what mischief his juju can do here!"

"None!" I said. "Surely you cannot believe in this nonsense!"

But his face made it clear that he did.

"You have said," I reminded him, "that you consider yourself also a Christian. Is this any way for a Christian to behave? Even when I studied under Drago, I never—"

He seemed suddenly unable to get his breath. "Did . . . did you say, 'Drago'?" he gasped.

"Yes, Doctor Drago of Lagos. Grandfather sent me to him some years ago."

The Honorable Mamuyo was managing to back away from me, even though he'd not gotten to his feet: He was kind of walking on the cheeks of his buttocks. He stopped only when he bumped against the wall. Instead of juju hex signs, he was now repeatedly making the sign of the cross at me, something he must have picked up from watching the Roman Catholics at their worship. At the same time, he was muttering, "In the name of Allah, the compassionate and the merciful," something the Moslems were always saying. Our African penchant for syncretism seemed to have reached new heights in him; he was taking no chances on ignoring any of the religions that were popular among us. I'd never seen a man so afraid.

"You . . . you nerer told me all this, Isaiah! I mean, Honorable Oke!"

"But it is all nonsense! I never even thought it worth mentioning." That wasn't strictly true, but my suppression of my past *was* more out of shame than any other reason. "There is no cause to fear juju," I said. "It is only silly superstition."

He had flattened himself against the wall like a leech. "Please, Honorable Oke," he burbled, "please, I did not know of your power; how could I know? I do not want to be in the middle of a battle for power between *babalawos*. Please, please: Take your juju feud elsewhere, I beg of you!"

I was becoming impatient with him. "I am no longer a *babalawo*. Besides, the whole thing is nonsense: I'm not involved in any 'juju feud.' And there is no 'power' to battle over!"

"No, no, of course not, just as you say, Honorable Oke." He was on his knees now, back against the wall, shaking and weeping. It was pointless to continue. I bowed respectfully, as one should to his future father-in-law, and let myself out.

There was blood smeared on the left post of my porch when I got home. Inside, the head of a small dog was on my sleeping mat and the air was full of the wretched smell of burned camphor bean plant. This juju, of course, was trivial and laughable; I could have just ignored it and gotten a good night's sleep anyway. But the fact that someone had been in my house left me feeling the way I imagine a woman would who has been pulled into the bush by an *egungun* and forced to have sex against her will.

The next day, Mr. Mamuyo failed to show up for the first time since I'd come to work for him. I tried to take over his duties as hiring master temporarily, but I was far less efficient at handing out the assignments than he was and the men grumbled at my slowness.

That afternoon, a strange man came and sat on one of the benches in the back of the shed. He spoke to no one, apparently content to wait around for quitting time. There was nothing distinctive about him: sunglasses, khaki shorts, a yellow tee-shirt, and a New York Yankees baseball cap. Except for his dreamy, almost beatific smile, he looked like any other unemployed local man looking for work. But from the way the other men moved aside to make room for him, it was obvious that he was important, though exactly why wasn't clear until his shirt rode up a little, exposing the pistol tucked into the waistband of his shorts. The fear on the part of the other men, the gun, and the unwavering smile meant that he was probably a member of the Ogboni "Fraternity." And there was no way that could mean good news for me.

The Ogbonis are our most politically powerful cult. They started out as another of our homegrown religions, a mixture of Christianity, Islam, and juju. But where the Ogbonis differed from all the rest was in their political astuteness. They invited practitioners of all other religions to join them on a non-exclusive basis. Because they seemed to welcome everybody equally, they developed a reputation for being diplomats, negotiators, "fixers." Soon, it became important for even *obas* to join this "fraternity" of like-minded men. The local Ogboni "House" became the political nerve center—the "Tammany Hall"—of every sizable town in Central Africa.

It was inevitable that the political power of the Ogbonis would extend to activities of an even more lucrative sort. Today all our officials can tell you proudly and honestly that we have no such thing as "organized crime" in Central Africa. We do, however, have what we refer to as Ogboni "Business." It includes all the usual: prostitution, drugs, big-time gambling. Of course, the Fraternity controls the unions that operate the hiring halls on the waterfront, as well; in effect, the unknown guy sitting quietly in back was my boss.

Finally, the last man gave up any hopes of getting work that day and shuffled out of the hall to fend for himself as best he could on the street. I pretended to busy myself with my paperwork. The Ogboni man walked casually to the front, hands in pockets. He stood by the side of the desk, humming almost inaudibly. When I felt I could no longer safely ignore him, I looked down. "Yes?"

He pulled off his cap and twisted it in front of his stomach, the way a nervous man and humble of the town might do. "I beg leave to speak with you, Brother Goat."

"You are Ogboni?" I asked him.

"Yes, Brother Goat, I have that honor. The Fraternity has sent me to discuss a matter with you." He smiled ingratiatingly, then hastened to add, "with your permission, of course!"

I pushed my work aside. "I am always pleased to have the council of the Fraternity."

He twisted his cap some more and then said, "Well, Brother Goat, to get to the heart of the matter . . . it is said that someone has something against you. It is said that there may be a juju feud."

"There will be no feud," I said with dignity. "I no longer take blood. I am no longer juju. I am Christian and only Christian. But I admit that some jujuman seems to have something against me."

"Ah! But you will not fight back? You will not turn your enemy's *epes* back on him?"

"I will not. Now, let me guess: For a fee, you will find this *babalawo* and 'reason' with him. Is that your pitch?"

He looked shocked, as if the idea had never occurred to him. "Why, you know, perhaps we could at that; perhaps we could. I would be most interested in discussing whether we could help you in that way, Brother Goat. But first, we must dispose of the matter that brings me here."

It was my turn to be surprised. "That is *not* why you wanted to talk to me?"

"No, Brother Goat, the matter involves a brother of ours who is deeply grieved. He is too embarrassed to face you; he fears your wrath. He fears trouble. And the Fraternity's first duty is to preserve peace among the brothers, is it not?"

"Whether that's so or not is not the point," I said testily. "I am not a member of your Fraternity. I am not one of your 'brothers.' "

He gave me the kind of peaceful, dreamy smile one sees only on those who know they are in control. "All men are brothers, Brother Goat. So I have offered to act on behalf of both of you. The Fraternity's only wish is to see everybody happy."

"And I can help this 'brother' be happy?" I asked.

"Ah, yes. You see, according to our brother, your work here has been exemplary, above reproach, perfect in every way." His smile broadened as he recited my virtues until he was positively beaming. He paused and his face fell, as if with regret. "That's why it's all the more difficult for him to let you go. He hopes you will understand."

I blinked. "You mean . . . I'm fired?"

He only twisted his cap harder and stared at the floor, mangling it with shame and regret.

I slammed my account book shut. "This is ridiculous," I said. "I cannot believe it. The Honorable Mamuyo would never be afraid to face me himself. Besides, how can he fire the man who is to wed his daughter?"

He wrenched his cap so hard the little button on top flew off. "Ah, well, as to that, Brother Goat . . . a man without a job, with no prospects, really ought to reconsider getting married, wouldn't you agree?"

I felt myself getting angry, but there was nothing I could do against the well-acted humility of an Ogboni. "Very well," I said, "you may tell your Fraternity that there will be no trouble; Oke is leaving."

I grabbed up my few personal effects and strode out, leaving him, his gun, and his smile in sole possession of the hiring shed; what happened to it was no longer my responsibility.

I arrived home to find my landlord on the porch.

"Out," he said. "Take your filthy juju and get away from my house. I won't have people like you living here."

"Wait," I said, "you don't understand—"

"I don't understand?" he shouted. "I don't understand that juju is the scourge of Africa? I don't understand that you people with your blood lusts and your drugs and your cruelty to animals and children keep us all in the dark ages? I don't understand that you jujumen would spread disease and killing around the world if you weren't penned up here?"

"But I—"

"No more talk!" he screeched. "You pretend to be a good Christian man, so I figure, 'Why not? Why not take a chance on him; he seems a nice fellow, even if he is a Christian.' Then, this!" He pointed to the blood on the porch post. "And this!" He toed the dog's head with disgust. "And this!" He tore down a cloth banner that hadn't been there that morning. It was covered with hex signs and excrement and blood.

I didn't know what to say. Neighbors all up and down the block were leaning out their front doors. They were all listening to him lambaste me, and several of them were throwing hex signs my way, as if to ward off the evil I might bring by being around. Even though I'd not done anything, I felt intensely ashamed. I just hung my head and nodded mutely.

"Here." He shoved a big sack at me. "Your clothes and belongings."

"My books," I said, "what about—"

"I'll send them on. Just get yourself and your poxy juju feud off my property. And don't ever come back. I'm not afraid of your mumbo-jumbo magic tricks, so you'll answer to me if you ever come back and molest any of the good people hereabouts."

I shouldered the pack and trudged off. My neighbors, who had asked me only the week before to run for the town council, watched me leave with a mixture of hatred and fear. It was impossible to tell which emotion dominated. To the landlord, they were all good Moslems: believers in one, true God and enemies of demonic possession and witchcraft. But they all signed juju curses at me as I went by.

I saw no reason to look back.

30

I spent that night in a pew of the mission church, even though I could have paid for lodging. But the hotel said they were "full up," in spite of the dozen keys dangling in plain sight from the board behind the desk. I also went to the houses of friends I thought I had made among the church congregation, looking for a place to stay. But no one was at home, at least not to me. Even though it made me feel paranoid, I couldn't shake the feeling that word had spread about me: "Have nothing to do with Oke. He's a *babalawo* involved in a juju war."

The feeling was reinforced the next morning when I started looking for a new job. Even though I was known around town as an excellent employee, none of my·contacts seemed to be hiring. In fact, one man who had tried to hire me away from Mamuyo only a few weeks earlier refused to see me when I called at his office.

It didn't take long to figure it out: These city people still believed strongly in juju. No matter how modern they wanted to appear, no matter how devoutly they claimed to embrace other religions, they were as much enslaved by fear of juju as the simple villagers back home had always been.

I stayed about another week in Port Harcourt, trying to put my life back together. But it was no good. My friends from church all found things they had to do and couldn't talk to me. The Honorable Mamuyo and his daughter were nowhere to be found. Even my pastor and his bishop were uncomfortable in my presence; the day after I asked them for help, there was a new lock on the church door. And they both refused to see me after that. I wondered if maybe there wasn't some basis in fact for what I had always before regarded as only a vicious slander: That in order to rise to the top in the Church Mission Society (which is the dominant Western church in Central Africa), one must be a secret jujuman.

Only one person spoke to me for more than a few seconds and he was a man I barely knew. He hunted me up, told me he'd heard of my plight, and asked after my health and well-being as a friend would do. He sympathized with me and offered to help me in any way he could. I was so happy I almost hugged him.

Then he asked me to work some juju for him—to curse his wife, who had become burdensome, so that she would die and leave her money to him. When I declined, he turned his back and walked away from me forever. The episode showed me that I probably could have made a rich living there as a *babalawo*. Selling potions, hexes, and charms from dark doorways. Taking money from guilty looking patrons to curse their friends for them in secret. Letting blood at forbidden rituals in cellars while a few *naira* convinced the police to look the other way. Working black magic from the shadows, just as jujumen do in other cities of the modern world.

I finally gave up and left town for good, disillusioned and feeling the need to "shake the dust of that place from my feet." Unlike the last time I had to run from juju, I had some money this time, so I was able to ride *inside* the bus.

But, just for the record, the inside of a cross-country Central African bus isn't a whole lot more comfortable than the outside. The ruts and potholes we kept hitting were like my tormentors: They made my life miserable even though I never saw them. Typical of all jujumen, my unknown assailants had done their work from the shadows and under cover of darkness. The only consolation I had was the knowledge that they must be tearing their hair out: None of their juju had worked on me. At least, not the way they planned.

I went up to Enugu, a good-sized place just south of our foothills. No one there knew me and I had a pouch full of *naira* notes, so I easily secured good lodging at the little hotel. It took me a couple of weeks, but I finally ran down a decent job with one of the international companies that exports the excellent tea and coffee grown in the highlands. I joined the local church and resolved to melt myself into the local scene so thoroughly that my juju enemies would never find me. I even assumed a new name: Nnaia Ojike, the given name of my old pal Speedy.

As time went on and I remained safe, my confidence grew. All I wanted was to live peacefully, free of juju's bloody interference in my life. And this time, I felt I could rest easy; I had gotten away clean. Besides, why would my tormentors want to pursue me? Hadn't they lost me my job? My friends? My fiancee? My whole contented life in Port Harcourt? I mean, even though their juju couldn't work on me the way they wanted it to, still, hadn't they done enough to satisfy their need for vengeance? Hadn't they?

Of course they had.

I went about the business of making a new life again. I became so busy and so confident that I almost forgot my unknown juju enemies. Until the morning a couple of months later that I woke up to find blood and tadpoles in the water pitcher in my room.

I flung open the door to the hall just in time to see a figure move out of sight into the darkness around the corner. Stark naked, I ran out into the second floor hallway of the International Hotel and gave chase. I rounded the corner fast and flung myself wildly in the direction of the figure. I may have yelled something like "Aha!" or "Oho!" But then again, I may simply have jumped in sinister silence.

In any event, the person I jumped onto turned out to be this little old gray-haired white lady from Boston. She screamed, fainted, and hit the floor with a loud thump. I'd only met her once before, in the lobby, when she told me she was in Enugu to help set up the new municipal library. So I figured right away that she would be justified in treating the present encounter as a diabolical liberty.

Feet started pounding up the stairs immediately so I decided that going for help was unnecessary. Instead, I knelt down by the poor lady's side, patting her hand to see if I could bring her around. She seemed to be breathing poorly, so I started to undo her blouse.

That, of course, was the exact moment when her traveling companion popped her head up over the top of the stairs. She was an equally gray librarian lady who also screamed and went over backward. She did not hit the ground, however, because her son was right behind her to catch her. He had told me when we met that he was something called a "middle linebacker" at Boston College. I had no idea what that was, but it clearly called for a great deal of size and strength. A certain quickness to anger also seemed an asset to that activity, judging by the look that came over his face.

I immediately sized up the situation. Seeing that an explanation might prove difficult, I dropped the old lady and ran into my room. I locked the door and barricaded it with a chest of drawers. Even so, I began to doubt it would stand long against the barrage of blows the son started laying on it. I tried to explain to him through the door how innocent it had all been, but I made a poor job of it. Under the circumstances, what could one expect? I just rambled on about juju and the "hit squad" that was after me and so forth.

Fortunately, someone came—the manager, I guess—and calmed him down. I couldn't hear everything that was said but I made out the words "juju" and "witch doctor" over and over again. After a while, the hall became quiet. I wondered briefly whether even college-educated white people from America could be scared by the possibility of juju black magic. Though it seemed more logical that the manager had simply been able to talk some sense into him. But in my heart, I still felt that he had been given the shameful message: "Have nothing to do with Oke; he is a *babalawo* involved in a juju feud." It was the whispered message that would ensure I stayed lonely and feared and hated as long as I lived.

I got dressed and packed my bag. But I waited until it was daylight before I dared move the chest of drawers. I opened the door just a crack, fully prepared to slam it at the first hint of any "middle linebacking," but all was quiet.

I hurried down to the desk, but the clerk hid behind the counter when he saw me. He refused to come out, even though I told him I simply wanted to pay my bill. I insisted loudly that I was no jujuman, that he should not fear me and hate me just because of vicious rumors. But the more I protested, the more he cringed back there. I finally counted out an amount that I guessed was about right and left it on the counter.

As I crossed the street, I looked back and saw the woman's son behind the curtains of their room. He no longer looked fierce and angry. In fact, he looked relieved, as if he was glad to be seeing the back of me. It was the same kind of look I'd gotten from my neighbors back in Port Harcourt.

*   *   *

This time, I took a train, hoping that train engineers talk to nosey strangers less than bus drivers apparently do. I took the first train north, into alien territory. Oh, it was still Nigeria, all right. But it was alien to me nonetheless.

The north of our country is as different from the south as it is from another country. For one thing, we in the south are a river and forest people; our terrain compares with that of America's Gulf Coast, especially around Louisiana. The north is much higher in elevation and receives only about a tenth our rainfall. It is, in fact, the border of the great Sahara Desert.

But there are more fundamental differences—the northern people are almost unanimously Moslems. They speak Arabic more readily than they speak our indigenous languages and their customs are similar to those of the Mediterranean peoples. Had the British not decided we were one country, we would happily be two.

The train stopped first at Kaduna, but only for a few hours. Then it went on to Kano, the end of the line in more ways than one. It is as far north as one can get and still say one is in Nigeria, and it is a dreadful place. I did not even leave the train station, wretched though it was. There was really no reason to: I was only running to confuse my tormentors, to "put mud across my trail," as we say back home. I stayed in the squalid, ramshackle station, sleeping on the filthy floor for two days until I could get a train going back south.

Finally, six long, miserable days after I left the International Hotel, I arrived back in Lagos. I knew it was uncomfortably close to home. But it was the only place in Africa anonymous enough for a man to lose himself, especially in the very heart of the city.

I knew I had to lay low, not only to prevent my identity being discovered, but also to avoid being accidentally spotted by any of Drago's people. That was the only part of building a new life that wouldn't present much of a challenge: How hard could it be to stay out of the way of a purple Rolls Royce? So, on the whole, I thought my decision to hide out in Lagos and make a new life there was a good one; Lagos was so crowded and so mobile that there was no way for my juju enemies to get to me, even if they knew I was there.

A week later, as I was walking to my new job at the big asbestos factory, I nearly tripped over two crossed *iki* wood branches somebody had laid in my path. Where the two joined together, a broken pop bottle filled with smelly juju-water had been set out. It startled me momentarily, but that was all. I kicked the assemblage apart, and the bottle bounced into the road, throwing its vile contents everywhere. I got through the day at the factory by telling myself that the juju had been laid for somebody else. That my juju tormentors had no idea where I was. That I was safe. And that juju was silly and harmless, anyway.

I had to stop telling myself all that, though, when I got back to the hotel that night. The dead dog just inside the door to my room had a rusty iron pipe shoved all the way through it—in at the anus and out from the mouth.

The ritual must have been done right there in the hotel room because the dog was laying in an pool of blood and other fluids, boxed in by black candles set at each point of the compass. There were scorches on the body, presumably from the same black candles. It must have been horribly painful for the poor beast. It must have been noisy, too, even though a blood-stained strap in the corner showed that they'd gagged the dog in an attempt to keep it quiet. And, yet, no one seemed to have complained.

Were all the other occupants of this big, international hotel jujumen? Or were they simply good people—Americans and Europeans on business—who just "didn't want to get involved"? Who found it easier to ignore those "strange noises" from down the hall? Who said, "It's none of *my* business what people do behind their own doors"? Juju depends on that kind of apathy; as it has truly been said, "All that is necessary for evil men to triumph is for good men to do nothing." And good people today find it more convenient to believe that juju does not exist than to confront it.

That was not so for me, of course. I was aching to confront my tormentors; it was just that I had no idea who or where they were. They had found me in three different cities now, these "hit men." Very well, there must be an underground network of some sort. And they'd obtained access to my hotel rooms, so they must have ways of coercing people, even Westernized people like the desk clerks in major hotels. They used juju that was favored by my clan, so they had to be kinsmen of mine from Inesi-Ile. And, of course, they worked in secret, out of shadows. Just like all jujumen.

Beyond that, I knew nothing. It wasn't much to go on. But it told me one thing: They had come and gone from the private parts of my life at will and there was no reason they should not do so again. They would follow me forever, to whatever place I tried to build a life for myself, and would ruin it. So I decided I had to figure a way at all costs to confront them and end their harassment of me. I decided I was through running from juju.

The next day, I went down to the factory as usual. But instead of going in the double doors marked "Laborers Only," I ducked into a nearby alleyway and returned to the hotel as surreptitiously as I could. It was a good thing my savings were still ample, because I missed a lot of work: I had to repeat my routine for about ten days before I finally caught my enemies in the act.

Resolution

31

Even from out in the hall, I could tell that someone was in my room. There were faint scuffling sounds from inside, and a smell like burning leaves hung in the air. I slipped my key in the lock and turned it so slowly that even I couldn't hear it. Then, with all my strength, I flung the door open.

One of the men was someone I'd never seen before. Before I could react, he bolted out the door, an obviously frightened hireling. The other man, the one in charge, was startled but not frightened. He looked up from the live rat he was tying, squeeking and spread-eagled, to the floor at the foot of the bed. It took me a moment to recognize him.

"Joshua!" I said.

The two years since I'd last seen him had not been kind. He was much leaner, and the loss of weight on his formerly muscular frame made him look gaunt. His cheeks were hollow and his eyes were shiny and fevered, like those of a bird. Not a fierce proud bird of prey, but perhaps an injured buzzard. The hot rage that had filled me so quickly out in the hallway disappeared, to be replaced by an almost tearful pity: One cannot remain angry with a man who has the "slim" disease.

He stood, and the smoke from the dishes of herbs he was burning swirled around him like a fog. The look of him reminded me of the last time I'd seen our grandfather, the same slack expression, the same exhaustion. And, when he spoke, the same flat tones.

"So," he said. "At last you know who is responsible for all your woes, son-of-my-father's-brother."

"Yes. And I'll make sure the authorities know, too. I'll make sure they see you red-handed." I didn't want him to make a break for it, as the first man had done, so I slipped the key into the lock, twisted it, and pulled up on it, breaking it off. "Now," I said, "you can't run."

He straightened his back, as prideful as though he'd won some great victory over a powerful foe. "I have no wish to run; I am not ashamed. For I am he who is responsible for all the evils that have come upon you. For your illnesses, for the flesh that rots off your body, for the worms that consume you from the inside out."

" 'Worms'? I have no 'worms,' Joshua; never felt better, in fact." I taunted him, patting my stomach in a self-satisfied way. "Your juju can no longer harm me, Joshua."

"Yes, yes, yes!" he cried. "Juju is deadly! Juju kills!" He insisted the way a child does, as if saying something loud enough, long enough, or often enough could make it true. "Terrible things have happened to you. I know!"

"Yes, Joshua. But there was no magic to any of it."

"No? You have no family. You have no friends." His confidence began to return. "Whose doing was it, if not mine? Tell me you do not fear the power of my juju."

"I've thought about that, Joshua. And you know what? If my friends ran and left me at the first sign of trouble from somebody like you, maybe they weren't worth much to begin with." His face clouded over again. " 'Fear' your juju, Joshua? Maybe I really ought to be grateful to you instead." And I experienced the immense pleasure of laughing at him.

He moved toward me and actually stumbled a bit under the weight of all the juju he was wearing: a heavy necklace of old iron doodads that hung almost to his ankles, stacks of iron bracelets all the way up both arms, an iron chest plate that seemed to be the floor pan from some old car or truck.

He looked ridiculous and I laughed at him again. Yet, there was a time when I couldn't have laughed, a time when I would have been frightened into a cringing silence. All the iron paraphernalia meant he was preparing for the "iron ritual," in which iron, the hardest material known to our ancestors, is endowed with the essence of *Ogun* himself. The iron that a jujuman wears when he performs the ritual is supposed to act like an accumulator of supernatural energy, which then is focused into one very special iron artifact: his *ida-agbara,* or "sword of power."

Every juju family has one. Usually, it's just an old knife that some ancestor long ago decided was sacred to *Ogun,* probably because its edge was especially sharp or because it was used to kill the family's meat animals.

Or maybe just because he liked it.

But, sometimes, as was the case with the clan Oke, the *ida-igbara* was something much grander. Ours was said to have been the personal property of His Excellency Gilbert Thomas Carter, Esq., Governor of the Colony of Lagos. The grandfather of my grandfather is said to have stolen it during a treaty signing ceremony in Abeokuta in 1893. It would be more glamorous, of course, if I could say that he won it in battle. But like most Central Africans, the Okes have always been farmers rather than warriors. Still, stealing the Governor's sword took its own portion of courage during the often harsh days of British rule.

And it was clear why my ancestor wanted the sword badly enough to risk stealing it from the British Governor: Long and thin, with a gracefully flared guard around its handle, it must have been a truly beautiful thing in those days. Of course, that was back when it was polished and oiled daily until the countless layers of beaten steel in its blade glistened like fresh running water in the Sun.

They say one could see the engraved hallmark of the Wilkinson Company on it for the longest time. But then, the corrosion that is a natural consequence of being buried in earth all the time finally made it illegible. Every "sword of power" must be buried when it's not in use because, as the *babalawo* tells it, "Only the Earth is fit to be your scabbard." To ensure that the sword does not go hungry during its long sleeps in the ground, the blade is fed male blood just before every burial.

The Oke *ida-igbara* lay beside Joshua now. He did not take it up, for there was no need to; the sheer power of the hatred directed through the metal was supposed to kill me. He just glanced at it and then looked back at me with a smile, as if I were supposed to fall down, paralyzed with fear, which was *exactly* what I was supposed to do, according to juju belief.

When I didn't keel over, Joshua looked surprised for just a second, as if he was wondering what could possibly have gone wrong with such powerful juju. Apparently he decided that the sword needed to be fed because he grabbed it up and swung it at the rat.

It was a big rat, a dull sword, and a sick man. I heard the rat's back break when the sword struck and then its head began thrashing around in agony. But the sword was so corroded that the blow didn't even draw blood. At this point, a Westerner would have recognized the old sword as useless. But Joshua couldn't give up on his juju: Rather than discard the ineffective sword, he squatted and half-cut, half-sawed, the poor rat's head off.

Then he rose and faced me. Slowly, almost lasciviously, he drew the flat of the rusted blade across his tongue, savoring the rat's blood. This was the kind of thing that always struck horror in a naive, uninitiated audience. "Now," he shouted, "see the all-powerful *ida-agbara* of the clan Oke! Look upon it and die!" He turned the point of the sword toward the floor and held it out in front of him stiff-armed, the same way my pastor back in Port Harcourt used to hold the big cross on Sundays.

He looked so preposterous standing there over his dead rat—mouth fouled with blood, clanking with iron like a living junkyard—that I just had to laugh again. I know it wasn't very charitable of me, but I couldn't help myself. I wasn't laughing only at him, of course, but at the whole pointless and silly history of juju.

Joshua did not take kindly to it. His nostrils flared in fury and he shook the sword in my direction a few times. It only made me laugh all the harder. "Just like a jujuman," I hooted. "Put a sword in his hand in the presence of his enemies and what does he do with it? Kills rats!"

He lowered the sword and studied it for a moment. Then he raised his fevered eyes and smiled at me. "Perhaps you are right, son-of-my-father's-brother," he said. "Perhaps there are better uses for a sword." His right hand went to the handle.

I backed away, no longer laughing, as he began to clank toward me. I grabbed at the doorknob and had only an instant to regret having broken the lock before the sword crushed the wood of the door frame just inches from my ear.

Joshua grinned at me maliciously while working the blade back and forth to free it from the wood and have another go. But there was a dull *snap,* like the sound of green firewood. Joshua turned away from me to gape numbly at the little stub of broken blade left in the handle of the mystical *ida-agbara.* The rest of the broken sword was still stuck in the door frame.

He blinked a few times and then staggered back, stunned at what he had done to the "sword of power." The useless remains of the sword slid from his grip. He fell to the floor, twitching as if possessed by a juju demon. He lifted his face toward the ceiling and his mouth and eyes opened wide.

I don't know the cause of what happened next. It could have been that he was overwhelmed with the guilt of what he must have regarded as sacrilege. Or it could have been simply that his disease had impaired his lungs and that stress had finally caused them to fail. But either way, he seemed to have lost the capacity to breathe.

Not that he couldn't take air into his body; he was gulping great heaving chestfuls, in fact. But he appeared unable to take oxygen from what he inhaled. He thrashed around the floor, gasping like a fish that had been pulled from the water and left on the dock. It almost seemed as if the harder he breathed, the less good it did him. He reached out toward me and I believe that, in spite of everything, he was looking to me for help.

"Joshua!" I yelled, going to his side. I had read somewhere of a way to force water from the lungs of someone who has drowned. That didn't seem to be Joshua's problem, of course, but I couldn't think of anything else to do. So I rolled him over and kneaded his back hard, working his lungs for him. It did no good at all. I rolled him over again, fearing that I might be doing more harm than good. After that, I didn't know what to do except kneel by his side, praying, but feeling otherwise helpless.

His agony lasted longer than I would have thought. It took several minutes for him to die before my eyes, still starving for air. Whether it was hysteria caused by breaking his sacred juju relic or whether it was his "slim" catching up with him, either way, juju had claimed still another victim in its long history of misery.

32

There wasn't much of an investigation. That's not to say that my people attach so little importance to the law that Joshua's death could be taken lightly. Rather, it demonstrates how common ritual-related killings are in our part of the world. Had Joshua been found dead in an alleyway of a gunshot wound and with an empty wallet, there's no question that the District Police would have been called in. But the local Town Constable who came round needed only one look at the accouterments of juju—Joshua's ritual "armor" and his shattered *ida-agbara*—to convince him that he needed no help in solving this case.

I spent that night under guard at the local clinic where they treated my injuries as well as they could. But I was suffering more from mental shock than from physical distress; time would have been the right medicine for what ailed me. Nonetheless, I was taken before the magistrate early the next morning.

Everything seemed to have been arranged in advance, as if there was a separate and well-defined procedure for dealing with legal problems involving juju. There were no preliminaries and no one asked me to speak. The magistrate just banged his gavel immediately and said I was guilty of "creating a public disturbance," during which an "innocent bystander" unfortunately died of heart failure; his words were dutifully recorded by his clerk. He then fined me ten *kobo*—about the same penalty as for a parking ticket. But he offered to tear up the official record if I would agree to clean up the room so that "there remains no trace of the nature of this most regrettable disturbance."

Shortly after, word reached me that Grandfather had died. Some say he died on the same day as Joshua. They say that he died just as I feared he would: with a juju curse for me on his lips. With both men dead, I should have felt myself beyond the long reach of juju, which had chased me all across Nigeria. Nevertheless, it was only after another full year went by without any further juju harassment that I dared to return to my home.

Inesi-Ile had grown considerably during the years I'd been away; there were strangers everywhere. It was the beginning of a population trend that eventually would extend through our entire society: People were starting to desert the country in favor of towns, even small towns like ours. The newcomers tended to be rootless. Not having the same ties to the land that we did, it was easy for them to pick up and move elsewhere. So the good opinion of their neighbors was of little value to them; they had no reason to fear the consequences of behavior that our more established families would find unacceptable.

Some of the social changes brought about by this influx of strangers were readily apparent, like increased prostitution and public drunkenness. Others were more subtle and, perhaps, more troubling for our society in the long run. For example, I noticed that locks began to appear on our doors for the first time. That may seem a small thing, but always before, it had been enough among us to simply to lay a stick on the ground in front of the doorway when leaving the house. It was not the stick that provided security; it was that everybody knew what the stick *meant* and respected it. But the newcomers didn't know our ways and had no reason to trouble themselves to learn them. If they disgraced themselves among our society, they thought, what of it? They could always move on.

I felt some of that same social disorientation when I first went back home, almost as if I'd never been there before. It certainly didn't feel the way home is supposed to feel to a prodigal son. Even my mother was more reserved toward me than I might have expected her to be. Her attitude hurt me at first, even though I vaguely understood that I had become somewhat of a stranger to the community. I knew it wasn't simply because I'd been away for so long; it was also because of my split from juju, the spiritual common ground of all the diverse people of Central Africa. Still, my mother's coldness confused me. Then one day, I found her crying alone.

"*Iya*," I said, much the way an American adult might try to cheer his or her mother by calling her "Momma." "What's wrong, *Iya*?"

She dabbed at her eyes. "You know my friend Akamba?"

I nodded without enthusiasm. Akamba was the town's self-appointed soothsayer and therefore an important personage. But in my view, she was little more than an old busybody, spending most of her day in gossip down by the river and going into a "trance" on the least provocation. Like most of our older citizens, she was distantly related to our family. So it was certain that her opinion about things would be very important to my mother.

"Well, Akamba says you are a thief."

"A thief? Me?" In our simple society, where there exists so little that can be owned personally, thievery is an odious offense. So I was stunned by the accusation, even though I'd picked up numerous hints that I was unpopular around town. That's our way: We Africans tend not to speak bluntly about personal matters. Buy I'd assumed all the dirty looks and hidden whispers were because Joshua had been a popular figure on the community and some people blamed me for his death. So there were many things that Akamba could have called me which wouldn't have surprised me. But to be called a thief was astonishing: There was absolutely no basis for such a charge. "How can she say such a thing, *Iya?*"

"Akamba says that Inesi-Ile was once a pleasant place, prosperous and happy, like a family, where everybody knew everybody. One knew one's place, then. But now," she spat on the floor, showing her displeasure, "now we fear each other. We take each other's goods without leave. And one's words can no longer be relied on to be true." She shook her head, clearly bewildered by the new problems of modern times. "The land has been bought up by the Ogboni so that we no longer own·our own farms, as our ancestors did. Yet there is not enough work for our men. They drink and gamble. Some of them lay with one another, men with men, so that women are in want of them. There is misfortune and poverty and illness everywhere." She lowered her voice, ashamed for what she was about to say, and looked both ways before going on. "We have even stopped addressing our elders with respect—could you ever have imagined such a thing?"

I shrugged. "This is sad, but some say it is the way of the new Africa. We are becoming like the rest of the world. This is 'modernization,' " I told her. "But what has it to do with Akamba calling me a 'thief,' *Iya?*"

"Akamba says that, of all people in our village, only *you* do not fear the ancestors or even the *orisha*. Akamba says that's why strife has come to our community: Because we no longer have the *orisha* to protect us from all that the evil spirits want to do to us. Akamba says that is because *you* have stolen them." She took a handful of dust from the ground and threw it over herself to demonstrate her grief and shame. "Akamba says you have stolen our gods."

I laughed and hugged her to me. " 'Akamba says, Akamba says . . . ,' "

I mocked. "Is this the reason my mother has been so distant to me, as if afraid of me?" I waggled a teasing finger at her. "Shame! What could be dearer to you than your own son?"

"Nothing," she replied with enormous dignity, "can be dearer to me than the ways of my people." She pulled away from me. "Not *even* my own son."

And that statement told all there is to know about religious life in Africa: We take it *seriously*. Far more seriously than people do in some other parts of the world. We do not know how to separate church and state, for example; our kings have always been our priests as well. In fact, it is one of our Oxford-educated kings who is currently the *Oba-Ooni* (or "chief of all juju priests"). According to tradition, he must perform blood ritual every day of the year but one. If they knew about his ritual obligations, his Western political and business associates would be shocked. But because they don't, they can continue to be at ease with this prime example of what they call the "new African."

But the new African exists only when Western eyes are around to observe him. Other times, the *real* African reemerges, the one who seeks protection from a threatening world through the power promised by the sympathetic magic of juju. Without that supernatural power, he believes himself and his family to be doomed. That's why juju rules in secret over his every thought and action.

So I had to admit to myself that, in a way, Akamba's charge against me was accurate. I had previously considered my renunciation of juju to be no one's business but my own. My apostasy was a sort of "victimless crime" in which I took only from myself and what I took was fear and superstition. But now, in my mother's shame, I saw that I had indeed taken something away from my people as well: the common tradition on which our social behavior is built.

I do not flatter myself that mine was the only voice raised against juju. But mine must have seemed very loud to my people, given the exalted conditions of my early life. Besides, from all those other reformers who disparaged our juju, we always got at least something in return—from the missionaries who came to convert us, we got medicine and monotheism; from the British who came to rule us, we got government and commerce; from the scholars who came to study us, we got literacy and science. I alone had defiled a vital part of my people's culture without giving anything in return. To the vast extended family that is a tribal man's life, I must have seemed like Judas, Brutus, and Benedict Arnold, all in one.

Still, there was a question of honor involved. I took my mother by the hand down to the river, to the spot where all the women gather to clean clothes and talk. In her presence—as well as that of most of the other adult women of the town—I confronted the slander.

"Akamba," I said, "you have called me, Isaiah of the clan Oke, a thief."

My challenge gave her leave to speak freely and she took advantage of it. "I have said so, Son of Better Men, and so it is." The other women clicked their tongues in encouragement.

"What do you say I have stolen?"

Her gums gleamed wetly in a false smile, her teeth having long since been sacrificed to her fondness for *djanga* root. "Why, as everyone here knows," she swept her audience with her skinny arm, "you have stolen our juju. I, Akamba, say it. But all here know it to be true." The women clicked their approval until they sounded like a field of locusts.

I opened my mouth to deny the charge angrily, as befits a man. Then I took another look at the wretched, resentful townswomen—most of them my kin—and said, "You speak truly, Akamba."

Everything stopped for a moment with the shock of my admission.

"But I will replace your juju with something better," I started. "A better religion and a better life." But I'm afraid I lacked the oratorical skill of the preachers I'd heard in the big city and I stuttered to a stop, wondering what in the world to say next. Sweat broke out on my forehead as I saw Akamba's look of derision out of the corner of my eye. "I will give you something better than juju," I repeated. "Something that does not urge you to abuse our children, to kill them for a momentary release or a chance at better luck. Something that does not spread 'slim' among us as a result of misusing blood."

But before I could really get going, Akamba cut me off very effectively by going into one of her "trances." She screamed once, sharply, which got everyone's attention. Her eyes were open so wide, I almost thought I heard the flesh around them creak with the tension. She began to shake all over and to emit low moans, like a cow left too long in the Sun.

She dramatically scanned the crowd, fascinating everyone. As she did, she gradually closed one eyelid while somehow contriving to leave the other absolutely motionless; it was like a motion picture of someone winking, only slowed down a hundredfold. Then her other eyeball rolled back into her head until her open eye looked like a white radish. I had no idea how she did it and I was as impressed by the sight as all the other onlookers. When she finally spoke again, it was through foam-covered lips and with the gravelly voice of a vulture.

"I am *Osain*," the voice rumbled. "Hear the message I bring."

There was a sharp intake of breath from the women. "*Osain! Osain!*" the whisper went round the terrified crowd. Surely, it was he, they must have thought—the one-eyed messenger of the *orisha*.

But never in all our history had *Osain* chosen to possess a women as the instrument for his message from the *orisha*. Several of the women became faint at the thought of such a miracle. Two of them even fell to the ground and began writhing in minor possessions of their own, to which nobody paid any real attention.

As for me, my only emotion was embarrassment for this poor old woman. I stood there watching her, as mute as all the other witnesses. Until I heard my name.

"Isaiah Oke lies as well as steals," Akamba/*Osain* said. "So say the *orisha*."

Those women who retained consciousness turned to stare at me. Some snarled. Akamba/*Osain* started bouncing back and forth in her ecstasy from one calloused foot to another. "Isaiah Oke says he has left the *orisha*. But this is his lie: He has *not* left the *orisha*."

"Now, see here, old woman," I said. "I ought to know whether I—"

"I say again: Isaiah Oke has not left the *orisha*. Rather it is the *orisha* who have left *him*," she said, getting more worked up by the moment. "Because this Isaiah has been found unworthy!"

The women began to close a circle around me. The foam flew from Akamba/*Osain's* mouth as she shouted, "The juju god *Orisha-Oko*, once incarnate in this Isaiah, has now chosen to go . . . ," she made a broad gesture, taking in all the four corners of the Earth, ". . . elsewhere."

For a moment, I wondered how she'd made the remark sound so ominous. But before I could think about it, the women around me intruded on my awareness. For the first time, I appreciated my situation: There were perhaps fifty or so of the village women drawing close around me, all angered and excited by Akamba/*Osain's* ravings.

Ironically, it was Akamba herself who saved me from a severe beating (at the least). As she neared the end of her energy, she shouted, "He is no longer a godling, this Isaiah! Now, he is just a man! He is just one of us!" Then, her last reserves spent, she slumped into a tired heap like the Wicked Witch from Oz.

The women stopped, undecided. They'd been primed to destroy a vicious, bigger-than-life heretic. But I'd just been classified as a poor struggling mortal, just like them. Just like everybody else.

They looked uncertainly to one other for guidance until my mother settled the issue. When she saw me standing there gaping like the women, she cuffed me smartly behind the ear, as befits a mother, and ordered me to scoop up poor, deluded old Akamba and carry her home. But she walked behind me with a shy smile all the way there.

It seemed she had her son again.

The Time of Christ

Ormond Edwards

The Time
of Christ

A Chronology of the Incarnation

Floris Books

First published in 1986.

British Library Cataloguing in Publication Data

Edwards, Ormond
The time of Christ: a chronology of the Incarnation.
1. Incarnation
I. Title
232′.1   BT220

ISBN 0-86315-030-6

Printed in Great Britain
by Billing & Sons Ltd, Worcester

Contents

Tables

Chronological Outline

Year		Jewish date	Julian date	Weekday	
BC	2	Nisan 1	April 6	Sunday	Annunciation (Matthew)
		Tishri 1	October 1	Wednesday	Annunciation of John's birth
	1	Tebeth 9	January 6	Tuesday	Birth of Jesus (Matthew)
		Tebeth 13	January 10	Saturday	Lunar eclipse (Josephus)
		Nisan 1	March 26	Friday	Annunciation (Luke)
		Tammuz 9	June 30	Wednesday	Birth of John
		Tebeth 9	December 25	Saturday	Birth of Jesus (Luke)
AD	12	Nisan 15	March 27	Sunday	Passover in twelfth year
	28	Heshvan 1	October 8	Monday	John's emergence
	31	Tebeth 23	January 6	Saturday	Baptism of Jesus
		c. Adar 3	c. Feb 15	(Thursday)	Temptation
		c. Adar 4–8	c. Feb 16–20	(Fri-Tue)	Calling of disciples
		Adar 16	February 27	Tuesday	Marriage at Cana
		Nisan 10	March 23	Friday	Cleansing of the Temple
		c. Sivan 9	c. May 20	(Sunday)	Samaritan Pentecost
		c. Tishri 7–8	c. Sept 13–14	(Thu–Fri)	Arrest of John
		Tishri 10	September 16	Sunday	Day of Atonement
		Tishri 16	September 22	Saturday	Healing of paralytic
		Tishri 30	October 6	Saturday	Opening of Galilean ministry
	32	Nisan 1	April 1	Tuesday	Death of John
		c. Nisan 16–20	c. April 16–20	(Wed-Sat)	Feeding of five thousand
		c. Sivan 6–11	c. June 2–8	(Mon-Sat)	Feeding of four thousand
		Tammuz 9	July 6	Sunday	Confession of Peter
		Tammuz 17	July 14	Monday	Transfiguration
		Tishri 15–22	Oct 10–17	Fri-Fri	Tabernacles
		Kislev 25	December 18	Thursday	Feast of Dedication
	33	Tebeth 15	January 6	Tuesday	At the Jordan (John 10:40)
		c. Adar 4	c. Feb 23	(Monday)	Raising of Lazarus
		Nisan 1	March 21	Saturday	New Jubilee cycle
		Nisan 10	March 30	Monday	Cleansing of the Temple
		Nisan 14	April 3	Friday	Crucifixion
		Nisan 16	April 5	Sunday	Resurrection
	34	Tishri 30	October 3	Sunday	Conversion of Paul
	70	Ab 9	August 6	Monday	Destruction of Temple

9

Abbreviations

AD   Anno Domini (in the year of our Lord). In this book always referring to Julian dates which were in use until the Gregorian calendar reform in the late sixteenth century. The Julian calendar has a leap year every four years, including centuries.

AE   Actian Era (dating from the Battle of Actium, September 2, 31 BC).

AM   Anno Mundi (in the year of the world, calculated from the Creation in the Old Testament as autumn 3761 BC). Used from about AD 360.

Ant.   Josephus, *Jewish Antiquities*

BC   Before Christ. Note that there was no year zero. The year before AD 1 was 1 BC. This must be taken into account when calculating time spans bridging BC/AD. Julian dates are used by historians, with a leap year every four years, beginning 1 BC, 5 BC, 9 BC, and so on.

BCE   Before Common Era. Same as BC, used by modern Jewish historians.

LXX Septuagint. The Greek version of the Old Testament.

SE   Seleucid Era. (Beginning autumn 312 BC Syrian reckoning, spring 311 BC Babylonian/Jewish reckoning).

War   Josephus, *The Jewish War*.

Acknowledgements

Unless otherwise stated, all quotations from the Bible are from the Revised Standard Version with kind permission of the National Council of Churches of Christ (New Testament © 1946, 1971; Old Testament © 1952).

Dates

All dates in this book are based on the Jewish calendar, where a day begins at *sunset*, the evening before the Julian date. Therefore the Julian equivalent given here should be thought of as beginning at the previous day's sunset.

References

The system used in this book quotes author and year of publication, followed by volume (if necessary) and page. The full title and publication details are in the bibliography.

Introduction

In setting out to investigate the chronology of the life of Christ we are brought to question the nature of time itself. Everyone knows times which seem barren because nothing happens. In contrast to the aridity of *chronos* the ancient Greeks had another word for time as the matrix of change and development, and the times and seasons which celebrate it: *kairos*. It is not so much a new chronology which we need as a new sense for living time.

In recent decades great advances have been made in the study of the diurnal, lunar and circannual rhythms which constitute the time-organism that is an essential part of the human, living body. The ancients too had once looked upon these rhythms of sun, moon and stars as projections into the macrocosmos of the rhythms which they observed in human growth, fluctuations in mood and in the alternation of waking and sleeping.

Within this living cosmos we can look for an understanding of the apparent conflict between the Christian view of creation and the biologist's account of human evolution. In seeking to become sensitive to the uniqueness of Christ's time, we shall also try to capture the biologists' concept of 'development time' as appropriate to our inquiry.

Consideration of the Gospels in the context of time has been pioneered by Oscar Cullmann. Not only in *Christ and Time*, but in all his writings he has placed the Incarnation as a process in time at the centre of our understanding of the world. Because it is central, it is necessary that we start with the historical life of Christ. When the Gospels are read aright, he is in effect saying, the life of Christ illuminates every facet of human evolution from the onset of hominization to the last days.

As in my earlier *A New Chronology of the Gospels* (1972), the central interest in this work is the duration of the life of Christ. But the scope of the inquiry has been so widened that the present book is a new work.

In *A New Chronology*, no account was given of the Star of

Bethlehem (Matthew) or of the registration under Quirinius (Luke). And the argument over the date of Herod's death had included no new evidence. But during the past ten years much has changed. Distinguished scholars have employed knowledge of Babylonian astronomy to interpret the star of the magi with striking success. And a newly revised English language edition of Emil Schürer, *A History of the Jewish People in the Age of Jesus*, has appeared since 1973.

We are immediately confronted by discrepancies between the Gospels of Matthew and Luke which seem incompatible with the historicity of the infancy narratives. For it cannot be overlooked that Matthew sets the nativity scene within the lifetime of Herod the Great, and Schürer's reviser has assembled overwhelming evidence that Roman taxation of Palestine could not have taken place during Herod's lifetime.

There remains a problem with Herod's chronology and here the revised Schürer is no help. It is not pointed out that there is a contradiction between Herod's 'received' chronology, derived from the Jewish historian Josephus in the first century, and the evidence of Herod's dated coins. As a first step, my 'Herodian Chronology' (1982) investigated the unresolved problems which again surface in the coins of king Herod Agrippa I (reigned AD 36–44).

It is not possible to establish the lengths of the Herods' reigns without a proper understanding of the calendars involved. In fact it should not have been necessary to resort to the coins to correct Josephus. A major new discovery published in 1954 led to a revision of Hasmonean (Maccabean) chronology by J. Schaumberger (1955). This perceptive scholar explained that in addition to the well-known Jewish calendar employed for all religious and internal purposes, there was a Hellenistic or Macedonian civil calendar used throughout the region west of the Euphrates for political and economic affairs. Schaumberger showed how, in the First Book of the Maccabees, the character of a happening, sacred or secular, determines which calendar is appropriate. And since the *ecclesiastical* year began some six months after the *civil* new year's day, an incorrect allocation of calendar can cause serious distortion.

When Herod was nominated king by the Romans, he purported to be no more than an aspirant to the throne. Steeped in the Hellenistic world of political power and an enthusiastic Hellenizer, Herod reckoned his *de jure* reign from the Hellenistic (civil) autumn new year 40 BC as his dated coin shows. Yet Josephus dated the reign from spring 40 BC as though Herod were already a legitimate Israelite king. Herod's capture of Jerusalem in 37 BC is then wrongly reckoned by Josephus to have taken place in his fourth *de jure* year. This conclusion that Herod's *de jure* years are reckoned in civil years eliminates the possibility that Herod could have died as early as spring 4 BC after reigning (as Josephus tells us) thirty-seven years. When calendar, coin and astronomical data are taken into account, it is found that the tyrant died early in 1 BC, not long after the lunar eclipse mentioned by Josephus, which is now identified as the total eclipse on January 10, 1 BC. A review of the historicity of the infancy narratives then becomes due.

The reality of the Incarnation necessitates a birth which was a historically real event. It can readily be understood that in the fourth century the newly fledged Church of the Roman Empire had no feeling for a delicate investigation of the circumstances surrounding the birth of Jesus of Nazareth. At a time when the alliance between imperial power and ecclesiastical authority was being forged, it was hardly opportune to emphasize the New Testament's clear distinction between divine authority and earthly power. The outcome was the traditional and highly unsatisfactory conflation of the Gospels of Matthew and Luke, which historically can no longer be sustained.

An invitation to explore the nativity accounts afresh is presented by the Dead Sea Scrolls discovered in 1947. Writings now known to be associated with the Essene community had already been found to have awaited not one but two Messiahs (and a prophet). But scholars, including notably R. H. Charles with his ingrained interpretation of the nativity accounts, had systematically amended all mention of Messiahs to the expected single Messiah. Charles had been most influential as an incomparable authority on writings of the inter-testamental period, and his systematic error had been pointed out by G. R. Beasley-Murray (1947) even

15

before publication of the Scrolls so strongly underlined the dual expectation of a royal and of a priestly Messiah.

Independently of the Scrolls research, G. Friedrich (1956) comes to the unexpected but convincing view that the Jesus of the Gospels answers to the expectation of the Messianic high priest. The Scrolls mention also a companion royal figure who would defer to the priestly Messiah 'at the Messianic banquet'. The Nativity of Matthew unmistakably relates the birth of a royal Messiah. We shall have to consider whether the solution to the mystery of the Nativity stories may not be found in the Essene expectation of, in all, three Messianic figures, prophet, priest and king. John would then be equated with the Prophet; Jesus of Nazareth (whose birth is recorded by Luke) with the priestly Messiah; and Matthew's princely Immanuel of Bethlehem with the transient but historically real figure of a royal forerunner. Some of the many historical puzzles connected with the physical birth will be further investigated in Chapters 8 to 12.

Determining the nature and timing of the star of Bethlehem belongs to the elucidation of Matthew's birth story. In Chapter 6 ancient and modern views on the star will be put forward. Among scholars who have specialized in the subject recently, opinions differ on the constellation appropriate to the royal Messiah. While it is agreed that the planet Jupiter constituted the hour hand of the zodiacal clock indicating the Messiah's advent, to which sign of the zodiac was it pointing as the magi made their journey?

At the time of Christ, Babylonian-Persian cosmic religion permeated Judaism and Hellenism. It would have been impossible to write the Gospels without using the thought-forms of pre-Christian religion. Yet, as the writings of the Gnostics exemplify, myth may embody a divine manifestation but it cannot tell how a divine being came to dwell in a human physical body. Its Docetism speaks merely of a semblance of an incarnation. Rudolf Bultmann and his followers have therefore energetically undertaken to demythologize the Gospels.

We should, however, be prepared to recognize that men have always pondered the same questions concerning the nature of man. The pre—Christian cultures influenced by the religious science of the magi — and all of them were deeply influenced — looked upon the heavens as the original home of mankind. Lacking a physical anthropology (fossil evidence of hominization) antiquity developed as a central doctrine its view of pre-existence, individual development (ontogeny) rather than the evolution of the human species (phylogeny). The modern science of man contrasts with the world-conception of antiquity in two respects. Pre-Christian ontogeny was macroscopic (the heavenly journey of the soul) where modern science focuses on the microscopic. Today the powers directing human behaviour are thought to be the expression of hormones, genes and chromosomes, where once the gods ruled over a paradisal world. An adequate history of ideas would be able to show the metamorphosis of the Garden of Eden into the theories of Darwin and Mendel. The god of the underworld is represented in evolutionary biology by 'natural selection' and the tempter has become the 'selfish gene'.

In order to relate the New Testament to our scientific view of the world, we may find it necessary to remythologize the Gospels, rather than demythologize them. For in the life of Christ the questions and answers which move us are anthropocentric and are less easily expressed in, say, the phraseology of evolutionary biology.

At the time of writing, scientific reports are appearing in rapid succession discussing what purports to be the earliest ancestor of man exhibiting the unmistakable hallmark of human nature, erect posture. Although the fossil record is highly imperfect, the finds of recent decades suffice to illustrate the main stages of hominization. About three-and-a-half million years ago, a hominid named *Australopithecus afarensis* walked upright. Some two million years ago *Homo habilis* had developed Broca's area, the speech centre, with expansion of the neocortex continuing in *Homo erectus* between one-and-a-half and half a million years ago. These hallmarks of humanity, of course, appear in species which are by no means yet *Homo sapiens sapiens*. A fourth stage begins with the awakening of a sense of personality, the *sine qua non* of modern man.

We should, however, bear well in mind that in human evolution, as in the young child, the essential steps of upright walking, speaking and thinking are themselves both biological evolution

17

and at the same time *learned*. It is in this context of learning to be human, that the expression 'Although he was a Son, he learned obedience through what he suffered' (Heb.5:8) may be considered most fruitfully. 'The most important confirmation of Hebrews' conception of Jesus' full humanity, however, is the statement that he *learned* obedience.' (Cullmann 1963, 97). The expression presupposes an inner human development, without which a life would not be fully or characteristically human. When Jesus 'learned obedience' even unto death, his life may be interpreted as a reiteration and completion of the process of hominization, with death and resurrection regarded as the last act in becoming human. 'Behold the man' said Pilate. The dimensions of the resurrection body may then be discovered in the 'dimensions' of upright walking, speaking, and thinking, revealed successively at Easter, Ascension and Whitsun.

In order to perceive the ministry as a development, a process of learning, we shall need a chronology sufficient at least to discern the major stages and turning points in the life of Christ. When we have considered these turning points, we shall be in a better position to examine the Christological significance of the pattern of the Incarnation. When we ask, 'How long did Christ's ministry last?' we encounter a plethora of conflicting opinions which seem to reflect a widespread feeling that the time-scale does not matter. This book is an attempt to show that it does matter. Time is of the essence and we need a calendar of the Incarnation to further our understanding of its purpose. Our aim is to learn to follow the course of the Incarnation as we would watch the development of an individual. We need to become alert to the possibility that there is an intrinsic time pattern in the Christ's 'becoming human'.

A development may unfold in a certain timespan. It can be dated only when the scale can be fixed through the use of astronomical data. Thus great attention should be paid to the two lunar eclipses which occurred around the time of the birth and death of Jesus. There was an eclipse shortly before Herod's death, to which reference has already been made, which therefore plays an important role in the chronology of the Nativity. The second eclipse occurred on April 3, AD 33.

The latter eclipse has not been recognized as significant in chronological discussion until very recently (Humphreys & Waddington 1983). These two Oxford scientists quote a number of examples from the ancient world in which 'the moon turning to blood' was used as the technical term for a lunar eclipse. At Pentecost, Peter quoted Joel (2:31), 'the sun shall be turned into darkness and the moon into blood' (Acts 2:20). The darkening of the sun relates to the darkness at noon which accompanied the Crucifixion, and the moon turning to blood to the partial eclipse of the full moon rising on the evening of April 3, AD 33 at the beginning of the Passover festival. During the years between 26 and 36, the only date on which the Passover moon rose (partially) eclipsed was Friday, April 3, AD 33.

We have embarked on a difficult voyage of discovery. At every stage our investigation has been immensely aided by guidance on specific points by a number of very distinguished scholars. Without implying that they would agree with any of my views, I would like to express my gratitude to Professor O. Neugebauer and Professor B. L. van der Waerden for their views on a matter of astronomical chronology indirectly connected with the Jewish civil calendar. Professor K. Ferrari d'Occhieppo has written on aspects of conjunctions of Saturn and Jupiter with an informative analysis of generous length, and Dr F. R. Stephenson, Dr C. J. Humphreys, Dr W. G. Waddington, and Dr N. P. Stroud have provided indispensable help with the astronomical basis of the Jewish calendars. On questions concerning Jewish coins I am indebted to Dr D. Bateson (Hunterian Museum, Glasgow), Arie Kindler (Kadman Museum, Tel Aviv), Dr Y. Meshorer (Israel Museum, Jerusalem) and Dr M. J. Price (British Museum). Dr Ernest Martin and Uwe Lemmer have been extremely kind in directing to me a flow of new material relating to the star of Bethlehem and Dr Colin Humphreys allowed me to see his article already in draft form. Among friends of longer standing, on matters astronomical I am deeply indebted to the late Willi Sucher, to Dr Georg Unger, and to their fellow-workers.

Others have been equally helpful in various other directions and I would like to thank Dr Andrew Welburn for his view on

Paulinism and Gnosticism; Mr A. A. L. Brown and Wim Viersen for their linguistic skills. I am unable adequately to express my gratitude to friends nearer home for much needed assistance with the manuscript.

Ormond Edwards
Aberdeen
Advent 1985

In Preparation

1 Gospel and Myth

'In the beginning was the Word . . .' In the opening sentences of his Gospel, John hears in the words of the Teacher from Galilee, the Logos, the heartbeat of creation. Matthew had an eye for a royal Messiah who would suffer an ignominious death. Mark sculpted the Lord of the seasons, where Luke depicted the divine shepherd of souls. But the Fourth Gospel is inspired by the rhyme and reason of the universe, the pre-existent Logos, the creative Word of God.

Once theologians claimed knowledge of the *Uroffenbarung*, the primeval wisdom of mankind, and used it to elucidate the Gospels. Our modern ideas on the nature of man and of the universe have evolved out of a much simpler yet more coherent view of existence which had its flowering in an earlier age. In its turn the naïve conception of the world was rooted in the great religious festivals of ancient Sumer some five thousand years ago, and the foliage of civilization's cultural Eden spread from Mesopotamia as cosmic religion. Between such lofty perspectives and our modern and highly adult fascination with the minutiae of the cosmos, and particularly with the intricate workings of the human body, there is great distance. But this gap is no greater than the distance which separates our own modern adult outlook from the world conception we share during the fleeting years of infancy.

In the early months of life, there is no sharp differentiation between the infant observer and the world he surveys. And at the dawn of civilization reality was similarly perceived as an objective-subjective unity, in the best manner of the atomic physicist today. Sumer was indeed far removed in spirit from the nineteenth century's cool distinction between the observer and the observed. In the eyes of antiquity, the self was ideally an exact image of the cosmos. Self-knowledge led inevitably to knowledge of the universe as living and ensouled. And conversely the soul was perceived swinging like a pendulum in response to the movement of cosmic bodies.

23

Opening the Gospels, we can soon become aware how the language of the Evangelists is imbued with the imagery of pre-Christian myth. The Greek language had absorbed much from past contact particularly with the older cultures of the Near East. The finest flowering of Hellenic culture in Platonism was, like post-exilic Judaism, strongly influenced by the Persian-Babylonian astral theology alternatively termed by B. L. van der Waerden (1974, 127–204) 'cosmic religion'. Since the Gospels have availed themselves so readily of the vocabulary of myth, Rudolf Bultmann and his followers set out systematically to eliminate from the Gospels all trace of the pre-Christian vision of the three-tiered world of Heaven, Earth, and Underworld. Here the well-known theologian is following in the more famous footstep of Galileo, who so persuasively demythologized space.

From the standpoint of his time, Bultmann was no doubt right, and his efforts have presumably alerted many to the employment by the Evangelists of myth. But a modern preference for abstraction is not the best qualification for sharing the intuitive conceptions of antiquity, and it would be well to understand the origins of the three-deckered conception of space before laying it aside.

When we travel backwards in time beyond the age of Plato, we find that everything and every idea had its location in the three-decker universe. There is no evidence that the Sumerians and Babylonians were less intelligent or less observant than ourselves, but they regarded the universe very differently. In their cosmogony they used the cosmos as an information storehouse, and their system of information retrieval was equally complex. This aspect of cosmic religion is now associated with the science of astrology.

Nowhere is the influence of ancient Sumer and Babylon more obvious than in the Jewish religious calendar. For it was during the Exile that the captive Jews adopted Babylonian month-names and, for all religious purposes, the Babylonian spring new year. The inherent mythology was not so much Babylonian as Sumerian, since the Semitic peoples of Mesopotamia adopted the Sumerians' entire culture, including the calendar, along with the Sumerian art of writing.

As Babylonian cosmology developed, the myths of the

Sumerian monthly religious festivals were projected on to the path taken by the sun each month, thus constituting the myths of the signs of the zodiac. After conquest by the Persians, Mesopotamian cosmic religion unfolded its vision of the heavenly journey of the soul. In the Avesta the soul (enters and) leaves earthly existence, journeying through three soul regions, Good Thought, Good Words, and Good Action. In later versions of the heavenly journey of the soul, the three regions are replaced by the seven planetary spheres.

Cosmic religion was brought to Greece by Pythagoras, in whose hands it became the basis of pre-Christian mysticism. In Pythagoreanism the journey of the soul is along the path of knowledge, and the three stages of higher consciousness are closely related to the threefold pattern of pre-existence. In Platonism, cosmic religion flowered as a spiritual psychology. But the old Heaven, Earth, Underworld has, in Plato's *Timaeus* (38) shrunk to the three seats of the human psyche in the head, the heart and the 'manger' of the metabolic system.

The early Church Fathers allowed that pre-Christian religion had been permitted partial revelations of the divine Word which had been fully incarnated in Jesus of Nazareth. And the Evangelist Matthew, by including in his Gospel an account of the adoration of the magi, summoned these priests of cosmic religion as witnesses to the Incarnation. Our understanding of this account has benefited enormously from knowledge of the magi's astral religion, contained in contributions by K. Ferrari d'Occhieppo (1977) and R. A. Rosenberg (1972).

When we come to the time of Christ, there is a sudden change. After the Crucifixion, the disciples were confronted with the fact that the manner of his death seemed utterly unconnected with the divine overtones of his life. Nothing drawn from the religion of their time or from Jewish Messianism, or even their understanding of his teaching, had prepared them for his sacrificial death. And when the first light of the Resurrection dawned within them, they found themselves on entirely new ground. Far from jettisoning their cultural heritage in order to enter into a comprehension of the new revelation, the disciples were moved to remember the instruction they had received during the Galilean ministry. They were alerted to previously unnoticed words of the prophets which brought the recent events into sharp spiritual focus.

The Gospels arose out of this endeavour. It would not be correct to say that the Evangelists sought light on the life of Christ in the Old Testament. It was the teaching of the risen Christ which reminded them both of the teaching the twelve had received while with him in Galilee, and of the readings from (Old Testament) Scripture, learnt as they heard together the scrolls read each sabbath in the synagogue.

Although still largely uncomprehended, the life of Christ was nevertheless felt by the disciples to belong to the history of mankind. But the Galilean teacher would have taken his place in the cultural history of mankind alongside other men of religious genius were it not for the Crucifixion. Holy Week has nothing of the sublimity of, for instance, the Buddha's exit. It is charged with the earthiness of death and the enormity of his brutal execution.

When the Apostles had at least partially come to terms with his death and Resurrection, they saw it as a death and rebirth of the divine world. Contrasted with the earlier spiritual life, the Crucifixion was a last act in a twilight of the gods which had spread through all the world's religions. And with the body of Jesus the divinities of antiquity were laid to rest. The Resurrection was to be understood not as a continuation but as a rebirth of the divine. 'When a woman is in travail she has sorrow, because her hour has come; but when she is delivered of the child, she no longer remembers the anguish, for joy that a child is born into the world.' (John 16:21).

The pre-Christian world-conception is perhaps best described as a cosmic embryology. There is nothing inorganic, no hint yet of death. Men sought their origin in a living and ensouled cosmos, sensing human life as the handiwork of the heavenly Father. But while man is born of the heavenly Father, he meets the Son as the Christ standing at the gate of death. The earlier picture of the soul as it was seen descending into earthly existence and again ascending after death is merged with the Christian concept of Father and Son. In the evolution of religion, the gods of mankind were once projected on to the distant stars and then, seen approaching mankind, they descended the planetary highway.

Continuing the same process of reduction and internalization, the post-Christian scientific world-conception today pursues the powers which rule over human nature into the realms of human physiology.

Men have at all times asked, 'What is man?' The age of natural science finds its answers in the language of enzymes, genes and chromosomes in the stead of signs in sun and moon and stars. Perusing Richard Dawkins' *The Selfish Gene*, the reader is left to conjecture whether this excellent writer is conscious that his 'selfish gene' differs not at all in character from the scientifically discredited Serpent in the Garden of Eden. It will be remembered that the Serpent tempted the first man with a fraudulent guarantee of immortality and instead implanted self-interest (Gen.3:4). As Dawkins sees them, genes are virtually immortal, surviving for millions of years in a ruthlessly competitive world. Strikingly reminiscent also of the ancient gods in Wagner's *Ring des Nibelungen*, the successful gene dupes the individual 'gene-host' into serving the gene's own purpose and then, having ensured the gene's own survival, discards the individual without compunction.

While the place of the Tempter is taken by the 'selfish gene', Satan, or Death as the king of the underworld, may be compared to the evolutionary biologist's concept of 'natural selection'. In mythology, the lord of the lower world is represented as grim and unpitying, a severe punisher of wrong. We may recall the classical image of the ruler of the dead also called Pluto, the Rich One, while reading the celebrated final paragraph of Darwin's *Origin of Species* for his picture of natural selection, where he pens a hymn of praise to the creative power of 'the war of nature, famine and death'.

Anyone wishing further to consider the subject of ancient myth and modern biology should not fail to read at least the second chapter of Stephen Jay Gould, *Ontogeny and Phylogeny* (1977, 13).

> The microcosm: ontogeny. The macrocosm: cosmic history,
> human history, organic development. This comparison may
> be the most durable analogy in the history of biology . . .
> The analogy of individual to cosmic history was favoured
> by many pre-Socratic thinkers. The nascent cosmos of

Anaximander, Anaximenes, and Democritus was
surrounded by an envelope resembling the amniotic
membrane . . .

In a sense, all culture, modern as well as ancient, is 'myth'. Pre-Christian religion revered the picture of the heavenly man. But for the founders of Christianity, pre-Christian culture was only a partial revelation, and the Incarnation alone is a full revelation of the *Uroffenbarung*. Our investigation will be conducted in the faith that the truths of the Incarnation will illuminate the mythology of the future (if the scientist will forgive such an expression) as well as illustrate the mythology of a vanishing world.

In theology, the term 'cosmic Christ' is nowadays somewhat less familiar than the 'pre-existent Christ', as designating the creator of man. When Christ speaks as the guide of souls upon the heavenly journey, we can hear the disbelief of his listeners that the divine could be involved in a human incarnation. For them epiphany and incarnation were mutually exclusive possibilities (John 6:41f):

> The Jews then murmured at him, because he said, 'I am the bread which came down from heaven.' They said, 'Is not this Jesus, the son of Joseph, whose father and mother we know? How does he now say, "I have come down from heaven"?'

We are able to feel something of his hearers' difficulty when we try to translate the language of a spiritual cosmology into the more familiar language of modern science. And there is at least an equal impediment to rendering the path of Incarnation in terms which have any meaning in human biology. True, scientists have been understandably most reluctant to represent human nature as determined simply by heredity. Yet there is no academic science of human individuality; the *ego eimi* is not determined by genetics.

In the following chapters, we hope to trace how the threefold revelation of the divine in the human nature of Jesus unfolded in *time*, where antiquity placed the divine in its three-dimensional *spatial* world.

2 Gospel and History

One of the major mysteries of Christianity is the absence of the Christ from the pages of history. The Herods, Pilate, Caiaphas, Augustus and Tiberius are chronicled as the great men of the day, but the greatest among them passes virtually unnoticed. The Evangelists, by contrast, devote their whole attention to the central figure with little reference to the public events of the day. Their task was to disclose the hidden nature of Jesus, the dimension withheld from the political historian or reporter, the 'open secret' of his earthly nature. A paucity of dates in the Gospels is, therefore, only part of a more general problem of bridging the gap between Gospel and history.

During the nineteenth century, innumerable attempts were made to write a historical biography of Jesus of Nazareth, stimulating a widespread interest in the chronology of his life. The results have proved very disappointing, and most scholars have come to the conclusion that there is no historical evidence upon which an adequate life of Jesus could be written. Certainly few, if any, of the chronological assumptions made 'in the quest of the historical Jesus' have stood the test of time. In the age of natural science, biblical scholars had set out on a different course. Unable to sustain the concept of Christ as man's Creator in the face of the advance of evolutionary biology, they adopted the methods of historical science. Academic theologians on the other hand speak of the 'pre-existent Jesus', meaning man's Creator, without venturing upon a single statement which would overlap with the scientific world conception.

A new approach has to be found. And although in the following pages our inquiry may seem to the non-specialist reader historical (in the loose sense of concern with the past), the intention is to remain open to the conception of the Incarnation as a creative power in human evolution.

When we embark upon a review of the historical material, the poverty of the documentary evidence immediately becomes apparent. Outside the New Testament, the earliest ostensible mention of Jesus is made by the Jewish historian Josephus. Written towards the end of the first century, his *Jewish Antiquities* (18.63f) contains the following strange words:

> About this time there lived Jesus, a wise man, if indeed one might call him a man. For he was one who wrought surprising feats and was a teacher of such people as accept the truth gladly. He won over many Jews and many of the Greeks. He was the Messiah. When Pilate, upon hearing him accused by men of the highest standing amongst us, had condemned him to be crucified, those who had in the first place come to love him did not give up their affection for him. On the third day he appeared to them restored to life, for the prophets of God had prophesied these and countless other marvellous things about him. And the tribe of the Christians, so called after him, has to this day still not disappeared.

This disputed passage is discussed in Schürer (1973, 428–41). Josephus goes on to identify James, the first Bishop of Jerusalem, as 'the brother of Jesus who was called the Christ', which seems to presuppose an earlier explanation of who Jesus was (*Ant.* 20.200–3). The earliest undisputed passage occurs in Tacitus (*c.* AD 55–120), 'Their originator Christ had been executed in Tiberius' reign by the governor of Judea, Pontius Pilatus.' (*Annals* 15.44).

A second and not unrelated mystery concerns the manifest reluctance of Jesus to demonstrate his Messianic nature publicly. The second quarter of the first century found Palestine suddenly alive with Messianic expectation. Yet until the week of his Passion, the ministry unfolds with the utmost reserve, an almost childlike reluctance to play the role expected of the Messiah. And when Jesus does reveal himself during Holy Week finally to fulfil his Messianic roles, his ignominious death immediately intervenes leaving his disciples utterly bewildered and aghast.

At the beginning of the last week of his earthly life, all reserve is suddenly cast aside. On Palm Sunday Jesus entered Jerusalem from the east, passing over the Mount of Olives where, in Judaism, the Messiah was expected to make his appearance. He

came 'not driving chariots like other kings, not demanding trib-
utes, not thrusting men off, and leading about guards, but
displaying his great meekness even thereby.' (Chrysostom *Hom.*
66). Here Matthew (21:5) quotes from the Old Testament
(Isa.62:11 and Zech.9:9):

Tell the daughter of Zion,

Behold, your king is coming to you,

humble, and mounted on an ass,

and on a colt, the foal of an ass.

This Old Testament quotation was Messianically interpreted also
at Qumran in the Dead Sea Scrolls (4QPatr. Bless.I). Matthew
does not directly quote Jacob's blessing (Gen.49:9–12), as he well
might. It is unnecessary. The prophetic blessing is enacted by the
Christ on Palm Sunday, 'Binding his foal to the vine, and his ass's
colt to the choicest vine . . .'

In the language of a cosmology, which had by that time
permeated all the religions of the world, this blessing is filled with
the cosmic imagery proper to kingship. To the crowds lining the
streets, it was evident that the Messianic king was taking
possession of his own city. Similarly, during this last week, in the
cleansing of the Temple, he entered as Messianic priest into his
own place. And in the Upper Room, Jesus celebrated the Last
Supper as Messianic prophet (Friedrich 1956).

Continuing with Palm Sunday, interpretation of Jacob's blessing
was dependent upon the Babylonian astral theology which had
permeated Judaism also with its cosmic imagery. We may today
find Babylonian imagery unfamiliar and yet be prepared to recognize that there is little in the Evangelists of the unreconstructed
historian. They were not trained in reportage but on the path of
discipleship. And we cannot come to terms with the historical
background of the Gospels without at least some understanding
of the relation between the event described and the consciousness
of the Evangelist. On the part of the Evangelists, it was not
possible for them to narrate, say, the entry into Jerusalem, without
having in themselves learnt to apply the symbolism of majesty to
the spiritual path.

Where Babylonian cosmology associated kingship with the
power of the sun at midsummer, sovereignty within is signified by

a circle of light surrounding the head, denoting wisdom. This crown of golden light is termed the 'halo', where the circle or disc of light invests the head of Christ or of the saints. 'Halo' is a Greek word meaning 'threshing floor', which seems at first sight unexpected. In the world-conception which reached its final flowering in Platonism, we referred to the metabolism as the 'manger' (*Timaeus* 38), the ox's stall. Without purification, 'oxlike' qualities make the head dull and obtuse. Yet unless the creative energy of the ox (bull) is restored to the head it is illumined only by the pale light of intellect. After purification, the power of the metabolism (ox) restores a royal strength to the head, endowing it with concentration and courage.

The Evangelists were able to record the life of Christ insofar as they themselves were able to develop their own spiritual qualities, to infuse their intellects with warmth and life. Their heads, untransformed, had too much winter in them. They needed in their mental faculties all the life and vigour of the spring and summer of human nature. Had the Evangelists strictly recorded 'how it was', we should have only a largely unrevealing portrait of Jesus of Nazareth (due to his reticence) moving amidst an uncomprehending group of companions who only began to perceive the divine dimension after his Resurrection. The accuracy of their depiction depended in the first place upon their own progress on the path of discipleship. The life of Christ which they set down is also the story of their own pilgrimage.

With their transformed consciousness the Evangelists were moved, after the Resurrection, to remember not only their own Hebrew culture (Matthew), but the very cradle of civilization (Luke). Their developing imaginative skill enabled them to employ or imply a wealth of imagery inherent in the ancient spiritual conception of the world. They could reach into the earliest cultural history, expressed in the opening chapters of Genesis. In the myths of creation, Eden, the Flood and so on, the Sumerians had recorded the thoughts and memories of man at the dawn of civilization, and these provide Genesis with its first eleven chapters. Drawing on the entire Old Testament, the Evangelists could avail themselves of the entire evolution of a culture, using the biography of a people to illustrate the life of Jesus.

It seems possible then that the Gospels represent a true historical record of the life of Christ only if there is an underlying connection between the pattern of the ministry and of the inner spiritual path of discipleship. It is not suggested that the Gospels set out the path of perfection of Jesus of Nazareth. But it is suggested that the converse is the case. The life of the Christ Jesus is itself the incarnation of the heavenly journey of the soul, his teaching being an important but not dominating part of his life. He retreads the path taken by humanity from the time when man first set foot on earth to the moment when he fully realizes his own mortality, when he becomes self-conscious.

Very soon after the age of Apostles, the inspiration of the Evangelists is only here and there in evidence in the writings of the Apostolic Fathers. Early Christian writers had no doubt that the Christ had already been partially revealed in pre-Christian culture. Stated less obviously, pre-Christian religion, cosmology and philosophy foreshadow the footstep, voice and thoughts of the Christ as he walked on earth.

Elsewhere profound insights into the life of Christ have been for centuries contributed by the great writers of each age. We shall merely attempt to heighten appreciation of the perspective of time, trusting that it will lead ultimately to a better grasp of the Gospels as history. We shall try to discern the unity between the Cosmic Christ, the creator of man, and the Jesus of history. For although his life may be set out as in any human biography, his life is the story of the new creation of humanity.

Biography normally explores the history of personality. The Gospels are not biographies in this sense. From various points of view they portray human nature before the dawn of personality obscures the pre-personality revelation of the human spirit. History's silence can be understood as witness that the Christ did not work through the power of a great historic personality, but through a quite new, inward and universally human quality. And a satisfactory chronology of Christ's life is possible only if the method takes full account of the uniquely universal which is nevertheless latent in every human being.

We need an ontogeny of Christ, a chronology of his becoming

human. We shall then try to discover whether this development-time, properly understood, can provide a bridge between the seemingly disparate worlds of the Gospel and the science of man. But our immediate aim must be to reconcile Gospel and history, in order to achieve a usable chronology.

3 Calendars and Festivals

It will be found that the possibility of extending our knowledge of Gospel chronology resides in a recognition that a number of important events in the Gospels are connected with particular religious festivals, although these are by no means always named. For instance, no new year festivals are identified as such by the Evangelists, yet it would seem that the Annunciation stories, the beginnings both of the Baptist's ministry and of the Christ's Galilean teaching ministry, as also the beheading of John the Baptist — all are connected with new year days.

The political framework is also important. Here we are concerned with the earthly life of an individual who was executed in Jerusalem while Pontius Pilate was Roman governor of Judea, John the Baptist's ministry beginning in the fifteenth year of Tiberius as Caesar. There is need, therefore, of an understanding of the political eras and of the civil calendar, especially during the Roman period. But we must first learn to distinguish between the political and religious calendars, and where they were applicable.

It will be suggested below that John the Baptist's ministry began in the autumn at the time of a pagan (civil calendar) new year's festival which was later adopted by Judaism as the rite of Tashlich. With regard to the Christ, our most certain information concerns the end of his earthly ministry. For the Crucifixion took place on a Friday, the eve of the Passover. Mention of other Passovers by the author of the Fourth Gospel enables us to determine the length of the Christ's ministry; and the internal chronology is constructed from a study of the sequence of festivals attended during this period.

The religious calendar

Judaism bred a profound concern with history which distinguished it from other religions. Other men might worship the revelation of God in nature, but the Jew revered the divine manifestation in the history of his people. Such an emphasis upon the historical Epiphany provided a progressive element absent in non-historical religions.

In his celebrated study *Christ and Time*, Oscar Cullmann distinguishes between 'linear' and 'cyclic' time. Development, evolution, progress emphasize the linear direction of time and this aspect of time is pre-eminent in biblical history. The advent of the Christ marks a qualitative change in the nature of time: *chronos* becomes *kairos*. *Chronos* (quantitative time) is the dry bed wherein once flowed the streams of Creation. *Kairos* (the qualitatively 'right' time) is the living water which springs up with the coming of the Christ. The flow extends backwards through time to the source of the original Creation as well as coursing through the future. For the Christian, the Incarnation is the starting point for understanding pre-Christian as well as Christian times: 'starting from that mid-point, the divine plan of salvation opened up in both a forward and backward direction.' (Cullmann 1951, 107).

If the Judeo-Christian conception of time is centred upon the Epiphany, Greek thought saw its most important aspect as a reflection of eternity. The regular motion of heavenly bodies reflects the 'circular' nature of eternity (Armstrong & Markus 1960, 119f):

> All living beings go through the familiar cycle of birth,
> growth, maturity, decay and death; and the same applies to
> the whole of the created universe, both in its parts and as a
> whole. Everything revolves in time according to number,
> and time itself revolves as the first of the moving things. The
> cycles are repeated until the whole cosmic cycle is fulfilled in
> the Great Year, that is to say, until the time when all the
> heavenly bodies, and hence the rest of the constituents of
> the cosmos, find themselves in the same relation to one
> another as they were in the beginning. And then a new
> cycle begins.

Professor Cullmann's distinction between linear and cyclic time is valuable in that it highlights the progressive nature of Judaism and Christianity. It would be a mistake to conclude that the cyclic element of time is unimportant. On the contrary, the order of

	Jewish	Equivalent	Babylonian
1	Nisan	March/April	Nisanu
2	Iyyar	April/May	Aiaru
3	Sivan	May/June	Simanu
4	Tammuz	June/July	Duzu
5	Ab	July/August	Abu
6	Elul	August/September	Ululu
7	Tishri	September/October	Tashritu
8	Heshvan	October/November	Arahsamnu
9	Kislev	November/December	Kislimu
10	Tebeth	December/January	Tebetu
11	Shebat	January/February	Shabatu
12	Adar	February/March	Addaru
	VeAdar	(intercalated month)	

Table 1. Jewish Month Names

Jewish worship and the path of Christian redemption run through the festival cycle of the sacred year.

In the rhythm of the seven-day week, the Mosaic pattern of Creation is ever and again unfolded just as Christianity relives each week the events of Holy Week. The days of the Jewish week, it may be mentioned, were numbered and not named. The months also were numbered (commencing in the spring) but, after the Captivity, Babylonian month-names were also employed (Table 1).

The *day* began after sunset when the stars began to appear. The *month* began with the observation of the first sickle of the new moon. According to Maimonides (1135–1204) (quoted by Finegan 1964, 42):

> Just as the astronomers who discern the positions and motions of the stars engage in calculation, so the Jewish court [Sanhedrin], too, used to study and investigate and perform mathematical operations, in order to find out whether or not it would be possible for the new crescent to be visible

37

in its 'proper time', which is the night of the 30th day. If the members of the court found that the new moon might be visible, they would be obliged to be in attendance at the court house for the whole 30th day and be on the watch for the arrival of witnesses. If witnesses did arrive, they were duly examined and tested, and if their testimony appeared trustworthy, this day was sanctified as New Moon Day. If the new crescent did not appear and no witnesses arrived, this day was counted as the 30th day of the old month.

The mean time between one new moon and the next is 29.530588 days which constitutes the synodic month. The new moon is, of course, invisible and the first sickle becomes visible in the evening at least 18 hours following the astronomical new moon. Finegan (1964, 74) relates from the Mishnah:

> In Jerusalem there was a special courtyard where the witnesses were examined and entertained . . . In the examination of witnesses they were interrogated with such questions as to whether the moon had been seen to the north or to the south of the sun . . . Rabbi Gamaliel II even had a diagram of the phases of the moon on a tablet hung on the wall of his upper chamber, and used it in questioning the witnesses.

Intercalation

The Jewish ecclesiastical year was parallel to but by no means always coincident with the Babylonian year. Where the Babylonians intercalated (added a month) to prevent their spring new year's day Nisanu 1 from falling before the equinox, the Jews intercalated to prevent Passover (Nisan 15) from falling before the vernal equinox. On average, therefore, the Jewish month began 14 days before its Babylonian namesake; that is, a month earlier nine times in 19 years. Failure to observe this distinction led a highly-regarded American historian of the Near East, A. T. Olmstead (1942a, 1942b) to write a life of Jesus based on the wrong calender.

A further difference between Babylonian and Jewish practice is to be found in the method of intercalation. In contrast to

Babylonian use of the regular intercalation *cycle*, the Jews retained into the fourth Christian century the *empirical* method of repeating the last month of the year to prevent Passover from falling too early.

Our authority for the Jewish empirical style of intercalation is Anatolius (d. AD 282), Bishop of Laodicea (in Eusebius, *Ch. Hist.* 7.32.16–19) who lists his supporting evidence:

> We can learn . . . from the statements of Philo, Josephus, and Musaeus, and not them only but still earlier writers, the two Agathobuli, famous as teachers of Aristobulus the Great . . . These authorities, in explaining the problems of the Exodus, state that the Passover ought invariably to be sacrificed after the spring equinox, at the middle of the first month; and that this occurs when the sun is passing through the first sign of the solar, or as some of them call it, the zodiacal cycle. Aristobulus adds that it is necessary at the Passover Festival that not only the sun but the moon as well should be passing through an equinoctial sign. There are two of these signs, one in the spring, one in the autumn, diametrically opposite each other, and the day of the Passover is assigned to the fourteenth of the month, after sunset; so the moon will occupy the position diametrically opposite the sun, as we can see when the moon is full; the sun will be in the sign of the spring equinox, the moon inevitably in that of the autumnal.

The Jews did not adopt the nineteen-year intercalation cycle until the fourth Christian century. Their previous custom is set out in the Talmud (Finegan 1964, 43).

> A year may be intercalated on three grounds: on account of the premature state of the corn crops; or that of the fruit trees; or on account of the lateness of the Tequfah [vernal equinox]. Any two of these can justify intercalation, but not one alone. . . The year may be intercalated on the ground that the kids or the lambs or the doves are too young. But we consider each of these circumstances as an auxiliary reason for intercalation.

An excerpt from a letter written by Rabban Gamaliel to the communities in Babylonia and Media reads (Finegan 1964, 43)

'We beg to inform you that the doves are still tender and the lambs still young and the grain has not yet ripened. I have considered the matter and thought it advisable to add thirty days to the year.'

Lastly, it should be noted that, in the present edition, the current practice has been adopted of stating dates of days from midnight to midnight, although in practice the Jewish day began in each case with the preceding sunset. For example, Nisan 14, sunset April 2, to sunset April 3, AD 33 is abbreviated to: Nisan 14, April 3, AD 33.

Festivals

The Jewish calendar was marked out by the movement of the moon in relation to the sun. The complement to this movement was the cycle of festivals which were celebrated with a wealth of religious artistry at salient points in the year. Judaism laid upon the devout an obligation to attend whenever possible the three annual pilgrim festivals in Jerusalem. These three feasts were closely associated with harvest celebrations: Firstly, the feast of Unleavened Bread (Passover) fell in the spring at the commencement of the barley harvest; secondly, seven weeks after the beginning of the barley harvest, Harvest or Weeks (Pentecost) was similarly connected with the wheat harvest; and thirdly, in the autumn, Tabernacles or Booths celebrated the ingathering of the year's harvest, and especially of the grape.

The first month of the ecclesiastical year (Nisan) was the month of Passover and Unleavened Bread. It opened without special ceremony, other than the usual sanctification of the new month by blowing trumpets. On Nisan 10 the sacrificial animals were brought to the Temple (the day of the Cleansing of the Temple). We are told that the day of the Crucifixion was Friday (the day of preparation for the sabbath, Mark 15:42) and also the eve of the Passover (the day of preparation for the Passover, John 19:14), that is Nisan 14. When Passover fell on the sabbath — a great and holy day — the daily evening burnt offering was slaughtered at 12.30 pm and offered at 1.30 pm. The Passover lambs were slaughtered in vast numbers thereafter (Mishnah, Pesachim 5:1).

The Feast of Unleavened Bread prescribed a diet of the 'bread of affliction' for seven days after all leaven had been removed. There is no agreement about the precise dates involved, but its beginning was connected with the commencement of the barley harvest. For calendrical reasons, the Pharisees insisted that the first sheaf of barley, the *omer*, was reaped on the day after Passover, that is Nisan 16, whereas the Sadducees and the Samaritans observed the Sunday after Passover for the same purpose. The practices coincided in 33, the year of the Crucifixion.

J. van Goudoever (1961, 18f) quotes from the Mishnah a lively account of the cutting of the first barley sheaf:

> The messenger of the court [Sanhedrin] used to call out on the eve of the festival and tie the corn in bunches while it was yet unreaped to make it easier to reap; and the towns near by all assembled there that it might be reaped with pomp. When it grew dark he called out, 'Is the sun set?' and they answered 'Yea!' 'Is the sun set?' and they answered 'Yea!' 'Is this a sickle?' and they answered 'Yea!' 'Is this a sickle?' and they answered 'Yea!' 'Is this a basket?' and they answered 'Yea!' 'Is this a basket?' and they answered 'Yea!' On the Sabbath he called out 'On this Sabbath?' and they answered 'Yea!' 'On this Sabbath?' and they answered 'Yea!' 'Shall I reap?' and they answered 'Reap!' 'Shall I reap?' and they answered 'Reap!' He used to call out three times for every matter and they answered 'Yea, yea, yea!'

The harvest begun in such impressive style lasted for seven weeks. The Jewish Easter festival provides a perfect example of the way in which the divine gift of human freedom (Passover commemorated the departure from bondage in Egypt) rested on the right relationship between the natural and the spiritual. Pentecost also had its agricultural basis. Since it fell seven weeks after the offering of the first barley sheaf, there was disagreement between the Pharisees who observed Sivan 6 and the Sadducees and Samaritans who celebrated Pentecost on the Sunday of Sivan 6–12.

J. van Goudoever (1961, 15) writes of Pentecost:

> The second of the three feasts is the Feast of Harvest or the Feast of Weeks. Some tables of the festivals prescribe the counting of the full seven weeks, others only mention the

last day, the feast itself. The seven weeks are counted from the beginning of the barley harvest; the fiftieth day, the Feast of Harvest, coincides with the end of the wheat harvest: the first fruits of the wheat harvest are brought in on this day.

When van Goudoever adds that the wave-offering, the *tenuphah* (meaning 'consecration') of two wheat (leavened) loaves, is offered at the Feast of Weeks to the Lord, he does not really clarify the picture. It is possible that he intended to state that Harvest coincides with the end of the barley (not wheat) harvest, since he makes it clear that we are concerned with the first-fruits of the wheat harvest. But he goes on to speak again of the end of the harvest being celebrated at Pentecost.

Perhaps the parallel between Pentecost (after forty-nine days) and the Jubilee (after forty-nine years) indicates that the common motif is release. Professor John Gray of Aberdeen explained to me that Pentecost was a festival offering of first-fruits, thereby deconsecrating the remainder of the crop so that it became available for the people.

Both Pentecost and Jubilee were a time of revelation and redemption. Historically, the feast of Pentecost commemorated the giving of the Law on Sinai. Philo (*Deca.* 46f) indeed, comes close to the New Testament picture of the festival of the Holy Spirit, whilst telling of the giving of the Mosaic Law.

> Then from the midst of the fire that streamed from heaven
> there sounded forth to their utter amazement a voice, for
> the flame became articulate speech in the language familiar
> to the audience, and so clearly and distinctly were the
> words formed by it that they seemed to see rather than hear
> them. What I say is vouched for by the law in which it is
> written, 'All the people saw the voice'.

Just as Passover was followed by the opening of the harvest season, the Feast of Booths, Tabernacles or Ingathering celebrated the end of the harvest season. Ingathering was preceded by ten days of prayer and penitence starting at the autumn new year's day, Tishri 1, and ending Tishri 10, the Day of Atonement (Yom Kippur). On new year, it is said, God opens three books. The first contains the names of the virtuous and pious, who are inscribed forthwith for life and blessing during the ensuing twelve months. The second contains the names of the irremediably wicked and impious; these are inscribed forthwith for death and disaster. In the third, however, are written the names of the 'betwixt-and-betweens' who are given the chance to determine their own fates by prayer and penitence, for the record is not sealed until twilight on Yom Kippur. After preparation on the Day of Atonement, the high priest on this day alone entered the Holy of Holies of the Temple. Wherever, on this single occasion in the year, the high priest reached the end of the Scriptural quotation, he uttered the otherwise ineffable name 'Yahweh', instead of the usual 'Adonai' (Lord).

Like Passover and Pentecost, the autumn festival was an occasion on which ideally all Israelites should make their pilgrimage to Jerusalem. During the summer, the first-fruits had been gathered of grain, wine, oil, honey, and all the produce of the field (2Chr.31:5), while the people lived in trellised-roofed cabins of intertwined branches of olive, myrtle, palm, carob and oleander. And at the autumn full moon they celebrated with great joy *the* feast of the Jews. They remembered also the time when the people had lived in tents up to the building of Solomon's Temple, the feast retaining the element of Temple dedication.

Lastly, at midwinter, the Feast of Dedication (Hanukkah) was celebrated for eight days, beginning on Kislev 25, to commemorate the victory of Judas Maccabeus over the Seleucid tyrant Antiochus Epiphanes, and the subsequent rededication of the Temple in 165 BC. On this day each year, Hanukkah is marked by the lighting of eight lamps at dusk. Usually one lamp is lit on the first evening, two on the second, and so on, providing Judaism with its counterpart to the lights on the Christmas tree.

There were in the sacred year of Judaism additionally four fast days. J. van Goudoever (1961, 45) says that the fasts were all associated with the siege and fall of Jerusalem in 587 BC under Nebuchadnezzar. They came into existence during the Babylonian Captivity and were revived after the destruction of the second Temple in AD 70. In which case it is understandable that the destruction of the Temple in AD 70 was mourned after the war with Rome, even though the days were overtly connected with the earlier tragedy.

THE TIME OF CHRIST

Tebeth 10 (midwinter)	Beginning of the siege
Tammuz 17 (9) (June)	Breach of the city walls
Ab 9 (July)	Destruction of the Temple
Tishri 3 (September)	Assassination of Gedaliah

Although it is often rightly emphasized that Judaism and Christianity share the concept of 'linear' time, of progress in history, we should not underestimate the role in all religious life of cyclic time. Redemption is the theme of biblical history and both the order of Jewish worship and the path of Christian redemption run through the festival cycle of the sacred year.

The civil calendar

The Seleucid era (SE) is the world's first era (beginning autumn 312 BC in Syrian reckoning, and spring 311 BC in Babylonian/Jewish reckoning). As cities won their independence from the Seleucid kingdom, they dated their years from their independence. After Pompey's overthrow of the Seleucids, events were officially dated by reference to the Roman Emperors (and their precursors) while the Seleucid Era remained in common use.

Octavian (Augustus) defeated Antony at the Battle of Actium on September 2, 31 BC, and subsequent events were often dated from this battle, making the Actian era (AE) (see Appendix 2).

While the Jewish religious calendar is more familiar to us, the civil calendar was used to record mundane happenings in the departments of fiscal, military and foreign affairs. In the modern British calendar, the beginning of the regnal year (for example Queen Elizabeth's 25th year) is followed some six months later by the beginning of the ecclesiastical year (on the first Sunday in Advent). Modern royalists and ecclesiastics appear to experience no difficulty in interpreting for example AD 1985/6 according to which new year is involved. In antiquity, the Jews similarly observed the opening of their ecclesiastical year some six months after their royal (or civil) year.

Biblical scholars have paid little attention to the Jewish civil calendar, believing it to belong rather to the province of Syrian political history. In fact the Seleucid Empire had imposed its Syro-Macedonian calendar on the Jews in 200 BC when Antiochus III

44

finally succeeded in incorporating Palestine into Syria's political orbit. Yet Biblical scholars profess themselves perplexed: (Schürer 1973, 18):

> Since there existed in both the Hellenistic world and among the Jews two rival calendars, with one New Year in the spring (1 Nisan) and one in the autumn (1 Tishri), it will surprise no-one that the chronology of the Maccabean works is beset with complex problems requiring individual consideration.

Fortunately new data published in 1954 enabled J. Schaumberger (1955) to clear up many of the misconceptions and uncertainties. Schaumberger showed that the author of the First Book of the Maccabees employed two calendars: the Jewish ecclesiastical calendar (with its spring new year) for all religious and internal purposes, and the Hellenistic or civil calendar for all political and external purposes. Ecclesiastical years ran parallel to the years of the Babylonian Seleucid era and were likewise numbered from the Babylonian starting-point spring 311 BC. The essential point is that the civil year (with its autumn new year) began some six months *earlier* than the equivalent ecclesiastical year. For the civil year ran parallel to Antioch's Syro-Macedonian year which was counted from the Syrian epoch of the Seleucid era autumn 312 BC. Correct interpretation of a date, then, requires correct identification of the calendar, sacred or secular.

When we come to examine the chronology of Herod the Great's reign, we shall find it crucial to decide whether, initially, Herod could have been considered a Hellenistic or an Israelite king. As a commoner, Herod had no legitimate claim to the throne in Jewish eyes. He had been appointed king by the Roman Senate *circa* December 40 BC and sought to gain his kingdom by force of arms. It will be shown that Herod's *de jure* years (40–37 BC) should be counted according to the *civil* calendar; his accession will then be dated Tishri 1, October 1, 40 BC.

At the outset of the Roman period Pompey finally destroyed Seleucid power, and Rome's domination of Antioch is dated from the epoch of the Pompeian era in Syria, autumn 66 BC. Later Roman coins (see Appendix 2) provide the Syrian epoch of the Caesarian era as autumn 49 BC. Similarly, the epoch of the Actian era in Syria is known to be autumn 31 BC. And it is also possible to equate years of the Actian era with years of Tiberius. A coin of *Q. Caecilius Metellus Creticus Silanus* (governor of Syria AD 12–17) is numbered 45 AE (autumn AD 14–15) and A (the first year of Tiberius). The further interpretation of the fifteenth year of Tiberius (Luke 3:1) will be discussed in Chapter 9.

Finally, the Crucifixion is everywhere attested to have been carried out under Pontius Pilate as procurator of Judea. His dispatch as successor to Valerius Gratus is recorded by Josephus (*Ant.* 18.35) dating his appointment AD 26. His recall is mentioned (*Ant.* 18.89) giving the date of his dismissal as AD 36: 'And so Pilate, after having spent ten years in Judaea, hurried to Rome in obedience to the orders of Vitellius, since he could not refuse.' Apart from the data in Josephus, there are coins of the procurator dated Tiberius 16, Tiberius 17 and Tiberius 18 (Meshorer 1967, Nos. 229–31 respectively), AD 29–32. Pilate's term of office was therefore AD 26 to AD 36.

We should further like to know whether the Trial scenes in the Gospels fit better into the earlier (AD 30) or later (AD 33) period of Pilate's rule. In the Gospels, the governor appears in a not unsympathetic light, weak and vacillating but inclined to be just. A nearly contemporary (AD 40) pen portrait has him provocatively anti-Semitic, naturally inflexible, a blend of self-will and relentlessness (Philo *Emb. G.* 299–305). Why, asks Stauffer (1960, 108f) are we not shown the mass-murderer, arbitrary and scornful of due process of law, when we read in the Gospels of the Trial? Stauffer's explanation is that Pilate was a creature of Tiberius' effective ruler, Sejanus. Exercising almost unlimited power in Rome, Sejanus was characterized by a strong anti-Semitism not shared by Tiberius. After the disgrace and death of Sejanus on October 18, AD 31, Tiberius took the government into his own hands again. Before autumn 31, Pilate was secure in Sejanus' favour, and even flagrant anti-Semitism in Jerusalem would have been applauded in Rome. After the death of Sejanus, Tiberius frowned upon signs of Pilate's misrule, as his ultimate recall shows. Stauffer's analysis is compatible with the Trial falling in the year 33 but not with the year 30.

4 The Time Approaching

'And the Jews and their priests decided that Simon should be their leader and high priest for ever, until a true prophet should arise . . .' In recognition of the Hasmonean family's valiant resistance to Seleucid persecution, the high priesthood was conferred on the brother of Judas Maccabeus in perpetuity. 'In perpetuity' meant that the office of high priest should pass to the house of Hasmon only until this provisional high priesthood should come to an end with the appearance of the Messianic prophet (1Macc. 14:25).

Simon was not accorded the royal title also, which was withheld pending the emergence of the royal Messiah. In Judaism prophet, priest, and king each had clearly defined spiritual roles, which could not be undertaken by a single individual without corruption unless he were perfect. At intervals during the period of Hasmonean rule, the separation of priestly and royal powers became a vital public issue, as Simon's descendants sought to enhance their personal power and prestige by combining them.

It was this issue which led to a breach between Simon's immediate successor John Hyrcanus (135–104 BC) and the Pharisees, and brought about his alliance with the Sadducees. Hyrcanus on one occasion incautiously solicited advice from the Pharisees. After offering the expected praise, one of them added, 'As you wish to know the truth, then know that if you wish to be righteous, lay down the office of high priest and content yourself with ruling the nation (*Ant.* 13.288–98). For Hyrcanus, his subsequent Sadducean alliance betokened a distinct weakening of the Hasmonean's religious interest in deference to his worldly aspirations. A. Schalit (1972, 290f) is well worth quoting at length.

> The Pharisees saw in the concentration of the two offices, the kingship and the High Priesthood, in the hands of this dynasty the ominous instrument with which the Hasmoneans were attempting to carry out their designs. Such concentration meant that the Hasmoneans not only

conducted the temporal affairs of the nation but — and
this the Pharisees considered far more important — they
also held the reins of religious affairs, so that they were in
a position to mold the nation's religious and moral character
in accordance with their secular ambitions.

The Pharisees regarded this state of affairs as intolerable,
and they were firm in their resolve to separate the two
offices. They insisted that the Hasmoneans content
themselves with the monarchy and relinquish the High
Priesthood. What was the political significance of this
demand? In order to understand this we must recall the
Pharisees' view of the role of religion in the life of the Jewish
people. The Pharisees regarded religion as the sum and
substance of the Jewish people. Religion in their opinion
should embrace the nation's life in all its manifestations; in
economic affairs and labor, art and thought, law and politics,
the life of society and of the individual . . . In the eyes of
the Pharisees, therefore, the Hasmonean state . . . which
had blurred the boundaries between Israel and the nations
and drawn the Chosen People close to the way of life of the
gentiles, had caused it to forget the cardinal fact in its life
which had determined its character forever: its existence as
a holy people. For this reason the state which the
Hasmonean dynasty had founded could not satisfy the
yearnings and the hope of the Pharisees. These could be
satisfied only by the kingdom of the Messiah of the House
of David. That kingdom alone they regarded as the fitting
framework for the life of the Chosen People.

The spirit of Messianism, which had been fired by the Maccabean revolt, subsequently underwent many changes. Schürer
(1979, 488ff) traces the changes in the older Messianic hope. Its
scale grew from national to global redemption. At the same time
the extension of hope for the future altered its focus from the
people at large to the just individual. And during the first Christian
century the Scriptures were searched diligently for illumination
on the coming of the Messiah — or several Messianic figures.

The Book of Daniel, thought to have been written during the
Maccabean uprising, proved vastly influential in shaping Messianic

expectations. In the Apocrypha and pseudepigraphical books of the Old Testament (Charlesworth 1983), on the other hand, Messianic hope played no great role. The hope of resurrection in the Second Book of the Maccabees marks an important development, and the Psalms of Solomon (Pompeian period) anticipates the Messianic king in fuller colour and sharper outline. There is also evidence of Messianism during the reign of Herod the Great in Josephus (*Ant.* 17.43ff).

It is unlikely to have escaped the Herodians that Virgil's *Fourth Eclogue* was composed just at the time of Herod's coronation in Rome. The occasion which prompted the poet was the (temporary) reconciliation between Octavian (Augustus) and Antony following the Treaty of Brundisium on October 2, 40 BC, which set the scene for Herod's unexpected triumph.

> Now there has come the last age of which the Cumaean
> Sybil sang; a great orderly line of centuries begins anew;
> now too the Virgin returns; the reign of Saturn returns; a
> new generation descends from the high heavens. Upon *the
> Child* now to be born, under whom the race of iron will
> cease and a golden race will spring up over the whole world
> . . . (Virgil, *Fourth Eclogue*, 4–9. Tr. Brown 1977, 566).

We need an outline history of Messianic expectation as well as a chronology of its fulfilment. But frequent quotation in the New Testament of Messianic passages from the Old Testament should not confuse. These Messianic connotations were for the most part recognized only after the Resurrection. How alien these interpretations were to contemporary Judaism is attested by the behaviour of both the disciples and of the opponents of Jesus (for example Matt.16:22, Luke 18:34; 24:21, John 12:34). There is no evidence that, at the beginning of our era, a suffering Messiah was expected.

In medieval Judaism we find the rabbinic doctrine of two Messiahs developed (Klausner 1956, and Sarachek 1968). But it is also now well-known that the Essene Order awaited both the Prophet and the Davidic King as forerunners of the priestly Messiah who would take precedence over them. The Prophet is mentioned explicitly only once (1QS 9:11), 'they [the members of the Community] shall depart from none of the counsels of the

Law . . . until the coming of the Prophet and the Messiahs of Aaron and Israel' (Schürer 1979, 550–54). Publication of the Dead Sea Scrolls confirmed that Qumran looked to the coming of a priestly Messiah as well as the more familiar figures of the Prophet and the royal Messiah.

They describe the Messianic banquet to be held when God would beget the Messiah to be with them (1QSa 2:11–22). The Priest will be accompanied by the Sons of Aaron, and the Messiah of Israel — as military commander — by his commanders. The Priest takes precedence over the Davidic Messiah in all spiritual matters. The earliest form of Essenic Messianism appears to have been the expectation of the priestly Messiah heralded by the Prophet. At what stage dual Messianism arose is not known, but it was probably in the Hasmonean period that sacerdotal Messianism coalesced with the traditional Davidic promise (Schürer 1979, 488–554).

Karl Georg Kuhn (1958, 60) explains:

> The concept of the two Messiahs, a priestly and a political one, is actually not as strange as it first appears to be. The entire structure of postexilic Israel shows the side-by-side position of the priestly hierarchy and a worldly political leadership. This structure is given already in the juxtaposition of the priests and the 'princes' as worldly leaders, found in Ezekiel 44–46. In Zech.4:14 (c. 520 BC) we see, side-by-side, the Aaronite Joshua, the high priest, and the Davidic Zerubbabel, the worldly leader of the Israelite community, as 'the two anointed ones'. In the final stage of development, more than 500 years later, during the second Jewish insurrection against the Romans (AD 132–135), the same juxtaposition occurs. The high priest Eleazar stands side by side with the political messianic leader of the uprising, Simon ben Kosba (bar Kokba). [Note: Bar Kokba (Son of Stars) was a Messianic interpretation of his name according to Num.24:17.] Here, however, contrary to the Essene order of precedence, the political head has the first place, while the high priest ranks second.

It is not difficult to see that Matthew's Nativity account corresponds to the expectation of a royal Messiah. It is the priestly

Messiah who seemed to be absent from the Gospels, although the Christ is portrayed as high priest in the Letter to the Hebrews and, less explicitly, in the Book of Revelation. After a thorough re-examination of the question, G. Friedrich (1956, 265ff) comes to an entirely different conclusion. He finds that the priestly concept is central to the Gospel picture of Jesus, even though it is not spelled out. 'Every period has its problems and its tasks. Earlier, Jesus had been seen first as Messiah, then as Son of Man, finally as Servant of God. The newly discovered Scrolls prompt an investigation of high priestly Christology in the Synoptics.' He goes on to say he believes 'that originally Jesus was regarded and revered exclusively as the high priest'.

Through a better understanding of Jewish Messianism, we are able to examine afresh the great divergences between Matthew's and Luke's Nativity accounts. The complete separation of the three Messianic offices was a prerequisite of the opening of the Messianic age. Only then could they be combined in one incorruptible individual. Later, Christian writers looked back upon the Incarnation as the investment of Jesus with the three Messianic offices. Eusebius (*Ch. Hist.* 1.3.10) regards all the high priests, kings and prophets of the Old Testament as foreshadowing the anointed one, 'Christs in image'. '. . . they all stand in relation to the true Christ, the divine and heavenly Word who is the sole High Priest of the universe, the sole King of all creation, and of prophets the sole Archprophet of the Father.'

5 Herod

Pompey's capture of Jerusalem in 63 BC was the long-delayed outcome of the pact with Rome made a hundred years earlier in a moment of despair by Judas Maccabeus. Although Pompey appointed the Hasmonean John Hyrcanus II high priest, Herod's father Antipater was already playing a powerful role as steadfast friend of Rome. When Rome's Parthian foes took possession of Jerusalem in 40 BC they deposed Hyrcanus and installed his nephew Antigonus as high priest and king. Herod had no option but flight and arrived in Rome not many days after Octavian (Augustus) and Antony had ceased hostilities and renewed their alliance at the Treaty of Brundisium on October 2, 40 BC. At their instigation, and without much ado, the Senate appointed Herod king of Judea.

Herod had hardly hoped for such an abrupt turn of fortune. His Idumean father had bequeathed on him the advantages of great wealth and political influence, but his descent endowed him with not a drop of royal blood. And the Romans normally were disinclined to look outside the royal houses for their client kings (Josephus, *Ant.* 14.386f):

> But this was the greatest sign of Antony's devotion to Herod, that not only did he obtain the kingship for him, which he had not hoped for — he had come to the capital not to claim the kingship for himself, for he did not believe the Romans would offer it to him, since it was their custom to give it to one of the reigning family, but to claim it for his (Hasmonean) wife's brother, who was the grandson of Aristobulus on his father's side and of Hyrcanus on his mother's . . .

After disqualifying his uncle, John Hyrcanus II, from priestly office by a technical mutilation, Mattathias Antigonus met both requirements — Hasmonean descent, and ecclesiastical acknowledgment — to be selected as high priest. As high priest and Israelite king (Rosh Hashanah 1.1), Antigonus would have reckoned his reign from the spring (ecclesiastical) new year preceding accession, Nisan 1, March 19, 40 BC (equivalent to 272 SE as in Appendix 2).

Herod was appointed king in about December 40 BC not by popular acclaim, nor by ecclesiastical assent, nor by virtue of descent. His candidature for royal power could then be admitted only in the Hellenistic sense of kingship. It was a purely political appointment by a foreign government and still to be effected by force of arms. His reign would then have been reckoned from the preceding civil (Hellenistic) autumn new year's day (conventionally stated as Tishri 1) September 14, 40 BC, and Herod's *de jure* year 1 is 273 SE.

As already put forward in Chapter 3, Schaumberger (1955) demonstrated that a sharp distinction is to be drawn between specifically Jewish and internal events, which were dated according to the Jewish ecclesiastical calendar in Nisan-to-Nisan years, and political and external events which belonged to the civil calendar and were dated in Tishri-to-Tishri years. Each date in the First Book of the Maccabees has to be interpreted according to this rule. The novelty in Herod's case is that the tyrant is not a Seleucid king but legally a Jew.

It is necessary both for the New Testament concept of the Messiah and for the chronology of Herod's reign to distinguish between Herod's ambitions and the nature of Israelite kingship. J. Gray (1969, 129n) observes,

> The king among the ancient Semites including the Hebrews was the temporal guarantee of the Order of God. As such among the Hebrews he was described as the son of God (Psalm 2). In Israel this described the social and moral relationship of the king to Divine authority. But in ancient Canaan and the pagan East it was capable of grosser interpretation.

Israel throughout its history had striven to distinguish between the king as protector of the faith, and the absolutist — a Pharaoh, an Antiochus IV Epiphanes, a 'divine' Caesar — whose pretensions made him an enemy of God.

After returning to Palestine in 39 BC, Herod vigorously prosecuted his campaign to win the kingdom during 39 and 38. In

53

January 37 BC an emphatic success afforded him an opportunity for a sudden assault on Jerusalem but he was thwarted by a violent winter storm (Josephus *War* 1.343). 'When the tempest abated, he advanced upon Jerusalem and marched his army up to the walls, it being now just three years since he had been proclaimed king in Rome.' Clearly Josephus is counting Herod's *de jure* years from the ecclesiastical spring new year Nisan 1, 40 BC. Accordingly the fall of the capital in July 37 BC would have occurred in Herod's fourth *de jure* year.

Herod issued a new coinage to commemorate his victory and its dating allows us to test the correctness of Josephus' Herodian chronology. Fortunately we are now able to turn for help to a new generation of highly expert Israeli numismatists for an opinion on Herod's dated coinage. Earlier Jewish coins had not been dated and the innovation is Hellenistic. Herod's predecessor, the Hasmonean Mattathias Antigonus, had preserved on his coins at least the proper distinction between his priestly and his royal roles. One coin (Meshorer 1967, No. 30), for instance, has on the obverse in Hebrew, 'Mattathias the high priest and the congregation of the Jews', and on the reverse in Greek, 'King Antigonus'. Herod's coins omit the Hebrew inscription and retain only the Greek, 'Herod the King'. These coins, which were dated 'Year 3', must have been minted in great abundance since they were to replace the entire Hasmonean currency. It is then hardly surprising to find a single year's issue exhibiting no less than four coin types. The Israel Museum's outstanding numismatist, Y. Meshorer, comments (1967, 66f) on the interpretation of the coin-date,

> . . . it must have been of decisive importance, as otherwise this date, and this one alone, could not have been emphasized to such an extent. Which was the third year of Herod's reign and what happened then?

> This question has been widely discussed and the explanation which has been suggested and is given here in brief appears to be quite logical. While in Rome in 40 BCE, Herod was appointed king of Judea, at a time when Mattityah Antigonus ruled over that territory. For three years Herod waged war against Antigonus until in 37 BCE

Julian date	Civil calendar			Ecclesiastical calendar		
	Seleucid Era	Herod civil	Herod's successors	Seleucid Era	Antigonus (High priest & king)	Herod eccl
BC 40 spring				272	1	
40 autumn	273	1				
39 spring				273	2	
39 autumn	274	2				
38 spring				274	3	
38 autumn	275	3				
37 spring				275	4	
37 autumn	276	4				
36 spring				276		1
36 autumn	277					
35 spring				277		2
35 autumn	278					
34 spring				278		3
34 autumn	279					
. . .	. . . . .			. . . . . .		. . . .
5 autumn	308					
4 spring				308		33
4 autumn	309					
3 spring				309		34
3 autumn	310		1			
BC 2 spring				310		35

Table 2. Herod's dates.

he conquered Jerusalem and became the effective ruler of Judea. Hence what was theoretically his third year was actually his first.

Counting from *spring* 40 BC, Herod's third year was equivalent to spring 38 – spring 37 BC. Counting from *autumn* 40 BC — as in the assessment of Herod's status as Hellenistic aspirant only — his third year is dated autumn 38 – autumn 37 BC. His capture of Jerusalem, commemorated on the coins dated Year 3, occurred in July 37 BC. The coin-date confirms the interpretation that Herod dated his reign from *autumn* 40 BC.

Josephus (*War* 1.665) carefully states the length of Herod's reign in an unusually complicated manner in that it implies two starting-points. 'He expired after a reign of thirty-four years, reckoning from the date when, after putting Antigonus to death, he assumed control of the state; of thirty-seven years from the date when he was proclaimed king by the Romans.'

In order to ascertain whether Josephus is here implying a Jewish coronation (after the death of Antigonus) as well as the Roman coronation in 40 BC, it is necessary to pay close attention to the events following Herod's capture of Jerusalem.

When victory had been achieved, Herod had crushed all active opposition and he had seen Antigonus taken away in chains to await Antony's pleasure. Yet the people would not submit to accept Herod as their legitimate king. Most of the Jerusalem inhabitants had supported Antigonus during Herod's three-year campaign for the kingdom. Retrospective recognition that he had been the legitimate ruler since 40 BC would have been tantamount to a confession of treason. Herod further antagonized his conquered subjects by appointing Ananel as high priest in the stead of Antigonus.

In order to achieve the far more durable status of an ecclesiastically acknowledged national king, Herod needed to eliminate his rival Antigonus and then offer, in exchange for a Jewish coronation, to restore the Hasmonean high priesthood. Herod had failed to browbeat the opposition (Josephus *Ant.* 15.2):

> When Herod got the rule of all Judaea into his hands, he showed special favour to those of the city's populace who had been on his side while he was still a commoner, but those who chose the side of his opponents, he harried and punished without ceasing for a single day.

Strabo (quoted in *Ant.* 15.9f) explains Antony's agreement to execute Antigonus,

> . . . since he believed that in no other way could he change the attitude of the Jews so that they would accept Herod, who had been appointed in his place. For not even under torture would they submit to proclaiming him king, so highly did they regard their former king.

Antigonus would represent Hasmonean rule as long as he lived. Herod therefore bribed Antony to execute his prisoner, and offered his subjects the irresistible concession of restoring the Hasmonean high priesthood. In return Herod sought and obtained recognition of his claim to rule not from 40 BC but 'from the date when, after putting Antigonus to death, he assumed control of the state'. In the political and military sense of 'the state' Herod had for months been in total possession of the reins of government. What he inherited after the death of Antigonus was the more subtle but very real spiritual power embodied in the Judaistic concept of kingship.

Herod acted as if to fulfil his side of the bargain. He restored the Hasmonean high priesthood by appointing his brother-in-law, Aristobulus, the handsome and extremely youthful brother of his wife Mariamne, in the place of Ananel. He had already brought back from Babylon the deposed John Hyrcanus II 'to share his kingship with him'.

The Hasmonean members of his own family were not so easily placated, and Herod suspected his mother-in-law of plotting his downfall, despite his conciliatory (albeit illegal) dismissal of Ananel from the high priesthood. Within months he fully justified her continuing suspicions. The popular young high priest Aristobulus was lost in a contrived bathing accident (*Ant.* 15:53–56). Mariamne was executed, closely followed by her mother. After the unpredictable Antony had left the public stage, Herod was free to eliminate the aged Hyrcanus, 'the only one left of royal rank' (*Ant.* 15.164). Before Herod's life had come to an end, he had dispatched all the sons whom Mariamne had borne him. Herod's successors should owe their position entirely to him, and not to their mother's Hasmonean blood.

Herod had transgressed most deeply against Jewish religious tradition by engineering recognition of himself as king in the Judaistic sense. As a child his future had been foretold (*Ant.* 15.373–76):

> There was a certain Essene named Manaēmus, whose virtue
> was attested in his whole conduct of life and especially in
> his having from God a foreknowledge of the future. This
> man had (once) observed Herod, then still a boy, going to
> his teacher, and greeted him as 'king of the Jews'. Thereupon
> Herod, who thought that the man either did not know who
> he was, or was teasing him, reminded him that he was only
> a private citizen. Manaēmus, however, gently smiled and

slapped him on the backside saying, 'Nevertheless, you will be king and you will rule the realm happily, for you have been found worthy of this by God. And you will remember the blows given by Manaēmus, so that they, too, may be for you a symbol of how one's fortune can change. For the best attitude for you to take would be to love justice and piety toward God and mildness toward your citizens. But I know that you will not be such a person, since I understand the whole situation. Now you will be singled out for such good fortune as no other man has had, and you will enjoy eternal glory, but you will forget piety and justice. This, however, cannot escape the notice of God, and at the close of your life His wrath will show that He is mindful of these things.'

We have seen that Herod's reign fell into two unequal parts. During the first *de jure* years, he fought successfully to replace Hasmonean rule which had endured since the Maccabean revolt. Military success, however, gave the victor no guarantee of permanency, and certainly no right to expect the establishment of a Herodian dynasty comparable to the house of Hasmon. Internationally, Herod had tied his wagon to Antony's evanescent star, and Herod's uncertain future under Octavian would demand unquestioned internal stability.

The second part of his reign began during the winter of 37–36 BC, when Herod sought Jewish recognition simply in order to enhance his chances of survival. Yet, even if his motives were entirely political, his destruction of the Hasmonean high priesthood had important Messianic implications. The Hasmonean high priesthood had been intended to endure until the appearance of a true prophet should inaugurate the Messianic age. After his death, Herod left behind the impression that the title he had usurped represented in itself a Messianic claim. Tertullian and Epiphanius asserted that this was the belief of the Herodians (*Presc.* 45): '*Herodiani Christum Herodem esse dixerunt* [The Herodians said, "Herod is the Messiah"].'

While the chronology of Herod's reign first requires that the early years be properly assessed in conjunction with the appropriate calendar, it is ultimately the death date which biblical scholars wish to ascertain. Table 2 shows that, following a reign of thirty-four years (after his Jewish coronation on Nisan 1, 36 BC) Herod died in his thirty-fifth year spring 2 – spring 1 BC. The date can be more narrowly defined by placing his death between the lunar eclipse of January 10, 1 BC (*Ant.* 17:167) and the following Passover at Nisan 15, April 10, 1 BC.

It is possible to state Herod's death date still more precisely, although not with the same degree of certainty. The *Megillath Taanith* (written after AD 70) mentions two festive days on which fasting was forbidden, without mentioning the occasions they commemorated: Kislev 7 and Shebat 2. In the Nisan-to-Nisan year 2–1 BC, Kislev 7 corresponds to December 5, 2 BC, and Shebat 2 to January 28, 1 BC. All chronologists who have dated Herod's death 1 BC have gone on to pinpoint Shebat 2. Thus E. L. Martin (1980, 53) quotes Burnaby, 'M. Moise Schwab, who studied the information about the scroll very intensively, felt that it was really the second of these, Shebat 2, that was the actual day which commemorated Herod's death.'

When calendrical, coin and astronomical data are given due weight, we find that Herod died certainly early in 1 BC, and probably on Shebat 2, January 28, 1 BC. The circumstances of his reign were not simple and the reader is referred to my 'Herodian Chronology' (1982) for a full examination of the detailed chronological argument.

6 The Star

When Jesus was born in Bethlehem of Judea in the days of Herod the king, behold, magi from eastern lands came to Jerusalem saying, 'Where is the new-born king of the Jews? For we have seen his star in the ascendant and have come to worship him.' When Herod the king heard this he was greatly agitated and all Jerusalem with him. And assembling all the chief priests and scribes of the people, he inquired of them where the Christ should be born. 'In Bethlehem of Judea,' they told him, 'for it is written by the prophet, "And thou, Bethlehem in the land of Judah, art not least among the princes of Judah; for out of thee shall come a prince, who will govern my people Israel".' Then Herod summoned the magi secretly and ascertained from them the time of the star's appearance. Then he sent them to Bethlehem saying, 'Go and search diligently for the child and when you have found him, send word that I too may come and worship him.'

When they had heard the king, they set out; and behold, the star which they had seen at its rising went before them until it came to rest over the place where the young child was. Beholding the star, they rejoiced with exceeding great joy. And going into the house, they saw the young child with Mary his mother and they fell down and worshipped him. And opening their treasures, they offered him gold, frankincense and myrrh. And being warned in a dream not to return to Herod, they departed to their own country by another way. (Matt.2:1–12 author's translation).

This chapter of Mathew is full of kings, for the magi were also called kings in classical times. In Jerusalem they met the false 'king of the Jews', before going on to Bethlehem to pay homage to the new-born Davidic heir to the throne.

Determining the nature and timing of the star of Bethlehem requires some knowledge of Babylonian astronomy. A great soul entering incarnation may have appeared to the spiritual eye of the magi as itself a radiant star (Zarathustra was called the 'golden star') but their spiritual experience was characteristically projected on to the cosmos. And the faith they professed is known today as 'cosmic religion' (see Waerden 1974).

Originally a Median priestly caste, the magi had since the fifth century BC served as the official priesthood of Zarathustrianism. Herodotus (*Hist.* 7.37) reports how Xerxes (*c.* 519–465 BC) made them the newly reformed religion's official priesthood at a critical moment in his campaign against Greece. When, at this juncture, 'the day was turned to night', the magi declared that the eclipsed sun indicated Greek decline, and the moon Persian fortune. Their combination of Zarathustra's reforming spirit and Babylonian cosmology carried cosmic religion throughout the ancient world, everywhere victorious.

Yet although the magi became Zarathustrian, they continued to revere the power of the cosmos to *determine* human fate. This doctrine, known as Astral Fatalism (Waerden 1974, 161–72), pronounced that 'everything depends on the stars'. When the stars return to the same place in the heavens at the end of a Great Year, everything on earth will begin again in exactly the same way as before. According to the early Pythagorean, Hippasus, there was a great year with a relatively short period of fifty-nine years (Censorinus, *Die nat.* 18.8). So short a timespan is obviously not a period of all the planets but it is, as van der Waerden observes, a period in which Saturn and Jupiter return to nearly the same place in the sky. It represents the interval of 59.58 years, which elapses between four conjunctions of Saturn and Jupiter (called Great Conjunctions).

The conjunction of Saturn and Jupiter in 7 BC is frequently linked with the star of Bethlehem and we need to discover why. This traditional interpretation, although made famous by Johannes Kepler (1571–1630), is found earlier in a commentary on the Book of Daniel by the Jewish savant Isaac Abrabanel (1437–1508), called *The Wells of Salvation* (1497). But where Kepler looked to the massing of the planets Saturn, Jupiter and Mars in the vicinity of 0° Aries in March, 6 BC, as the star of Bethlehem, Abrabanel regarded the conjunction of Saturn and Jupiter at 330° (0° Pisces)

Adam to the Flood	1656 years
The Flood to the birth of Isaac	392
The birth of Isaac to the Exodus	400
Adam to the Exodus	2448 years

Table 3. Chronology of the Seder Olam Rabba.

as signifying the advent of the Messiah and identified the 'mighty' conjunction in AD 1464 as having Messianic significance.

In the thirteenth century, Pseudo-Ovidius' *De Vetula* contains observations on the proximity of the 7 BC Great Conjunction to 0° Aries, seemingly the first Christian writer to have concerned himself with the conjunction. Before examining Abrabanel's source, mention may be made of the earliest Jewish writing on the subject. B. L. van der Waerden (1963) writes, 'The Jewish astrologer called Mashallah (Messehalla in the West) was closely connected with the Persian tradition. He, like Abu Ma'shar, came from Balkh, the city associated with Zoroaster.'

Van der Waerden discusses both groups who were very much interested in planetary conjunctions. Abu Ma'shar, in his book on conjunctions, deals at length with the calculation of Saturn-Jupiter conjunctions and their astrological significance (Kennedy 1958, 78:259). He continues,

> . . . Ibn Hibinta connected the conjunctions with important events, such as the Deluge, the birth of Christ, the religion of Islam, etc. Just so, our sources connect the Deluge and the religion with conjunctions. The conjunction of all the planets in −3101 (=3102 BC), which forms the basis of the Persian System, is a 'mighty conjunction' in the sense of the astrological theory.

Solomon ibn Gabirol (*c.* 1022 – *c.* 1070), the 'Jewish Plato', essayed to make the Redemption contingent upon the conjunction of the two highest planets Saturn and Jupiter. Abraham bar Hiyya (*c.* 1065 – *c.* 1136) in the *Megillat-ha-Megalleh* (The Scroll of the Redeemer) has a full exposition of the system (Sarachek, 1968).

Sign*	Heliot	Date	Significance according to Abraham bar Hiyya
Pisces	265°	1397 BC	Birth of Moses; Torah
Aries	295°	1159	
Taurus	330°	920	
Gemini	12°	682	
Cancer	54°	443	
Leo	94°	205	
Virgo	134°	AD 34	Beginning of Israel's tragedy; disciples of Jesus; spread of the new faith;
Libra	173°	273	Constantine; Mani
Scorpio	207°	511	Muhammad
Sagittarius	237°	749	
Capricornus	267°	988	
Aquarius	300°	1226	
Pisces	332°	1464	Downfall of the Gentiles; salvation of the Hebrew peoples

Notes *The signs are given as in Hiyya's system with 'grand' conjunctions occurring every 2859 years in Pisces.
†Conjunctions of Saturn and Jupiter (Heliocentric) calculated by P. Treadgold.

Table 4. Major conjunctions of Saturn and Jupiter (according to Abraham bar Hiyya).

Abraham's chronology stems from the second Christian century *Seder Olam Rabba* and is given in Table 3.

From the 3761 BC epoch of the Jewish Era of Creation (*Anno Mundi*), the birth of Moses is dated AM 2368 (=1393 BC). Abraham calculated that a conjunction of Saturn and Jupiter had occurred in the sign of Pisces in 1396 BC, portending, said Abraham, the birth of Moses and the promulgation of the Law. Approximately every 238 years after this 'mighty' conjunction, a 'major' conjunction appears in successive signs, Aries, Taurus, Gemini and so on, until a 'mighty' conjunction (that is in the sign of Pisces in Abraham's system) recurs in AM 5224 (=AD 1464), presaging the coming of the Messiah. It will mark the downfall of the Gentile powers and the salvation of the Hebrew people. The world will then return to its original state of innocence, and the marvellous things that have been created and concealed from the beginning of the world will be made manifest (Table 4).

We now need to ask the question why Jewish scholars, not traditionally preoccupied with astrology, regarded the Great Conjunction as signalling the appearance of the Messiah. An important and influential paper by Roy A. Rosenberg (1972, 108f) explains how the conjunction of Saturn and Jupiter was interpreted in the light of Magian religion. In it he pointed out that in antiquity Saturn and Jupiter were widely regarded as representative of the divine Father and his Son:

> There is yet another element in the picture, however, one which illumines with even greater clarity the reason why this planetary phenomenon is so significant. Yahweh, the God of Israel, was from a very early period identified with El, the high father-god of Canaan and Phoenicia. We know from Sanchuniathon, the priest of Beirut who left an extremely valuable account of Canaanite religion, that El was the god of the planet Saturn, the 'Kronos' of the Greeks. In Greek religion, of course, Kronos had been dethroned by his son Zeus, manifest in the planet Jupiter. This is paralleled in Canaanite religion by the story of the rivalry between El and Baal. But, nonetheless, in Greek thought it is Kronos who gives to Zeus, continuously, 'all the measures of the whole creation', because it is he who is 'the originator of times'. If the Greek material reflects a Canaanite idea, then it is quite possible that in Jewish astrological tradition too the conjunction of Saturn and Jupiter signified the transfer of power from one planetary *daemon* to another. To the Greeks and Phoenicians, El (Kronos) had given over all his powers to his son Baal (Zeus). But in Jewish theology El or Yahweh was still the universal ruler, and the transfer of powers symbolized by the periodic planetary conjunction meant something a bit different: Yahweh was giving to his Messiah a portion of his power and authority, so that he, the Messiah, might shatter the wicked principalities that hold

sway over the earth, condemn them to punishment and exalt the righteous in their stead. The planet Saturn in this cosmic drama represents Yahweh, while the planet Jupiter, called [in Hebrew] Ṣedeq [righteousness], represents his 'son', the Messiah.

The magi, it may be imagined, when they arrived in Jerusalem, would have explained to the chief priests and the scribes the significance of the triple conjunction of Saturn and Jupiter in 7 BC, very much along the lines laid out by Rosenberg. It was incumbent upon them to explain to the Jewish theologians the Messianic significance of this relatively rare phenomenon. Saturn was the star-sign of Old Testament religion (Amos 5:26), and Jupiter would have been recognized as the planet of the Messiah. They would have given their interpretation of the Great Conjunction, signifying a transition from the Father (Yahweh) religion to the 'Son' religion of the Messiah.

Jerusalem's priesthood might well have been impressed by the magian science yet at the same time have declined to accept their proclamation of the Messiah's advent. For it was well known to them that the Messianic prophet would first appear and, according to the chronology developed below, John's birth had not yet happened. David Hughes (1979) provides an ideal survey of every aspect of the subject. He shares the view of Rosenberg and the distinguished astronomer K. Ferrari d'Occhieppo in the identification of the triple conjunction as the star of Bethlehem. Jewish tradition, albeit late, is cited by Hughes in support of the Messianic significance of the sign of Pisces. It is also possible that the early Christian association of the Christ with the sign of the Fish derives from the constellation of 7 BC. It is, therefore, possible to agree with these remarkable scholars concerning the Messianic significance of the triple conjunction in that year, *without* being prepared to accept that 7 BC was the year in which the magi made their journey.

In the Gospel of Matthew (2:1–11) we are left in no doubt that the overt reason for the magis' visit was to show reverence upon the birth of the *royal* Messiah. 'Where is the new-born king of the Jews?' is the only question they ask outside the private deliberations of priests in conclave. 'We have seen his star' informs

Jerusalem that it is the planet Jupiter which the magi have been observing. It must have seemed to Matthew almost superfluous further to specify the constellation intended.

We need to take account of the style of Matthew's narrative of the adoration of the magi. It is singularly devoid of the exaggerations and embellishments to be expected had pious inventiveness prevailed. If Matthew had composed his second chapter as a *midrash*, a sermon woven from Old Testament prophecies (as some commentators allege) how could he have failed to quote all the more obvious passages? Why did he not quote from Numbers (24:17)?

> I see him, but not now;
>> I behold him, but not nigh:
> a star shall come forth out of Jacob,
>> and a sceptre shall rise out of Israel

Or from Genesis (49:8–11):

> Judah, your brothers shall praise you;
>> . . .
> Judah is a lion's whelp;
>> . . .
> He stooped down, he couched as a lion,
>> and as a lioness; who dares rouse him up?
> The sceptre shall not depart from Judah,
>> nor the ruler's staff from between his feet,
> until Shiloh [Messiah?] comes;
>> and to him shall be the obedience of the peoples.
> Binding his foal to the vine
>> and his ass's colt to the choicest vine . . .

The blessing on Judah is full of symbolism, employing starnames in use since Sumerian times. The lion's whelp is identified as Leo Minor. And Mul Apin, an ancient Babylonian star catalogue, calls Leo the 'heart of the lion' (couched) and 'king'. The ruler's staff between the lion's feet is the king-star, Regulus. And next to Leo is the sign of Cancer, which was earlier called 'the Asses' Crib' by Aratus (*c.* 315–*c.* 240 BC).

While Matthew does not quote from the blessing of Jacob (Gen.49:8ff) it is *enacted* ('. . . mounted on an ass, a colt, the foal of an ass') in the Entry into Jerusalem, demonstrating that the promise to the royal house of Judah had been kept. The royal nature of the Messiah is fully and publicly acknowledged on Palm Sunday; but the astral symbolism concerns not Pisces but Leo.

E. L. Martin (1980) identifies Jupiter as the planet of the Messiah, in agreement with other experts. Resting his case on the Old Testament prophecies quoted above, he differs from them in identifying the star-sign as Leo; Jupiter passing through Leo four or five years later than 7 BC when it was in Pisces. Jupiter passes through the sign of Leo every twelve years, of course. It was accordingly still necessary that the magi should have been alerted by a sight of much greater rarity than this regular occurrence, and there seems little question that their interpretation of the triple conjunction in 7 BC performed this function. But the visit of the magi can have happened only several years later after Jupiter had entered the sign of Leo.

Jupiter entered the sidereal sign of Leo on September 18, 3 BC (Tuckerman 1962). About November 29, 3 BC, the planet came to rest and then began its retrograde motion. After looping Regulus (in Babylon, looping Regulus signified a change of ruler in the East; the Parthian king Phraates IV duly died in 2 BC), Jupiter re-entered Leo on May 16, 2 BC.

During the following months, Jupiter moved forward through the sign of Leo and into Virgo, entering the sidereal sign of Virgo on October 17, 2 BC, coming to rest between December 24, 2 BC and January 3, 1 BC. We would date the arrival of the magi in Jerusalem during these days.

7 The Enrolment

In those days a decree went out from Caesar Augustus that all the world should be enrolled. This was the first enrolment [*apographē*], when Quirinius was governor of Syria. And all went to be enrolled, each to his own city. And Joseph also went up from Galilee, from the city of Nazareth, to Judea, to the city of David, which is called Bethlehem, because he was of the house and lineage of David, to be enrolled with Mary, his betrothed, who was with child. (Luke 2:1–5).

This much-discussed passage presents exceptional difficulties to the historian. P. Winter lists five issues (Schürer 1973, 399–427):

1. History does not otherwise record a general imperial census in the time of Augustus.
2. Under a Roman census, Joseph would not have been obliged to travel to Bethlehem, and Mary would not have been required to accompany him there.
3. A Roman census could not have been carried out in Palestine during the time of King Herod.
4. Josephus knows nothing of a Roman census in Palestine during the reign of Herod; he refers rather to the census of AD 6–7 as something new and unprecedented.
5. A census held under Quirinius could not have taken place in the time of Herod, for Quirinius was never governor of Syria during Herod's lifetime.

Luke makes additional mention of the census in Acts 5:37: 'After him Judas the Galilean arose in the days of the census [*apographē*] and drew away some of the people after him; he also perished, and all who followed him were scattered.' Since the Gospel account is much more complex, we shall begin with the reference in Acts. It is most interesting that in Luke's report of Gamaliel's speech, the enrolment is connected with the origin of the Zealot movement headed by Judas the Galilean. Since Josephus attributed the destruction of Jerusalem by the Romans in AD

If you are interested in other publications from Floris Books, please return this card with your name and address.

Name _____

Address _____

_____

_____

_____

☐ Please send me your catalogue once
☐ Please send me your catalogue regularly

Postcard

Floris Books
21 Napier Road
EDINBURGH
EH10 5AZ
Great Britain

70 to the unbridled fanaticism of these Zealot movements, we are able to trace their origins in his history. If we can date the beginning of the Zealot movement, we would help to establish the timing of the census.

In Josephus (*Ant.* 18.1–4) also, the taxation under Quirinius in AD 6–7 is linked to the rebellion of Judas.

> Quirinius, a Roman senator . . . arrived in Syria, dispatched by Caesar to be governor [or judge] of the nation and to make an assessment of their property . . . Quirinius also visited Judaea, which had been annexed to Syria, in order to make an assessment of the property of the Jews and to liquidate the estate of Archelaus. Although the Jews were at first shocked to hear of the registration (*apographē*) of property, they gradually condescended, yielding to the arguments of the high priest Joazar, the son of Boethus, to go no further in opposition. So those who were convinced by him declared, without shilly-shallying, the value of their property. But a certain Judas, a Gaulanite, from a city named Gamala, who had enlisted the aid of Saddok, a Pharisee, threw himself into the cause of rebellion. They said that the assessment carried with it a status amounting to downright slavery . . .

Schürer (1973, 381) identifies Judas of Gamala with Judas son of Hezekiah (Ezekias), who already figured in *Antiquities* (17.271f). Ezekias, a dangerous adversary, had been unceremoniously executed by the young Herod (*Ant.* 14.159). His son Judas was prominent in the disturbances which followed Herod's death.

Varus, Roman governor of Syria at the time of Herod's death, intervened when the rapacious Sabinus, the procurator of Caesar, set out to 'take charge' of Herod's property. This was at least half the kingdom, it is estimated. Josephus (*Ant.*17.271f) continues:

> Then there was Judas the son of the brigand-chief Ezekias, who had been a man of great power and had been captured by Herod only with great difficulty. This Judas got together a large number of desperate men at Sepphoris in Galilee and there made an assault on the royal palace, and having seized all the arms that were stored there, he armed every single one of his men and made off with all the

69

property that had been seized there. He became an object of terror to all men by plundering those he came across in his desire for great possessions and his ambition for royal rank, a prize that he expected to obtain not through the practice of virtue but through excessive ill-treatment of others.

Varus sent his son to fight against the Galileans, and Sepphoris, the most important city in Galilee which was the centre of the rebellion, was burnt to the ground and its inhabitants sold into slavery. At the same time, Varus proceeded to Samaria where he encountered no opposition (*Ant.* 17.288f). On the single occasion when Augustus is recorded (*Ant.* 17.319f) as intervening in Palestinian fiscal affairs, Augustus in the determination of Herod's testament rewarded Samaria for its loyalty with a tax remission.

[Herod] Antipas [second surviving son of Herod the Great] received the revenue of Peraea and Galilee, which yielded an annual tribute of two hundred talents . . . To Archelaus [first surviving son of Herod] both Idumaea and Judaea were made subject and also the district of the Samaritans, who had a fourth of their tribute remitted by Caesar; this alleviation he decreed because they had not joined the rest of the people in revolting.

Archelaus had sent his steward to bring accounts of Herod's property to Augustus (*Ant.* 17.228). Caesar Augustus is thus seen involved in an assessment of Herod's kingdom, as required by Luke's narrative. Before the Roman annexation of Judea in AD 6, the taxation system was controlled by the Herods. As Schürer (1973, 416) observes, Herod acted throughout independently with regard to tax and there is no sign whatever of his paying any dues to the Romans. He remitted and even exempted from taxation at will. Indeed one of the complaints made to Augustus by the Jewish deputation before his adjudication of Herod's testament concerned 'the collecting of the tribute that was imposed on everyone each year', for Herod's demands were excessive and his methods irregular and arbitrary. On this occasion Augustus was sufficiently involved that he did not rely on the accounts of Archelaus' steward. It is distinctly stated that he received revenue reports from Varus and Sabinus (*Ant.* 17.229).

When Caesar had read these letters and also the reports of
Varus and Sabinus concerning the amount of the property
and the size of the annual revenue, and had looked at the
various letters sent by Antipas in an effort to obtain the
kingship for himself, he called together his friends to give
their opinions. Among them he gave first place at his side
to Gaius . . .

At this time Gaius was about nineteen years old and favoured
to succeed his grandfather Augustus. He was about to take up his
proconsular appointment in Syria and it was obviously beneficial
to his authority to be seen by his subjects appearing at the side
of the Emperor. To raise the esteem of the inexperienced youth
in the eyes of the soldiery, Gaius was married to the empress's
grand-daughter Livilla presumably in Rome before his departure
with a distinguished entourage. Among them was Publius Sulpicius Quirinius.

On their journey to the East, Tiberius was visited on the island
of Rhodes. In an obituary notice penned later by Tacitus (*Annals*
3.46), the presence of Quirinius at this meeting is noted. 'A little
later, Tiberius asked the senate to award a:

public funeral to Publius Sulpicius Quirinius. He came from
Lanuvium, and had no connexion with the ancient patrician
Sulpician family. But he was a fine soldier, whose zealous
services had earned him a consulship and honorary
Triumph from the divine Augustus. Later, appointed adviser
to Gaius Caesar during the latter's Armenian commission,
Quirinius had treated Tiberius, then living at Rhodes, with
respect — as the emperor now told the senate. But others
had less agreeable memories of Quirinius, who was a mean,
over-influential old man, and (as I have mentioned) had
persecuted Aemilia Lepida.

Gaius and his principal advisers Lollius and Quirinius, arrived
in Syria to replace Varus as governor. In most sources, therefore,
Gaius is listed as governor from autumn 1 BC. Actually, only a
single source (Orosius *Hist*. 7.3) implies clearly that Gaius Julius
Caesar was specifically in charge of Syria. Schürer (1973, 259)
observes, 'There is no definite reason to think that Gaius replaced
the normal governor of Syria during this period.'

Whatever his title, there is no doubt that Quirinius was the ideal man to clear up the disorder left by Varus. Lollius was required to remain at the side of Gaius, and Quirinius combined administrative competence of a high order with a taste for the unpleasant business of the registration. When, a few years later, Archelaus was deposed, Quirinius was again charged with the task.

We may now consider whether:

1. The *apographē* is supposed to have been a Roman taxation conducted at some time during Herod's lifetime.
2. The *apographē* was a valuation of Herod's estate made in the months following his death in 1 BC.
3. Luke's *apographē* was the taxing of Judea in AD 6–7 by Quirinius, recorded by Josephus.

The first possibility seems to be excluded by points 4 and 5 in Schürer's excursus (p. 68). Josephus knows nothing of a Roman census in Palestine during Herod's lifetime. If in 8 BC Herod suffered a fall from Augustus' favour, the penalty could have been a financial imposition on Herod, but, as a *rex socius*, certainly not the direct intervention of a Roman taxation of the people. Nor was Quirinius at any time in Herod's reign governor of Syria. It has often been argued that Quirinius was also earlier governor of Syria before AD 6. We know from coins that Varus was governor 7–4 BC, and that Varus was governor of Syria at the time of Herod's death in 1 BC. The idea that in this time Quirinius served a first term is excluded.

When we consider the second possibility, that the *apographē* was a Jewish assessment of Herod's property supervised by the Romans, we are again faced with the fact that there is no evidence of Quirinius (or anyone else) having served two terms as governor of Syria. On the chronology of Herod summarized above, perhaps Luke 2:2 has to be understood as stating that Quirinius was governor following Varus. Schürer (1973, 258) comments,

> This thesis has seemed to be supported by the inscription from Tibur (ILS 918) which records *int. al.* the unnamed senator whose career is described '*(legatus pr. pr.) divi Augusti iterum Syriam et Ph(oenicem) optinuit)*'. In spite of the recent doubts of A. N. Sherwin-White, (1963, 163f) this

will, however, mean not that the man was twice *legatus* of Syria, but that his second legateship was that of Syria. The inscription more probably relates to L. Calpurius Piso.

Schürer considers it likely that L. Calpurnius Piso was governor *c.* 4–1 BC. But my 'Herodian Chronology' (1982) has demonstrated that the governor of Syria at this time was Varus, not Piso. Perhaps we should revert to the possibility that Quirinius was governor before AD 6, following Varus in 1 BC.

To sum up, Luke's enrolment should be identified not with the taxation of Judea in AD 6–7 (which would not have affected the Galilean subjects of Herod Antipas) but with the assessment of Herod's estate following his death. Although supervised by the Romans, it was conducted along traditional Jewish lines according to tribes and genealogies. It was completed in the months after Varus had ceased to be governor of Syria in 1 BC. During this transitional period in early winter 1 BC practical authority for administration was probably divided between Gaius' principal aides, Lollius and Quirinius. In the circumstances it is likely that Quirinius would have been given full authority to settle the affairs of Palestine in the winter of 1 BC.

F. Heichelheim (1938, 160ff) dismisses the possibility that Luke was mistaken in placing the nativity in the setting of an enrolment. Writing in the first century only a generation or so after the life of Christ, Luke could and would have been refuted or corrected by both non-Christians and Christians living near Bethlehem and also by the family of Jesus living there. There was no Roman census before Quirinius, 'but it is generally forgotten that half or two-thirds of Herod's kingdom was his private domain, and that a census must have been held [after his death] in these regions to facilitate the collection of poll and land taxes which were directly owed to the king.'

Luke, on the above analysis, need not be corrected on any specific point if something like the following paraphrase is deemed to be permissible:

In the days following Herod's death, Caesar Augustus ordered that Herod's entire kingdom should be assessed for tax purposes. This was the earlier of two enrolments conducted while Quirinius was governor of Syria. And all went to be enrolled for the poll and property tax, each to his own ancestral city, in the Jewish manner. And Joseph also went up from Galilee, from a settlement called Nazareth, to Judea, to the city of David, which is called Bethlehem, because he was of the house and lineage of David, to be enrolled with Mary, his betrothed, who was with child.

The Nativities

8 Matthew

As already related in Chapter 4, there was a persistent expectation in Judaism — in later rabbinic writings as well as in the Dead Sea Scrolls — of two Messiahs and a Messianic Prophet. This expectation is not encountered in the Gospels. Yet the divergence between the birth narratives in Matthew and Luke is so great, that we need to ask whether the two accounts do not in fact correspond to the dual expectation.

Biblical scholars do not need to be reminded of the necessity of considering the narratives of Matthew and Luke quite separately. We have for a time to lay aside the familiar and much-loved Christmas picture composed from Matthew and Luke with notable additions from Francis of Assisi and from the Victorians. We shall then ask, Do the Gospels exclude the possibility that there was a royal forerunner, parallel to John, the prophetic forerunner of the Messiah in the history of the Christ Jesus, which could explain the great differences between the nativity stories?

K. Stendahl (1962, 770f) observes,

> The genealogy in Matthew differs considerably from that in
> Luke 3:23–28. In Luke the line goes back to Adam, the
> 'Son of God', and it goes back via David's son Nathan. In
> Matthew the line goes from Abraham via David and
> Solomon . . . [Matthew 1:17] makes clear what is Matthew's
> intention with the genealogy. Abraham and David are the
> significant ancestors. There is no interest in anything going
> beyond Abraham, the father of the Israelites. And Jesus is of
> royal descent. He is a son of David. Among the three
> Messianic figures of the Qumrân community, the Prophet,
> the Messiah of Aaron and the Messiah of Israel (1QS
> 9:10–11), the genealogy identifies him with the last, the
> royal and Davidic, the non-priestly Messiah.

The early Church Fathers were soon engaged in trying to explain why Matthew's genealogy of Jesus begins with Abraham giving, via David and Solomon, the royal line of the House of

Judah, where Luke's genealogy gives a quite different line from David and Nathan. Already by AD 200, we find the Lucan genealogy associated with the priestly tradition. Ambrose (*c.* 339–397) commented (Goudoever 1961, 232), 'Both Gospels have reported the truth, Matthew proving that Jesus' descent comes from the royal line; Luke deriving a descent from God through the priestly line.' Ambrose found confirmation in the calf symbol connected with Luke, as representing the priest's sacrificial role. Hippolytus of Rome (*c.* 170 – *c.* 235) in discussing the four symbols of the Gospels had come to the same conclusion: the Bull means the priestly glory depicted by Luke; the Lion means leadership and royal dignity which comes forth from the line of Judah and is depicted by Matthew. Hippolytus was acquainted with a twofold descent of the Christ: the Christ from the tribe of Levi and of the tribe of Judah (Goudoever 1961, 232).

The family in Matthew is *domiciled* in Bethlehem until the flight into Egypt, and Nazareth is mentioned for the first time by Matthew on the return from Egypt. In Luke's Nativity, the family is forced by the enrolment to travel from Nazareth at the time of the birth. After the birth of the Lucan child, the family does not flee to Egypt but visits the Temple in Jerusalem before continuing on the homeward journey to Nazareth.

There seems to be a clear choice between either (a) rejecting one or both of the infancy Gospels as unhistorical, or (b) accepting both narratives as historical, and of reconsidering the three nativity stories in the Gospels in the light of the fact, highlighted by discovery of the Dead Sea Scrolls, that three Messianic figures were awaited.

King Herod, the magi and the star shining over the house in Bethlehem, with the journey into Egypt, furnish the Matthean account with its characteristic details, just as the enrolment, and the shepherds coming to the stable are features of the Lucan nativity. The star has been interpreted above as physically manifest as Jupiter, the planet of the Messiah entering and coming to rest in Virgo, in the early days of January 1 BC. Herod's death is dated January 28, 1 BC, not long after the total eclipse mentioned by Josephus, which occurred on January 10, 1 BC. We shall now concentrate on Josephus' account of the days leading up to the lunar eclipse, during which — on the above reckoning — the advent of the magi occurred. This is the only eclipse mentioned by Josephus and it occurred at the termination of a vigorous disturbance in the Temple (*Ant.* 17.149–67):

Judas, the son of Sariphaeus, and Matthias, the son of Margalothus, were most learned of the Jews and unrivalled interpreters of the ancestral laws, and men especially dear to the people because they educated the youth, for all those who made an effort to acquire virtue used to spend time with them day after day. When these scholars learned that the king's illness could not be cured, they aroused the youth by telling them that they should pull down all the works built by the king in violation of the laws of their fathers and so obtain from the Law the reward of their pious efforts. It was indeed because of his audacity in making these things in disregard of the Law's provisions, they said, that all those misfortunes, with which he had become familiar to a degree uncommon among mankind, had happened to him, in particular his illness. Now Herod had set about doing certain things that were contrary to the Law, and for these he had been reproached by Judas and Matthias and their followers. For the king had erected over the great gate of the Temple, as a votive offering and at great cost, a great golden eagle, although the Law forbids those who propose to live in accordance with it to think of setting up images or to make dedications of (the likeness of) any living creatures. So these scholars ordered (their disciples) to pull the eagle down, saying that even if there should be some danger of their being doomed to death, still to those who are about to die for the preservation and safeguarding of their fathers' way of life the virtue acquired by them in death would seem far more advantageous than the pleasure of living . . .

With such words, then, did they stir the youth, and when a rumour reached them that the king had died, it only made the scholars' words more effective. At mid-day, therefore, the youths went up (to the roof of the Temple) and pulled down the eagle and cut it up with axes before the many people who were gathered in the Temple . . . [Forty of the

young men were speedily arrested and brought before
Herod.] Thereupon the king had them bound and sent to
Jericho where he summoned the Jewish officials, and when
they arrived, he assembled them and lying on a couch
because of his inability to stand, he recounted his strenuous
efforts on their behalf, and told them at what great expense
to himself he had constructed the Temple, whereas the
Hasmonaeans had been unable to do anything so great for
the honour of God in the twenty-five years of their reign
. . . this was supposedly an insult to him, but in actual fact,
if one closely examined their actions, was sacrilege.

   . . . Herod . . . dealt rather mildly with [them] but
removed the high priest Matthias from his priestly office as
being partly to blame for what had happened . . . As for the
other Matthias, who had stirred up the sedition, he burnt
him alive along with some of his companions. And on that
same night there was an eclipse of the moon.

Could Matthew and Josephus have been describing the same
event? If the insurrection, disclosed by Josephus, ended before the
lunar eclipse which heralded Herod's death, then the disturbance
evidently flourished around the time (6 January) traditionally
associated with the adoration of the magi. Writing in 1880, Florian
Riess already identified the 'sedition' with the arrival of the magi
which so 'startled' Jerusalem. If we accept his conclusion, we have
a latest date for the Matthean Nativity.

Earliest mention of the commemoration of the Baptism is made
in about AD 194 by Clement of Alexandria, who also supplies the
date of the Nativity (*Misc.* 1.21.145.1–6. *ANCL* 4:445):

From the birth of Christ, therefore, to the death of
Commodus [December 31, AD 192] are, in all, a hundred
and ninety-four years, one month [30 days], thirteen days.
And there are those who have determined not only the
year of our Lord's birth, but also the day; and they say that
it took place in the twenty-eighth year of Augustus [August
29, 3 BC to August 28, 2 BC on the Egyptian reckoning], and
in the twenty-fifth day of Pachon [May 20 (Clement also
mentions Tybi 15, January 10, and Tybi 11, January 6)].
And the followers of Basilides [the famous Gnostic who

flourished in Alexandria about AD 117–138] hold the day of his baptism as a festival, spending the night before in readings.

Holzmeister (1933, 43) interprets Clement's implied date of the Nativity as November, 3 BC. But K. Ferrari d'Occhieppo is no doubt correct in assuming that Clement here employs 194 Egyptian years of 365 days without intercalation. Then Clement's date of the Nativity is January 6, 2 BC.

Clearly this traditional date of the Nativity on January 6, relates to Matthew's birth narrative since the date is linked to the adoration of the magi, and therefore falls in Herod's lifetime. Herod was startled at the news of the magi because his highly efficient intelligence system would have been expected to have reported without delay anything so untoward as the birth of a possible Davidic pretender to the throne. If the child was only newly born at the time of the magi's visit, this consternation is comprehensible. The massacre of the innocents would then have coincided with the uprising in the Temple.

We date the Matthean Nativity, on the grounds given above, Tebeth 9, January 6, 1 BC, according with Eastern tradition of the day and the month (but not the year).

9 Luke

In the third Gospel, Luke devotes much attention to the birth of both John and Jesus, narrating the circumstances of annunciation and birth at some length. Luke dates the annunciation of John's birth 'in the days of Herod, king of Judea' (1:5). Yet when we read of John's birth itself we can feel that the atmosphere has changed from the charged mood of Herod's last days as in the Matthean birth story. At the end of Herod's life, the air was heavy with the fear of widespread bloodshed (*Ant*. 17.174).

The emotional spectrum of Luke's depiction of events should also be noted. Awe, doubt, astonishment, humility, exaltation, tribulation, rejoicing and wonder abound. But of Herod's insane instinct to slaughter and of the fear it engendered, there is in Luke's birth narratives no trace. Freedom from this fear can have only one cause: the tyrant is dead. General excitement greeted John's birth as the news swept through the land. Lack of any official reaction stands in total contrast to the secrecy and threatening violence of Matthew's account. The only conclusion is that the births of John and of Jesus, according to Luke, followed upon Herod's death. It will be remembered that in Chapter 7 it has already been shown that a birth occurring at the time of the registration can only have taken place after Herod's death. Luke's indication, then, 'in the days of Herod the king' applies to John's conception but *not* to the birth of John and of Jesus of Nazareth.

John the Baptist

We shall first examine a little more closely the timing of the annunciation of John's birth. Luke (1:5,8) states that, at that time, John's father Zechariah was serving in the Temple belonging, as he did, to the priests' course of Abijah. Chronological interpretation of this statement is not unproblematic. According to the First Book of the Chronicles (24:7–19) the first course to serve in the rota was Jehoiarib, which was appointed to serve for a week

Jewish date	Julian date	Course
Ab 8–14	August 5–11	1 Jehoiarib
Ab 15–21	August 12–18	2 Jedaiah
Ab 22–28	August 19–25	3 Harim
Ab 29–Elul 6	August 26–Sep 1	4 Seorim
Elul 7–13	September 2–8	5 Malchijah
Elul 14–20	September 9–15	6 Mijamin
Elul 21–27	September 16–22	7 Hakkoz
Elul 28–Tishri 4	September 23–29	8 Abijah

Table 5. Priests' courses due to serve in AD *70.*

commencing on the sabbath, before being relieved by the next course. The course of Abijah, to which Zechariah belonged, was the eighth of twenty-four courses. Unfortunately we are not told the time of year when each course served.

We do know, however, that the first course of Jehoiarib was serving on Ab 9, August 6, AD 70 when the Temple was destroyed by the Romans. In both Talmuds, the Tosefta (a Tannaitic collection only less ancient than the Mishnah) and in the Chronicle *Seder Olam Tabbah*, Rabbi Jose ben Halafta (*c.* AD 150) is reported on this point (Beckwith 1977, 82). 'Rabbi Jose said, "Fortunate things happen on a fortunate day, and evil things on an evil day. For as the first temple was destroyed on a Sunday, the year after a sabbatical year, when the course of Jehoiarib was on duty, on Ab 9, so it was with the second temple".' Had the Temple not been destroyed in AD 70, they would have continued to serve as in Table 5.

We have already interpreted Luke (1:5) as placing the annunciation of John's birth prior to Herod's death (January 28, 1 BC) and John's birth subsequent to that date. Each course served one week twice during a year, apart from the joint participation of all courses at the time of the pilgrim festivals. Table 5 shows that Abijah was due to serve at the new year in the autumn of AD 70. Assuming that the pattern repeats each year Zechariah also would have served at new year in 2 BC. This corresponds to a birth at the traditional midsummer.

Luke informs us that a large number of people were present while Zechariah was making the offering, 'the whole number of people' presumably implying that the day was of more than ordinary importance. Early Christian writers sometimes treated Zechariah in an unwarranted fashion as the high priest entering the Holy of Holies on the Day of Atonement, Tishri 10. Table 5 would identify the special day as the autumn new year's day Tishri 1, October 1, 2 BC. John's birth would then follow nine months later around Ab 9, June 30, 1 BC.

Jesus of Nazareth

Luke (1:26) places the annunciation of the birth of Jesus six (lunar) months after that of John, that is on Nisan 1, March 26, 1 BC. The resultant date of the Nativity, which was in antiquity reckoned to follow after a gestation period of 10 sidereal months (273 days) is Tebeth 9, December 25, 1 BC.

Urbanus Holzmeister (1933, 41) dates the earliest mention of the Feast of the Nativity on 25 December in Rome in AD 354. In this year an entry in the *Depositio Martyrum* reads, '*VIII Kal. Ianuarii natus Christus in Betleem Iudeae*'. Celebration of the Feast of the Nativity on 25 December is thought to have begun before the middle of the fourth century.

Again the dating of the Nativity is much earlier than its commemoration. It should be remembered that Christmas was not singular if it was not celebrated on a certain day much before the middle of the fourth century, since the same is largely true of other comparable festival days. The Christian year came into being at that time, after the end of the first three centuries. Hippolytus (c. 170 – c. 235) in his *Commentary on Daniel* (4), dated the birth of Jesus eight days before the Kalends of January (December 25), a Wednesday, in the forty-second year of the reign of Augustus, 5500 years from Adam. Hippolytus also gave April 2 as well as the date of March 25 (which corresponded to birth on December 25) for the *Genesis Christou*.

Perhaps nothing militates against acceptance of the historicity of the Infancy Gospels so much as the imputation (in both Matthew and Luke) of the Virgin Birth. The modern mind is amenable to argument and persuasion on the degree to which human nature is determined by the forces of heredity. It might be conceded that, apart from mathematical and musical genius, greatness of spirit has not much to do with the genetic component of the human make-up. It is suggested that we interpret hints of a Virgin Birth not as denial of paternity, but in the way of antiquity, which minimized the influence of earthly factors and emphasized the spiritual element. The Virgin Birth is the Nativity seen through the eyes of one beholding the descent of the Spirit at the Baptism of Jesus. It is an important Christological statement which was not intended to be accepted over-literally.

If the Nativity, especially in Luke's Gospel, is rightly understood in this fashion, it should be seen as a portrayal of the paradisal birth of the last Adam. The scene recalls the Genesis scene of Adam in the garden of paradise. 'So out of the ground the LORD God formed every beast of the field and every bird of the air, and brought them to the man to see what he would call them; and whatever the man called every living creature, that was its name' (2:19). This scene recalls the later Christian view of Adam as prophet, priest and king, here baptizing the animal kingdom before the entrance upon the scene of Eve. Luke's setting of the Nativity in a manger was later elaborated (incongruously, in the apocryphal *Pseudo-Matthew Gospel*, a Latin compilation attributed to Jerome, which seems to have appeared in the eighth or ninth century) with a detail from Isaiah (1:3), 'The ox knows its owner, and the ass its master's crib'.

Totally lacking outer ecclesiastical trappings, the Lucan nativity comes close to the heart of the religious experience evoked by the Temple ritual. It tells of the coming of a Messianic high priest who would, on entering the Temple on Palm Sunday, substitute self-sacrifice for animal sacrifice. The Temple's adornment with the imagery of the heavenly journey of the soul shines through the inner nature of Jesus. The Book of Revelation (1:12–16) contains a vision of the Son of Man which unites the aspect of the Messianic high priest with the image of the high priest of the universe.

Then I turned to see the voice that was speaking to me, and on turning I saw seven golden lampstands, and in the midst of the lampstands one like a son of man, clothed with a long robe and with a golden girdle round his breast; his head and his hair were white as white wool, white as snow; his eyes were like a flame of fire, his feet were like burnished bronze, refined as in a furnace, and his voice was like the sound of many waters; in his right hand he held seven stars, from his mouth issued a sharp two-edged sword, and his face was like the sun shining in full strength.

The theme of the Christ as Messianic high priest is evident in 'the high priestly prayer' in John 17 and is explicitly treated in Hebrews.

While unfolding the Nativity scene, Luke gazes on the whole of humanity and sees the poverty-stricken birth in Bethlehem as the story of man and his celestial origin. He is born not in a human habitation but in a dwelling normally reserved for beasts. He looks back to a time when once man and beast were companions not foes. The depths of Luke's strikingly simple imagery have in recent decades led scholars to abandon the apparently fruitless search for historicity and instead to read the Nativity narratives for their theological import. Luke has written of a new genesis of mankind, an aim which cannot detract from the story's historicity unless we demur from Luke's estimation of the Christ.

10 Summary of Opinion

Nearly every book on the life of Christ includes a chronological table. Even a casual comparison reveals a wide divergence of opinion. In order to form an impression of the range of opinion on the date of the Nativity, the numbers of writers, ancient and modern, listed by Urbanus Holzmeister (1933, 31–34 & 15–17) favouring each year between 12 BC and AD 9 are tabulated in Table 6.

J. Finegan (1964, 229) names early Christian sources favouring dates between 4 BC and AD 1 as in Table 7.

Largely governed by prevailing notions of the date of Herod's death, the great majority of modern scholars place the birth of

Year	Number of Writers		Year	Number of Writers	
	Ancient	Modern		Ancient	Modern
12 BC	0	4	5/4	0	1
10	0	2	4	7	2
9	0	1	4/3	4	0
9/8	0	2	3	11	3
8	0	2	2	8	4
8/7	0	1	2/1	2	0
7	0	10	1	2	2
7/6	0	2	1 BC/AD 1	1	0
7/5	0	7	AD 1	1	1
6	0	5	8	2	0
6/5	0	1	9	3	0
5	1	8			

Table 6. Ancient and modern opinion on the date of the nativity (after Holzmeister 1933)

Source:	Date:
Alogi (heretics)	4 BC
Irenaeus	4/3
Cassiodorus Senator	3
Clement of Alexandria	3/2
Tertullian	3/2
Origen	3/2
Africanus	3/2
Hippolytus of Rome	3/2
'Hippolytus of Thebes' (one fragment)	3/2
Eusebius	3/2
Epiphanius	2
'Hippolytus of Thebes' (another fragment)	2/1
Chronographer of the Year 354	AD 1

Table 7. Dates of the birth of Jesus in early Christian sources (after Finegan 1964, 229).

Jesus before 4 BC. No single Church Father dates the Nativity so early. The idea that Herod died as early as 4 BC seems to have been unfamiliar in early Christian times.

Table 8 summarizes the conclusions reached when the differences between Matthew and Luke on the date of the Nativity are fully respected. Both Gospels are here read as dating the birth Tebeth 9. Tebeth 9, 1 BC could have been interpreted in the Eastern Church as equivalent to January 6, 1 BC; it is equally possible to interpret the same date as December 25, 1 BC, the date adopted in the Western Church.

To summarize: Matthew and Luke contain three annunciation stories and three corresponding births. The Eastern tradition of the January 6 birth-date coinciding with the adoration of the magi is placed within the lifetime of Herod early in 1 BC. The Western traditional date of December 25, 1 BC is retained with respect to

	Annunciation	Birth
Jesus (Matthew)	2 BC Nisan 1 April 6	1 BC Tebeth 9 January 6
John the Baptist	2 BC Tishri 1 October 1	1 BC Tammuz 9 June 30
Jesus (Luke)	1 BC Nisan 1 March 26	1 BC Tebeth 9 December 25

Table 8. Dates of the Nativities in Matthew and Luke.

Luke's nativity of Jesus of Nazareth, six lunar months after the birth of John.

It is concluded that:

1. On their arrival in Jerusalem the magi proclaimed the opening of the Messianic Age as heralded by the triple conjunction of Saturn and Jupiter in 7 BC.
2. Explaining the Messianic significance of the triple conjunction to the authorities in Jerusalem on their journey to Bethlehem, the magi followed the movement of Jupiter through the royal sign of Leo until Jupiter came to rest in Virgo, at which time the magi paid homage to the new-born son of the House of David.
3. The three births — of royal Messiah, the Prophet, and of the priestly Messiah — constituted the introit into the Messianic Age. Up to the Baptism of Jesus of Nazareth (whose birth Luke alone narrates) all three Messianic figures are in some sense forerunners of the Christ Jesus. At the Baptism in the Jordan, all three Messianic roles were conferred on the unique figure of Jesus of Nazareth. Thirty years earlier three individuals had each represented a single Messianic role in the inauguration of the Incarnation. The mystery is how these three roles were first associated with three distinct individuals, and ultimately devolved on the unique Jesus of Nazareth.

11 The Way

From about 150 BC, religious tradition in Judaism was represented by three philosophies, practised by the Essenes, Sadducees and Pharisees. We have grown accustomed to dwell on the exaggerated other-worldliness of the Essenes, the earthy realism of the high priestly party of the Sadducees, and the hypocrisy of the Pharisees. We shall try to redress this one-sidedness with an impression of the original genuinely religious impulses cultivated within these orders.

In their positive expression, the Pharisees sought to emulate within the context of everyday life the ritual purity of the Temple by consecrating themselves to obedience to the written and unwritten Law. The Sadducees were conservative in religion but liberal in their Hellenistic cultural sympathies. This aristocratic priesthood dismissed progressive interpretation of the Law which expanded the scope of religion to all aspects of life. And in their desert retreats, the Essenes strove to observe only the sovereignty of God in order to be united with the divine. While the Pharisees propounded, and the Sadducees rejected, their version of the Law, the Essenes in their 'exclusive' desert retreats led their life of devotion to God.

With some notion of these aspects of Judaism's three orders, we can also look at their spiritual practices against a more general background of a widely shared pattern of the spiritual life. M. Smith (1981, 22) defines the stages of the development of spiritual consciousness under the heading of 'mysticism', which may without too much distortion be applied to the inner core of Judaism's three orders. 'The stages of the Mystic Way vary somewhat in the different religions of East and West in which Mysticism has taken root, but the threefold division which has been accepted in the West will, to a large extent, cover the stages of the Way as set forth in the religious systems of the East.' Adding our interpretation of the Jewish religious orders, we continue with M. Smith,

These three stages are of the Purgative life [Pharisees], the Illuminative life [Sadducees] and the Unitive life [Essenes]; and the old Sufi teacher who said that Renunciation, which is the keynote of the Way, should be (1) renunciation of that which is unlawful [Pharisees], (2) renunciation of that which is lawful [Sadducees], and (3) renunciation of all save God Himself [Essenes] was describing the three stages of the Mystic Way fairly accurately.

The language of mysticism has not changed essentially since pre-Christian times. When we trace its development back to early Pythagoreanism, we see how the three stages of the Path evolved out of the stages of the heavenly journey of the soul as the ascending stages of consciousness in mysticism. In the Pythagorean order, for instance, the corresponding terms of higher consciousness were termed *kátharsis* (purification), *kósmos* (cosmic illumination) and, highest, *theōría* (contemplation).

In the Gospels, we meet the Pharisees devoting themselves to the maintenance of ritual purity outside the Temple precincts. They invited the people to submit to the discipline of consecration without enjoying its protective blessing. Obedience was demanded to the implications as well as to the letter of the Law and, in time, their interpretative zeal gave rise to a vast body of unwritten Law. After the Maccabean uprising had restored Judaistic values, the Pharisees took a leading role in upholding public morality, when outer appearance came to seem of greater importance than the soul's inner state. As the order played a more and more prominent part in public life, the Pharisees laid themselves open to the accusation of fostering purity only in an external sense.

It is of course not true that the New Testament invariably casts the religious orders in a bad light. When the Christ addresses Nicodemus (John 3:1f) as a leading member of the Pharisaic order, his expectation of him is correspondingly high.

> Now there was a man of the Pharisees, named Nicodemus, a ruler of the Jews. This man came to Jesus by night and said to him, 'Rabbi, we know that you are a teacher come from God; for no one can do these signs that you do, unless God is with him.'

Scrupulous observance of the laws of purity had opened the

eyes of Nicodemus to the significance of Jesus' actions. Earlier, his order had surveyed the work of the Baptist and listened carefully to John's replies to his examination by priests and Levites (John 1:19–28). The Pharisees asked John, 'Then why are you baptizing, if you are neither the Christ, nor Elijah, nor the prophet?' As a prophetic order, the Pharisees were no doubt particularly interested in John's practice of purification by baptism. The role of the prophet may be compared with the work of the Paraclete, the Spirit who leads into all truth (Cullmann 1963, 37). Following John's baptism, Jesus had assumed the prophetic mantle of John.

Nicodemus may have wished to explain the limits of the knowledge which could be attained through the practice of purification. We can interpret Christ's reply as indicating the further stages of the path. Self-knowledge should extend far beyond introspection and introduce the soul into the inner sanctum of human nature recessed behind the veil of personality. Self-knowledge is not to be achieved through 'wisdom with age' but by reversing the normal direction of maturation. The individual is led thereby to reunite with his universal Self, which pre-exists personality.

Personality is the psychological counterpart to biological specialization. In evolutionary biology, the process whereby specializations are abandoned in favour of a more general nature is called 'neoteny'. We might refer to Christ's description of spiritual development as a psychological neoteny, as J. B. S. Haldane once remarked (Gould 1977). Neoteny implies the abandonment of adult features in favour of a childlike strategy and is an essential precursor of major advances in evolution. 'Truly, truly, I say to you, unless one is born anew, he cannot see the kingdom of God.' Jesus' response to Nicodemus introduces him to the second stage of spiritual development, termed cosmic or illuminative consciousness. Jesus proceeds to guide the Pharisee 'by night' through the cosmic imagery of the Temple and its meaning.

A fourth-century rabbi later asserted, 'The land of Israel is the middle of the earth. Jerusalem is the middle of Israel. The Temple is the middle of Jerusalem. The Holy of Holies is the middle of the Temple. The Holy Ark is the middle of the Holy of Holies. And the Stone of Foundation [*Even Shetiyah*] is in front of the

Holy of Holies.' (Comay 1975, 49). This legend that the Temple contained Jacob's Pillow [the *Even Shetiyah*] has its continuation in the Stone of Scone beneath the coronation throne in Westminster Abbey. It epitomises the function of the Temple as the embodiment of the ladder leading up to heaven, the planetary journey of the soul.

The first great gate of the Temple was, Josephus tells us, covered with gold, representing the boundless expanse of the heavens. Hanging in front of the Holy of Holies was the veil, the Babylonian tapestry woven in colours which represent the elements: scarlet (fire), blue (air), purple (water) and fine linen (earth) (*War* 5.213). The veil was an image of the universe. Worked into the tapestry was the whole vista of the heavens except the signs of the zodiac. And before it were

> . . . three most wonderful works of art, universally renowned: a lampstand, a table, and an altar of incense. The seven lamps (such being the number of the branches from the lampstand) represented the planets; the loaves on the table, twelve in number, the circle of the Zodiac and the year; while the altar of incense, by the thirteen [the number of sidereal months in the year] fragrant spices from sea and from land, both desert and inhabited, with which it was replenished, signified that all things are of God and for God. (*War* 5.216–18).

A similarly cosmic interpretation of the Temple and of the high priest's vestments is given elsewhere by Josephus (*Ant*.3.180f) and also by Philo.

To anyone familiar with the all-pervading cosmic religion of post-exilic times, the Temple's decoration would have seemed to illustrate the essence of its worship. As B. L. van der Waerden (1974) informs us, the heavenly journey of the soul was the centrepiece of cosmic religion, with Plato its high priest. Just as in the Gospel of John (3:2) the sight of the kingdom of God is afforded to those who cross the threshold of birth, in Plato's *Republic* (10.614f) a glimpse of the heavenly journey is granted to a hero who returns from the dead.

> 'I shall tell you,' I said, 'a story, not of Alcinous, but of a valiant man, Er, son of Armenius, of the race of

Pamphylia. Once upon a time he fell in battle. On the tenth day they took up the dead, who were now stinking, but his body was found fresh. They took him home, and were going to bury him when on the twelfth day he came back to life as he was lying on the pyre. When he had revived, he told them what he had seen yonder. His soul, he said, departed from him, and journeyed along with a great company, until they arrived at a certain ghostly place where there were two openings in the earth side by side, and opposite them and above two openings in heaven. In the middle sat judges. These, when they had given their judgment, ordered the just to take the road to the right, which led upward through heaven, first binding tablets on them signifying their judgments. The unjust they ordered to take the road to the left, which led downward. They also had tablets signifying all that they had done bound on their backs. When it came to his turn they told him that it was laid upon him to be a messenger to men concerning the things that were there, and they ordered him to listen to and look at everything in the place. Then he saw there souls departing, after judgment had been delivered upon them, by one of the openings of heaven and one of earth; by the other, two souls were arriving, on the one side coming up out of the earth, travel-stained and dusty, on the other coming down from heaven, shining pure. They all seemed on their arrival to have come a long journey, and were glad to turn aside into the meadow. There they encamped as in an assembly, and those who were acquaintances recognised one another . . .'

Just as the Sadducees made the Temple their spiritual province, the Essenes may be linked with the Tabernacle in the wilderness. Before the followers of Moses had abandoned their nomadic existence for settlement in Palestine, they had worshipped in the tent of desert religion, and the Essenes like them found their spiritual home in the desert. They excelled in purity and were no doubt at home in the spiritual cosmology represented in the Temple of Jerusalem. But their *theōría* filled heaven and earth with all the beings of light and darkness.

Their Messianic expectation was much more concrete and explicit than their contemporaries otherwise could articulate. It may be believed that John the Baptist was brought up in the Essene Dead Sea settlements. There is no reason to believe that John became a professing member of the order but there is no doubt that he must have been a familiar figure in their midst. John's baptism for all penitents would have posed a major challenge to the order. Either it was a betrayal of their sacred and exclusive baptismal rite; or John could have been recognized by them as the Prophet who was to come, in which case their order could hardly have continued untouched by his Messianic impact. Meanwhile, here in the desert was their Holy of Holies, and they prepared assiduously for the Messianic high priest who would enter it.

12 John the Baptist

In the days of Herod, king of Judea, there was a priest named Zechariah, of the division of Abijah; and he had a wife of the daughters of Aaron, and her name was Elizabeth. And they were both righteous before God, walking in all the commandments and ordinances of the Lord blameless. But they had no child, because Elizabeth was barren, and both were advanced in years.

Now while he was serving as priest before God when his division was on duty, according to the custom of the priesthood, it fell to him by lot to enter the temple of the Lord and burn incense. And the whole multitude of the people were praying outside at the hour of incense. And there appeared to him an angel of the Lord standing on the right side of the altar of incense. And Zechariah was troubled when he saw him, and fear fell upon him. But the Angel said to him, 'Do not be afraid, Zechariah, for your prayer is heard, and your wife Elizabeth will bear you a son, and you shall call his name John.

And you will have joy and gladness,
and many will rejoice at his birth;
for he will be great before the Lord,
and he shall drink no wine nor strong drink,
and he will be filled with the Holy Spirit,
even from his mother's womb.
And he will turn many of the sons of Israel to the Lord
    their God,
and he will go before him in the spirit and power of
    Elijah,
to turn the hearts of the fathers to the children,
and the disobedient to the wisdom of the just,
to make ready for the Lord a people prepared.'
And Zechariah said to the angel, 'How shall I know this? For I am an old man, and my wife is advanced in years.'

And the angel answered him, 'I am Gabriel, who stand in the presence of God; and I was sent to speak to you, and to bring you this good news. And behold, you will be silent and unable to speak until the day that these things come to pass, because you did not believe my words, which will be fulfilled in their time.' And the people were waiting for Zechariah, and they wondered at his delay in the temple. And when he came out, he could not speak to them, and they perceived that he had seen a vision in the temple; and he made signs to them and remained dumb. And when his time of service was ended, he went to his home.

The fullness of Luke's account (1:5–23) of the annunciation of John's birth is commensurate with its great significance to contemporary Judaism. Gabriel's proclamation signals the end of the provisional order, instituted at the start of the Hasmonean era until the prophet's coming. It is frequently argued that the solitary date in the Gospels of the fifteenth year of Tiberius must attach to something more important than the beginning of John's prophetic ministry (and that the Baptism of Jesus fell in the fifteenth year of Tiberius). But the suggestion that John's appearance is of minor importance misses entirely the epoch-making impact of the advent of *the* Prophet, so long awaited.

We have seen how Luke's account of the birth of Jesus evokes the paradisal springtime of human life on earth. It is very different with the birth of John. Like Sarah, the mother conceived not in the spring freshness of youth but in the autumn of life when Eros has lost his strength. Man's genealogical tree puts out a last shoot which is to embody all its finest powers. John is the greatest born of woman, the finest flower of heredity. Now far from the garden of paradise, the last of the hunter-gatherers (eating hard fruit and wild honey) looks around on the desolate wilderness, a natural world depleted by man's depredations and with his food supply restricted to the bread produced by arduous toil and eaten 'in the sweat of your face' (Gen.3:19). Natural egotism reinforced by the ever present threat of hunger has proved a mighty force in man's conquest of nature. When at length the spiritual rains fail, the prophet has the duty to prescribe to his people an egotism-free diet.

The First Book of the Kings (17:10–16) tells how the prophet Elijah responded to famine induced by drought. He was directed to Zarephath,

> . . . and when he came to the gate of the city, behold, a widow was there gathering sticks; and he called to her and said, 'Bring me a little water in a vessel, that I may drink.' And as she was going to bring it, he called to her and said, 'Bring me a morsel of bread in your hand.' And she said, 'As the LORD your God lives, I have nothing baked, only a handful of meal in a jar, and a little oil in a cruse; and now, I am gathering a couple of sticks, that I may go in and prepare it for myself and my son, that we may eat it, and die.' And Elijah said to her, 'Fear not; go and do as you have said; but first make me a little cake of it and bring it to me, and afterward make for yourself and your son. For thus says the LORD the God of Israel, "The jar of meal shall not be spent, and the cruse of oil shall not fail, until the day that the LORD sends rains upon earth." ' And she went and did as Elijah said; and she, and he, and her household ate for many days. The jar of meal was not spent, neither did the cruse of oil fail, according to the word of the LORD which he spoke by Elijah.

After his beheading, John was identified as Elijah. 'For all the prophets and the law prophesied until John; and if you are willing to accept it, he is Elijah who is to come' (Matt.11:13f).

Jesus spoke earlier of Elijah, at the opening of his Galilean teaching ministry (Luke 4:14–30), perhaps thinking of the period just past in which John had been continuing his prophetic ministry after the baptism of Jesus. 'But in truth, I tell you, there were many widows in Israel in the days of Elijah, when the heaven was shut up three years and six months, where there came a great famine over all the land; and Elijah was sent to none of them but only to Zarephath in the land of Sidon, to a woman who was a widow.' (4:25f) From the beginning of his work to his death, John's ministry is estimated below to have lasted three and a half years also (compare Thiering 1981).

The emergence of John the Baptist

The political backcloth to the emergence of John can be found in Josephus' history. As the expectation of the Messiah approached flashpoint, Pilate was flaunting the unbridled power of Rome in the face of the Jews, and Herod Antipas (tetrarch of Galilee) was prepared for any rival who might prove inconvenient to him.

The beginning of John's ministry in the fifteenth year of Tiberius as Caesar can also be viewed against the background of the Essene sect's quest for spiritual perfection in the remoteness of the desert. At Qumran, as we have envisaged it, John was a familiar figure. Far from the complacent cities, they bestowed their baptism on the few who had reached the requisite degree of perfection. Yet John's first audience seems to have been made up largely of soldiers and tax-collectors (Luke 3:12). What were these religious untouchables doing down by the Jordan when John began his ministry?

It is generally and rightly thought that John began his work in the autumn season, when the intense summer heat was abating and attention turned to the religious festivals of repentance and atonement. At that time the faithful should have been attending the solemn ceremonies in the Temple. But the soldiers and tax-collectors would hardly have been made welcome there. What were they doing down at the Jordan when John began his preaching? A historian's portrait of the scene only adds emphasis to the question (Olmstead 1942a, 52f).

> The surrounding view was sheer desolation. At John's feet twisted and turned the Jordan in its narrow, deep-sunk trough. No longer was its water bright, clear green, as when it left the Lake of Galilee; its rapid flow deeper and deeper into the earth, to which it owed its name of 'Descender', had charged its waters with mud to the point of saturation. A few streams coming down from the hills through deep-cut gorges showed a thin line of green. On the western side, one small mass of verdure marked out the palms and the precious medical balsams which clustered around Jericho's copious spring. Elsewhere the valley terraces showed bare

alkaline soil, baked and cracked by the sun, horrible for
walking with unshod feet.

To either side, valley and sea were shut in by lines of
unscalable hills, broken rarely by gorges through which
trails climbed up by the plateau. The rocks were almost
unbelievably barren, thrown about in wild confusion, tilted,
contorted, and overturned by the titanic earth movements
which produced this long double fault, extending . . . one
sixth of the distance round our globe. Closer in, marl cliffs
add a ghostly effect by their pale tints. In winter, wind
passed over snow-covered Hermon at the valley head and
whistled down the narrow trough; in summer the hills shut
in an intolerable heat the few unfortunate peasants who
tended Jericho's balsam wealth for absentee landlords. To
the heat and the ever-present malaria was added the
unrealized but not unfelt atmospheric pressure, which
makes mere breathing a misery, for the spot is actually the
lowest open to the sun on earth, almost thirteen hundred
feet below the level of the sea.

The rite of baptism

To John's hearers, the tax collectors and soldiers, the devotions
of the Essenes would be as unapproachable as the great chasm
was forbidding. What were these religious outcasts doing at such
a spot? For John could not have begun his preaching without a
congregation (presumably assembling for another purpose). A
theologian provides an answer which is partially satisfying (Levertoff & Goudge 1928, 3:129).

The weeks preceding the Day of Atonement were always
a time of preparation for that great fast, and the Jewish
motif of that season was 'teshubah' (repentance) and 'Malkut
Shamayim' (the Kingdom of Heaven) . . . The baptism of
John thus heralded the approach of the establishment of the
New Covenant founded on forgiveness of sins
(Jer.31:31–34), as the Old Covenant on Sinai was preceded
by 'sanctification' (Exod.19:10), which in the earliest
Midrash is actually called 'baptism' (cf. my edition of *Sifre*,

92). One of the prophetic lessons for this season was the latter portion of Micah 7; cf.[v.]19, 'and thou wilt cast all their sins into the depths of the sea.' (This verse has given rise at a later date to a quaint Jewish custom retained until this day. On one of the days between New Year and the Day of Atonement the people go down to any neighbouring sheet of water and shake their garments into it, thereby symbolically disposing of their sins. This little drama is called *Tashlich* — 'thou wilt cast'). As straws are capable of indicating the quarter from which the wind blows, so these small matters suggest the probability that John began his ministry about this season.

Theodor Gaster (1952, 121–3) provides a historical perspective on the origins of *Tashlich*.

In the afternoon of the first day of New Year (or of the second day, if the first happens on a sabbath), it is the practice of orthodox Jews to repair to the nearest body of flowing water and there recite in Hebrew the closing words of the Biblical book of Micah,

God will again have compassion upon us;
He will tread our iniquities under foot;
And Thou wilt cast all their sins into the depths
    of the sea.

The ceremony is called *Tashlich*, from the Hebrew word 'Thou wilt cast'; and while the verses are being recited, it is customary to shake crumbs from one's pockets into the water.

The custom is first attested in the fifteenth century, and it is explained in a purely homiletic manner. According to one's view, the sight of the water on New Year's Day is intended to recall the fact that the world was created out of watery chaos; while another insists that the purpose of visiting flowing streams is to observe the fish and thereby to be reminded that, in the word of the Preacher, mankind is 'as the fishes that are caught in an evil net' (Eccles.9:12). Yet a third interpretation sees in the custom an allusion to the ancient legend which relates that when Abraham was speeding to Mount Moriah in obedience to the divine

101

commandment to sacrifice his son Isaac — an event which was said to have taken place on New Year's Day — Satan interposed a turbid stream to impede his progress. The patriarch, however, would not be stayed, but strode through it undaunted!

The true origin of the ceremony is probably to be found, however, in the common custom of throwing sops to the spirits of rivers on critical days of the year. The Romans, for example, used to cast straw puppets into the Tiber at the Ides of May; in European folk-usage, such offerings are (or were) often made to Rhine, Danube, Rhone, Elbe and Neckar on New Year's Eve. The Jews would thus have adopted the custom from their Gentile neighbours, reinterpreting it in accordance with their own outlook and tradition.

Levertoff and Goudge associated the beginning of John's Baptism with *Tashlich*, and Gaster traced *Tashlich* to an earlier pagan rite practised on the New Year's Eve in the autumn early in our era. Like the Jewish new year, the pagan or civil new year also had its rite of repentance. The tax collectors, soldiers and the multitudes were, we suggest, adopting the method of salvation of surrounding Gentile cults. The words of the Baptist lend themselves to this reading. 'You brood of vipers' is a particularly vituperative way of referring to the Serpent spirit which played such a role in pagan rites. And upon these offspring of the Serpent, John conferred the sacred baptism of the exclusive Essenes. No more dramatic emergence could be imagined.

Matthew (3:1ff) recalls a later scene. John is dressed in his winter cloak, and now it is the Pharisees and Sadducees who constitute his audience. They had bound themselves to observance of the Law (tablets of *stone*) which was in them purely external. For them a change of heart would indeed be a momentous change. To all his hearers, John speaks with the same voice, Drive out the Serpent from your souls.

We date John's emergence then to the *civil* new year's day, Heshvan 1, October 8, AD 28. L. Girard (1953, 58) confirms that the fifteenth year of Tiberius is equivalent to AD 28–29, saying that it is certain that the Latin authors Tacitus, Suetonius, Pliny, the Christian chronologists Julian Africanus, Hippolytus, Tertullian, Lanctantius, Eusebius, the Jewish historian Josephus . . . in a word the whole of antiquity, pagan, Jewish and Christian have known but one chronology of Tiberius in which AD 14–15 is always the starting point from which the fifteenth year of Tiberius is always reckoned as AD 28–29.

As the Fourth Gospel tells (1:19–28), the priests wished to establish whether John was the returning Elijah.

> And this is the testimony of John, when the Jews sent priests and Levites from Jerusalem to ask him, 'Who are you?' He confessed, he did not deny, but confessed, 'I am not [ἐγὼ οὐκ εἰμὶ] the Christ.' And they asked him, 'What then? Are you Elijah?' He said, 'I am not [οὐκ εἰμὶ].' 'Are you the prophet?' And he answered 'No.'

Even these diminuendo denials served to remind his interrogators that it is the mission of the prophet to preach self-denial. John's teaching had the power so to concentrate the minds of his listeners that they could begin to see through the veil of personality the impending incarnation of the Christ. The Messianic prophet had been expected to return baptizing. For John continues with the Pharisees asking the question that concerned them. 'Then why are you baptizing, if you are neither the Christ, nor Elijah, nor the prophet?'

John's baptism of Jesus is dated according to second-century tradition on January 6. It has been reasonably conjectured that the date must have derived from a tradition concerning the length of the Christ's ministry. Such sometimes inconsistent traditions are to be found set down side by side, for instance, in Dionysius Exiguus (c. 500 – c. 560), inaugurator of the Christian Era (whereby we number years Anno Domini, 'in the year of our Lord'). In a passage quoted more fully in Chapter 13, Dionysius writes, '. . . and from when he was baptized Jesus Christ our Lord were two years and 90 days, which are 820 days . . .' Counting forward from January 6 yields a date of 5 April, easily recognizable as April 5, AD 33, the date of the Resurrection, stated below. Two years and ninety days earlier (820 days) the Baptism of Jesus is accordingly dated 6 January AD 31. It should also be pointed out that the same interval of 820 days (two and a quarter years) has elapsed between our date of the beginning of John's ministry October 8, AD 28 and the date of the Baptism of Jesus, January 6, AD 31.

Paul seems to place the baptism of Jesus relatively late in John's ministry. 'Before his coming John had preached a baptism of repentance to all the people of Israel. And as John was finishing his course, he said, 'What do you suppose that I am? I am not (οὐκ εἰμὶ ἐγώ) he. No, but after me one is coming, the sandals of whose feet I am not worthy to untie.'

By the end of AD 30, John's task had largely been accomplished. In the hearts of great numbers of people a recognition of the nearness of the divine had been kindled. Silent for centuries, the voice of an authentic prophet had awakened men to the coming of the Christ. In other men, John's preaching and baptism induced catharsis. In Jesus of Nazareth, the Baptism was the starting point of the indwelling of 'all righteousness'. John's baptism could illuminate the Messianic consciousness of the penitents only because the Incarnation was imminent. In Jesus, the Baptism similarly brought illumination so that he could see his future life and death. For thereafter Jesus speaks of his death as his 'baptism' (Luke 12:50). When he stepped into the Jordan he took upon himself the sins of humanity, which the people had cast upon its waters. These sins bore within them the guarantee of death. At his Baptism, the divine Spirit began to perfect the human nature of Jesus. That its operation is not confined merely to the soul is, ultimately, shown in the Resurrection.

After the Baptism

After the Baptism of Jesus, John continues to work. Following the Passover of AD 31, John and Jesus are shown in close proximity again (John 3:22–4:3).

> After this Jesus and his disciples went into the land of Judea; there he remained with them and baptized. John also was baptizing at Aenon near Salim, because there was much water there; and people came and were baptized. For John had not yet been put in prison.
>
> Now a discussion arose between John's disciples and a

	Year	Jewish date	Julian date	Weekday
John's emergence	AD 28	Heshvan 1	October 8	Monday
Baptism of Jesus	AD 31	Tebeth 23	January 6	Saturday
Arrest of John	AD 31	c. Tishri 7–8	c. Sept 13–14	(Thu-Fri)
Death of John	AD 32	Nisan 1	April 1	Tuesday

Table 9. The ministry of John the Baptist

Jew over purifying. And they came to John, and said to him, 'Rabbi, he who was with you beyond the Jordan, to whom you bore witness, here he is, baptizing, and all are going to him.' John answered, 'No one can receive anything except what is given him from heaven. You yourselves bear me witness, that I said, I am not the Christ, but I have been sent before him. He who has the bride is the bridegroom; the friend of the bridegroom, who stands and hears him, rejoices greatly at the bridegroom's voice; therefore this joy of mine is now full. He must increase, but I must decrease.'

He who comes from above is above all; he who is of the earth belongs to the earth, and of the earth he speaks; he who comes from heaven is above all. He bears witness to what he has seen and heard, yet no one receives his testimony; he who receives his testimony sets his seal to this, that God is true. For he whom God has sent utters the words of God, for it is not by measure that he gives the Spirit; the Father loves the Son, and has given all things into his hand. He who believes in the Son has eternal life; he who does not obey the Son shall not see life, but the wrath of God rests upon him.

Now when the Lord knew that the Pharisees had heard that Jesus was making and baptizing more disciples than John (although Jesus himself did not baptize, but only his disciples), he left Judea and departed again to Galilee.

During these months following the Baptism, Jesus and his disciples acted at first almost as part of the Baptist movement. Jesus had received the prophetic mantle but the Evangelist shows that there was no intention of competing with or, indeed, terminating John the Baptist's work. And until after the Baptist's arrest, Jesus did not begin his public teaching. From Matthew (4:12–17) we learn that the news of John's imprisonment was the cause of Jesus' withdrawal into Galilee.

> Now when he [Jesus] heard that John had been arrested,
> he withdrew into Galilee; and leaving Nazareth he went
> and dwelt in Capernaum by the sea, in the territory of
> Zebulun and Naphtali, that what was spoken by the
> prophet Isaiah might be fulfilled:
> 'The land of Zebulun and the land of Naphtali,
> towards the sea, across the Jordan,
> Galilee of the Gentiles —
> the people who sat in darkness
> have seen a great light,
> and for those who sat in the region and shadow of death
> light has dawned.'
> From that time Jesus began to preach, saying, 'Repent, for
> the kingdom of heaven is at hand.'

E. Stauffer (1960, 66) conjectures that Herod Antipas (son of Herod the Great) was making his customary pilgrimage to attend the rites of the Day of Atonement and Tabernacles in Jerusalem when he halted to hear the famous preacher (see Chapter 15). The point of John's fearless denunciation of Antipas concerned his marriage to Herodias. Herodias, daughter of Aristobulus (second son Herod the Great and Mariamne I) had already married another uncle, Philip, son of Herod the Great and the second Mariamne. Since her first husband still lived, her second marriage was a scandal in Jewish eyes.

After his confinement in the fortress-prison of Machaerus, John languished for several months before his life was ended at Antipas' 'birthday'. The date of Herod's natural birthday is not known but the narrative portrays an official occasion. The presence of Herod's lords, captains and chief stewards (Mark 6:21) is adequate evidence of that. The official birthday or accession day prescribed in Judaism was the 'New Year for kings', in that year (32) Nisan 1, April 1. From the date proposed for the beginning of John's ministry Heshvan 1, October 8, AD 28, three and a half years had elapsed, a period which also occurs in the life of Elijah (Luke 4:25).

A portrait of John is also provided by the political historian Josephus (*Ant.* 18.117–19) and it is interesting to compare it with the Gospel picture.

> For Herod had put him to death, though he was a good man and had exhorted the Jews to lead righteous lives, to practise justice towards their fellows and piety towards God, and so doing to join in baptism. In his view this was a necessary preliminary if baptism was to be acceptable to God. They must not employ it to gain pardon for whatever sins they committed, but as a consecration of the body implying that the soul was already thoroughly cleansed by right behaviour. When others too joined the crowds about him, because they were aroused to the highest degree by his sermons, Herod became alarmed. Eloquence that had so great an effect on mankind might lead to some form of sedition, for it looked as if they would be guided by John in everything they did. Herod decided therefore that it would be much better to strike first and be rid of him before his work led to an uprising, than to wait for an upheaval, get involved in a difficult situation and see his mistake. Though John, because of Herod's suspicions, was brought in chains to Machaerus, the stronghold that we have previously mentioned, and there put to death, yet the verdict of the Jews was that the destruction visited upon Herod's army [in AD 36] was a vindication of John, since God saw fit to inflict such a blow on Herod.

Only shortly after John's death, according to the Gospel account, the feeding of the five thousand took place. Matthew connects the two events closely (14:12–15).

> And his [John's] disciples came and took the body and buried it; and they went and told Jesus.
>
> Now when Jesus heard this, he withdrew in a boat to a lonely place apart. But when the crowds heard it, they followed him on foot from the towns. As he went ashore he saw a great throng; and he had compassion on them, and healed their sick. When it was evening, the disciples came

to him and said, 'This is a lonely place, and the day is now over; send the crowds away to go into the villages and buy food for themselves.'

In the feeding of the five thousand, we are led back into the condition appertaining to the first temptation (discussed below).

Now it is through the twelve that the temptation is renewed to buy earthly sustenance for the disciples and followers of John, sorrowing and suffering from lack of food and sleep. Jesus had earlier, after his Baptism, remained a part of the Baptist circle. With John's death and the feeding of the five thousand, the Spirit of the Baptist is integrated into the teaching ministry of Jesus that men shall live 'by every word that proceeds from the mouth of God' (Matt.4:4).

As guardian of the Old Covenant, Elijah fed the widow and her son; his Spirit is now not far distant from the distraught and famished crowd. The feeding of the five thousand was, of course, no ordinary meal. As in the Eucharist which it foreshadowed, physical food was present only in token quantities. The combination of fasting and grief awakened the spiritual perception of the twelve. They saw how the words of Christ nourished the souls of those who came to him. With the death of John, the Spirit of Elijah was freed from incorporation in a single human vessel to serve as the messenger of the New Covenant. Under his inspiration, the twelve had now to learn to recognize Jesus not merely as a national redeemer but as the creator of a new humanity.

The Incarnation

13 The Baptism

Quite early the Church lost a full understanding of the Baptism of Jesus. At first the Evangelists appear to have used the birth narratives (Annunciation or Nativity) to illuminate the nature of the Baptism. In the fourth and fifth centuries the doctrine of the Incarnation led to a supposed conflict between the weight to be attached to these two major moments in the birth of the divine Son. When opponents of the Patriarch of Constantinople, Nestorius (d. *c.* 451), revered Mary as the *Theotokos*, the Mother of God, the Nestorians felt themselves precluded from attaching significance to the Baptism as a divine begetting, as indicated by reference to Psalm 2.

Luke speaks of the Baptism of Jesus as an 'anointing' (Acts 10:36–38):

> You know the word which he sent to Israel, preaching good news [the Gospel] of peace by Jesus Christ (he is Lord of all), the word which was proclaimed throughout all Judea, beginning from Galilee after the baptism which John preached: how God anointed [ἔχρισεν] Jesus of Nazareth with the Holy Spirit and with power [δυνάμει].

Anointing, in the Old Testament, was the symbol of consecration alike in the case of the prophet (1Kings 19:16b), priest (Lev.8:12) and king (1Sam.10:1).

Eusebius also makes explicit the connection between anointing and the Baptism, quoting the Coronation Psalm (2:7) invoked by the voice from heaven (Luke 3:22 Western text, *Ch. Hist.* 1.3.5):

> The Lord said to me, 'You are my Son;
> I have today begotten you.'

Eusebius goes on to make a further important point (*Ch. Hist.* 1.3.11):

> He did not receive the symbols and patterns of the high priesthood from anyone; He did not trace his physical descent from the acknowledged priests; He was not

promoted by the soldiers' weapons to a kingdom; He did not become a prophet in the same way as those of old; He did not receive from the Jews any rank or pre-eminence whatever.

From the moment of Baptism, the anointing of Jesus is different from the baptism of John's other followers. For them the Baptist was the personification of purification. He was also the waning moon reflecting the glory of the rising sun of Christ. Through John the entry of 'all righteousness' into a human vessel became conscious. The process is opposed to the unrighteous prince of this world who exercises his government through fear of death. All righteousness enters into Jesus when the thin shell of self-consciousness is sundered by suffering total immersion in the waters of the Jordan.

A glance back at John's call to repentance reminds us of the mighty impact of submersion. In John's baptism of the penitents, a particular state of consciousness was built up in the candidates by his compelling instruction and then earthly consciousness was suddenly extinguished by total immersion in the Jordan. His call (μετανοεῖτε) sought a total spiritual reorientation and a reversal of the normal direction of earthly experience. It is often recounted how a shock sustained through near drowning can cause a flashback vision of the past life. As the account from Plato's *Republic* well illustrates, a close encounter with death was a primary source of knowledge concerning pre-existence. In Plato's grand myth, the soul travels back in time and enters upon the heavenly journey before being called back to resume life on earth. In the Baptist's rite the eyes of the soul were at the same time opened to the nearing of the pre-existent Christ. The Baptist's cry of 'The kingdom of heaven is at hand' marks the transition between the heaven of the ancients, identified with outer space, and the 'heaven within' of the Christ. To the ears of the Baptist's followers, the voice of John sounded, proclaiming the pre-existent Logos, 'In the beginning was the Word . . .'

From the beginning, the Baptism was regarded in conjunction with the death and resurrection of the Christ Jesus. Cullmann asks (1963, 67):

What is the meaning of baptism for forgiveness of sins for

Jesus himself? The other Jews went to John the Baptist to be baptized for their own sins. But when Jesus is baptized just as all the others were, he hears a divine voice which implicitly says to him, 'You are not baptized for your own sins, but for those of the whole people. For you are the one whose vicarious suffering for the sins of others the prophet predicted.' This may also be the sense of Jesus' words in Matt.3:15 about 'fulfilling all righteousness'. But this means that Jesus is baptized in view of his death, that on the cross he will accomplish a general baptism of his people. He takes on himself all the sins which the Jews bring to the Jordan. In this way the whole plan of salvation which he has to realize is openly laid before him.

This explanation of Jesus' baptism is confirmed by the only two sayings of Jesus which contain the verb βαπτισθῆναι, Mark 10:38 and Luke 12:50, For Jesus, 'to be baptized' means the same as 'to die'.

From the human viewpoint, the descent of the Holy Spirit might be visualized as a huge accession of consciousness of immortality. But to the divine Spirit now entering earthly consciousness the experience was an intimation of mortality. And it is from this divine perspective that the Baptism is felt as a birth. As his bodily nature emerged from the waters the new-born being of the Christ Jesus was projected into the hard light of day.

When we come to consider the Resurrection, a comparison with a later point in human development suggests itself. During the two or three years following the Baptism, the disciples are called, trained and shown what is to come, but they are again and again revealed as lacking the faculty of comprehension. It is only after the Resurrection that they begin to remember and understand. In early childhood, these faculties begin to operate after the birth of self-consciousness, a change which will be compared with the transformation in the disciples which began at the first Easter.

In the final part of this book, 'Christology and Chronology' we shall look again at the interpretation of the ministry as a revelation of human nature before the birth of personality and make the comparison between firstly, the baptism and physical birth, and secondly, the Resurrection and the birth of self-consciousness.

113

The chronological problem further explored below is to connect possible models of the Incarnation with the data in the Gospels, and with extant traditions concerning the duration of the ministry. On the latter point Dionysius Exiguus (*c.* 550 – *c.* 560) collected disparate strands of wildly conflicting traditions (*Paschate*, Arg.15):

> From 25 March to 25 December the days number 271. From the resultant number of days Christ our Lord was conceived on the day of the Lord (Sunday) 25 March and born on Tuesday 25 December. On the day of his Passion 133 (*sic!*) years and 3 months had passed, which is 12,414 days. Again it is stated that he was born on Tuesday 25 December and died on Friday 25 March. Counting from the Baptism were two years and 90 days, or 820 days from the day on which he was baptized Thursday 6 January and suffered on Friday 25 March, as already stated.

Among the examples provided by Dionysius, the ministry is stated as beginning on January 6 and ending on March 25 after an interval of 820 days. But 820 days from January 6 brings us to April 5, not March 25. The nearest approximation to the figures is achieved by dating the Baptism Saturday January 6, AD 31 and — after 820 days — the Resurrection on Sunday April 5, AD 33. There is no tradition of the *year* of the Baptism and it is supposed that the date January 6 was deduced from a tradition relating to the length of the ministry.

The earliest tradition of the date January 6 is found in Clement of Alexandria (*c.* 150 – *c.* 215) (*Misc.* 1.21): 'And the followers of Basilides [Gnostics of a Petrine school] hold the day of his baptism as a festival, spending the night before in readings. And they say that it was in the fifteenth year of Tiberius Caesar, the fifteenth day of the month Tubi; and some say that it was the eleventh of the same month,' that is, January 6 or 10.

Never explicitly stated in antiquity, there seem to have been two traditions which hover over many statements of early Christian writers. Firstly, the crucifixion is connected with the day of the Annunciation, March 25 according to Western tradition. Secondly, the Baptism was linked with the date of the Nativity in the Eastern tradition of January 6.

114

14 The Temptation

Mark gives a characteristically terse account of what happened immediately after the Baptism (1:12f): 'The Spirit immediately drove him out into the wilderness. And he was in the wilderness forty days, tempted by Satan; and he was with the wild beasts; and angels ministered to him.' Mention of the wild beasts recalls the picture of the first man in paradise surrounded by beasts who are not yet wild. In due time paradise becomes the setting for temptation and Adam's animal companions are represented by the Serpent. The image of the wild beasts allows this twofold interpretation.

The first temptation

During the days following the Baptism, earthly sustenance must have seemed the least urgent of needs for so mighty an indwelling Spirit. As Luke says, in those days he ate nothing and only afterwards was hungry (4:2). After forty days' fasting the Father's bounty, in the form of bodily reserves, has been totally exhausted and the body's demands become insistent. Matthew and Luke both order first the temptation to feed himself. Matthew (4:1–4) begins with his reaction to hunger:

Then Jesus was led up by the Spirit into the wilderness to
be tempted by the devil. And he fasted forty days and forty
nights, and afterward he was hungry. And the tempter came
and said to him, 'If you are the Son of God, command
these stones to become loaves of bread.' But he answered,
'It is written,
"Man will not live by bread alone,
but by every word that proceeds from the mouth
of God." '

Fasting played an immensely important role in the spiritual life of antiquity, and in the modern world-conception the threat of hunger has figured with equally great effect. Since we can then

115

examine the first temptation from both ancient and modern vantage points, we can observe both the common ground and the contrasts between the two points of view.

In the ancient world, prolonged fasting was undertaken for the sake of the visions thereby obtained. Certainly these visions were distorted sometimes wildly by hallucinations arising from a physiology under extreme stress. But a strict regime of mental self-control and prayer was practised in order to subdue the wild beasts and devils assailing the hallucinating soul. Once bodily appetites had been completely subjugated, eating could then become a mildly unwelcome interruption to the pursuit of sanctity. Yet the conquest over the appetites was achieved only near the point of death from starvation and, as has been illustrated above, it was the proximity to death which brought spiritual knowledge of pre-existence and life after death.

In connection with the Temptation, Marcus Dods recalls a tale of fasting, changing paradise to nightmare (Hastings 1906, 2:715):

> It seems that in the East, or at any rate in Persia, there is a traditional custom called 'the subjugation of the *jinn*'. In order to achieve this victory, the candidate retires to a desert place, fasts for forty days, and when the jinns appear in the forms of a lion, a tiger, and a dragon, he must hold his ground fearlessly. Doing so, power over the demons is attained.

Since spiritual exercises of this extreme kind produce visions and hallucinations emanating from the condition of the organs of the body, it can be appreciated that these painful experiences were made to yield a (spiritual) science of physiology. Through fasting, the organs were induced to 'speak' in the form of the visions encountered. Although many animal forms are mentioned, they were grouped into the classic Eagle (above), Bull (below) and on either hand Man and the Lion. When the power which binds the organs of the body into the human whole, the human form is at its weakest, the body is represented as a composite animal figure in the form of the sphinx.

This intimidating figure appears most memorably in the struggle between Oedipus and the Theban sphinx. Oedipus is a hero of royal blood whose life is predestined much in the manner of modern writings on genetics. The sphinx ('throttler') possessed a woman's head, lion's body, serpent's tail and eagle's wings, the body being constructed in the image of the four cardinal signs of the zodiac. The contest between Oedipus and the monster concerns the nature of man. 'What being, with only one voice, has sometimes two feet, sometimes three, sometimes four, and is weakest when it has the most?' When Oedipus solves the riddle, the sphinx hurls herself down from the mountain into the ravine below (second temptation). The drama of Oedipus conveys the spiritual predicament of man in pre-Christian terms.

The nightmares induced by hunger in antiquity were echoed in Thomas Malthus (1766–1843) and his contemplations of the influence of hunger on population size. No less than in antiquity, his observation laid the foundation for many of the most potent ideas of the age, which became known as 'the nineteenth-century nightmare'. For Malthus it was a natural progression from his observations of the effects of scarcity to becoming the world's first professor of economics, in which capacity he succeeded in turning Adam Smith's optimism into 'the dismal science'. His ideas were to prove no less fruitful in the evolutionary biology of Alfred Russel Wallace and Charles Darwin.

Malthus concentrated his attention on years of scarcity, when the struggle to survive would make self-interest an essential attribute. Economics is the science of the allocation of scarce resources and, viewed of course from a purely earthly point of view, in a situation of scarcity, self-interest is the only rational behaviour of *Homo economicus.*

In the first temptation, Jesus was tempted to feed himself: to subject himself to the law of self-preservation which prevails for every creature on earth. Here is the first great challenge of his ministry: to proclaim his teaching of altruism with the power to overcome self-interest in economic life to the extent that altruism can become a biological reality.

An illuminating view of the temptations is given by Gerhard Friedrich (1956, 265ff). He regards the Christ's first encounter as the temptation to act as false *prophet.* A god-given faith in the future is the prophet's indispensable gift, even though his insight into the future can also see the inevitable consequences of present evils. His modern counterpart is the economist, despite his false oft-heard protestations of 'I am no prophet'. Expectations of the future are the common currency. Self-interest demands quick returns, while altruism invites identification with the future of mankind as a whole. As a representative of the spiritual life, the prophet maintains that the greatest good for the greatest number ultimately cannot be assessed merely as competitive success in earthly life. From the beginning of hominization (human evolution), upright walking was accompanied by food-sharing. The latest evidence of palaeontology is that the early putative ancestors of man were vegetarian rather than carnivorous, co-operative rather than competitive. And man's specifically human behaviour is altruistic rather than egotistic.

The second temptation

Matthew relates the second temptation (4:5–7):
> Then the devil took him to the holy city, and set him on the pinnacle of the temple, and said to him, 'If you are the Son of God, throw yourself down; for it is written,
>> "He will give his angels charge of you,"
> and
>> "On their hands they will bear you up,
>> lest you strike your foot against a stone." '

The location in the holy city and the Temple corresponds to Gerhard Friedrich's interpretation of the temptation to appear as false *priest*. The vertical movement in 'throw yourself down' envisages the priest's task as soul-guide, the conductor of souls into and out of earthly existence. While the soul remains in the hands of the angels he is prevented from falling precipitously and prematurely into his specialized earthly role. The Christ is 'tempted' as a divine being to play his role without allowing the time and space necessary for men to reject or follow him: to retain their freedom. The Christ has to learn that learning itself is the way in which we become human.

In the second temptation we have an excerpt from the spiritual account of incarnation and excarnation, expressed in spatial terms characteristic of the ancient world. Movement downwards corresponds to entry into life and accommodation to earthly conditions. Movement upwards corresponds to the heavenly journey of the soul. The tempter here urges the Christ to enter into his earthly task as Messianic high priest without reservation or delay. In his last public word at the end of the ministry, Jesus returns to the same image. 'Truly, truly, I say to you, unless a grain of wheat falls into the earth and dies, it remains alone; but if it dies, it bears much fruit' (John 12:24). In the Incarnation, the time for patient waiting has now (early in Holy Week) ended. His public manifestation as Messiah, after the reticence of the previous ministry, is represented as the wheat grain falling to the ground. Acceptance at last of his special role publicly and openly leads immediately to his earthly death.

We can take a further look at the parable of the falling wheat grain in the light of what is known of the evolution of the wheat plant. The cultivated grain with which we are familiar differs from the ancestral grasses in that the latter shed their seeds as soon as they are ripe. Collectors of the wild seed as food would have preferred the occasional plant where the seed had not yet fallen and the head could be gathered intact, suggesting the way in which the cultivated variety may have evolved. Of course, the head may lack the ability to fall and the 'suicidal mutation' then prevents germination (Hawkes & Woolley 1963, 271). In both man and his vital food-grain, maturation is retarded as much as possible. When the time has come, the seed is decisively released so that its death and resurrection can occur.

Antiquity's spatial imagery of the process of incarnation has its counterpart in modern developmental biology as expressed in the dimension of time. In the first temptation, we could say that the egotist is impatient for reward where the altruist behaves patiently. In the second temptation, the impatience of the egotist 'accelerates' the adoption of his specialized, adult role. 'Retardation' which is a particular characteristic of human evolution, prolongs the period of preparation, giving expression to the general type (humanity) while holding back personality and its special skills. We have already commented (in Chapter 2) on the reticence which is so marked a feature of the ministry. Retardation, if we may use the biological term, during the ministry

119

gives way to acceleration (falling to earth and dying) only after the same episode in which the parable of the seed is told: the casting out of the (unrighteous) prince of the world, who plays the part of the tempter in the third temptation.

If the temptation to turn stones into bread may be related to the role of the prophet (economist), the second temptation to alter the course of individual development unfolds in a different province of life. Nowadays the priest's responsibility in this sphere is shared by the biologist (physical development or ontogeny) and the psychologist (psychological development). No doubt at least Jungian psychologists are aware of the precursors in Gnosticism of modern theories of the soul. Archbishop Philip Carrington (1952, 52) finds an antecedent to Freud in the second-century influential Gnostic philosopher, Valentinus. We can find elements paralleled in the second temptation: 'The twelfth aeon . . . was a female named Sophia, who fell from her high place into the *kenoma* or void, and this fall set going those causes which led to creation. (Note: The myth of the Fall of Sophia in Valentinian Gnosis is identical with the psychological "theory" of S. Freud.)'

The third temptation

The third temptation (Matt.4:8–11) is better understood.
> Again, the devil took him to a very high mountain, and
> showed him all the kingdoms of the world and the glory of
> them; and he said to him, 'All these I will give you, if you
> will fall down and worship me.' Then Jesus said to him,
> 'Begone, Satan! for it is written,
>> "You shall worship the Lord your God
>> and him only shall you serve." '

Here the danger is for spiritual capacities which promote leadership (epitomized in the royal Messiah) to be employed to subjugate men into submission to the ruler of this world.

According to Gerhard Friedrich (1956), the Christ would have been trapped in the temptation if he had made premature or otherwise improper use of his spiritual powers to appear as false prophet, false priest or now as false *king*. Where contemporary

Judaism had expected of the royal Messiah a national redeemer, Jesus is plain that his kingdom is not of this world. Their concept of the King-Messiah crucially did not involve a sacrificial death, and his kingdom would be of this world. It is this interpretation of his mission which Jesus most vehemently rejected. In the face of the expectations of all the disciples and the faithful adherents of Judaism, Jesus from the beginning of his ministry consciously faced death. Satan's potent weapon is the fear of death. The death penalty is the state's ultimate sanction and the final source of its authority. Since the Christ is unwilling to place himself in the service of earthly domination, he is able to enter Jerusalem on Palm Sunday as the king of peace. Palm Sunday is a prelude to Easter Sunday, and the Christ's 'kingly' powers are those which ultimately bring resurrection. These are opposed to the forces of heredity which transmit the human clay laid aside at the Resurrection.

When we turn to the science of life, we find fear of death allocated a most potent role in evolution. It is the natural response to the operation of natural selection. Natural selection is governed, in Darwin's words by 'the war of nature . . . famine and death.' Through the threat of death a make-up is selected which is most responsive to terrestrial conditions.

Summary

The three temptations of the New Testament represent the most potent agents in general evolution. We have characterized them as:

1. Self-interest supplanting altruism (in the biological and ethical sense) as man's central motive.
2. Premature adult drives at the cost of individual development.
3. The instinct for self-preservation and adaptation induced by the fear of death.

In the life of Christ the Temptation illuminates the purpose of the Incarnation by drawing attention to the powers against which the spiritual resources of the Christ were arraigned. Perhaps the contrast between the Spirit and the opposing powers can be delineated by distinguishing between the cultural and physical components of change. In the life of Christ the spiritual faculties of imagination, idealism and creative morality are directed against the forces which operate through man's tellurian nature. The Christ's invisible powers become apparent only when they strike physical or biological resistance to change.

The three temptations depict the attempt to rob man of his divine form. We shall later show that these temptations are renewed at the onset of each term of the ministry.

1. The Baptism at the beginning of the silent ministry initiates a prolonged fast which leads to the first temptation.
2. The opening of the Galilean ministry precipitates the attempt to cast Jesus down from the brow of the hill on which Nazareth was built (Luke 4:29), which can be interpreted as an echo of the second temptation.
3. The third temptation is renewed in Peter's rejection of the Passion.

15 The Silent Ministry

The term 'silent ministry' (*die stillen Monate*) is used by Stauffer (1957, 61) of the period between the Baptism and the beginning of the Galilean or public teaching ministry. It is silent in as much as it contains as yet no public instruction and each Evangelist contributes to give an impression of its duration.

Luke tells that, while the Baptism took place in Judea, the preaching ministry began in Galilee. The passage has already been quoted in connection with the Baptism of Jesus (Acts 10:36–38 'You know the word which he sent to Israel, preaching good news of peace by Jesus Christ (he is Lord of all), the word which was proclaimed throughout all Judea, beginning from Galilee after the baptism which John preached: how God anointed Jesus of Nazareth with the Holy Spirit and with power.' Matthew and Mark connect the beginning of the Galilean ministry with the arrest of John the Baptist: 'Now when he heard that John had been arrested, he withdrew into Galilee . . . From that time Jesus began to preach, saying, "Repent, for the kingdom of heaven is at hand." ' (Matt.4:12,17). Similarly Mark (1:14): 'Now after John was arrested, Jesus came into Galilee, preaching the gospel of God'.

After the Baptism of Jesus, John continued to work. In the first five chapters of John's Gospel there are various references to the overlapping ministries of John and Jesus in the time following the Baptism. Early Christian tradition connected John's Gospel with the intention of repairing the Synoptic Gospels' failure to describe the silent ministry. The assumption that the life of Christ *prior* to the arrest by John the Baptist is recorded by John is shared by the Church Fathers, Jerome, Eusebius and so on. Their source may have been the Latin Preface found by Lucinius of Baetica (*c.* 391) (Eisler 1938, 15):

John the Apostle whom the Lord Jesus loved most wrote as the last of all (his) gospel . . . (the) motive for (the

	Year	Jewish date	Julian date	Weekday
Baptism of Jesus	AD 31	Tebeth 23	January 6	Saturday
Temptation		c. Adar 2	c. February 15	(Thursday)
Calling of disciples		c. Adar 4–8	c. Feb 16–20	(Fri-Tue)
First journey from Judea to Galilee				
Marriage at Cana		Adar 16	February 27	Tuesday
Cleansing of the Temple		Nisan 10	March 23	Friday
Samaritan Pentecost		Sivan 9	May 20	Sunday
Second journey from Judea to Galilee				
Arrest of John		c. Tishri 7–8	c. Sept 13–14	(Thu-Fri)
Healing of paralytic		Tishri 16	September 22	Saturday
Third journey from Judea to Galilee				

Table 10. The silent ministry (AD 31).

composition) of his writing his gospel: when he read the scrolls of Matthew, Mark and Luke, he approved the text of (their) story, and confirmed that they had told the truth, but that they had woven together only the history of the one year in which He suffered, after John (the Baptist) had been arrested. Leaving aside therefore the one year, the facts of which had been set forth by the three, he narrated the deeds (of the Lord) during the time before John (the Baptist) was locked up in prison, as it can be clearly perceived by those who read the scrolls of the gospels carefully.

While the Fourth Gospel is said to have 'narrated the deeds (of the Lord) during the time before John was locked up in prison', it makes no explicit mention of the Baptist's arrest. In an attempt to ascertain the time-span of the silent ministry, we shall follow the course of events in John's Gospel prior to the death of John the Baptist, which Mark and Matthew place shortly before the feeding of the five thousand. In other words: when, in the context of the events narrated by John (1–5, prior, that is, to the feeding of the five thousand in Chapter 6), did Jesus hear of the arrest of

John and thereupon set out for Galilee to open his teaching ministry?

In John's Gospel the calling of the disciples follows the Baptism in the Jordan. When, after the Resurrection, the time had come for the selection of Judas Iscariot's replacement, Peter referred back to the time immediately following the Baptism: 'So one of the men who have accompanied us during all the time that the Lord Jesus went in and out among us, beginning from the baptism of John . . .' (Acts 1:21f). We must carefully distinguish this first summons from the later calling of the twelve, when Peter and his companions abandon their nets to become fishers of men. Whereas it is likely that the first calling began already on the banks of the Jordan not long after the Temptation the calling of the twelve occurred in Galilee after the teaching ministry had been initiated in the aftermath of the Baptist's arrest, and is recorded by the Synoptists. If the length of the interval between the first calling and the marriage at Cana is for the present passed over, there are two further time indications in John's Gospel (2:12f).

Firstly, 'After this he went down to Capernaum, with his mother and his brothers and his disciples; and there they stayed for a few [οὐ πολλὰς, literally 'not many'] days.

Secondly, 'The Passover of the Jews was at hand . . .' This is the first Passover mentioned in John's Gospel, and in AD 31 it would have fallen on Nisan 15, March 28. If, as some suppose, the marriage at Cana occurred a full year after the Baptism, then the interval between marriage feast and Passover would be about eighty days, which seems overlong for 'not many days'.

The marriage at Cana

Karl Friedrich Althoff (quoted below) has dated the marriage near the end of February in the same year as the Baptism. His estimate of 'not many days' from the marriage to the Passover is thus barely a month (29 days) and supports the notion that Baptism, Temptation, calling of the disciples, marriage at Cana and the cleansing of the Temple follow fairly closely upon one another.

Shortly before his death in 1980, Professor Althoff wrote (in a personal communication) giving his understanding of John (2:1): '*On the third day* there was a marriage at Cana in Galilee.'

The Greek Καὶ τῇ ἡμέρα τῇ τρίτη corresponds to the Hebrew of Genesis (1:13): 'And there was evening and there was morning, *a third day*.' John has previously introduced the three earlier scenes with 'on the next day' (ἐπαύριον 1:29,35,43). It is then not possible to count the days and alight on the day of the marriage feast as the third day. It would be the fourth day in that case. Even today in Greece τρίτη, and in Israel *yom shelishi* (referring to the third day of creation) simply means 'Tuesday'.

Althoff sees in 'the third day' also a premonition of the day of resurrection, which is one of the keys to the mystery of this 'wedding'. He continues,

Now, Jewish couples, from olden times up to the present, have always preferred Tuesday as the day of their wedding because, on the third day of creation, 'God saw that it was good' (twice! Gen.1:10,12). This is the reason why Tuesday is regarded as a 'day of luck and prosperity' and the right day for a wedding. Therefore I should think it not mere chance that the text of this wedding begins by mentioning 'Tuesday'. The marriage at Cana points, in my view, to the seed of the Eucharist, the introduction of a new seed (Ulfilas's Gothic *mana-seths*, world) in the midst of a dying earth — as starting point (Cana means 'acquisition'). And the text follows — in its composition — in twelve sentences, seven steps, four stages as in the composition of the Act of Consecration of Man [the Eucharist of The Christian Community].

Most significantly the 'third day' occurs also in Genesis (22:4) in connection with the consecration of Isaac, 'On the third day Abraham lifted up his eyes and saw the place afar off.' So I thought that, as after the Baptism in the Jordan on January 6, there are the forty days in the desert: perhaps from 7 January to 15 February or later (8 January to 16 February?). Then comes the return to the place of the Baptism, with John testifying 'on the next day' (John

1:29,35). Thereafter comes the transition of the two disciples from John to Jesus, their walk to Qumran (only a few miles from the place of the Baptism in the Jordan), and the journey to Galilee lasting some days. I thought Tuesday, February 27, AD 31 should not be too early and not too late for the marriage at Cana.

With the journey which ended at Cana, we have followed Jesus and his disciples on their *first* journey from Judea into Galilee.

The cleansing of the Temple

It is puzzling to find the cleansing of the Temple occurring twice (John 2:13, and secondly Matt.21:12; Mark 11:15 and Luke 19:45) near the beginning and near the end of the ministry. It is sometimes explained that every time Christ entered the Temple, he cleansed it. Certainly it is an over-simplification to assert that John has misplaced the episode. For John (2:20) takes care to date this Passover by his mention of 'forty-six years'. The word translated as 'Temple' here is *naos*, meaning 'the inner sanctuary'. Apart from the rock altar, it contained the altar of incense, the seven-branched lampstand, the table of shewbread, and the Holy of Holies which was screened by a veil. Josephus (*Ant.* 15.421) says, 'The temple itself [*naos*] was built by the priests in a year and six months'. There is no question, then, of the sanctuary having taken forty-six years to build, as many translations imply.

Josephus (*Ant.* 15.380–423) gives a very detailed account of Herod's reconstruction of the second Temple. It followed upon the visit Augustus paid to Syria when Herod had completed his seventeenth year (*Ant.* 15.354). Appendix 1 shows Herod's eighteenth year (in the civil calendar appropriate to the visit of Augustus to Syria) as autumn 20 – autumn 19 BC. Dio Cassius (*Rom. Hist.* 54:7) dates Augustus' visit to Syria in the consulship of Marcus Apuleius and Publius Silius, which fell in 20 BC. Josephus (*Ant.* 15.380) continues, 'It was at this time, in the eighteenth year of his reign, after the events mentioned above, that Herod undertook an extraordinary work, (namely) the reconstructing of the temple of God . . .' In the ecclesiastical calendar (appropriate to the Temple's reconstruction) Herod's eighteenth year was spring 19 – spring 18 BC (Appendix 1). Josephus (*Ant*. 15.421) describes how after vast preparations for the rebuilding operations, 'The temple itself was built by the priests in a year and six months' adding that the Temple was completed by the anniversary of the king's accession, Nisan 1. If we estimate eighteen months (spring 19 to autumn 18 BC) for the preparation, the inner sanctuary would have been completed by spring 16 BC. By spring AD 31, the inner Temple had been standing forty-six years, as John (2:20) may be understood to state.

The second journey

Continuing our study of the journeys in the early chapters of John's Gospel to try to locate the arrest of John, we hear, following the Passover, 'After this Jesus and his disciples went into the land of Judea; there he remained with them and baptized. John also was baptizing at Aenon near Salim, because there was much water there; and people came and were baptized. For John had not yet been put in prison.' (John 3:22–24). As comment on the situation, John adds (4:1–3), 'Now when the Lord knew that the Pharisees had heard that Jesus was making and baptizing more disciples than John (although Jesus himself did not baptize, but only his disciples), he left Judea and departed again into Galilee.'

Here we have the *second* journey from Judea to Galilee and the motive for Jesus' departure from Judea is made abundantly clear. Not only is there as yet no word that John has been arrested, but Jesus leaves Judea expressly because John is not in prison and is still working.

On this second journey, while Jesus and his disciples were passing through Samaria, the conversation with the Samaritan woman at the well took place (John 4:7). Afterwards he said to his disciples, 'Do you not say, "There are yet four months, then comes the harvest"? I tell you, lift up your eyes, and see how the fields are already white for harvest.' (John 4:35).

There is some indication that the Palestinian natural year was divided into three seasons of equal length, of four months each. The New Year for Trees, Shebat 1, (January/February) marked

128

the beginning of spring (germination). Spring ended with the blossoming fruit trees at Pentecost, Sivan 6 (May/June) in the Pharisaic calendar. Duration of the spring season was four months and five days, that is 123 days.

The conversation with the woman of Samaria is frequently connected with Pentecost, when the fields stand ripe awaiting the harvest. In the Samaritan calendar (*see* Goudoever 1961), Pentecost fell each year on a Sunday and the conversation may have been about Sivan 9, May 20, AD 31.

The arrest of John the Baptist

Apart from the healing of the courtier's son (4:46–54) possibly at midsummer, only the visit to 'a feast of the Jews' in Jerusalem (5:1) remains in John's account before the feeding of the five thousand (6:1–14) by which time John the Baptist is already dead. When does the arrest occur? The last mention of John the Baptist at work was in John 4:1ff. The Evangelist has previously narrated the calling of the disciples during the first journey from Judea to Galilee. John makes very clear that the reason for the second journey is precisely the fact that John is still baptizing. The only journey remaining to be investigated is that which is due at the conclusion of Chapter 5 and which is itself not described in the Fourth Gospel.

The autumn Tabernacles festival is the setting for all that occurs in John 5. It was *the* great feast of the Jews which was preceded by the days of penitence in preparation for the Day of Atonement. On the sabbath day during Tabernacles Jesus healed a man who had been paralysed for thirty-eight years, and there follows during a major discourse on his own future task a summary and assessment of the work and mission of John, but now in the past tense (5:33–36).

> You sent to John, and he has borne witness to the truth. Not that the testimony which I receive is from man; but I say this that you may be saved. He was a burning and shining lamp, and you were willing to rejoice for a while in his light. But the testimony which I have is greater than that of John; for the work which the Father has granted me to

accomplish, these very works which I am doing, bear me
witness that the Father has sent me.

The tone is unmistakably that of a retrospect, with the listeners
admonished to direct their attention to the future, and we agree
with Stauffer that John had been arrested a few days before
Atonement and the Feast of the Tabernacles.

According to Stauffer (1960, 66), Jesus evidently first learned
of the arrest of John at the feast of the Jews (John 5:1), namely
Tabernacles. Stauffer envisages that Herod Antipas was embarked
on a pilgrimage to celebrate the Day of Atonement and Tabernacles in Jerusalem when he sought out John. In that case John
would have been arrested immediately before the Day of Atonement which in AD 31 was on Sunday, Tishri 10, September 16.

At the time of the feeding of the five thousand, which followed
six months later, Mark (6:14) reports Antipas' opinion of Jesus
as John raised from the dead. Cullmann (1963, 32) comments that
not only Herod but others too failed to notice Jesus during the
silent ministry, while both were working together.

This agrees also with what the Synoptics tell us about the
date of Jesus' beginning his public activity: he began it for
the first time when the Baptist was sent to prison. Between
the time of his baptism and John's imprisonment, Jesus
seems to have worked in the shadow of the Baptist. Perhaps
he appeared at first more or less a disciple of the Baptist.

According to John's Gospel, the duration of this period of the
ministry cannot have been long, nor closely observed. This is
revealed also by Antipas' view that Jesus was the risen Baptist.

The third journey

The Fourth Gospel then, having narrated the deeds of the Lord
during the time before John was locked up in prison, ends its
narrative of the silent ministry, and it is the Synoptists
(Matt.4:12ff, Mark 1:14f, Luke 4:14f) who mention the *third*
journey from Judea to Galilee for the inauguration of the Galilean
teaching ministry: 'Now after John was arrested, Jesus came into
Galilee, preaching the gospel of God, and saying, "The time is
fulfilled, and the kingdom of God is at hand; repent, and believe

in the gospel." ' (Mark 1:14f). In Luke, the parallel passage (4:14–16) reads,

> And Jesus returned in the power of the Spirit into Galilee, and a report concerning him went out through all the surrounding country. And he taught in their synagogues, being glorified by all.
>
> And he came to Nazareth, where he had been brought up . . .

Conclusion

We have proposed that the silent ministry is the subject of the first five chapters of John's Gospel. These eight or nine months are silent in the sense that they form a prelude to the teaching ministry in Galilee. When, after the Resurrection, Peter and his earliest companions referred to Jesus not yet as the Christ but as παῖς, the 'Child' (Acts 3:13,26; 4:25,30) it is a question how far this first Christological conception has embedded in it the foundation of the Gospels. In the child, we may remember, there are eight or nine months 'silence' before he begins to articulate words. The infant does not speak during the months following birth, but he is by no means uncommunicative. Nor is the Messianic character of the ministry of Jesus obscure in the silent period. While in Jerusalem, Jesus strongly asserts his Messianic nature at all times. The Temple is cleansed at this early stage perhaps not so much as a demonstration of the high priesthood of Jesus, but that the coming of a true prophet, John, has brought to an end the provisional (1Macc.14:41) legitimacy of the Temple high priesthood and its animal sacrifice.

16 The Year of Grace

We are left in no doubt by the Gospels that news of the Baptist's arrest was the prelude to a major new development in the Christ's ministry.

Healing the paralytic on the sabbath

As the most radical exponent of the Law was led away in chains, Jesus deliberately and very publicly broke the sabbath law. Since a human being was forbidden to heal on the day of rest, the raising of the paralytic on the sabbath (John 5:2ff) was either an act of God, or of a man blasphemously playing the role of the divine. With the words, 'Rise, take up your pallet, and walk', the Christ commands that the law of the sabbath should be broken. Unhesitatingly, the Great Council (Sanhedrin) intervened. His sabbath offence warranted prosecution. But his defence, 'My father is working still, and I am working' was to the Sanhedrin sheer blasphemy, punishable by death.

Jerusalem's religious authorities had not moved against John, who had declared to his disciples that Jesus was 'the Son of God'. Now that Herod had proceeded against John, Jesus not only broke the sabbath but also called God his Father. Before delivering his verdict on John's work (John 5:33ff), Jesus summed up the silent ministry. From the moment of his baptism in the Jordan, he is doing the will of the Father. Most marvellous among the works wrought by the Father is the gift of life. And at the gate of death judgment upon life is entrusted into the hands of the Son, the guide of the souls of the dead. 'Truly, truly, I say to you, he who hears my word and believes him who sent me, has eternal life; he does not come into judgment, but has passed from death to life' (John 5:24). We are given an anticipation of Christ's teaching ministry heard through Johannine ears. The words of Jesus spring directly from the pre-existent Word. Ancient cosmic theology had been built around the knowledge of pre-existence and John (1:51)

132

comes close to expressing its spiritual cosmology, 'Truly, truly, I say to you, you will see heaven opened, and the angels of God ascending and descending upon the Son of man.' The teaching of Jesus has divine substance (John 4:34). 'My food is to do the will of him who sent me.' The marvellous *work* of the Father will be expressed in the marvellous *words* of the Son.

The time has now arrived for the teaching ministry to begin. The raising of the paralytic is reminiscent of the stage in childhood when the child has learnt to stand erect but not yet to walk. Achievement of erect posture facilitates the onset of speech. 'The pattern of learning to speak closely parallels the pattern of postural control' (Hurlock 1964, 221). The 'sign' language of gesture is now to be translated into verbal form. The silent ministry has reached a comparable stage with the raising of the man who had lain so long.

The Galilean ministry

At this point, therefore, upon hearing of John's arrest, Jesus returned to Galilee. John's task of describing the period of the ministry preceding John's imprisonment is accomplished and Luke continues (4:14–21):

And Jesus returned in the power of the Spirit into Galilee, and a report concerning him went out through all the surrounding country. And he taught in their synagogues, being glorified by all.

And he came to Nazareth, where he had been brought up; and he went to the synagogue, as his custom was, on the sabbath day. And he stood up to read; and there was given to him the book [scroll] of the prophet Isaiah. He opened the book and found the place where it was written,

'The Spirit of the Lord is upon me,
because he has anointed me to preach good news to the poor.
He has sent me to proclaim release to the captives and recovering of sight to the blind,
to set at liberty those who are oppressed,
to proclaim the acceptable year of the Lord.'

133

And he closed the book, and gave it back to the attendant, and sat down; and the eyes of all in the synagogue were fixed on him. And he began to say to them, 'Today this scripture has been fulfilled in your hearing.'

Many questions arise out of this passage. Can this sabbath be dated? Is the reading from Isaiah specially selected by the Christ or, if not, can it be placed in the Jewish reading cycle? Above all, what is meant by the 'acceptable year of the Lord' and does it have chronological implications?

Some of these questions find their answer in a closer knowledge of the Jewish synagogue service for the sabbath. F. W. Farrer (1874, 1:22f) visualizes the scene:

> . . . there were seats on one side for the men; on the other, behind a lattice, were seated the women, shrouded in their long veils. At one end was the *tebhah* or ark of painted wood, which contained the sacred scriptures; and at one side was the *bîma*, or elevated seat for the reader or preacher. Clergy, properly speaking, there were none, but in the chief seats were the ten or more *batlanîm*, 'men of leisure', or leading elders; and pre-eminent among these the chief of the synagogue, or *rôsh hak-kenéseth*. Inferior in rank to these were the *chazzân*, or clerk, whose duty it was to keep the sacred books; the *shelîach*, corresponding to our sacristan or verger; and the *parnasîm*, or shepherds, who in some respects acted as deacons.

> The service of the synagogue was not unlike our own. After the prayers two lessons were always read, one from the Law called *parashah*, and one from the Prophets called *haphtarah*; and as there were no ordained ministers to conduct the services . . . these lessons might not only be read by any competent person who received permission from the *rôsh hak-kenéseth*, but he was even at liberty to add his own *midrash*, or comment.

The service is that of the sabbath morning. We need to know whether the passage concerning the acceptable year of the Lord (Isa.61:1f) was a reading appointed to be read every year (already at the time of Christ) in the sabbath service of the synagogue in a regular lectionary cycle. A considerable Jewish scholar, J. Mann

(1971, xvi), says that the passage seems to imply that though the choice of the scroll was determined by custom or the synagogue authorities, Jesus was free to select any text in the book of Isaiah that he wished. It is also argued elsewhere that Isaiah 61:1f was never a *haphtarah* (Strack & Billerbeck 1922–28, 4.1:169ff). Mann (1971, 288), however, finds 'ample evidence' that at the time of Christ, Isaiah 61:1f formed part of the Jewish lectionary cycle, as indicated in Luke 4. And, says Mann, its very mention in the Gospel later led to its elimination from the Jewish lectionary cycle, being substituted by Isaiah 43:1ff. Since Isaiah 43:1ff is due to be read towards the end of Tishri, Guilding (1960, 125) follows Mann when dating the opening of the Galilean ministry, 'It seems likely, therefore, that our Lord's synagogue sermon was preached shortly afterwards, at the end of Tishri or the beginning of Cheshvan [Heshvan].' In the year 31 this sabbath is dated Tishri 30, October 6.

At the beginning of the 'acceptable year', better known as the year of Grace or as the year of the Jubilee, a new beginning of the world was envisaged. Slaves were to be set at liberty and land restored to its original divine owner. The year was to be proclaimed on Tishri 1 (Mishnah) or 10 (Lev.25:9). Mention of it led early Christian writers to postulate that the entire period from the Baptism to the Passion lasted twelve calendar months. J. van Goudoever (1961, 271) points out that the year of the Jubilee begins in the autumn and lasts until the spring new year inaugurates a new Jubilee forty-nine-year cycle. The Jubilee 'year' thus lasts eighteen months.

The Jubilee year's proclamation eighteen months before the new year of the Jubilee cycle possessed astronomical-calendrical significance, even though there is little sign of the Jubilee period having been used for intercalation purposes. J. G. Franke (1778, 13) pointed out that the difference between forty-nine lunar and forty-nine solar years is very nearly eighteen lunar months. After a Jubilee year of eighteen months, both lunar and solar new years would be brought into alignment. We have already seen that, on other grounds, van Goudoever allows the Jubilee year 18 months. If we assume that Nisan 1, AD 33 (shortly before the Crucifixion) was the first year of a new forty-nine-year Jubilee cycle, then the

Jubilee year began eighteen months earlier on Heshvan 1, October 7, AD 31, which closely agrees with the date, on the lectionary hypothesis, of Saturday, Tishri 30, October 6, AD 31.

In conclusion, we would date the beginning of the Galilean teaching ministry from the synagogue sermon (Luke 4:14ff). Coming after Tabernacles (September 21–28, AD 31), we have dated the sabbath service in question Tishri 30, October 6, AD 31.

In Luke's writing, there is a correspondence between the proclamation of the Jubilee (after forty-nine lunar years) which opens the teaching ministry of the Gospel, and the gift of the spirit at Pentecost (after forty-nine days) in Acts, which opens the apostolic ministry.

The Transfiguration

The 'acceptable year' of the Lord reached a high point in the Transfiguration. There are two traditional dates: Tammuz 17 at the end of June and, in the modern calendar, August 6, and we can hazard a guess at the tradition which is expressed in these divergent dates. Translated into the historical year in question, these commemorative dates correspond to Tammuz 17, July 14, and Ab 9, August 6, AD 32.

Both dates are connected with the fall of Jerusalem. In the Mishnah both the first fall of Jerusalem in 587 BC and the second fall in AD 70 are commemorated on 17 Tammuz. It seems probable that the burning of the Temple was seen by early Christians as an image of the Transfiguration. For the Temple was destroyed on Ab 9, August 6, in AD 70. And in the year of the Transfiguration AD 32, Ab 9 is (as in AD 70) August 6. The conflagration which engulfed the Temple of Jerusalem in AD 70 must indeed have been an awe-inspiring spectacle.

Witnessing the destruction by fire of the Great Castle in wartime Stuttgart, Emil Bock (1981, 136) saw it as a vivid illustration of the course of the Incarnation. An incendiary bomb had lodged in the roof and ignited. The conflagration spread throughout the building, beginning with the roof and penetrating each floor from above. Bock viewed the ministry as the penetration as if by fire of the Christ Spirit from above working downwards ultimately to

	Year	Jewish date	Julian date	Weekday
Opening of Galilean ministry	AD 31	Tishri 30	October 6	Saturday
Death of John	32	Nisan 1	April 1	Tuesday
Feeding of five thousand	32	c. Nisan 16–20	c. April 16–20	(Wed-Sat)
Feeding of four thousand	32	c. Sivan 6–11	c. June 2–8	(Mon-Sat)
Confession of Peter	32	Tammuz 9	July 6	Sunday
Transfiguration	32	Tammuz 17	July 14	Monday
Tabernacles in Jerusalem	32	Tishri 15–22	October 10–17	Fri-Fri
Feast of Dedication	32	Kislev 25	December 18	Thursday
At the Jordan (John 10:40)	33	Tebeth 15	January 6	Tuesday
Raising of Lazarus	33	c. Adar 4	c. February 23	(Monday)
New Jubilee cycle	33	Nisan 1	March 21	Saturday

Table 11. The Year of Grace (AD 31-33).

the physical body. Bock had a picture of 'storeys' corresponding to three stages in Christ's ministry. Early Christianity's vision also connected the burning of the Temple with the fire of the Spirit consuming Christ's body.

Faced with a choice for the date of the Transfiguration between the Julian equivalents of Tammuz 17 and Ab 9, the Church of Jerusalem seems to have chosen Tammuz 17, July 14, while the Greek Church preferred Ab 9, August 6. The Jewish background to the Transfiguration appears to be the appearance in glory of Moses. Goudoever (1961, 251f) comments,

> Both stories took place on a mountain; on which mountain Jesus is transfigured, however, is not said. The Second Epistle of Peter calls it a holy mountain.
>
> *Jesus* was transfigured (μετεμορυώϑη), and his garments became glistening, intensely white as no fuller on earth could bleach them. The skin of *Moses*' face shone (δεδόξασται) (Exod.34:29f. LXX) . . .

137

Only in Matthew can the expression be found that Jesus' face shone *like the sun*. Philo writes about Moses, 'His face shone like the rays of the sun' (*Life of Moses* 3:2) . . . These rays from Moses' face are later depicted as the horns of Moses. Moses' glorification on the mountain is to be considered as a fore-shadowing of his death, according to the Biblical Antiquities [Ps. Philo]: Moses died on the same liturgical day as he was glorified, on Tammuz 17.

Even in Eastern Churches, where the feast of the Transfiguration is celebrated on August 6, the Old Testament readings refer to Moses' transfiguration. In the Greek lectionary, the following lessons are read:

Exodus 24:12–18 (Moses on the mountain);

Exodus 33–34 (in part) (Moses asks to see the Glory of the Lord, which passes by Moses forty days after the revelation on Sinai);

1 Kings 19:3–16 (in part) (The Lord passes by Elijah on Mount Horeb after forty days).

While the date of Tammuz 17 may be associated with the practice of the Armenian Church, Goudoever (1961, 209) assesses it in comparison with the tradition of August 6 in the Greek Church. 'If the Armenian lectionary, as edited by Conybeare, may indeed be considered representative of the liturgical tradition of the fifth century in Jerusalem, then the celebration of the Transfiguration on Midsummer day is as important as its commemoration on 6 August.' In AD 32, as we have seen, the two dates under discussion are Tammuz 17, July 14, and Ab 9, August 6. Since the Transfiguration followed the confession of Peter after an interval of only about a week, it would be useful to try to establish independently the date of Peter's confession.

The confession of Peter

Philip Carrington (1952) interpreted the numbers in the margin of early Gospel manuscripts. One of the oldest, *Codex Vaticanus*, is divided into 62 narrative portions, allowing 48–49 units for reading each Sunday, with an additional 13–14 units to be read at the time of the Passion. Resembling the annual cycle of Torah readings which began in the autumn, Carrington's Marcan cycle commences in the autumn with its account of the work of John the Baptist.

As Goudoever (1961, 240ff) comments, Carrington's reconstruction is remarkable, because number 25 in the margin of *Codex Vaticanus* comes at the feeding of the five thousand, half way through the year in the Passover season. Seven weeks later at Pentecost, number 32 has the feeding of the four thousand, number 36 has Peter's confession, and number 37 has the Transfiguration. On this hypothesis we can allocate these readings to a place in the calendar:

Feeding of the five thousand	Lection 25	Nisan 16–22	(April)
Feeding of the four thousand	32	Sivan 6–12	(June)
Confession of Peter	36	Tammuz 4–10	(July)
Transfiguration	37	Tammuz 11–17	(July)

Carrington (1952, 168) adds that the Gospel divides mathematically into two halves between lections 36 and 37, according to another system of enumeration. In both cases this half-way point in Mark's Gospel is close to the midsummer solstice.

> Every day, beginning from the midwinter solstice, the sun rises higher in the firmament and makes his way north. The midsummer solstice marks his highest point of glory. From this moment he must decline; he turns and begins to retreat southward. Mark's story follows a similar course. The Transfiguration is its highest peak of glory; the movement of the story turns and moves southwards towards Jerusalem. The Son of Man must go there to die.

Carrington explicitly associates the Transfiguration pericope with the Jewish fast of Tammuz 17. The preceding pericope containing the confession of Peter and the first proclamation of the Passion would then be associated with the date Tammuz 9, which in the Jewish tradition is often connected with Tammuz 17. Matthew (17:1) places the Transfiguration at an interval after the confession of Peter defined as 'after six days', Mark (9:2) likewise. Luke (9:28) mentions 'about eight days after'. Peter's recognition of Jesus as the Messiah brings forth the proclamation of the

Passion which characterizes the last period of Christ's earthly life. The confession and the proclamation constitute a major turning point in the ministry, from which the way up to his Passion and death in Jerusalem opens up. We would date the turning point Tammuz 9, July 6, AD 32.

17 Dating the Crucifixion

It is wholly appropriate that the culmination of the Incarnation should also be the most important event in dating it historically. Ancient and modern opinion concerning the year of the Crucifixion is compared in Table 12.

A positive dating

In the main two possibilities for the year of the Crucifixion are favoured by modern biblical chronologists; AD 30 and AD 33. Following normal practice, the result obtained depends on the interpretation placed upon the fifteenth year of Tiberius and the estimated length of the ministry. Before setting out the analysis, we shall first examine a new solution to the perennial problem.

In a *Nature* article of unusual interest, C. J. Humphreys and W. G. Waddington (1983) have attempted the first positive dating of the crucifixion. A quotation from the Old Testament prophet Joel in Peter's first Pentecost sermon (Acts 2:14–20) provides the starting point:

> But Peter, standing with the eleven, lifted up his voice and addressed them, 'Men of Judea and all who dwell in Jerusalem, let this be known to you, and give ear to my words. For these men are not drunk, as you suppose, since it is only the third hour of the day; but this is what was spoken by the prophet Joel:
>
> > "And in the last days it shall be, God declares,
> > that I will pour out my Spirit upon all flesh,
> > and your sons and your daughters shall prophesy,
> > and your young men shall see visions,
> > and your old men shall dream dreams;
> > yea, and on my menservants and my maidservants in those
> >   days
> > I will pour out my Spirit; and they shall prophesy.
> > And I will show wonders in the heaven above

Year	Ancient	Modern	
	(a)	(a)	(b)
AD 21	1	2	0
22	0	0	0
23	0	0	0
24	0	0	0
25	0	1	1
26	0	1	1
27	0	0	0
28	1	2	0
29	2	24	19
30	6	37	51
31	6	7	7
32	14	3	1
33	9	26	30
34	0	3	3
35	0	4	3

Table 12. Ancient and modern opinion on the year of the Crucifixion. Sources (a) Holzmeister (1933, 172–74 & 158–61), (b) Girard (1953, 59f).

> and signs on the earth beneath,
> blood, and fire, and vapour of smoke;
> The sun will be turned into darkness and the moon into
> blood,
> before the day of the Lord comes,
> the great and manifest day." '

The quotation is from Joel (2:28–32), which says that 'the sun shall be turned to darkness, and the moon to blood before the great and terrible day of the Lord comes'. Humphreys and Waddington write,

> The quotation from Joel provides a telling commentary on
> the recent events of the first Easter. The outpouring of
> Spirit commenced at Pentecost and 'that great and glorious
> day' refers to the resurrection. 'The sun will be turned to
> darkness' (Acts 2:20) is a clear reference to the three hours
> of darkness at the crucifixion (Matt.27:45), and would be
> understood as such by Peter's audience. Since the darkened
> sun occurred at the crucifixion, it is reasonable to suppose
> that 'the moon turned to blood' that same evening.

It seems unlikely, the authors say, that Peter should proclaim as the first words uttered with the inspiration of the Whitsuntide

Spirit an Old Testament quotation without particular application to events less than two months old.

Humphreys and Waddington (1983, 745) believe that Peter's Joel quotation at Pentecost refers to the darkness at noon on the day of the crucifixion and, on the same day, an eclipse of the moon. The article shows the moon 'turning to blood' to be in ancient times a not unusual description of a lunar eclipse. The following examples are cited:

1. The lunar eclipse of September 20, 331 BC occurred two days after Alexander crossed the Tigris, and the moon was described by Curtius (IV, 10 (39), 1) as 'suffused with the colour of blood'.

2. The lunar eclipse of August 31, AD 304 (probably) which occurred at the martyrdom of Bishop Felix, was described in *Acta Sanctorum* as 'when he was about to be martyred the Moon was turned to blood'.

3. The lunar eclipse of March 2, AD 462 was described in the *Hydatius Lemicus Chronicon* thus: 'on March 2 with the crowing of cocks after the setting of the Sun the Full Moon was turned to blood'.

This forms the basis of the argument that at Pentecost Peter quoted Joel (2:31) in connection with an eclipse of the Passover moon at the Crucifixion. F. R. Stephenson (1969, 224) already identified this quotation as referring to a lunar eclipse.

There is in the Book of Revelation (6:12) a prophecy which closely resembles Joel's, 'there was a great earthquake; and the sun became black as sackcloth, the full moon became like blood'. The point of interest in this quotation is that it is the *full* moon that becomes like blood. Astronomically, only the full moon can be eclipsed, just as only a *new* moon can eclipse the sun. The apocalyptist by mentioning the full moon reveals that he does not attribute the darkening of the sun to a solar eclipse. And by the same token the blood-red full moon most likely indicates that he has a lunar eclipse in mind. Yet if Peter's hearers understood his words in this way, is it not puzzling that this interpretation is not found much more prominently stated in early Christian literature?

The Assumption of Moses, dating from the beginning of the

first Christian century, elaborates Joel: 'The sun shall give no light and the moon . . . shall change into blood and the circle of the stars shall fall into disorder.' (Schürer 1979, 506).

The *Report of Pilate* is a fourth-century Christian work (James 1924, 154): 'At his crucifixion the sun was darkened; the stars appeared, and in all the world people lighted lamps from the sixth hour till evening; the moon appeared like blood'. Another reference is made by the fiercely orthodox fifth-century Archbishop Cyril of Alexandria (quoted by Driver 1965, 333) to the *skotos*, the darkness, at the time of the Crucifixion, that 'something unusual occurred about the circular rotation of the moon so that it even seemed to be changed into blood'. As historical evidence of an eclipse at the time of the Crucifixion third, fourth and fifth-century sources are valueless, but the quotations show that in those days it was fairly widely thought that the Joel quotation applied to the appearance of the moon on the day of the Crucifixion.

Regarding the darkening of the sun, Luke and his contemporaries were perfectly well aware that a solar eclipse at the full moon was an astronomical impossibility. The verb *ekleípein* 'to fail', while a technical term for an eclipse, is also used to describe the sun's (or moon's) light failing for whatever reason. It is generally thought that the darkness at noon was caused by a khamsin storm which is not unexpected during the fifty days between Easter and Pentecost. *Khamsin*, an Arabic word meaning 'fifty', is an extremely dry, hot and dust-laden wind, which blows up from the desert. Also called 'simoom', at its most intense the dust-storm causes a darkening which in some ways can be compared to the effect of a total solar eclipse.

The pale yellow devil of the *khamsin* is viler than the black stormwind. Clouds of dust swirl skyward out of the Arabian Desert while the air at ground level scarcely stirs. It is felt only in the mouth filled with grit, in the effort of breathing, the reddened eyes . . . Through the dirty-yellow murk, the red sun peers bleakly like a ball of blood . . . The day has become an oven. Seeping up from the Dead Sea, the acrid odour of brimstone, asphalt and pitch spreads over the city . . . Grasses wilt and flowers sag limply. Bird-song ceases.

Sheep bleat out their misery and the oxen bellow their
distress. Dogs pant with discomfort and men are filled with
a grim sense of impending tragedy . . . (Merezhkovsky,
Death and Resurrection, quoted by Bock 1978, 238f).

During the Crucifixion, the sun was blotted out. Since the darkness lasted only three hours, there must have been a fresh wind
clearing the thick atmosphere at the time of the earthquake which
rent the veil of the Temple at about 3.00 pm, the hour of Christ's
death (Matt.27:51).

Other arguments

These, in outline, are the grounds for accepting that at Pentecost
Peter quoted Joel in conjunction with the eclipse of the Passover
moon at the Crucifixion. For the first time positive evidence has
been advanced for the date of the Crucifixion: while Pontius Pilate
was procurator of Judea, between AD 26 and 36, the Passover
moon was eclipsed only on the night of Friday–Saturday, Nisan
15, April 3–4, AD 33.

Some biblical scholars may prefer a demonstration that the data
is not compatible with any other year than AD 33. It is then
first necessary, to recapitulate our inquiry into the calendar, to
appreciate the relationship between the two major new years.
Years were counted from the autumn new year in the civil (Syro-
Macedonian) calendar. The corresponding year in the ecclesiastical (Babylonian-Jewish) calendar begins from the spring new
year following some six months later. This relationship is well
known to have obtained in the Hellenistic (Hasmonean) period,
but is unaccountably ignored by scholars studying the Roman
(Herodian) period. We have seen how this requirement, in
conjunction with the coin evidence and the lunar eclipse
(mentioned by Josephus) alters the date indicated for Herod's
death from 5 or 4 to 1 BC.

Given the revised date of Herod's death, it becomes evident
also that the Roman governor of Syria, Varus, continued his long
term of office until autumn 1 BC. Since the Nativity of Luke took
place under Quirinius, it cannot be dated much earlier than winter
1 BC/AD 1. Luke (3:23) says, 'Jesus, when he began his ministry,

was about thirty years of age'. In which case, Jesus was aged thirty in winter AD 30–31.

Many scholars have thought the date Tiberius 15 so important that Luke (3:1) must have applied it to the baptism of Jesus, and not merely to the opening of John's ministry. Following their argument, the three Passovers mentioned in John (2:13, 6:4 and 19:14) are accordingly dated spring AD 28, 29 and 30. Although this interpretation is not supported by J. K. Fotheringham (1932) it can in fact be reconciled with his interpretation of the fifteenth year of Tiberius: 'Technical chronology proves just as decisively that the fifteenth year of Tiberius was the year AD 28–29. Regnal years were always reckoned from the New Year's Day of the local calendar and the January New Year was not in use in the eastern Roman Empire.' Fotheringham's elimination of the reckoning of Tiberius 15 from the January new year is important for us. In his day, however, the relationship between the civil and ecclesiastical calendars in Palestine had not yet been clarified. After correctly identifying Tiberius 15 in the civil calendar as autumn AD 28–29, he then defines the corresponding ecclesiastical year as spring AD 28–29: 'The only question is whether the fifteenth year of Tiberius began in Nisan of AD 28 or in the autumn of that year.'

The identification of Tiberius 15 in the civil calendar with autumn AD 28–29 is confirmed by a coin date of *Q. Caecilius Metellus*, governor of Syria AD 12–17. The coin is numbered 45 (of the Actian era) and bears the letter A (equivalent to Tiberius 1). Since the beginning of first year of the Actian era is dated autumn 31 BC in Syria, Actian 45 is equivalent to Tiberius 1 which began in autumn AD 14, and Tiberius 15 began in autumn AD 28 (see Appendix 2). When Fotheringham's opinion is corrected with the help of Schaumberger (1955) the year in the ecclesiastical calendar corresponding to autumn AD 28–29 is spring AD 29–30. We would interpret this conclusion by referring to the connection between the beginning of John's ministry and the pagan (autumn) new year ceremony discussed above. The consequence of equating autumn AD 28–29 with spring AD 29–30 means that the earliest possible Passover of the ministry is spring AD 29. Unless we are prepared to limit the ministry to a single year AD 29–30, it is impossible to date the Crucifixion as early as AD 30.

146

We can now summarize the principal data:

1. The Crucifixion occurred on the Day of Preparation of the Passover — Nisan 14 (John 19:14).

2. The Crucifixion occurred on the Day of Preparation of the sabbath — Friday (John 19:31).

3. Pontius Pilate was procurator of Judea between AD 26 and 36 (Josephus and coin dates).

4. During the years of Pilate's rule, only Tiberius 16 (AD 30) and Tiberius 19 (AD 33) satisfy (1) and (2).

5. Since John mentions three Passovers during the ministry of Jesus, and the earliest possible Passover of the ministry is Tiberius 15, Tiberius 16 is excluded as the year of the Crucifixion and Tiberius 19 remains as the only possibility.

There remains then Friday, Nisan 14, April 3, AD 33 as the only possible date of the crucifixion.

Christology and Chronology

18 The Resurrection

We cannot now fathom the depths to which the disciples were cast down by the Crucifixion. The death of their teacher must have rested on their souls like a load too crushing to be borne in consciousness. For them all hope in the future had been removed. Indeed, the future itself had been entirely taken from them, and they had no alternative to a review of what had come to pass. At the same time another process takes place, which sometimes may be initiated by the sudden termination of all hope of continued life on earth. Awaiting execution in a wartime jail, Sjovald Cunyngham-Brown (1975, 120) tells how he was affected.

> For those who may not so far have had this experience I should mention that when all hope of further survival is gone, a sensation of great peace and weariness overcomes the mind. This was the end. One had reached the bottom at last.
>
> . . . In these circumstances the mind, unable to move forward, turns back; and lying all day and night for months at a stretch in the green gloom, one unwound, as it were, the thread of one's life — starting from here and moving slowly and steadily back to one's earliest beginnings.

Yet the disciples were not condemned men awaiting execution. The death of Jesus had left the remaining disciples at liberty, and the authorities in no mood to persecute these miserable fugitives. After all the disciples had opted for survival just as the guardians of public order and their ecclesiastical counterparts had acted in self-preservation. For months the disciples had refused to accept the doctrine later enunciated by Caiaphas that it was expedient for one man to die for the people. The training of the disciples had culminated in Peter's recognition of Jesus as the Christ. Peter and his companions now had to learn why his confession had provoked so prompt and so severe a rebuke.

At the close of the Galilean teaching ministry, it had still been arguable that Jesus might yet have been acknowledged by the Temple. Or at least the Council might have demurred at procuring his death. It was also possible that the leaders of Judaism would reject him. Jesus had already been excommunicated as a punishment for breaking the sabbath law. Yet even if he were to incur the death penalty on religious grounds, there remained an apparently inviolable shield against its execution: the Romans had removed from the Sanhedrin the right to inflict capital punishment. 'The Jews said to him [Pilate], "It is not lawful for us to put any man to death." ' (John 18:31).

To the disciples the Crucifixion could be viewed as a totally unacceptable miscarriage of justice. They had not been helped by the expectations prevailing in contemporary Judaism which had entertained no notion that the national saviour would suffer a sacrificial death. When Peter acknowledged the Christ at Caesarea Philippi, he had evidently reached, but not surpassed, the Jewish concept of the Messiah, according to Mark (8:31–33). Matthew (16:16–23) affirms that Peter was also able to add, 'the Son of the living God'. To this perception Jesus could only respond, 'Blessed are you, Simon Bar-Jona! For flesh and blood has not revealed this to you, but my father who is in heaven.' It is Peter's 'God forbid, Lord! This shall never happen to you' which merits the terrible rebuke, 'Get behind me, Satan'.

Peter's words are a renewal of the third temptation. The first two temptations had been directed at the Son of God. As in the words of Peter quoted by Mark, the third temptation omits this form of address. The temptation is not so much a call to misuse his divine power as an insistence that he submit to earthly law, to obey the Prince of this world who wields his power through the fear of death. Rejecting the constraints and imperatives imposed by the realities of earthly life, Jesus quotes the Law (Deut.6:13), 'You shall worship the Lord your God and him only shall you serve.' (Matt.4:10).

Resisting the temptation to wield earthly power, the entry of Jesus into Jerusalem on Palm Sunday demonstrated that his royal role was entirely devoid of earthly aspiration. John (12:14–16) allows an insight into the way in which the event was later remembered in the light of the Resurrection. To his account of the ride into the city, John adds this comment, 'His disciples did not understand this at first; but when Jesus was glorified, then they remembered that this had been written of him and had been done to him.' Here John adds a third strand to the memory process which enveloped the disciples after he 'was glorified'. Reliving their own lives they traced back the steps they had taken during the Galilean ministry, visiting the synagogues in each town on the sabbath. In their recollection they could hear again the readings from the Law and the Prophets, but now with a growing comprehension. Passages read each year throughout Judaism began for the first time to yield their Messianic meaning.

After the entry into Jerusalem, the rejection of the third temptation is taken to its triumphal conclusion: the ruler of this world is cast out (John 12:27–33). John goes on to explain with the utmost clarity that the casting out of the ruler of this world is tantamount to earthly death. ' "Now is the judgment of this world, now shall the ruler of this world be cast out; and I, when I am lifted up from the earth, will draw all men to myself." He said this to show by what death he would die.' Christ's victory over death can only manifest itself after death has failed to persuade him of its terrors. Without an Easter science it is difficult indeed to approach the mystery of the resurrection body and envisage the form life takes when the *sarx* (flesh) but not the *sōma* (body) has been returned to the earth.

Our technical civilization betrays its shortcomings when we come to consider life before birth and life after death. Even theologians who speak of the 'pre-existent Christ' may also deny human pre-existence. It is agreed that the body of the risen Christ contained no particle of the earthly body of Jesus. Yet we often try to comprehend the resurrection body without any clear idea about the nature of the human physical body. A distinction has to be drawn between the corporeal component whose proteins are similar in all primates, built according to the instructions of the genetic code, and the form of the human body which is not inscribed in the genetic code. It is this 'human form divine' alone which constitutes the resurrection body. Normally we are bound to think of flesh and bodily form as inseparable. It might be said that the Christ lived and died to release this 'inseparable' bond and rescue the human form from the fate of what Paul called 'the man of dust' (1Cor.15:47).

In setting out to explore the significance of the life and death of Jesus, the disciples were entering a new domain, far removed from the mythical experience of earlier generations. Yet a certain similarity of pattern can be observed between their awakening and the stages of spiritual development in both pre-Christian and Christian mysticism. Unique to the disciples was the presence of the risen Christ in their midst. And between their sense of his presence and their own growing self-knowledge something like a continuing dialogue arose which became known as the 'teachings of the risen Christ'. We may visualize stages in the Resurrection experience of the disciples which may be compared with the stages on the path of higher knowledge (described earlier in Chapter 11).

Resurrection	Pythagoreanism	Medieval Mysticism
Memory	Catharsis	Purgative consciousness
Teachings of the risen Christ	Cosmic consciousness	Illuminative consciousness
Presence in the resurrection body	Contemplation	Unitive consciousness

To what degree can the presence of the risen Christ have been remembered and yet be real? We can only appeal to experience, without denying that the aftermath of the Crucifixion was, as the scientists say, non-repeatable. Sjovald Cunyngham-Brown in his condemned cell felt his own life retrospect as an escape from imprisonment in time and the material world. At the same time his impression was that he was being instructed again by an erstwhile spiritual teacher. Following this instruction he imagined in the corner of his cell a fresh red rose growing which he describes (1975,122f),

I could see the glorious red velvet of its petals — could gaze

at its indented green leaves and its sharp downward-turning
thorns, so black-red at their base and grading off to pale
amber at their tips; could glory in the freshness of the dew
as each minute droplet shone like a diamond in a light
brighter than the sun.

At the beginning of his autobiographical sketch (1975, 5) he tried
to characterize the quality of his early childhood with words which
anticipate his later experience,

. . . my mother must have woven the fabric of my material
habitation suffused with a love of life and of this world, for
my earliest recollections are of a singing joy and excitement
with my own body and with the earth. Colour and scents,
the delight of air and space in the blue light of dawn,
birdsong and ivy-leaves spangled with dew, all these form
the initial framework of my thinking.

From such examples we can learn how deeply a life retrospect
can draw on the memories of early childhood. It is not merely the
outer facts which are recalled. It is a rediscovery of the little
child's immediate perception of the colours and tones which
constitute the infant's paradise. For the disciples this infant paradise was re-entered in the Upper Room until they were again
surrounded by the hills of their early homeland and again gazing
on the play of sun and wind on the lake of Galilee. In such a way
Mark can be understood, 'But go, tell his disciples and Peter that
he is going before you to Galilee; there you will see him, as he
told you' (16:7).

19 On the Third Day

After the Resurrection, the disparity between the disciples' despair at the Crucifixion and their experience of the risen Christ must have seemed to them an unbridgeable chasm. Luke depicts the sequence of emotions evoked in them during the forty days of Easter. Perplexity greets the discovery of the empty tomb. The appearance of two men in dazzling apparel causes fright and awe, followed by the key sentence, ' "Remember how he told you, while he was still in Galilee, that the Son of man must be delivered into the hands of sinful men, and be crucified, and on the third day rise." And they remembered his words . . .' (24:6–8).

On the road to Emmaus, Cleopas and his companion expressed their expectation: 'But we had hoped that he was the one to redeem Israel' (24:21). Clearly their expectation of Israel's redeemer had not envisaged his sacrificial death. After upbraiding the disciples for being 'slow of heart to believe all that the prophets have spoken,' the Christ teaches 'And beginning with Moses and all the prophets, he interpreted to them in all the scriptures the things concerning himself' (24:25–27).

Luke again stresses the role of the Old Testament readings interpreted by the Christ during his public ministry:

> Then he said to them, 'These are my words which I spoke to you, while I was still with you, that everything written about me in the law of Moses and the prophets and the psalms must be fulfilled.' Then he opened their minds to understand the scriptures, and said to them, 'Thus it is written that the Christ should suffer and on the third day rise from the dead . . .' (24:44).

The reference is to Hosea (6:2):

> After two days he will revive us;
> on the third day he will raise us up,
> that we may live before him.

These words of Hosea, 'on the third day' speedily entered into the heart of the Christian creed, although the New Testament does not explicitly ascribe the saying to the prophet. We see how their first awareness of the presence of the risen Christ revives memories of the instruction of the disciples during the Galilean ministry and of his interpretation read each sabbath in the synagogue. The prophets are now to be understood showing that the Christ would suffer and die. The apparently unbridgeable chasm between the crucified and the risen Christ is crossed by referring back to the Old Testament and the childhood of Israel.

Students of the Jewish lectionary may be interested in knowing whether Hosea (6:2) would have been read in the normal course of Saturday morning synagogue services. It may be noted that the verse was due to be read with Leviticus (15:1ff) in the Palestinian triennial cycle of readings, according to B. Z. Wacholder (in Mann 1971, lix). The cycle is, however, of a later date than the Gospel, and its inclusion in the lectionary cycle is mentioned merely to illustrate that Hosea (6:1ff) was later considered sufficiently important a passage to warrant inclusion.

Earlier on Easter morning, the women who came to the tomb had been addressed by the two men in dazzling apparel, 'Remember how he told you, while he was still in Galilee, that the Son of man must be delivered into the hands of sinful men, and be crucified, and on the third day rise.' Luke continues to emphasize the incredulity of the apostles: 'but these words seemed to them an idle tale, and they did not believe them. But Peter rose and ran to the tomb; stopping and looking in, he saw the linen cloths by themselves; and he went home wondering at what had happened' (24:6f,11f).

Referring again to Luke, it has already been commented that apart from Matthew (16:16) the other Evangelists do not report Peter at Caesarea Philippi confessing the 'Son of the living God'. Luke's Gospel (9:20) speaks of 'the Christ of God' and so the words 'flesh and blood has not revealed this to you, but my Father who is in heaven' are not included by Luke.

Luke corrects a possible impression that Jesus would meet his end in Galilee in the tetrarchy of Herod Antipas and again the third day is stressed (13:31–33):

At that very hour some Pharisees came, and said to him, 'Get away from here, for Herod wants to kill you.' And

157

he said to them, 'Go and tell that fox, "Behold, I cast out
demons and perform cures today and tomorrow, and the
third day I finish my course. Nevertheless I must go on my
way today and tomorrow and the day following; for it
cannot be that a prophet should perish away from
Jerusalem." . . .'

Seeking an understanding of the Crucifixion, we are led back
to the climax of the Galilean ministry. And in Chapter 9 Luke
omits sundry important scenes in order to highlight three events
of surpassing significance: the feeding of the five thousand, the
confession of Peter, and the Transfiguration. The chapter begins
with the commissioning of the twelve and their sending out. After
the death of John, they return accompanied by thousands looking
towards a new shepherd. Bethsaida becomes a desert place where
a new Moses feeds a new Israel in the 'Last Supper of the Galilean
Ministry' as it is called by John Marsh (1962, 761).

The teaching ministry has fed the souls of the people with the
images upon which the soul thrives, and the feeding of the five
thousand conjures up the figure of a new Moses calling down
manna from heaven (John 6:31–35).

'Our fathers ate the manna in the wilderness; as it is written,
"He gave them bread from heaven to eat." ' Jesus then
said to them, 'Truly, truly, I say to you, it was not Moses
who gave you the bread from heaven; my Father gives you
the true bread from heaven. For the bread of God is that
which comes down from heaven, and gives life to the
world.' They said to him, 'Lord, give us this bread always.'
Jesus said to them, 'I am the bread of life. . .'

As teacher Jesus is the new Lawgiver and his Law had been given
in the Sermon on the Mount.

We have already seen how the second episode in Luke's
Chapter 9, the confession of Peter, is inwardly connected with the
Crucifixion. For it was crucial that recognition of the Christ should
have involved an acceptance of the Passion. Peter's confession is
followed immediately by the proclamation of the Passion and
then, a week later, by the Transfiguration. Some modern scholars
have concluded that the Transfiguration is a displaced account of
the post-Resurrection appearance of the risen Lord. Professor

Marsh deduces the Evangelist's intention of identifying the teacher who walked through Galilee with the risen Christ walking in the resurrection body (1962, 761). The composition in Luke suggests the comparison:

Feeding of the five thousand	Last Supper
Confession of Peter (and proclamation of the Passion)	Crucifixion
Transfiguration	Resurrection

When we try to penetrate the mystery of the first Easter Sunday, we are led initially into a reassessment of the Galilean teaching ministry. We are thereby introduced into a re-examination of familiar and unfamiliar passages from the Old Testament. It is necessary to learn to read them as though discovering for the first time their relevance to the New Testament.

20 Paidology

What would have happened if Jesus had accepted his mission entirely according to prevailing expectation? His genealogy alone (as in Matt.1:1–16) would readily have assured his acceptability as Messiah. Had he not withstood the temptation to become king with earthly power (Matt.4:8), his role would have been quickly construed in political terms. Resistance to this temptation resulted in his divine energy being channelled entirely into the transformation of human nature, eventuating in the Resurrection. Otherwise a Christianity without the Passion would have come about dispensing a subjective morality, while leaving what William Blake called 'the human form divine' entirely subject to the working of the material world.

Peter's numb bewilderment can be understood more easily when we grasp that he had shared in a more general failure to anticipate that the Suffering Servant of God (*'ebed Yahweh* of Isaiah 53) portrayed the Messianic destiny. Judaism as a whole had entertained no clear expectation that tragedy had so great a part to play in his life. In the last weeks and after the raising of Lazarus, Caiaphas addressed the Sanhedrin. We can hear partially concealed beneath his biting tones the unexpected strain of his pronouncement (John 11:49–53).

'You know nothing at all; you do not understand that it is expedient for you that one man should die for the people, and that the whole nation should not perish.' He did not say this of his own accord, but being high priest that [crucial] year he prophesied that Jesus should die for the nation, and not for the nation only, but to gather into one (*synagágē*) the children of God who are scattered abroad. So from that day they took counsel how to put him to death.

Again and again in the Gospels it is made apparent that it was this unthinkable outcome prophesied in Christ's teaching that the disciples failed to apprehend. Even though Peter and his companions had followed Jesus since his Baptism, their capacity to recollect these mysterious and terrible predictions did not awaken before the light of the Resurrection began to shine in their perception. In the first rays falling on the most recent events in Jerusalem they began to remember what they had been taught in Galilee.

A week earlier Palm Sunday had brought them close to the heart of the matter. The crowds thronging the route had been drawn by the raising of Lazarus. 'The crowd', says John (12:17f), 'that had been with him when he called Lazarus out of the tomb and raised him from the dead bore witness. The reason why the crowd went to meet him was that they heard he had done this sign.' Through rejecting involvement in the imperatives of earthly power, Jesus came in the course of his life to command a spiritual power which finds expression in the raising of Lazarus. It is not coincidence that the decision to put him to death was taken immediately after the raising of Lazarus. And we can at least dimly perceive how his rejection of the third temptation leads to the Crucifixion. Jesus was able to enter Jerusalem as the rightful Messianic king, *not* subject to Satan's geopolitical sway, because he had attained lordship over the physical body (symbolized by his riding on an ass) by withstanding the temptation of earthly power (Matt.4:8).

John (12:20ff) reveals Christ's hidden struggle with the power of death just at this point near the beginning of Holy Week (while the Synoptists depict him as taking possession of the Temple). After death was overthrown the disciples could look back on the Galilean teaching ministry as a whole, which began in the synagogue in Nazareth. It was followed without pause by a violent scene which could be interpreted as a reiteration of the second temptation (to appear as false priest). 'When they heard this, all in the synagogue were filled with wrath. And they rose up and put him out of the city, and led him to the brow of the hill on which their city was built, that they might throw him down headlong. But passing through the midst of them he went away' (Luke 4:28–30).

The third temptation (Matt.4:8–11) is re-enacted at Caesarea Philippi (Matt.16:13–20) with Peter's confession. Cullmann (1963, 74f), comments,

> According to Mark 8:32, he was the very one who in
> Caesarea Philippi showed so little understanding of the

necessity of Jesus' suffering. It was he who took Jesus aside to tell him, 'This shall never happen to you,' so that Jesus, who saw in Peter the same Tempter who once before tried to divert him from his way, had to rebuke him with the words, 'Get behind me, Satan!' We can understand that the same apostle, who according to 1Cor.15:5 was later the first to see the risen Christ, was also the first after this experience to proclaim in the light of the resurrection the necessity of the suffering and death of Jesus. He, who had wanted to hear nothing of it during the lifetime of Jesus, made Jesus' suffering and death the very centre of his explanation of Jesus' earthly work.

In response to Peter's acclamation of Jesus as the (royal) Messiah, Jesus reveals himself for the first time as the Servant or Child of God who would suffer many things, and be rejected by the elders and the chief priests and scribes, and be killed, and after three days rise again. The proclamation in Mark (8:30ff) becomes, after the Resurrection, of paramount importance for the disciples and above all for Peter. Their immediate recourse, in pursuing an understanding of the Resurrection, to the prophets of the Old Testament, may be connected with the early post-Resurrection view of Jesus as pre-imaged by Moses.

It appears that this figure of a Moses *redivivus* was applied to Jesus (as in Acts 3:22 and 7:37 which recall the Messianic prophecy of Deut.18:15f and the hostility shown to Moses). The new Moses is now identified with the Suffering Servant of God, who is portrayed by Isaiah (53), providing Peter with a model of the Incarnation. Moses leading his people through the Red Sea foreshadows the baptism. And in Matthew's Gospel the Books of Moses serve as the pattern of Christ's teaching ministry, at least in the opinion of some biblical scholars. W. D. Davies (1964, 14–108), conducts a thorough investigation of Pentateuchal motifs in Mathew's Gospel.

Following a tradition traced back (by B. W. Bacon 1930, 80ff) possibly to the second century, Matthew's Gospel is found to contain five sermons corresponding to the five Books of Moses. Apart from the Prologue (Matt.1–2) and the Epilogue (Matt.26–28), the remainder of the material in the Gospel falls into five 'books' each of which is terminated by a formula, which occurs in almost identical forms at 7:28, 11:1, 13:53, 19:1, 26:1.

The Gospel thus presents the following structure:

Preamble or Prologue: The birth narrative. (1–2).
Book 1: (a) Narrative material. (3:1–4:25)
  (b) The Sermon on the Mount. (5:1–7:27).
  Formula: '*And when Jesus finished these sayings*, the crowds were astonished at his teaching, for he taught them as one who had authority, and not as their scribes.' (7.28f, our italics).
Book 2: (a) Narrative material. (8:1–9:35).
  (b) Discourse on mission and martyrdom. (9:36–10:42).
  Formula: '*And when Jesus had finished. . .*' (11:1).
Book 3: (a) Narrative and debate material. (11:2–12:50).
  (b) Teaching on the kingdom of heaven. (13:1–52).
  Formula: '*Now when Jesus had finished these parables*' (13:53).
Book 4: (a) Narrative and debate material. (13:54–17:21).
  (b) Discourse on church administration. (17:22–18:35).
  Formula: '*Now when Jesus had finished these sayings*' (19:1).
Book 5: (a) Narrative and debate material. (19:2–22:46).
  (b) Discourse on eschatology; farewell address. (23:1–25:46).
  Formula: '*When Jesus finished all these sayings*' (26:1).
Epilogue: From the Last Supper to the Resurrection. (26:3–28:20).

A similar fivefold division of the Gospel on the model of the Pentateuch is discussed by C. Rau (1976, 70–72). It seems entirely possible that the experience of the risen Christ laying out the meaning of the Pentateuch lent the life, teaching and death of Moses and especial significance, suggesting to the Evangelist a framework for this account of the ministry. Further parallels between the Books of Moses and Matthew's Gospel may be noted. The comparison between Noah's Flood and the Baptism was a favourite with early Christians.

Matthew narrates nothing of the silent ministry after the Temptation, but divides the remainder of the ministry into two equal sections (Rau 1976, 19–21):

From 4:17: '*From that time Jesus began to preach* saying. . .'

From 16:21: '*From that time on Jesus began to show. . .*'

163

This twofold division of the Gospel strikingly resembles the pattern of the second and third periods of the ministry of Jesus emerging in teh chronological analysis given above.

This threefold subdivision of the genealogy (Matt.1:1–17) provides a further parallel between Old and New Testament. In the genealogy the history of Israel is the book of the genesis of the royal Messiah. The first fourteen generations from Abraham to David covering the migration of Abraham and his descendants can be compared to the jorneying Christ of the silent ministry. After the people's migration had ended with David taking possession of Jerusalem, a second phase opened with the building of Solomon's Temple, the house of the Word, which may be likened to the beginning of the teaching ministry. After returning from the Babylonian captivity, the growing awareness of the people's Messianic destiny may prefigure the question of the role of the Messiah first raised by Peter at Caesarea Philippi.

'Paidology' is the term used by Cullmann (1963) for Peter's post-Resurrection perception of the Christ as the Suffering Servant of God 'ebed Yahweh (Hebrew) or Child of God, pais tou theou (Greek). Acts 3:13, 26 and 4:2, 30 reveal that the 'Child' was the commonest way in which the Christ was denoted. And the first Christians addressed each other as 'Children'. Cullmann (1963, 74) comments that it is probably no accident that of the only four passages in the New Testament which call Jesus pais, two occur in a speech attributed to the apostle Peter, and two are spoken in prayers of the Church in the presence of Peter.

We see the early dawn of a 'paidology' or Petrine Christology in the first Resurrection appearances to the disciples. During the post-Resurrection period before the calling of Paul, the developing understanding of the life of Christ centred on Peter. We will adopt the term 'paidology' for the incipient understanding of the risen Christ which awakened in the disciples in the period between the first Easter and Paul's conversion. This period during which the Christ appeared to the disciples and 'last of all' to Paul, it transpires, was surprisingly short.

21 The Birth of Christ

Birth is the converse of death and in many ways the view from above sees earthly life as a reversed and upside-down world. Death is the consequence of the endeavour to seize hold of immortality within the context of life on earth. And through unreserved self-sacrifice the immortal framework of human existence is reborn. The idea that the birth of the risen Lord was the inner aspect of his death on the cross is implicit in the earliest Creed, received and repeated by Paul in his Letter to the Romans (1:3ff) as the Gospel of God that had been 'promised beforehand through his prophets' concerning his Son 'who was descended from David according to the flesh and designated Son of God in power according to the Spirit of holiness by his resurrection from the dead, Jesus Christ our Lord'. We follow Lauenstein (1971, 27) in discerning three (rather than two) statements concerning the birth of Christ:

Nativity — Baptism — Resurrection

They represent the birth of the divine being of the Christ as occurring in three stages: Nativity, Baptism and Resurrection, three 'births' which may be compared with each other.

A beginning can be made by seeking an explanation of the role played in the birth narratives of the concept of the virgin birth. For, although the virgin birth is found connected with Nativities in both Matthew and Luke, it cannot readily be reconciled with his descent physically, which is stressed in both Gospels, 'according to the flesh from David'. For the Evangelists it is of paramount importance that the physical reality of the Incarnation is presented with the utmost clarity. Why then should these writers weaken the impression of historicity by introducing a mythical element in their allusions to a virgin birth? Matthew (1:18–25) and Luke (1:26–38) provide the only first-century references to the virgin birth. If these assertions had been interpreted literally, it would have been logically necessary to assume Mary's descent from David and for that no evidence exists.

165

Both Matthew's Nativity account and what we might call a Matthean interpretation of the Baptism of Jesus may be likened to a coronation (compare Psalm 2:7). And Matthew emphasized the hereditary aspect of kingship by accentuating his descent from Abraham. Luke (3:23–38) portrays Jesus as the 'son of God' as Adam was 'the son of God'. Luke's Nativity (with the descent via Nathan through a line containing a number of priestly names) views the Baptism rather as an ordination.

By introducing the concept of the virgin birth into the Nativity narratives, Matthew and especially Luke wish to minimize the influence of heredity in their portrait of the nature of Jesus. Then the essential component of his human nature comes not from the earthly (heredity) but from above. In both the annunciation of the birth of Jesus (conception) and in the Baptism of Jesus by John, the Spirit descends from the heavenly Father. By the Gospels' straightforward logic, since the virgin birth is a fitting picture of the Baptism ('today I have begotten thee'), it is also a good representation of the spiritual aspect of conception.

Other than in Matthew and Luke, the earliest reference to the virgin birth is contained in the shorter Epistle of Ignatius to the Ephesians (18), written by the Apostolic Father in the second century. It is interesting that the conception (and birth) is considered in conjunction with the Baptism: 'For our God, Jesus Christ, was, according to the appointment of God, conceived in the womb by Mary, of the seed of David, but by the Holy Ghost. He was born and baptized, that by His passion He might purify the water.' To the Smyrneans (1, shorter) Ignatius wrote, 'with respect to our Lord, that He was truly of the seed of David according to the flesh, and the Son of God according to the will and power of God; that He was truly born of a virgin, was baptized by John, in order that all righteousness might be fulfilled by Him.'

John (3:5–6) speaks of the Baptism using the spiritual imagery of birth (born of water and of the breath of the spirit) and we can see that the body emerging from the waters is equally suitable as a depiction of birth as of the Baptism. Paul (Acts 13:30–33) extends the similitude to the Resurrection:

> But God raised him from the dead; and for many days he
> appeared to those who came up with him from Galilee to

Jerusalem, who are now his witnesses to the people. And we bring you the good news that what God promised to the fathers, this he has fulfilled to us their children by raising Jesus; as also it is written in the second psalm,

'Thou art my Son,
today I have begotten thee.'

Why do the Evangelists use references to conception and birth to convey the principal features of the Incarnation? And why should the conversation with Nicodemus circle around the same theme of birth and rebirth? If John's readers were less familiar with the words to Nicodemus (3:1ff), would they not better share the bemusement of the great teacher of the Pharisees? It can be explained that the Bible uses the word 'begetting' as a cultic term for 'coronation' or 'ordination', just as in the parables of Jesus the nature of the kingdom of heaven is drawn entirely in pictures from everyday life. Consecration removes the individual from his economic and social setting in the everyday world in order to become a conductor of the spiritual power to engender life. Nicodemus' question could be put more prosaically into scientific language: 'We know that the brain determines how I think, but how can the way I think affect the way the brain functions? How can the body become an instrument for the spirit?' The fact of the Resurrection demands that the body changes and ultimately is transformed in response to the working of the Spirit. During the ministry the disciples had been prepared to follow Jesus as a figure capable of changing the cultural climate of mankind. They were evidently not yet ready to recognize in him the power to fashion human nature anew even down to the physiological foundations of consciousness. On the third day the disciples began to feel the presence of the Lord of all, a being with a role in the biological as well as the cultural evolution of man.

If we can keep in mind the picture of a nature which directs human life rather than being subject to its dictates, we have a notion of the implication in antiquity of the 'virgin birth'. Biology was expected to be obedient to divinity. There was no quarrel with the materialist explanation of human conduct but its operation was regarded as disobedience, a term which figures largely in Paul's thinking.

After Pentecost the first Christians continued their exploration of the dimensions of the Resurrection. Perhaps Luke intends Stephen's great exposition before the high priest (Acts 7) as a progress report on the development of Petrine Christianity during the interval between the first Easter and the day of Paul's calling. Although Stephen headed the first mission to men who had come from outside Palestine, he still addresses Jews from the Diaspora and not yet Paul's future congregation of non-Jews.

It is noteworthy that, facing the charge of blasphemy (Acts 6:14) 'for we have heard him say that this Jesus of Nazareth will destroy this place, and will change the customs which Moses delivered to us,' he offers in defence the Old Testament's history of the Jewish people. Stephen, like Matthew's Gospel, goes back to Abraham as the beginning of his story. Broadly the narrative (Acts 7) is an account of the disobedience of Israel, not yet the Pauline view of the disobedience of mankind (represented by Adam).

In three phases (3 × 40 years) of his life, Moses emerged to lead and instruct the people, prophesying, 'God will raise up for you a prophet from your brethren as he raised me up.' But the people turned to the old faith, symbolized by 'the star of the god Rephan' (Saturn). The prophets, however, were slain when they announced beforehand the coming of the Righteous One.

How far Stephen's speech presents a stage in the development of a Petrine Christology may be gauged by comparison with the words of Peter (Acts 3:13–15) when the Apostle also quotes the prophecy of Moses from Deuteronomy (18:15f). 'The God of Abraham and of Isaac and of Jacob, the God of our fathers, glorified his child Jesus, whom you delivered up and denied in the presence of Pilate, when he had decided to release him. But you denied the Holy and Righteous One, and asked for a murderer to be granted to you, and killed the Author of life, whom God raised from the dead.'

If Peter's understanding of the Resurrection of the 'Child Jesus' be termed 'paidology' *pace* Cullmann, it already contains a conception of the cosmic Christ which Paul was later to expand. Translating his and Stephen's words into the language of cosmic religion, Judaism had reverted to the old Saturn religion and rejected the new 'Jupiter' religion of the Righteous One, the Author of life. Peter's message contained a powerful appeal, 'God, having raised up his child, sent him to you first, to bless you . . .' (Acts 3:26). At its heart was the identification of Isaiah's depiction of the Suffering Servant (Child) of God with Jesus. Yet in turning back to the nativity of the Jewish people, Peter and Stephen express a principle theme in the Gospels. We may say that Matthew is written against a background of Jewish history from the time of the patriarchs beginning with Abraham. Luke's Gospel displays its more universal character against the background of the story of mankind beginning with Adam. In the genealogies and in the Nativity stories the whole Gospel is contained.

Peter's central doctrine of the childhood of Jesus is also capable of a reversed exposition. For just as the story of the Incarnation as a whole is contained in the infancy narratives, the report of the ministry of Jesus is likened to the birth and early development of the child. On one view it is the Baptism in the Jordan which can be compared with the Annunciation, and the death and Resurrection which is like a birth. The story of the Temptation after forty days in the wilderness particularly lends itself to such comparison, considering the parting of the ways between human and animal (primate) development which takes place at this juncture in the formation of the foetus. Much easier to grasp, and much closer to the world-conceptions with which the Evangelists could have been familiar is a comparison which derives from regarding the Baptism in the Jordan as a Nativity. The death and Resurrection is then connected with the birth of the human personality.

The life of Christ presents human nature before it has been diminished and hidden beneath the earthly mask of personality. The growth of self-awareness which culminates in the third year of life (after birth) is at the same time a process of dying for the universal nature which is summed up in the word 'Child'. It is not, of course, claimed that a twentieth century reading of the Gospels such as this was already present in the minds of the Evangelists. It is claimed that the concept of paidology is inherently capable of a development which takes us nearer to the heart of the Gospel.

22 Paul's Conversion

We are most familiar with the tradition that tells of the appearance of the risen Christ during the forty days after the Resurrection until the Ascension. Yet it is evident that the appearances of the risen Christ to his disciples did not cease with the encounters described in the Gospels, but continued. '. . . he appeared to Cephas, then to the twelve. Then he appeared to more than five hundred brethren at one time, most of whom are still alive, though some have fallen asleep. Then he appeared to James, then to all the apostles. Last of all, as to one untimely born, he appeared also to me.' (1Cor.15:5–8).

One later tradition, not encountered before the third century (in Gnostic writings preserved in Coptic) gives a period of twelve years during which the Christ remained with his disciples. This, G. Ogg (1968, 28ff) explains, emerged out of the tradition that after the Resurrection the Apostles remained together in Jerusalem for twelve years before they went their several ways to preach the Gospel in other lands. This period corresponds to the tradition that the mother of Jesus lived in Jerusalem with the beloved disciple for eleven years until her death in her fifty-ninth year.

There is another widespread and early tradition that the risen Christ appeared to his disciples for eighteen months after the Resurrection (Westberg 1911, 50ff, and Harnack 1912, 673–82).

Of the first stage of Paul's life after his conversion, G. Ogg (1962, 731) writes,

> In its early pentecostal days the church grew rapidly and
> soon came into conflict with Jewish authorities. While it
> may be doubted if passages such as *Ascension of Isaiah*, 9.16
> and Irenaeus, *Adversus haereses* 1.30.40 embody
> trustworthy tradition regarding the period from the
> Resurrection to Paul's conversion, the events of Acts 1–8
> may have occupied but one and a half years and Paul's
> conversion have taken place in 34 or 35.

G. Ogg dates the Damascus event from Galatians (1:15–18), which tells of Paul's escape from the threat of arrest by the Nabatean king, Aretas:

> But when he who had set me apart before I was born, and had called me through his grace, was pleased to reveal his Son to me, in order that I might preach him among the Gentiles, I did not confer with flesh and blood, nor did I go up to Jerusalem to those who were apostles before me, but I went away into Arabia; and again I returned to Damascus.
> Then after three years I went up to Jerusalem to visit Cephas, and remained with him fifteen days.

The story of Paul's escape is told in the Second Letter to the Corinthians (11:32–3): 'At Damascus, the governor under King Aretas guarded the city of Damascus in order to seize me, but I was let down in a basket through a window in the wall, and escaped his hands.'

Schürer (1973, 581f) writes: 'These events thus occurred at the end of the reign of Tiberius, AD 36–7. The flight of Paul from Damascus took place not long after this, when the city seems to have been governed by an *ethnarches* of King Aretas.' R. Jewett (1979, 100) concurs with the opinion of G. Ogg (1968) '. . . the conversion can be set in early October 34, and the first Jerusalem visit in October of 37, with the escape from Aretas immediately before this.'

The tradition that the appearances of the risen One lasted eighteen months is found in no less than four sources, Christian and Gnostics, deriving from early Christian times.

(1) Irenaeus (*c.* 130 – *c.* 200) gives as the teaching of the Ophites, an early Gnostic sect (*Her.* 1.30.14):

> But after his resurrection he tarries (on earth) eighteen months; and knowledge descending into him from above, he taught what was clear. He instructed a few of his disciples, whom he knew to be capable of understanding so great mysteries, in these things, and was then received up into heaven.

(2) Irenaeus (*Her.* 1.3.2) states the doctrine of the disciples of Ptolemaeus, school of Valentinus. Valentinus (second century)

founded a Gnostic sect with a widespread following. His disciples claimed that he had been educated by Theodas, a pupil of Paul: 'The other eighteen Aeons are made manifest in this way: that the Lord (according to them) conversed with His disciples for eighteen months after His resurrection from the dead.'

(3) The *Apocryphon of James* (Jewett 1979, 29) refers to resurrection appearances for 550 days.

(4) *Ascension of Isaiah* 9:16 (a second century Jewish-Christian work) says (Hennecke 1963–65, 2:657):

> And when he [the Son of Man] has made spoil of [despoiled] the angel of death, he will arise on the third day and will remain in that world 545 days.

Since the quality of the sources is not impressive, the question must be whether the eighteen months period is corroborated by the evidence of Pauline chronology *in toto*. It is noted, however, that a tradition shared by Gnostic and Christian writers cannot be late. G. Ogg (1968, 29) comments that the *Ascension of Isaiah* is an apocryphal writing,

> . . . but its author was neither a heretic nor Gnostic. Here then we have a datum that had a place alike in Gnostic and ecclesiastical tradition. It does not owe its existence to metaphysical speculation, and must be rooted in history; and what Harnack suggests is that originally it referred to the period between the Lord's Resurrection and his appearance to Paul on the Damascus road.

R. Jewett (1979, 99f) dates Paul's conversion August–October AD 34. In his closely argued analysis, he writes,

> An even more precise designation of dates is possible when one correlates this framework with a final fragment of evidence that no chronology since the time of Adolf von Harnack has been able to incorporate successfully. As recounted in Chapter 2, he correlated early Christian and Gnostic references to eighteen months of resurrection occurrences with 1Cor.15:8, producing a date of October 3 or 8, 34, for Paul's conversion. No one would wish to accord such a datum deriving from tenuous oral tradition a pivotal point in NT chronology. Yet its correlation with the new hypothesis is stunning. It falls precisely within the

date-range for the conversion that resulted from the interlock between the three well-documented dates and the seventeen year time-span. It is hard to believe that mere chance could account for so precise a fit in details deriving from such a wide variety of sources. The probability of a workable conjunction between the Harnack datum and the other three dates with a seventeen year time-span over a twenty year period is 1 to 474,591. The fact that Harnack's inference correlates so exactly with the chronological interlock provides it a kind of systemic authenticity. The result of accepting such a datum is that the conversion can be set in early October, 34, and the first Jerusalem visit in October of 37, with the escape from Aretas immediately before this.

Account should now be taken of the fact that — also exactly eighteen months after the first Easter — on 3 October AD 34 a conjunction of Saturn and Jupiter took place. Our question is this. Could this Great Conjunction, so important in the interpretation of the star of Bethlehem, have signposted Paul's Damascus experience? We should ask: While Paul journeyed to Damascus could he possibly have been unmindful of the approaching conjunction of the major planets? And could he, as a learned Pharisee, have been ignorant of the message of the magi?

We may recall Roy A. Rosenberg's generally accepted explanation that on their visit to Jerusalem the magi would have alerted Jewish scholars to the Messianic significance of the Great Conjunction of 7 BC: Yahweh is handing over to his Messiah a portion of his spiritual power and authority. Compare Paul on his conversion (already quoted from Galatians 1:16): '[Yahweh] was pleased to reveal his Son to me . . .' Paul's long apprenticeship as a Pharisee at the feet of the famous Rabban Gamaliel must have familiarized Paul with so memorable a pronouncement as made by the magi. If eighteen months (545 days) after the Resurrection, October 3, AD 34, may be considered as the date of Paul's conversion, the Great Conjunction of AD 34 would then be the outer sign accompanying Paul's encounter with the risen Christ. The record (Acts 9:3) does not rule out this interpretation: 'Now as he journeyed he approached Damascus, and suddenly a light from heaven flashed about him.' Further detail is added (Acts 22:6–14):

> As I made my journey and drew near to Damascus, about noon a great light from heaven suddenly shone about me . . . Now those who were with me saw the light but did not hear the voice of the one who was speaking to me . . . And when I could not see because of the brightness of that light, I was led by the hand by those who were with me, and came into Damascus.
>
> And one Ananias, a devout man according to the law, well spoken of by all the Jews who lived there, came to me, and standing by me said to me, 'Brother Saul, receive your sight.' And in that very hour I received my sight and saw him. And he said, 'The God of our fathers appointed you to know his will, to see the Just One and to hear a voice from his mouth. . .'

If the date of Paul's conversion and of the Great Conjunction are related, the words of Ananias offer some confirmation of the interpretation. The Greek word translated as 'the Just One' is *Dikaios*. R. A. Rosenberg (1972, 109) points out its use in Acts 3:14, 7:52 and 22:14, where Jesus is called 'the Righteous One' (*saddiq*). As quoted in Chapter 6, Rosenberg mentioned that the Hebrew word *çdq* (*saddiq*) means both 'righteousness' and also the planet Jupiter.

All the evidence adduced converges on October 3, AD 34 as the date of Paul's conversion. Without wishing to put too much weight on any particular strand of the evidence, we would judge that it is very rare for a spiritual experience which has no place in the secular calendar to have such a variety of sources all pointing to the same date.

It may be that the sight of the approaching Great Conjunction in AD 34 raised in Paul no more than a question concerning the magian prediction of the Messiah. The testimony of the magi has always been regarded as the witness of the pagan world. It would have been entirely suitable that the Apostle to the Gentiles had been subtly persuaded by the magi, representing the Gentile world. The magian consciousness projected its spiritual perceptions so strongly that all qualities and spiritual beings were visualized and identified with the visible objects of the material universe. For Paul it was of the utmost importance that his meeting with the risen Christ would not be confused with anything perceptible to the senses. His task was to cultivate the ground which lay between Jewish abstraction and pagan observation of natural phenomena. But only with his firm grasp of the nature of the Resurrection appearance could he embark on his exploration of the nature of the resurrection body.

23 After Damascus

Twenty years after his calling, Paul set out in his First Letter to the Corinthians (15:3–8), like a hymn to the new creation, the young Christian community's experience of the Resurrection. Closely linked to his great theme of the resurrection body is his treatment of temptation as a cosmic force forging the earthly destiny of man. Paul powerfully contrasts the temptation ('disobedience') of the first Adam with the 'obedience' of the last Adam. Disobedience or temptation is presented as the negative of the creation of man. The ministry of Jesus (the 'obedience of Jesus') reveals the positive picture of the process of becoming human. Jesus had not insisted upon his divinity but through 'learning obedience' he poured his divine form into the human framework of the ministry.

Paul's picture of Christ

Paul's conception of the Christ is the subject of a key passage in the Letter to the Philippians (2:5–11, author's translation):

Think what you too see in Christ Jesus,

Who, although in form divine,
did not seize upon
equality with God,

But emptied himself,
taking on the form of a servant
becoming like man.

And found in human fashion
he humbled himself
obedient unto death, death on a cross.

Therefore God has highly exalted him
and bestowed on him the name
which is above all names,

That at the name of Jesus
every knee should bow
in heaven and on earth and under the earth,

And every tongue confess
that Jesus Christ is Lord
to the glory of God the Father.

In Paul's portrait, the Christ relinquishes his *morphē theou*, his divine form, to assume human form on the Cross. Here we can see how close Paul remains to the pre-Christian spiritual conception of the world: above, on earth, and below. In order to understand this aspect, we would have to trace back to our earliest experience of it the three dimensions of space, until they meet in us, as we feel our position in space quite concretely. Particularly the Babylonians loved to be concrete and placed man archetypally facing south at the centre of the world. Indeed before Plato everything and every idea had extension in space. Man was central and his universal form was the image of the form of God. In the form of the Cross we can still see the three dimensions of space represented in the form of the human body. Paul tells of the pure human form which appears as the resurrection body after the Crucifixion when the dust, the material component of the body, is laid in the grave.

This passage (Phil.2:5–11) is essential to our understanding of Paul's view of the resurrection body in the First Letter to the Corinthians (15:35ff). O. Cullmann (1963, 177) continues his discussion of the *eikon*, the image of God:

We should relate all these texts to Phil.2:6. They are far
more relevant to its interpretation than all Gnostic
parallels. Only from this point of view do we understand
that by the 'form' of God in which Jesus Christ existed at
the very beginning is meant precisely the form of the
Heavenly Man, who alone is the true image of God.

A distinction is made between 'form' (*morphē*) which is of the essence, and the transitory *schema*, the human appearance (to other men). Closely related to the opposition of *morphē* to *schema* is the opposition of *sōma psychikon* to *soma pneumatikon* (1Cor.15:44). *Psychikon* is difficult to translate into English, and the Revised Standard Version's 'physical body' would have been more accurately rendered as 'sense-perceptible body'. What is meant is the mortal body insofar as it bears the sickness of sin within it, the baleful aftermath of the psyche's wilful perturbations. Adam's transgression consists in the development of the personality in thought, word and deed in an arbitrary manner, and not in conformity with the divine, cosmic order.

Modern biology

Modern biology also distinguishes two elements in the human *physis*: the form and the fabric. The fabric is constructed according to the information contained by the set of genes possessed by each cell. But geneticists are widely agreed that the form, the architectural plan, is not contained in the genetic body-building instructions. This is important for us because it corresponds to the distinction drawn in the New Testament by Paul between the heavenly form and the earthly fabric.

Classically man shared his divine form with the cosmos, itself constructed in the image of its Maker. The rhythms of the cosmos everywhere detectable in nature tell us that the same divine plan underlies all nature. But in modern man especially these annual, monthly and daily biorhythms work more weakly. We can trace their decline as *Homo sapiens* changed his occupation from hunter/gatherer to herdsman/farmer to trader/city-dweller. In three great steps man has succeeded in escaping from his unquestioning obedience to these heavenly powers. When Paul speaks of 'Adam's disobedience', he can be interpreted as alluding to the thrall of cosmic rhythm which orchestrates the earthly life of all creatures to a greater or lesser extent, but least of all in today's city-dweller.

Before Paul could understand the resurrection body, he had to go back to the origins of mankind and consider the nature of the human body. Unfortunately, Paul could not avail himself of a theory of human evolution. The ancient world was able to speak of human origins only in the language of folk memory (received from the Sumerians) or of pre-existence. The story of Adam in the garden of Eden is a blend of Sumerian ancestral tradition and memory of the pre-existent soul recalling the paradisical state before its entry into the material world.

As the modern counterpart to the creation myth of Genesis we have the theory of hominization. The creation of *Homo sapiens sapiens* proceeded in three stages:

1. Learning to walk upright, with the hands used for food-sharing.
2. Learning to speak, with the hands used for tool-making.
3. Learning to utilize the bilateral development of the brain.

These three clearly defined stages in the far-distant ancestry of modern man precede the very recent appearance of *Homo sapiens sapiens* only some forty thousand years ago. Whether the story of becoming human is told by Moses in Genesis, in the pages of the Gospels, or in the 'paidology' of the anthropologists as they discover the cradle of mankind, they relate a similar story. The theory of natural selection has robbed the pre-existent Christ of his role as the creator of human nature, but its failure to account for hominization should reopen the question. There is nothing anti-Christian in the view that natural species are guided on the genetic level by self-interest. It is only when the theory is promoted as the sole agency in human evolution that the Christian view of the genesis of human nature is ruled out. Of course, man is powerfully affected by egotism but we would see altruism as his underlying characteristic. If man's earthly (hereditary) nature is the seat of self-interest (in the biological sense of the term), altruism can be seen as the sign of his heavenly or spiritual nature.

When primeval man or his ancestor first raised himself into an erect posture, human consciousness began to appear on earth. The same power operates in each one of us in the months which follow birth. Our own lives contain the secrets of the creation of human nature and each one can read the story of man's genesis in the language of his own development. In this first phase of hominization, standing upright, man exerts his will against gravity, the god of the underworld. The vertical plane becomes the plane of his will and when he walks, his movement is relative to this plane. His independent stance had been won at the cost of consciousness of the divine: the divine withdraws from man's will leaving him heir to freedom and the possibility of error. With his

179

head aloft, the human gaze is lifted to the stars and in this same (vertical) plane the face of man, his physiognomy, becomes visible.

Stages of evolution

For the anthropologist, erect posture is the first step in human evolution achieved (some three-and-a-half million years ago) before the dawn of self-consciousness (in the last hundred thousand years). *Three* stages in the evolution of man may be glimpsed in the hominid sequence proposed by palaeontologists: Firstly *Australopithicus afarensis*, secondly *Homo habilis*, and thirdly *Homo erectus* (Johnson & White 1979).

Stage 1. The onset of hominization is marked by the acquisition of erect posture without as yet speech or enlarged brain capacity. 'Hominization is not initiated by the upright posture' says L. Bolk (1926). But because the form becomes human, the bodily posture becomes vertical. Self-interest would not have preferred bipedalism since, 'the adoption of non-saltatory bipedal progression is disadvantageous because both speed and agility are reduced' (Lovejoy 1981, 342).

Among the primates, quadruped locomotion is an adaptation which is advantageous in the struggle for existence. It can therefore be attributed to the operation of self-interest monitored by natural selection. The abandonment of competitive advantage represented by the adoption of upright walking should then be attributed to the operation of altruism. Altruism is here not limited in concept to selfless *behaviour* but is regarded in connection with the human *form*. Biologically speaking, the provision of food is a first necessity. Although it can be circumscribed by self-interest, the food-sharing made possible by use of the hands freed by man's upright bearing is the 'altruistic strategy' for escaping the Malthusian dilemma. Again self-interest versus altruism should be examined in relation to the *form* of the body.

In the Gospels, the temptation to feed oneself is overcome, and food-sharing is revealed as the epitome of altruism in the Last Supper.

Stage 2. A second stage in hominization is taken among man's ancestors with a further marked retardation. Maturity is post-poned, former physical specializations and (from the human point of view) premature solutions to the problems of earthly life are abandoned and the period of learning is prolonged. Tool-making begins to replace the utilization of the body as an implement. Anthropologists are confident that the evolution of verbal and material culture went hand-in-hand.

We have already interpreted the second temptation as an imagination which is readily applicable to the concept of neoteny resulting from retardation. Here Jesus resists the impulse to reveal his spiritual stature in the Temple without allowing the time needed for the human development appropriate to the priestly Messiah. During Holy Week, his success in overcoming the second temptation makes his cleansing of the Temple possible. His driving out of the sacrificial animals bought and sold there is a perfect representation of a neoteny consequent upon retardation. The non-human specializations are eliminated and the true man takes possession of the temple of the body.

> In the temple he found those who were selling oxen and
> sheep and pigeons, and the money-changers at their
> business. And making a whip of cords, he drove them all,
> with the sheep and the oxen, out of the temple; and he
> poured out the coins of the money-changers and overturned
> their tables. And he told those who sold the pigeons, 'Take
> these things away; you shall not make my Father's house a
> house of trade.' (John 2:14–16).

The Synoptists lay more stress on the Temple as a house of prayer in their narratives of Holy Week.

Homo habilis represented a stage in hominization more advanced than the upright-walking *Australiopithicus afarensis*. Apart from signs of tool-making, evidence of a major advance has been found illustrated in a skull cast of the famous fossil numbered 1470 (Leakey & Lewin 1977, 205):

> Probably the most intriguing discovery comes directly from
> the brain itself, or rather from the imprint it leaves on the
> inside of the skull. In studying a number of endocasts from
> hominid skulls, Ralph Holloway made a specially detailed
> search around the bumps and muffled wrinkles on the left

side. His search, of course, was for Broca's area, the brain centre that organizes words into a grammatical format and initiates the muscle control required in making the precise speech sounds. During a visit to Nairobi, Holloway looked for this critical sign in the 1470 skull. Though it is more than two million years old, he found the Broca's area, immediately apparent as a small bump on the front left side of the cast.

Stage 3. If modern man's sense of identity is his chief characteristic, then the most evolved of the three hominids corresponds to the last stage of development before the birth of self-consciousness. In *Homo erectus* it is brain enlargement which predominates. Nor, as in the earlier hominids, have fossil remains been found only in the narrow cradle of the Great Rift Valley. They are distributed at sites over a very wide area of the Old World. Where his forebears had been content to dwell by the lakeside, for *Homo erectus* the mobility to migrate converted the whole world into one gigantic lake about which he distributed himself. Before Lyell and Darwin, these hominids would have been described as antediluvian. Today we can see them as enacting the stages of mankind's infancy.

The Old Testament crowns its story of the expulsion from paradise with the Flood account. The birth of self-consciousness necessitates the cutting of an umbilical cord. And this cord is the magical link which obtains between the imagination and nature's dance. Otherwise man would experience in the ferocity of the elements the uncontrolled power of his own egotism unleashed. As the 'Flood' subsides, towards the end of the last Ice Age, the new *Homo sapiens sapiens* looks upon a new world from which he has to a unique degree extricated his consciousness, achieving the alienation necessary to increasing self-consciousness.

Self-consciousness is modern man's specific characteristic and Paul was quick to point out that the cost of this earthly consciousness is death. Evolutionary theory recognizes fear of death as a very powerful guiding principle in earthly life. But true humanity requires that man should exorcise from his soul the very 'war of nature, fear of famine and death' which governs natural life on earth. As a picture of the total mastery of the fear of death the Gospels present Christ's entry into Jerusalem on Palm Sunday manifesting a human nature which has utterly resisted the (third) temptation to submit to the dominance of Pluto's dark realm.

In the Temptation of Jesus, the powers were displayed which sought to bind the *morphē*, man's divine form, to his transient flesh (Paul's *schema* or 'man of dust'), threatening that the divine form should not survive beyond the dissolution of the body. In the garden-grave the last remains of the 'man of dust' were eliminated and the human form divine finally wrested from the snare of death. From this viewpoint we may regard the death and Resurrection of the Christ Jesus as the last act in 'becoming human'. The divine form of the resurrection body is then to be discovered in the purely spiritual dimensions of upright walking, speaking and thinking.

Learning humanity

Hominization or 'becoming human' is the result of two processes operating simultaneously, contrasted biblically as creation and temptation. In the life of the Christ Jesus, it is his ability to withstand temptation that is singular. Jesus refuses the dictation of self-interest to generate altruism. In order to restore the child within human nature, he declines to reveal himself as the prefected adult human being. Jesus is unwilling to subject himself to the laws of this world, whether physical (genetic) or cultural (political). In consequence the process of the Incarnation becomes largely an internal development through the course of the ministry. Becoming human is itself a learning process. The Christ had to *learn* to be human just as each one of us has to *learn* to walk, to speak and to think. Jesus similarly exhibited his humanity as a development. Yet the life of Jesus would not really be divine unless the development it manifests is at the same time a new step in human evolution.

From the Baptism to the Resurrection, we see the life of Christ unfold on two levels. Outwardly, it is the culmination of Jewish religious Messianism when he ultimately adopted his Messianic roles as anointed prophet, priest and king. These may be called the 'adult' aspect of the Incarnation. His uniqueness may be compared with the uniqueness of an individual's personality which matures in adulthood. When we penetrate behind personality formation to the earliest years of earthly life we encounter the stages in human development which are learned, but at the same time also are biological when the child learns to walk upright, to speak and to think. In the child these juvenile stages illustrate the phases of hominization, the creation of man. And we should expect to discern their pattern in the life of the creator of man when he himself becomes human (Steiner 1950).

Paidology

There is perhaps no need to consult books on the chronology of early child development since the evidence is everywhere close to hand. The question left to the reader is whether the chronology of child development resembles the chronology of the Incarnation. By about thirty-seven weeks after birth the child has so far completed the co-ordination of its motor-sensory system that it can raise itself to the vertical. From the Gospels the raising of the paralytic (John 5:1ff) is dated above thirty-seven weeks after the Baptism. At the culmination of the first, 'silent' part of the ministry, the Christ restores man's upright bearing and instructs him to walk. The first five chapters of John tell how he walks in repeated journeys between Judea and Galilee. The creator Spirit, no longer hovering over the waters, walks with the increasing confidence found in the young child learning to set foot upon earth.

Speech readiness in the child comes somewhat later than 'motor readiness'. Between the sixth and seventh months, just after the baby has mastered the skill of sitting alone 'babbling' begins. The baby says his first words at the end of the first year, at approximately the time when he is standing alone. There is evidence that speech readiness occurs between the ages of twelve and eighteen months in most babies. (Hurlock 1964, 219). 'The pattern of speech development is marked by spurts and resting periods – times when no apparent improvement occurs.'

Only when the child has learnt to stand erect, albeit still with external support, is he ready to undertake the most active phase

184

in learning to speak. Yet during the child's most active period of learning — from twelve to eighteen months — words are few and sentences are limited to one-word utterances. The immediate consequence of the child's learning to speak is the formation of Broca's area, the speech centre in the brain. And only after this psychogenic development has been accomplished (at about seventeen months) does the child begin to formulate structured sentences.

When, nine months after the Baptism, the Christ Jesus begins to teach in the synagogue in Nazareth (Luke 4:14ff), he does not at first find his own idiom but quotes from the Scriptures. The transition from quotation to self-expression is to be seen in the Sermon on the Mount (Matt.5:21) 'You have heard that it was said to the men of old . . . but I say to you . . .' His Galilean teaching marks the transition from the Old Testament's law of obedience to the will of the Father to the Son's rule of the heart. The old law is not abrogated. It is in the mouth of Christ that it becomes the language of the heart. When the Christ speaks to the multitude, it is nature as the handiwork of the Father that replaces quotation from the Old Testament. During the Galilean ministry, the grain of wheat (as a picture of the word) falls to the earth but as yet even to the disciples the instruction falls short of the words, '. . . and dies'. In our Gospel chronology we have connected the end of the Galilean ministry with the confession of Peter and the first proclamation of the Passion.

The further development of the child is the subject of a recent Harvard University study by J. Kagan (1981, 131 & 67):

> Much of the development takes place during the second year but it is expressed in language somewhat later. The change of a child's phraseology from speaking of self as subject does not take place — or, but rarely so — till the third year . . .
>
> By 22 months, when the pronoun *I* or the child's name appeared, the most common usage was *I* plus an action predicate ('I go', 'I do', 'I play') . . . By the final visits [in Kagan's study], at 26 and 27 months, self-descriptive utterances were sophisticated, including phrases like, 'I step on my ankle' or 'I do it myself'.

Out of experience, the study of self-awareness was designed to end at 27 months. At this age the difference between two and three years is enormous.

The final stage of the ministry, beginning with the proclamation of the Passion and ending with the trial and condemnation of Jesus, is centrally concerned with the question of the identification of the Messiah. With reference to the Messianic self-consciousness of Jesus, it may be noted that six out of seven statements ('I am the bread of life, I am the light of the world' etc) of the 'I am' occur during the last nine months. The conflict over the Messianic claim and counterclaims reached their climax during Holy Week in the trial before Caiaphas and Pilate. During the last part of the ministry, the focus is upon the fate of the human personality at a stage when the issue of mortality presents itself inexorably.

Dimensions of humanity

Three models of 'incarnation' have been proposed, interpreted as referring firstly to the life of Christ (the ministry), secondly to hominization (phylogeny), and thirdly to individual development (ontogeny). With the aid of such comparisons, the dimensions of emergent human nature can be discerned. If the expectation is correct that early man repeated as adult the stages of early childhood, we should expect that the earthly life of Christ would exhibit a similar pattern. Comparison is made with the stages of the ministry already outlined above:

Life of Christ	Early Childhood
1. Silent ministry	1. Upright posture
2. Teaching ministry	2. Speech
3. Messianic self-consciousness	3. Growing self-consciousness

We should expect that in the life of Christ the forces operating in evolution should also be prominent, even though their aspect is culturally conditioned. Modern science has replaced the serpent of Genesis by the 'selfish gene', but the inculcation of self-interest is the object of both agents. Man's soul is a battleground between self-interest (which we share with the animal kingdom) and the specifically human quality of altruism. It is necessary to uphold the uprightness of man as the physical expression of altruism.

Man's erect posture is fundamental to human life on earth, but it is the consequence, not the cause, of his becoming human.

A second dimension of humanity relates to the characteristic retardation which extends childhood and makes learning a dominant trait. In the third and last phase, retardation gives way to a confrontation with fear of death. In nature, fear of death through natural selection engineers the adaptations to earthly life. In man fear of death has played a comparable role in the evolution of personality. In the life of Christ the first proclamation of the Passion which accompanied Peter's confession marks a great and decisive turning point in the ministry.

Although it is possible to compare the trial of Jesus with the culmination in childhood of dawning self-consciousness, the grim reality of the Crucifixion seems utterly remote from the enchantment of childhood. Nevertheless, the Crucifixion should be seen in conjunction with the birth of personality which itself can be regarded as the death of the pre-personality universal 'Son of God' revealed in early childhood. In their life of Jesus, the Gospels tell how he sustained a resistance to the forces that otherwise fashion earthly life. When fear of hunger, self-protectiveness and fear of death are excluded from human life, earthly existence is threatened. In his death on the cross, what Paul called the 'man of dust' is laid aside but the dimensions of the heavenly man remain united with his experience of earthly life, as the wounds in the hands and the side of the risen Christ show.

When the child first becomes conscious of his identity, the brain is far from fully grown. It is more like a growing plant still responding to the influence of external stimuli in a very flexible way. The brain has not yet been sufficiently finished that it can act passively merely as an apparatus continuously recording personal memory. The brain's plasticity continues into the fourth year of childhood until, as the completion of growth approaches, the Tree of Life becomes the Tree of Knowledge. In the appearances of the risen Christ to his disciples after the first Easter, Paul tells us that the Christ appeared 'last of all' to himself on the road to Damascus. Of course, the presence of the Christ was still experienced both in the celebration of the Eucharist and in personal encounters with Paul and others after Damascus. Yet Paul underlines the qualitative difference between encounters before and after Damascus. Following Westberg and Harnack, we have dated Paul's calling three years nine months after the Baptism of Jesus. In the fourth year of childhood the developmental biology of the child's nervous system loses plasticity, leading to the more passive recording of long-term memory. Possibly the feeling of the presence of the risen Christ after this time became less formative, a less overwhelming experience.

After the conversion of Paul, the Christ was no longer called 'the Child'. We have interpreted the earthly life of Christ as a revelation of the inner reality of human nature as it unfolds in childhood, an extension of what might broadly be termed the mystery of birth. This aspect of the ministry is a revelation of the Father who is manifest in springtime growth and in birth. In his death Jesus identified himself totally with the destiny of the human personality. In the Resurrection mortal man is enabled to reunite with his immortal self which works deep below the surface of intellectual consciousness in the early years of childhood. Our forgotten experience of the 'lost' years of early childhood constitutes a gap which separates earthly man from his spiritual origins. The Gospel account of the Incarnation portrays the hidden way of individual development which once had formed the pattern of the creation of man.

For in effect the writings of the Evangelists restore to the receptive reader the divine impulse which once brought him into being. At no time do they pretend to provide historical evidence in the documentary sense. Yet since the life of Christ is concerned with the transformation of human nature, a chronology of his life is required in order to glimpse how the mystery of the Incarnation has its own intrinsic timespan. This timespan then becomes part of the revelation of the nature of man. The Gospels tell the story of an individual development in which the evolution of all mankind is inlaid. For man they become of all-consuming interest when he begins to recognize in them the power to rediscover his own true being.

Appendix 1

The civil and ecclesiastical calendars of Jerusalem (3–1 BC and AD 26–36), calculated by visibility of new moon. The first visibilities of the moon have been computed by Colin J. Humphreys (Jesus College), and W. Graeme Waddington (Department of Astrophysics), Oxford University, for Jerusalem in conformity with Schoch's criteria. They are published here with their kind permission. The Palestinian new year's day (asterisked), Tishri or Heshvan 1, coincides with the first day of the seventh Babylonian month Tashritu 1.

APPENDIX 1

Year BC/AD	Tishri	Heshvan	Kislev	Tebeth	Year BC/AD	Shebat	Adar	VeAdar	Nisan	Iyyar	Sivan	Tammuz	Ab	Elul
3 BC	Sep 12	Oct 12*	Nov 11	Dec 10	2 BC	Jan 8	Feb 7	Mar 8	Apr 6	May 6	June 4	July 3	Aug 2	Sep 1
2	Oct 1*	Oct 31	Nov 29	Dec 29	1	Jan 27	Feb 26		Mar 26	Apr 24	May 24	June 22	July 22	Aug 20
1	Sep 19*	Oct 19	Nov 17	Dec 17	AD 1	Jan 15	Feb 14		Mar 16	Apr 14	May 13	June 12	July 11	Aug 10
AD 26	Oct 1*	Oct 31	Nov 30	Dec 30	AD 27	Jan 28	Feb 27		Mar 28	Apr 27	May 26	June 24	July 24	Aug 22
27	Sep 20*	Oct 20	Nov 19	Dec 19	28	Jan 18	Feb 16		Mar 17	Apr 15	May 15	June 13	July 12	Aug 11
28	Sep 9	Oct 8*	Nov 7	Dec 7	AD 29	Jan 6	Feb 4	Mar 6	Apr 5	May 4	June 3	July 2	July 31	Aug 30
29	Sep 28*	Oct 28	Nov 26	Dec 26	30	Jan 24	Feb 23		Mar 25	Apr 23	May 23	June 21	July 21	Aug 19
30	Sep 18	Oct 17*	Nov 16	Dec 15	31	Jan 14	Feb 12		Mar 14	Apr 12	May 12	June 10	July 10	Aug 9
31	Sep 7	Oct 7*	Nov 6	Dec 5	32	Jan 3	Feb 2	Mar 2	Mar 31	Apr 30	May 29	June 28	July 28	Aug 27
32	Sep 26*	Oct 25	Nov 24	Dec 23	33	Jan 21	Feb 20		Mar 21	Apr 19	May 19	June 17	July 17	Aug 16
33	Sep 15	Oct 15*	Nov 13	Dec 13	34	Jan 11	Feb 9		Mar 11	Apr 9	May 8	June 7	July 6	Aug 5
34	Sep 4	Oct 4*	Nov 3	Dec 2	35	Jan 1	Jan 30	Feb 28	Mar 30	Apr 28	May 27	June 26	July 25	Aug 24
35	Sep 23*	Oct 23	Nov 21	Dec 21	36	Jan 19	Feb 18		Mar 18	Apr 17	May 16	June 14	July 14	Aug 12

Appendix 2

Eras and regnal years in Syria and Palestine 70 BC to AD 46.

Julian date	Seleucid civil	eccl	ERAS Pompeian (civil)	Caesarian (civil)	Actian (civil)	REGNAL YEARS Emperor (civil)	Herod civil eccl
BC 70 spring		242					
70 autumn	243						
69 spring		243					
69 autumn	244						
68 spring		244					
68 autumn	245						
67 spring		245					
67 autumn	246						
66 spring		246					
66 autumn	247		1				
65 spring		247					
65 autumn	248		2				
64 spring		248					
64 autumn	249		3				
63 spring		249					
63 autumn	250		4				
62 spring		250					
62 autumn	251		5				
61 spring		251					
61 autumn	252		6				
BC 60 spring		252					
60 autumn	253		7				
59 spring		253					
59 autumn	254		8				
58 spring		254					
58 autumn	255		9				
57 spring		255					
57 autumn	256		10				
56 spring		256					
56 autumn	257		11				
55 spring		257					
55 autumn	258		12				
54 spring		258					
54 autumn	259		13				
53 spring		259					
53 autumn	260		14				
52 spring		260					
52 autumn	261		15				
51 spring		261					
51 autumn	262		16				

APPENDIX 2

Julian date	Seleucid civil	Seleucid eccl	Caesarian (civil)	Actian (civil)	Emperor (civil)	Hasmonean (eccl)	Herod civil	Herod eccl
BC 50 spring		262						
50 autumn	263							
49 spring		263						
49 autumn	264		1					
48 spring		264						
48 autumn	265		2					
47 spring		265						
47 autumn	266		3					
46 spring		266						
46 autumn	267		4					
45 spring		267			Augustus			
45 autumn	268		5		1			
44 spring		268						
44 autumn	269		6		2			
43 spring		269						
43 autumn	270		7		3			
42 spring		270						
42 autumn	271		8		4			
41 spring		271						
41 autumn	272		9		5	Antigonus		
BC 40 spring		272				1		
40 autumn	273		10		6		1	
39 spring		273				2		
39 autumn	274		11		7		2	
38 spring		274				3		
38 autumn	275		12		8		3	
37 spring		275				4		
37 autumn	276		13		9		4=1	
36 spring		276						1
36 autumn	277		14		10			
35 spring		277						2
35 autumn	278		15		11			
34 spring		278						3
34 autumn	279		16		12			
33 spring		279						4
33 autumn	280		17		13			
32 spring		280						5
32 autumn	281		18		14			
31 spring		281						6
31 autumn	282		19	1	15			
BC 30 spring		282						7
30 autumn	283		20	2	16			
29 spring		283						8
29 autumn	284		21	3	17			
28 spring		284						9
28 autumn	285		22	4	18			
27 spring		285						10
27 autumn	286		23	5	19			
26 spring		286						11
26 autumn	287		24	6	20			

193

Julian date	ERAS Seleucid		Caesarian	Actian	REGNAL YEARS Emperor	Herod	Herod's successors
	civil	eccl	(civil)	(civil)	(civil)	(eccl)	(civil)
BC 25 spring		287				12	
25 autumn	288		25	7	Augustus 21		
24 spring		288				13	
24 autumn	289		26	8	22		
23 spring		289				14	
23 autumn	290		27	9	23		
22 spring		290				15	
22 autumn	291		28	10	24		
21 spring		291				16	
21 autumn	291		29	11	25		
BC 20 spring		292				17	
20 autumn	293		30	12	26		
19 spring		293				18	
19 autumn	294		31	13	27		
18 spring		294				19	
18 autumn	295		32	14	28		
17 spring		295				20	
17 autumn	296		33	15	29		
16 spring		296				21	
16 autumn	297		34	16	30		
15 spring		297				22	
15 autumn	298		35	17	31		
14 spring		298				23	
14 autumn	299		36	18	32		
13 spring		299				24	
13 autumn	300		37	19	33		
12 spring		300				25	
12 autumn	301		38	20	34		
11 spring		301				26	
11 autumn	302		39	21	35		
BC 10 spring		302				27	
10 autumn	303		40	22	36		
9 spring		303				28	
9 autumn	304		41	23	37		
8 spring		304				29	
8 autumn	305		42	24	38		
7 spring		305				30	
7 autumn	306		43	25	39		
6 spring		306				31	
6 autumn	307		44	26	40		Archelaus
5 spring		307				32	(8 years)
5 autumn	308		45	27	41		Antipas
4 spring		308				33	(43 years)
4 autumn	309		46	28	42		Philip
3 spring		309				34	(37 years)
3 autumn	310		47	29	43		1
2 spring		310				35	
2 autumn	311		48	30	44		2
1 spring		311					
BC 1 autumn	312		49	31	45		3

194

APPENDIX 2

Julian date	Seleucid civil	Seleucid eccl	Caesarian (civil)	Actian (civil)	Emperor (civil)	Herod's successors (civil)	Roman Procurator (civil)
AD 1 spring		312			Augustus		
1 autumn	313		50	32	46	4	
2 spring		313					
2 autumn	314		51	33	47	5	
3 spring		314					
3 autumn	315		52	34	48	6	
4 spring		315					
4 autumn	316		53	35	49	7	
5 spring		316					Coponius
5 autumn	317		54	36	50	8	1
6 spring		317			Archelaus dep.		
6 autumn	318		55	37	51	9	2
7 spring		318					
7 autumn	319		56	38	52	10	3
8 spring		319					Ambibulus
8 autumn	320		57	39	53	11	1
9 spring		320					
9 autumn	321		58	40	54	12	2
10 spring		321					
10 autumn	322		59	41	55	13	3
AD 11 spring		322					Annius Rufus
11 autumn	323		60	42	56	14	1
12 spring		323					
12 autumn	324		61	43	57	15	2
13 spring		324					
13 autumn	325		62	44	58	16	3
14 spring		325			Tiberius		
14 autumn	326		63	45	1	17	4
15 spring		326					Val.Gratus
15 autumn	327		64	46	2	18	1
16 spring		327					
16 autumn	328		65	47	3	19	2
17 spring		328					
17 autumn	329		66	48	4	20	3
18 spring		329					
18 autumn	330		67	49	5	21	4
19 spring		330					
19 autumn	331		68	50	6	22	5
20 spring		331					
20 autumn	332		69	51	7	23	6
AD 21 spring		332					
21 autumn	333		70	52	8	24	7
22 spring		333					
22 autumn	334		71	53	9	25	8
23 spring		334					
23 autumn	335		72	54	10	26	9
24 spring		335					
24 autumn	336		73	55	11	27	10
25 spring		336					
25 autumn	337		74	56	12	28	11

Julian date	ERAS Seleucid civil	eccl	Actian (civil)	Emperor (civil)	Herod's successors (civil)	(civil)	Roman Procurator (civil)
AD 26 spring		337		Tiberius			Pontius Pilate
26 autumn	338		57	13	29		1
27 spring		338					
27 autumn	339		58	14	30		2
28 spring		339					
28 autumn	340		59	15	31		3
29 spring		340					
29 autumn	341		60	16	32		4
30 spring		341					
30 autumn	342		61	17	33		5
AD 31 spring		342					
31 autumn	343		62	18	34		6
32 spring		343					
32 autumn	344		63	19	35		7
33 spring		344					
33 autumn	345		64	20	36		8
34 spring		345					
34 autumn	346		65	21	37		9
35 spring		346		Philip dies			
35 autumn	347		66	22	38		10
36 spring		347		Gaius		Agrippa	Marcellus
36 autumn	348		67	23=1	39	1	1
37 spring		348					
37 autumn	349		68	2	40	2	2
38 spring		349					
38 autumn	350		69	3	41	3	3
39 spring		350					
39 autumn	351		70	4	42	4	4
40 spring		351		Claudius	Antipas dep.		Agrippa, King
40 autumn	352		71	1	43	5	=5
AD 41 spring		352					
41 autumn	353		72	2			6
42 spring		353					
42 autumn	354		73	3			7
43 spring		354					
43 autumn	355		74	4			8
44 spring		355					Cuspius Fadus
44 autumn	356		75	5			1
45 spring		356					
45 autumn	357		76	6			2
46 spring		357					

Bibliography

Abrabanel, Isaac. 1497. *Wells of Salvation*.

Abraham bar Hiyya Savasorda. *Megillat-ha-Magelleh*.

Africanus, The Extant Writings of Julius. 1869. Vol. 9 of *ANCL*.

ANCL. Ante-Nicene Christian Library. 1867–1971. Ed. A. Roberts and J. Donaldson. Edinburgh: T & T Clark.

Armstrong, A. H., and R. A. Markus. 1960. *Christian Faith and Greek Philosophy*. London: Darton, Longman & Todd.

Bacon, B. W. 1930. *Studies in Matthew*. New York, and London: Constable.

Beasley-Murray, G. R. 1947. Two Messiahs in the Testament of the Twelve Patriarchs. *Journal of Theological Studies*. 48: 1–12.

Beckwith, R. T. 1977. Christmas and the Priestly Courses at Qumran. *Revue de Qumran*, 9 (1): 73–94.

——. 1982. The Pre-History and Relationships of the Pharisees, Sadducees and Essenes. *Revue de Qumran*. 14 (11): 33–46.

Bickerman, E. J. 1968. *Chronology of the Ancient World*. London: Thames & Hudson.

Billerbeck, P., *see* Strack, H. L., and P. Billerbeck.

Bock, Emil. 1978. 5 ed. *Cäsaren und Apostel*. Stuttgart: Urachhaus.

——. 1981. 6 ed. *Die drei Jahre*. Stuttgart: Urachhaus.

Bolk, L. 1926. *Das Problem der Menschwerdung*. Jena: G. Fischer.

Brown, Raymond E. 1977. *The Birth of the Messiah*. London: Chapman.

Brown, S. Cunyngham, *see* Cunyngham-Brown, S.

Bruce, F. F. (Ed.). 1963. *Promise and Fulfilment*. Edinburgh: T & T Clark.

Bühler, Walter, 1983. *Der Stern der Weisen. Vom Rhythmus der grossen Konjunktion Saturn-Jupiter*. Stuttgart: Freies Geistesleben.

Burrows, E. 1938. *The Oracles of Jacob and Balaam*. London: Burns & Oates.

Carrington, Philip. 1952. *The Primitive Christian Calendar. A Study of the Making of the Marcan Gospel*. Vol. I. Cambridge: University Press.

Cassius, Dio, *see* Dio Cassius.

Censorinus. *De die natali*.

Charlesworth, J. H. (Ed.). 1983. *The Old Testament Pseudoepigrapha*. London: Darton, Longman & Todd.

Chrysostom, *see* John Chrysostom.

Clement of Alexandria. *The Miscellanies*. 1867–69. Vol. 4 and 12 of *ANCL*.

Comay, Joan. 1975. *The Temple of Jerusalem*. London: Weidenfield & Nicolson.

Cullmann, Oscar. 1951. *Christ and Time*. London: SCM.

——. 1963. 2 ed. *The Christology of the New Testament*. London: SCM.

——. 1976. *The Johannine Circle*. London: SCM.

Cunyngham-Brown, Sjovald. 1975. *Crowded Hour*. London: Murray.

Darwin, Charles. 1902. 6 ed. *The Origin of Species*. London: Murray.

Davies, William D. 1962. *Christian Origins and Judaism*. London: Darton, Longman & Todd.

——. 1964. *The Setting of the Sermon on the Mount*. Cambridge: University Press.

Dawkins, Richard. 1978. *The Selfish Gene*. London: Paladin.

Dead Sea Scrolls. (English translation by Theodor H. Gaster. 1957. London: Secker & Warburg.)

Dio Cassius. *Roman History*. 1905. Ed. Herbert Baldwin Foster. Troy, New York: Pafraets.

Dionysius. *Liber de Paschate*. Ed. Migne. Vol. 67 of *Patrologiae*

Driver, Godfrey Rolles. 1965. *Journal of Theological Studies* 16:327.

Dubberstein, W. H., *see* Parker, R. A. and W. H. Dubberstein.

Edwards, Ormond. 1972. *A New Chronology of the Gospels*. London: Floris.

——. 1982. Herodian Chronology. *Palestine Exploration Quarterly*. (January–June): 29–42.

Eisler, Robert. 1938. *The Enigma of the Fourth Gospel*. London: Methuen.

Eusebius. *History of the Church*. 1965. Tr. G. A. Williamson. Harmondsworth: Penguin.

Farrar, Frederick William. 1874. *The Life of Christ*. 2 vols. London: Cassell.

Ferrari d'Occhieppo, K. 1977. 2 ed. *Der Stern der Weisen – Geschichte oder Legende*. Wien: Herold.

Finegan, J. 1964. *Handbook of Biblical Chronology*. Princeton: University Press.

Fotheringham, J. K. 1932. Letter to *The Times*. December 31.

——. 1934. Evidence of Astronomy and Technical Chronology for the Date of the Crucifixion. *Journal of Theological Studies*. 35: 146–62.

Francke, J. G. 1778. *Novum Systema Chronologiae Fundamentalis*. Göttingen.

Friedrich, Gerhard. 1956. Beobachtungen zur messianischen Hohepriestererwartung in den Synoptikern. *Zeitschrift fur Theologie und Kirche*. 53:265–311.

Gaster, Theodor H. 1952. *Festivals of the Jewish Year*. New York: Sloane.

Ginzel, F. K. 1899. *Spezieller Kanon der Sonnen- und Mondfinsternisse*. Berlin: Mayer & Muller.

Girard, L. 1953. *Le cadre chronologique du ministère de Jésus*. Paris: Gabalda.

Gore, Charles (Ed.) 1928. *New Commentary on the Holy Scripture.* London: SPCK.

Goudge, H. L., *see* Levertoff, P. P., and H. L. Goudge.

Goudoever, J. van. 1961. 2 ed. *Biblical Calendars.* Leiden: Brill.

Gould, Stephen J. 1977. *Ontogeny and Phylogeny.* Cambridge: Harvard University Press.

Gray, John. 1969. *A History of Jerusalem.* New York: Praeger.

Guilding, A. 1960. *The Fourth Gospel and Jewish Worship.* Oxford: Clarendon.

Harnack, Adolf von 1912. Chronologische Berechnung des 'Tages von Damaskus'. *Sitzungsberichte der preussischen Akademie der Wissenschaft zu Berlin.* 37:673–82.

Hastings, James. 1906. *Dictionary of Christ and the Gospels.* 2 vols. Edinburgh: T & T Clark.

Hawkes, J. J., and L. Wooley. 1963. *History of Mankind, Cultural and Scientific Development.* Vol. 1 of *Prehistory and the Beginnings of Civilization.* London: Allen & Unwin.

Heichelheim, F. M. 1938. Roman Syria. In Vol. 4 of *An Economic Survey of Ancient Rome.* Ed. Tenney Frank. Baltimore: Hopkins.

Hengel, M. 1974. *Judaism and Hellenism.* 2 vols. London: SCM.

Hennecke, Edgar. 1963–65. *New Testament Apocrypha.* 2 vols. London: SCM.

Herodotus. *History.*

Hippolytus. *Commentary on Daniel.* 1868. Vol. 6 of *ANCL.*

Hiyya, *see* Abraham bar Hiyya.

Hoehner, H. W. 1979. *Chronological Aspects of the Life of Christ.* Grand Rapids, Mich.: Zondervan.

Hoerner, Wilhelm. 1978. *Zeit und Rhythmus: Die Ordnungsgesetze der Erde und des Menschen.* Stuttgart: Urachhaus.

Holzmeister, Urbanus. 1933. *Chronologia Vitae Christi.* Rome: Scripta Pontificii Instituti Biblici.

Hughes, D. 1979. *The Star of Bethlehem Mystery.* London: Dent.

Humphreys, C. J., and W. G. Waddington. 1983. Dating the Crucifixion. *Nature.* 306.743–46. December 22/29

Hurlock, E. 1964. 4 ed. *Child Development.* New York: McGraw Hill.

Ignatius. *Epistle to the Ephesians.* 1867. In Vol. 1 of *ANCL.*

——. *Epistle to the Smyrneans.* 1867. In Vol. 1 of *ANCL.*

Irenaeus. *Against Heresies.* 1868–69. Vol. 5 and 9 of *ANCL.*

James, Montague Rhodes. 1924. *The Apocryphal New Testament.* Oxford: Clarendon.

Jewett, R. 1979. *Dating Paul's Life.* London: SCM.

Johanson, D. C., & T. D. White. 1979. A Systematic Assessment of Early African Hominids. *Science.* 203 (4378) (January 26): 321–30.

John Chrysostom. *Homilies.*

Josephus, Flavius. *Jewish Antiquities.* 1930–65. Loeb Classical Library. 7 vols.

——. *The Jewish War.* 1927–28. Loeb Classical Library. 2 vols.

Kagan, J. 1981. *The Second Year, the Emergence of Self Awareness.* Cambridge: Harvard University Press.

Kelber, Wilhelm. 1958. *Die Logoslehre von Heraklit bis Origenes.* Stuttgart: Urachhaus.

Kennedy, E. S. 1958. In *Journal of American Oriental Society.* 78:259.

Kennedy, E. S., and D. Pingree. 1971. *The Astrological History of Masha'allah.* Cambridge: Harvard University Press.

Kennedy, E. S., *see* Waerden, B. L. van der, and E. S. Kennedy.

Kirk, G. S., and J. E. Raven. 1963. *The Presocratic Philosophers.* Cambridge: University Press.

Klausner, Joseph. 1956. *The Messianic Idea in Israel.* London: Allen & Unwin.

Kuhn, Karl Georg. 1958. The Two Messiahs of Aaron and Israel. *The Scrolls of the New Testament.* Ed. K. Stendahl, 54–64. London: SCM.

Langdon, S. 1933. *Babylonian Menologies and the Semitic Calendars.* London: British Academy. (Reprinted 1980. München: Kraus.)

Lauenstein, Diether. 1971. *Der Messias.* Stuttgart: Urachhaus.

Leakey, R., and R. Lewin. 1979. *People of the Lake – Man, his Origins, Nature and Future.* London: Collins.

Lemmer, U. 1980. Neuere Betrachtungen zum Stern von Bethlehem. *Stern und Weltraum.* 19 (December): 404–6.

Levertoff, P. P., and H. L. Goudge. 1928. Mathew. *New Commentary on the Holy Scripture.* Ed. C. Gore. London: SPCK.

Lewin, R. *see* Leakey, R., and R. Lewin.

Loeb Classical Library. London: Heinemann, and Cambridge: Harvard University Press (pre 1931 New York: Putnam's Sons).

Lovejoy, C. O. 1981. The origin of man. *Science.* 211 (4480) (January 23): 341–50.

Machen, J. G. 1958. 2 ed. *The Virgin Birth of Christ.* London: James Clarke.

Malthus, T. [1798] 1970. *An Essay on Population.* Ed. Anthony Flew. Harmondsworth: Penguin.

Mann, J. 1971. 2 ed. *The Bible as Read and Preached in the Old Synagogue.* Vol. 1. New York: Ktav.

Markus, R. A., *see* Armstrong, A. H. and R. A. Markus.

Marsh, John., 1962. The theology of the New Testament. *Peake's Commentary.* 756–68.

Martin, E. L. 1980. 2 ed. *The Birth of Christ Recalculated.* Pasadena, Calif., and Newcastle-upon-Tyne: Foundation for Biblical Research.

Meshorer, Y. 1967. *Jewish Coins of the Second Temple Period.* Tel-Aviv: Am Hasefer & Masada.

Murray, G. R. Beasley, *see* Beasley-Murray, G. R.

Occhieppo, K. Ferrari d', *see* Ferrari d'Occhieppo, K.

Ogg, G. 1940. *The Chronology of the Public Ministry of Jesus.* Cambridge: University Press.

——. 1962. Chronology of the New Testament. *Peake's Commentary*. 728–32.

——. 1965. The Chronology of the Last Supper. *Historicity and Chronology of the New Testament*, 75–96. London: SPCK.

——. 1968. *The Chronology of the Life of Paul*. London: Epworth.

Olmstead, A. T. 1942a. *Jesus in the Light of History*. New York: Scribner's.

——. 1942b. The chronology of Jesus' life. *Anglican Theological Review*. 24:3.

Orosius, Paulus. *Historiarum Adversus Paganos*. 1936. Tr. I. W. Raymond. New York: Columbia University Press.

Ovid (Pseudo-Ovidius). *De Vetula*. 1968. Ed. Paul Klopsch. Leiden & Köln.

Parker, R. A. and W. H. Dubberstein. 1956. 3 ed. *Babylonian Chronology 626 BC–AD 75*. Providence, R. I.: Brown University Press.

Peake's Commentary on the Bible. 1962. Ed. Mathew Black & Harold Rowley. London: Nelson.

Philo, Judaeus. *Decalogue*. 1937. Loeb Classical Library.

——. *The Embassy to Gaius*. 1972. Loeb Classical Library.

Philo. (Pseudo-Philo) *Biblical Antiquities*.

Pingree, D. 1968. *The Thousands of Abu Ma'shar*. London: Warburg Institute.

Pingree, D., *see* Kennedy, E. S., and D. Pingree.

Plato. *Republic*. 1935. Tr. A. D. Lindsay. London: Dent.

——. *Timaeus*. 1929. Tr. R. G. Bury. Loeb Classical Library.

Rau, Christoph. 1976. *Das Matthäus Evangelium*. Stuttgart: Urachhaus.

Raven, J. E., *see* Kirk, G. S., and J. E. Raven.

Riess, Florian. 1880. *Das Geburtsjahr Christi*. Freiburg.

Rosenberg. Roy A. 1972. The 'Star of the Messiah' reconsidered. *Biblica*. 53:105–9.

Sarachek, J. 1968. 2 ed. *The Doctrine of the Messiah in Medieval Jewish Literature*. New York: Hermon.

Schalit, Abraham. (ed.) 1972. *The World History of the Jews. First series: Ancient Times*. Vol. 6. *The Hellenistic Age*. Jerusalem: Masada. (Reprinted 1976. London: W. H. Allen.)

Schaumberger, J. 1955. Die neue Seleukiden-Liste BM 35603 und die makkabäische Chronologie. *Biblica*. 36:423–35.

Schürer, Emil. 1973. *The History of the Jewish People in the Age of Jesus Christ*. Vol. 1. Edinburgh: T & T Clarke.

——. 1979. *The History of the Jewish People*. Vol. 2.

Seyrig, H. 1954. *Syria*.

Sherwin-White, A. N. 1963. *Roman Society and Roman Law in the Testament*. Oxford: University Press.

Silver, A. H. 1959. *A History of Messianic Speculation in Israel*. Gloucester, Mass.: Boston, Beacon.

Smith, M. 1981. The nature and meaning of mysticism. *Understanding Mysticism*, ed. R. Woods, 19–35. London: Athlone.

Stanley, Steven M. 1981. *The New Evolutionary Timetable*. New York: Basic, and London: Harper.

Stauffer, Ethelbert. 1957. *Jesu Gestalt und Geschichte*. Bern: Francke.

——. 1960. *Jesus and His Story*. London: SCM.

Steiner, Rudolf. [1909 September 15–24, Basel] 1964. *The Gospel of St. Luke*. London: Steiner.

——. [1911] 1970. *Spiritual Guidance of Man and Humanity*. New York: Anthroposophic.

Stendahl, K. 1962. Matthew. *Peake's Commentary*, 769–98.

Stephenson, F. R. 1969. The date of the Book of Joel. *Vetus Testamentum*. 19:224–29.

Strack, H. L., and P. Billerbeck. 1922–28. *Kommentar zum Neuen Testament aus Talmud und Midrasch*. 4 vols.

Tacitus. *The Annals of Imperial Rome*. 1956. Tr. M. Grant. Harmondsworth: Penguin.

Tertullian. *The Prescription Heretics*.

Thiele, E. R. 1951. *The Mysterious Numbers of the Hebrew Kings*. Chicago: University Press.

Thiering, B. E. 1981. The three and a half years of Elijah. *Novum Testamentum*. 23 (January): 41–55.

Tuckermann, B. 1962. *Planetary, Lunar, and Solar Positions 601 BC to AD 1, and AD 2 to 1649*. Philadelphia: American Philosophical Society.

Waddington, W. G. *see* Humphreys, C. J. and W. G. Waddington.

Waerden, B. L. van der. 1974. *Science Awakening II. The Birth of Astronomy*. Leiden: Noordhoff, and New York: Oxford University Press

Waerden, B. L. van der, and E. S. Kennedy. 1963. The world-year of the Persians. *Journal of American Oriental Society*. 83: 315–27.

Westburg, F. 1911. *Zur neutestamentlichen Chronologie und Golgatha Ortslage*. Leipzig:

White, A. N. Sherwin, *see* Sherwin-White, A. N.

White, T. D., *see* Johanson, D. C., and T. D. White.

Wooley, L., *see* Hawkes, J. J., and L. Wooley.

Index of biblical references

Index

INDEX

Resurrection 26, 113, 151–55
——, as birth of Christ 166f
resurrection body 153, 175, 177

sabbath law 132
Sabinus (Procurator) 69, 70
Sadducees 90f, 102
Samaritan woman at well 128
Satan 27
Saturn 61, 65
Sejanus (Roman ruler) 46
Seleucid era 44
self-consciousness 182
'selfish gene' 27
Serpent (of Garden of Eden) 27
Silius, Publius (consul) 127
Simon Maccabeus 47
Solomon ibn Gabirol (*c.* 1022 –
    c. 1070) 62
speech 180f
Stone of Foundation (*Even Shetiyah*)
    92f
Star of Bethlehem 60–67
Stephen 168
Suffering Servant of God 162, 164

Tabernacles, Feast of 40, 42f
——, (AD 31) 129
Tacitus, mention of Jesus 30
Tashlich (Jewish custom) 100–102
Temple (in Jerusalem) 93
——, cleansing of 127f

——, destruction (AD 70) 83
——, reconstruction of second 127
Temptation of Jesus 115–22
——, first 115–18, 161
——, second 118–20, 161
——, third, 120f, 152f, 161f
Tiberius, Emperor 46, 71, 146
time, nature of 36
Transfiguration 136–38

Unleavened Bread, Feast of
    (Passover) 40f

Varus (Roman governor of Syria) 69,
    70, 71, 72, 73, 145
virgin birth 165f, 167

Waddington, W. G. 19, 141–43
week 37
Weeks, Feast of (Pentecost) 40, 41f

Xerxes (d. 465 BC) 61

Yahweh 43
year, Babylonian 38
——, Jewish civil 53
——, Jewish religious 38, 53
Yom Kippur (Day of Atonement) 42f

Zarathustrianism 61
Zarephath, widow of 98, 108
Zechariah (father of John) 82f, 96f

207